Imperfect
Perfection

Imperfect
Perfection

Motherhood - you always love the ones you hurt

Nicola Dunn

First published in the United Kingdom in 2012
by Dunnsix Publishing

ISBN 978-0-9571362-0-5

Produced by
The Choir Press, Gloucester

1

Natasha sat all alone on the stairs of her family home, her palms clammy, her hands shaking. She'd had a nervous sweat all day. Feeling a breeze she leant forward to see where it was coming from. Her black blouse creased at the front as she pushed her body forward. The thought of looking messy irritated her; it was an important day. She sat up straight and pressed the creases out with her hand. The breeze was coming from the open window of the dining room. She could see the large clock which had hung over the fireplace ever since she could remember. It was all she could hear, the ticking that seemed to echo through the large hall where the elegant crystal light shade hung from the high ceiling. She had never really taken much notice of the the clock before; it was as if she was seeing it for the first time, above the brick fireplace, though it had been the focus of the family dining room. It was there through everything, each second passing, the hours and days that had ticked by, as being part of the family. She wiped a tear from her face. She was only twenty and wondered why she should feel so alone. She was becoming chilly, sitting for so long. She rubbed her hands gently up and down her legs, taking care not to ruin her expensive black silk tights. The pain inside her was unbearable. She let out a desperate screech, trying to hold back, afraid of screaming too loudly. Her head fell to her knees and she held on to her legs with her long fingers, as if to drain all the life from them. She began to cry again, crying as though her life depended on it, her head beginning to hurt. She thought no one could see or hear her; there was no one to stand in judgement. How could she let them know she was so very broken inside? They wouldn't understand.

The breeze from the open window reminded her of the hours she spent outside as a young girl; she just managed a smile, but then quickly held it back. The family garden: apple trees as far as the eye could see, a maze of colour, a collection of hiding places that were always found, they had to be found. The flowers and trees still grew there, the people she loved now rested there, undisturbed, listening to the rustling of the leaves. It wasn't fair. The garden seemed so very different now. She could stay out there for as long as she wanted.

There were so many things in her life that she had forgotten – she had hidden them away for so long. She was fearful the hurt would remain inside for ever. She wanted to remember. Dare she open herself enough? She needed to.

Her father came quietly into the hall to see her sitting alone with her head upon her lap. He stood in front of her and placed his strong hands on her shoulders. It startled her. Gazing up at him she smiled with all the strength she had. She shuffled up for her father to sit next to her, and as he sat his body gave her a sense of protection. He creased his suit jacket as she had her blouse, as he squeezed into the small space. He put his arm around her back, pulling her gently to him, and kissed her softly on the top of her head. His gentle touch seemed to squeeze more tears from her. She sobbed, her head now on his chest, his crisp white shirt wet from her tears. The tears she had held inside for years. Her father's pain also began emerging from deep inside. He cried as he held his daughter close, his strong fingers pushing into her arm. Two people allowing their sorrow to finally escape into the world.

"I need to remember, Dad." She tried to speak through her tears, her ribs aching.

"Me too." Her father spoke with a gentleness she had never heard before. She finally felt at ease being held by him. Hoping today was the day her father could find peace with himself. She closed her eyes and remembered as far back as her memory would allow. Her father closed his eyes as well as they both sat on the chilly stairs, ready to speak about their lives.

She could almost smell her mother's cooking, the aroma of apple pie. Imagining the sweet taste made her mouth water. Her memories became more vivid.

"Natty, get your sisters for me sweetheart." Their mother spoke softly but assertively, her voice echoing through the house, as she wiped her hands across her favourite apron. The apron she wore for the inspection was a gift from their father. She always had it wrapped around her, cooking or not, tying it around her small waist very tightly, almost taking her breath away. As if to feel him, hoping to remember the days he would hold her close. They did love each other long ago. They had danced together, never letting each other go long enough for a breath to be taken. She'd glance into his eyes each time she saw him and it was as though it was the first time. Not daring to miss a single moment. Sharing everything with him. Their father was the same. They were so in love, until one day their mother put her foot out and tripped him up. He fell to the ground so hard that it pushed the wind from him. She never put her hand out to help him up. She just left him lying there, struggling to regain any dignity and respect that was lost with the fall. They never held hands again. Only three threads now held them together emotionally, and they were Natty, Glenn and little Ruth.

"OK Mother. I'll go and get them down for you, just so you can send us all back up the stairs again," Natty said under her breath as she turned to leave the room. She knew how lucky she had been that their mother hadn't heard her. Her name had been shortened to Natty; she hated it, and she also hated being the responsible one in charge, which was a great burden for a girl of thirteen.

"Ruth, Glenn, mummy dearest wants you," Natty called, feeling fed up. She stopped outside her youngest sister's bedroom. Ruth looked up, her expression changing into a face of fear. She was younger than Natty by five years, but for some reason she behaved as though she was the eldest.

"Ruth, Mum wants you!" Natty stepped slowly into her bedroom. She could see her sister as she looked up from her favourite book of fairy tales.

"Yes Natty, I heard you the first time." Ruth got up from her rocking chair and placed her book back neatly on the shelf.

"Why do you always have to be so rude? It's not my idea to hassle you. You're only small so stop getting too big for your boots." Natty was becoming irritated with Ruth. She tapped her fingers on the white door frame, hoping her sister would hurry.

3

"Oh what a surprise, too small. I feel like being rude, that's all."
Ruth took her hairbrush from her antique dressing table, and then
placed her dolls back onto her bed which was always flawlessly
made. She liked to hold them while she read, sometimes out loud,
pretending to be a teacher.

Glenn walked quietly into Ruth's beautiful bedroom, hitting
Natty's bottom with the back of her hand. She was younger than
Natty by two years.

"How is Mother, the lady of the manor?" Glenn asked as she
began to straighten up her clothing, brushing frantically at any
specks that might be on her tartan skirt. She could nearly see her
reflection in her shoes, they shone like glass.

"Time will tell." Natty took a glance at herself in the full-length
mirror behind Ruth's door.

"Why don't you all make yourselves at home in my room?"
Ruth's voice was slightly raised. She brushed her hair, pulling it
back to make an extremely neat plait. The red ribbon she used to
tie it was from a box of chocolates she had been given by her father
one birthday.

"Your room's so much better than ours, don't you think Natty?"
Glenn smirked.

"Um, yes, I think so but really this isn't the time for chatting,
Mother's waiting." Natty was filled with apprehension and dread,
as she left the pretty bedroom.

Glenn and Ruth looked at each other for a moment, both letting
out a huge sigh, then they followed her. They all gathered at the top
of the staircase, contemplating the soft blue steps which would take
them down to either smiles or sorrow. Each step they would take
as if it were their last, three young hearts beating quickly. Ruth's
hands were clenched and sweating. She was praying deep inside she
could be taken away at that very moment, knowing they would all
be at the bottom soon. But the nearer she got her little face would
show how frightened she was. Glenn put her hand on Ruth's
shoulder, holding it as tight as she could without creasing her
sister's white blouse. Her stomach began to feel heavy; the anger
she felt bubbling up inside for having to go through the anguish had
to stay there, she would have to wait until she was in her luxurious
bedroom again to punch the pillows.

4

"It will be OK this time, honey." Glenn's voice was so quiet she was almost whispering. She hoped Natty would back her up in her lie.

Natty frowned, already full of diminished hope, knowing exactly what was going to happen. How she wanted to be wrong, even if it was only for one day. If only she could protect her younger sisters, if only they didn't have to go into the kitchen.

"Let's just get dinner, eh?" Natty's stomach had been rumbling since she missed breakfast. Her voice began to sound a little weak.

Smells from the kitchen became more intense as they waited together in the hall. It was lovely to pretend their own welcome would be as homely. Fear consumed their young bodies as they entered the shining kitchen. It was the most immaculate room you could ever see, with reflections from the shining cutlery like mirrored mobiles. They stood at the table, waiting together to see their mother's mood and the impact it would have on their evening. Their mother stood strong and independent in the centre of the room; she didn't smile and deep down they knew she wouldn't. It was if she were guarding a fort from any unwanted enemies. As they lined up side by side they prayed she wouldn't hurt them too much this time. Pretending she could be nice they stood still as soldiers, very young soldiers waiting to go into battle without any chance of returning.

Natty, Glenn and Ruth held their hands out for inspection with every effort not to show any sign of their shaking bodies. In their mother's eyes this wouldn't have been acceptable whatever the situation. She would scrutinise every fingertip with a fine-tooth comb.

"Turn your hands over!" Their mother's voice was stern and full of anger.

In sequence they all turned their hands to reveal their sweaty palms. Ruth held her breath in desperation as she could see the remains of an old pen mark in the middle of her hand, from her homework earlier. Her head began to thump with sheer terror.

"Ruth, your parting is not straight. Head down! Do I have to do everything for you?"

The howling of her voice vibrated through them.

"Glenn your head down, you should know by now!" Their mother's face was nearly touching hers. Glenn waited for the criticism and the punishment she knew was to come. She could feel

5

herself getting angry, mixed with emotions of sadness. She couldn't stand it. She wished she could mess her hair up right in front of their mother's nose, that would have shown her.

"Natty what are you doing? You're meant to be sorting these girls out for me, you are exactly like your father!" Their mother was snarling at Natty.

They could see how much anger was stirring up in her petite body; it didn't matter how small she was, the power she had over them was immense.

"You and your father have no responsibility, no idea whatsoever about anything!"

She yanked Natty's head, pushing it down and looking as though she was to drown her under the deepest of waters. Ruth was swaying with nerves, her pen mark still in full view of their mother. She was trying so hard to stay still. It was too late, their mother had caught her movement and without any warning Ruth received a blow to her face from the back of their mother's hand. The force knocked her backwards but she quickly composed herself again. She didn't want to upset their mother further. She stood with her feet close together, imagining they were fixed with glue. Ruth put her shaking hands out again, not wanting their mother to find another excuse to hit her, but remembering the blue ink. Their mother could not distinguish between love and cleanliness. There was nothing they could do about it – how could they? Three beautiful girls alone with such a woman; the person who created such beauty was such a woman to destroy it, bit by bit. Their father had managed to make his escape. The only thing on his side was that he was an adult; he had managed to release himself from her.

Ruth started to sob inside, her tears too scared to appear from her eyes. She would hold them back until all the beating was over, her heartbeat in rhythm with the clock, which ticked through everything, a silent witness to the atrocities. Glenn sighed, gaining a slap to her face. Her beautiful grey eyes would glisten with tears. They would always sparkle, like her father's. Every time their mother looked into them she would see their father watching everything she was doing.

"Mother, please can we eat now?" Natty knew she had trodden on unwelcoming ground.

It was forbidden to speak when it was inspection time, let alone plead. The sneer from Glenn confirmed what was coming to them extra hard. Their mother's beautiful hands came down on them, she kept pounding them with all her force. She had the most beautiful hands – she always kept them soft and polished – but how she used them each and every day was a different matter entirely. There was a sudden silence from the crying and screams which echoed through the kitchen. She had stopped and was standing red and flustered, staring at them, her eyes cold. All they could see was hatred and how she was yet again blaming them for her sudden unacceptable behaviour.

"It's quite obvious to me you're not hungry. I don't know why you have to do this to me. Go back upstairs to your little hideaways at once. If you come down in this awful state again your supper will go in the trash. I do not ask a lot from you, any of you. So do not let me down again!" Their mother's voice was becoming broken as she shouted at the top of her voice.

Their mother was left alone in the kitchen, her cheeks flushed, and she was breathing heavily. Her hair fell out of place. She patted it down with her tired hands, before straightening her apron. She composed herself as she waited for her daughters to return for the wonderful supper she had prepared. She knew how much they loved steak and kidney puddings. She had made an extra large apple pie for them, to go with vanilla ice cream. It was going to get wasted again – if only they didn't want to continue hurting her, she thought.

Hurrying up the stairs the girls returned to a place of relative safety.

"Mum's going to hit us again Natty, what are we going to do? I can't get myself any cleaner, and I can't look beautiful." Poor Ruth, she was only eight and yet already saw herself as an adult. Nearly succeeding in her quest with the way she spoke, the thoughts she would sometimes share with her sisters were vastly beyond her years. She would brush her blonde hair many times. It was extremely long so she gave it extra attention. Her blue eyes would sparkle like glass, especially when she thought of her father, her wonderful sweet father. She longed for the day when she was to visit him, a glorious day, but always a day full of secrets. Ruth

7

loved being the smallest when her father would hold her in his strong arms. She loved to sit and stroke his arms and sing lullabies, as singing was never allowed at home. Any voice was not allowed. Ruth loved to wear red, it made her feel like a beautiful rose. Her father loved her in red too. It always looked pretty against her blonde hair and he knew it made her smile. She'd be his special little flower. She informed her father one day she was going to marry a prince, and then she'd always be someone's special princess.

Her castle was to be filled with scented roses from all around the world. She could never share the reality of her home life with her father, her day of escape with him was too amazing to bring any sadness. At her tender age she already knew the difference she was going to make in her life. She liked to walk through the jigsaw of apple trees and flowers in the garden, imagining her prince lifting her away from the wicked witch inside. Her walks and dreams would always have to come to a sudden end when Natty or Glenn came to find her. Her sisters felt like they were searching forever, finding her eventually. Sometimes they would find her promptly and for a quick daring moment they'd sit together on the shaded grass, holding each other tight, listening to the trees, smelling the air and dreaming together.

Natty could never really let herself go completely. She would just be entering her dream when their mother shouted from the garden door. It would rattle them, making the chance to relax impossible. Natty wanted to be left alone to dream as her sisters did. She was always the one having to look after them, the one trying to make them understand the situation they were in, even though she found it hard to understand herself. Natty loved her sisters very much but felt a little resentful because they were so pretty; often she would look at them in admiration. She wasn't as pretty. Her wiry brown hair would tangle in the slightest of winds, it was always so frizzy. Natty knew even if she brushed it all day it never was going to be straight. Her eyes were a light brown and she was considering wearing a little mascara when she went to their father's house, hoping she could make them look a little bigger. Natty did love being tall but her waistline could almost have been classed as skinny, to the extent of being transparent; she felt there wasn't really much going for her. She was hoping she would have a chance to turn into the beautiful swan, just like the story from Ruth's book. Glenn resembled her mother the most facially but had never dared admit it. She kept her black hair short. Her plump lips were a cherry red, she was beautiful. She was always the hardest to find in the garden, but being eleven she had much more of an idea where all the best hiding places were. She didn't hide to dream or even annoy Natty. She only hid because there was nowhere else to go.

They all sat alone in their bedrooms, waiting for their mother to call them down again, fear still consuming their sore shaking bodies, sitting waiting to hear their mother's voice echo through the house, giving them a chance to redeem themselves.

"Girls, down here!" Their mother's voice was gentle but raised. That was it, their rehearsal time was over. They all slowly emerged from their rooms in unison, taking the desperate journey down to their fate once more, Ruth holding back her tears, Glenn reassuring her and of course Natty leading the way.

2

She was the most beautiful thing he had ever seen; for years such beauty could only possibly exist in his imagination. The sun's reflection glimmered from the mane of black hair falling around her petite shoulders as she walked to her table. Matthew Hopkins had never seen anyone so perfect; the young lady's smile and poise was compelling.

Eve Browning laughed with her friends at her local coffee bar. It was a regular Sunday morning gathering. They all had to be up early on Monday mornings so socialising after the hour of six o'clock was always a no go. Packing fish was not Eve's ideal career but it paid enough to cover the rent of her one bedroom apartment, just a stone's throw away from the permanent fish aroma. Her apartment was extremely basic, but Eve Browning didn't care much for plush surroundings, and why should she? She was beautiful and free and associated with friends who cared for her very much. What else could she possibly want at twenty-eight? She found it extremely hard to brush aside the stares from across the booth, almost enjoying the glances from the strong young man and feeling slightly uncomfortable at the same time. She couldn't bring the situation to the attention of her friends. They were constantly telling her that being alone was not healthy for a girl in her prime, trying to convince her she needed some attention. They would have her married to him with six children before their coffee had gone cold.

Clutching his newspaper in one hand and holding a fresh coffee to go in the other, Matthew managed to build up enough courage to approach her. Each movement he made was subconsciously thought by him. Was he looking respectable? Had he combed his hair enough times that morning? He stood strong over the booth, as he looked at the four girls who sat there. Taking a deep breath, he hoped that with the next release he could produce the right set of words. Through the giggles he could hear the busy surroundings of the smoky coffee bar: the clattering of spoons and cups being washed, a steaming coffee machine sounding like a jet wash, soft voices merging into mumbles. Trying to guess the number of coffee lovers by the ringing of the bell as they closed the glass door, he forced himself to focus again. There was no turning back now, he was already in front of her.

"It's lovely to see someone like you here." What kind of greeting was that? He may as well have said, "I am finding you completely adorable." Everything always had to be just so for Matthew but he never seemed to say the right thing at the right time.

"Yes, can I help you?" Eve replied, blushing, trying to look calm and holding back her nerves, but her giggles were about to bubble over like the coffee machine.

"You can actually . . . I was wondering if you wish . . . or shall I just say would you like to meet here maybe next Sunday? I would be very pleased if you would allow me to buy you coffee." He had said it successfully, completed the task in hand. If it made sense it really didn't matter, it was her turn, and the ball was in her court.

He waited for her response. "On your bike" would have been normal for him to hear. It was the usual thing many women had muttered.

"I do hope that includes a bagel too?" Eve was somewhat pleased with her reply. Beat that one, gorgeous, she thought.

"OK, a bagel it is. I'm Matthew by the way."

"Eve, by the way." Her friends were all smiles, like three Cheshire cats sitting waiting to pounce on the poor little mouse.

"Twelve noon, if you wish?" Matthew was gaining confidence by the second.

Eve nodded in agreement to his choice of time, turning away from him towards her friends who were waiting for the handsome man to depart so they could all give him the once over. Matthew left quickly so as not to ruin any of his hard work. Looking back he saw the calendar behind the counter. 23rd September 1950. He smiled to himself; it was going to be a day to remember.

3

The last candle had been placed into the moist chocolate sponge cake that had been made by their mother. Fifteen wonderful pink and white candles placed perfectly to avoid the delicately iced roses and pink ribbon. Natty crept up to the open kitchen door and cautiously leaned against the wood, feeling a warm sense of gratitude for her mother's skills as she stretched her neck just enough to see without attracting any attention.

Natty watched her mother smile. She seemed full of admiration for her own efforts.

"Natty." Soft whispers came from the top of the stairs. Ruth and Glenn were peeping through the banisters trying to get their sister's attention, resembling monkeys in a cage.

"Quickly, up here, you're not meant to see it yet." Ruth was so very excited at the idea of having all the family back together, anyone would have thought it was her birthday. Glenn's quiet giggling prompted Ruth to join in. Natty crept up to her sisters, every creak on the stairs making the situation funnier. They all grabbed hands and scurried excitedly to Glenn's bedroom. As they jumped up and down, their party dresses floating around them, the soft carpet turned into an imaginary trampoline. Natty hated her dress with lilac flowers showered all over it and a huge lilac sash tied around her waist, which was hard to ignore as it seemed to be holding the whole thing together. But it wasn't important, today was her day and it was going to be great. Together they were swirling around holding hands, all looking as pretty as could be. Any little girl who loved frilly knickers and bows would have been eternally grateful for the three masterpieces.

"Daddy's coming today Natty, he's coming home and he's coming to see us all." Yearning so much like every birthday, Ruth was sure that this time their father would be able to stay, and she was full of anticipation. It was going to be different today, she was sure of it.

"Ruth he has to go, he isn't going to stay with us, not with Mother. He isn't ever." Natty became irritated and unclasped her hands from theirs. She sat carefully on Glenn's superbly made bed.

"What makes today any different? Because it's my birthday, your birthday or god damn Glenn's birthday? It's never going to happen. Pretending you're so happy in your frills, what will happen when he leaves? You both know. We'll do as always, smile for Dad's sake!"

Without any warning the fun and excitement disappeared and they came back to reality. Glenn pulled Ruth to her side, holding her close, annoyed at Natty for taking Ruth's moment away from her.

"What's your problem? You're upsetting her." Glenn became the protector. It was a first.

"For goodness sake, I haven't got one. It's you two dreamers who have the problem. Why can't you both be honest?"

Natty rushed out of the bedroom with her head in her hands, becoming tearful.

"Daddy's here!" Ruth and Glenn were shouting as they dared to kneel on the bed. Side by side they watched as he walked steadily to their home. Glenn couldn't help herself – she hit the window as hard as she could and then began waving frantically.

"Oh goodness!" Natty stopped in her tracks before running into her bedroom in a panic to tie her purple sash yet again. Her hair needed to be tidied as her fingers had ruffled it. She stood at her mirror pinching her cheeks, trying to add a little colour. She seemed paler than usual recently, she hadn't eaten a lot and it was starting to show. Her complexion wasn't her doing, surely? At least she couldn't get the blame for not looking after herself. The last visit she had with her father hadn't gone too well; she'd felt upset with him that day, both for leaving them and especially for not noticing there was something wrong. Thinking maybe he did know what was happening but didn't really care enough to say. They'd managed to exchange two words to each other all day, hello and goodbye being the exact two.

Glenn stepped into the bedroom.

"Come on Natty, it's your day remember, don't ruin it."

"Can I make a wish today Glenn?" Natty asked with a dreamy look.

"Birthdays *are* for wishing, but remember, you can't tell us."

"I wish Glenn, I wish Mother would disappear. Do you think my wish will come true?"

"No such luck girl, no such luck." Glenn sighed, if only Natty had kept the wish to herself. It wasn't coming true, not this birthday.

They all gathered at the top of the stairs, Natty managing to hold the tears back once again. One sister behind the other all in perfect formation, each step they made taking them closer to their father. The open door to the kitchen enabled them to enjoy the wonderful sight of their mother and father standing side by side, as they used to. The birthday present their father had brought Natty filled most of the table, obscuring the view of the fabulous birthday cake. He smiled, leaning forward to kiss them as they passed. Tickling each one in turn, grabbing at their waist, his strong fingers pushing into their ribs as if he wanted to turn them inside out.

They all admired how well groomed he was, his face was smooth and looked soft. His shiny waxed hair was always in place, slightly greying at the sides which made him look even more handsome. He always wore a crisp white shirt with short sleeves, slightly touching his elbow, never an inch longer, black trousers immaculately pressed, and of course highly polished black shoes, which were his favourite.

The girls had never seen their father any other way. Whatever his attire he made a wonderful job of it. Not bad for a man of forty-nine.

"Happy birthday Natty, How is my grown-up girl? You look wonderful." His energy filled the air.

Natty's only thought was how could anyone look so wonderful in such a stupid dress?

"Fine thank you, Dad. I've missed you so much, I'm very sorry how I behaved the last time I saw you." Her response was soft and polite.

The interchange between father and daughter was interrupted abruptly. The wonderful birthday present was quickly removed from the elegant table. Their mother began to feel agitated as it had taken her so long to get it looking wonderful for them all. She wondered why they didn't care, their father could have chosen to put the present anywhere.

"Let's eat, girls, and then you will have time to talk properly, you can tell your father what you've been up to." Turning away from them all she placed the gift on the floor.

Natty was sure her mother hadn't meant what she had said – they were never doing much of anything apart from the usual hiding away in fear.

"Natty, are you going to say thank you to your father for your gift?" Their mother took a deep breath as she repositioned the tablecloth, checking over every detail one more time before they sat. Each knife and fork spaced equal distance apart. As always the cutlery sparkled, it took all morning to polish. The finest dinner service money could buy. It was a wedding present, only coming out on special occasions. This was always special for their mother, all her family together giving her a chance to show her marvellous skills, enjoying making their day truly memorable.

"Wait, wait, it's not right yet!" The panic from their mother was almost squeezing from her body, blowing her fringe up as she huffed and puffed. Her eyes quickly swept over every detail of the table and then her girls.

"Thank you Dad, it looks great." Smiling as she pulled her father's chair out for him to sit, Natty noticed her mother's stares as her hands were being checked from a distance. They were in total view of her father. It felt like her heart skipped a beat. Surely she wouldn't react, not while their father was there to protect them?

"Natty and I will open it later, but let's do as your mother says, eating sounds a good idea. It smells good enough to eat anyway." He spoke nervously.

Their mother had prepared a feast of roast chicken, mashed potatoes, a mixture of vegetables to give the plates a ray of colour, and hot steaming gravy blending all the yummy flavours together. Natty noticed the lack of conversation between her parents causing a cloud of tension over the magnificent table. But seeing them together made up for everything. She held her stomach in, feeling unsettled and praying her mother would behave herself. She could cope with the pretence that they were eating as a family and it certainly wasn't the hardest thing she'd ever had to endure. They all ate silently, maybe an odd word or the smallest smile only to break the monotony. Their mother could have been sitting with a remote control. They were almost programmed in their table manners, including their father.

"Natty, I think it is present time!" Their father pushed himself from the table, wiping his mouth on the starched napkin as he stood. The excitement he felt earlier returned in his voice.

"Mother, can we be excused please?" Ruth's joy and eagerness couldn't be contained as she was dying to know what was inside the box, which now belonged to her lucky big sister.

Picking up the box, their father led the way to a room which was only used for admiring. Eating in there was completely forbidden. The girls were told over and over. Their mother was allowed to go in whenever she wished. Often they would see her sneaking in a plate of biscuits and a cup of tea. They were all allowed in there when their father came.

For once Natty wasn't the biggest one leading the way. Standing behind her strong father was wonderful – she could be the child. Always being in front of her sisters and leading the way would scare her sometimes.

They sat on the floor underneath the large clock, all peering at the wonderfully wrapped present, every join taped down with precision.

"Go on Natty, open it." A gentle request from her father; wanting to help her he was touching the edges more enthusiasticly than she. Natty slid her thin fingers between the joins, tearing them slowly as not to damage the surprise held inside. She successfully completed her task to reveal a shiny silver box. She couldn't bear the anticipation or the thought of the moment ending. She released the white satin bow, bringing her thoughts back to the dress she had had to wear all day. She eventually found the dress of all dresses. The gasps around her confirmed how beautiful it really was. The dark blue silk would sit perfectly upon her small shoulders and it was long enough to cover her long, skinny legs. It would disguise her whole body with complete elegance. She was mesmerised. Neither she nor her sisters had ever seen a dress so beautiful.

16

"Oh Dad, it's wonderful, so wonderful, how did you know?" Natty had often seen such dresses in her mother's magazines where she would take a quick peek if her mother left the room. But they were only imaginary.

Holding it up against her body and pretending to wear it, Natty began gliding and twirling around, holding the straps with one hand, pressing it down around her waist with the other. She began to glide with ease around the dining room, the glistening soft silk accompanying her every move. Ruth's eyes lit up, her sister was a princess and she desperately wanted Natty to put it on. Glenn knew it would be her turn one day to receive such a luxury. But in the meantime she could only look forward to seeing how she looked in it.

From that moment the time they all shared together passed very quickly. Their mother just let them be, she had spent most of the day flitting in and out making sure her standards were not going to drop for the length of their father's visit. From beginning to end it would be flawless.

"Right girls, time's up. I have to make a move now, you know what it's like – long journey and everything." Their father's voice softened as he rose from the armchair looking down at the floor, a sense of guilt as always overwhelming him. Having to slide Ruth from his lap first. That was it. The clock had struck twelve, the girl's fairy tale was over. With a sickening feeling they all knew they would soon be back to reality. It was there, hitting them straight in the face again, like the slaps from their mother earlier that day.

"Dad, please don't go, please stay for a little longer!" Glenn pleaded with him, something she had never dared to do before, as she quickly glanced at her mother. Natty looked at her amazing gift and could almost feel it disappearing with him, feeling as if she was about to wake from a wonderful dream.

"Say goodbye girls, you know your father is a busy man." Their mother's voice was shaky, she sounded tearful, but she stood with her shoulders back.

He kissed each of them goodbye, holding their faces and then pulling them forward to him gently, as he looked into their eyes.

"Goodbye Ruth, your prince will come to your castle soon.

Goodbye Glenn. Be good for your mother. Goodbye Natty, happy birthday, look after your sisters." Their father smiled awkwardly as he looked at the floor again. He left them standing still as they watched their strong, kind father desert them once more. Their mother followed him out. Natty wondered why she couldn't just grab him back, how she could simply let him go.

Their father turned to their mother for a brief moment, gazing deep into her eyes for longer than necessary.

"Goodbye Eve, it's been lovely."

4

Matthew sat in the same booth that he had seen her walking to with her coffee. He remembered her face as if it were only yesterday. It seemed longer than a week since he had finally seen such beauty. It was fate, he knew it. Normally he would grab his coffee and go, but for some reason he had felt like staying. He could still smell her perfume. Matthew felt very tense in an excited kind of way, as he brushed the debris from the reused table. He began blowing salt granules onto the floor, feeling a little downhearted that it was so messy, but he wanted to sit in the same place she had. Having to make it just right for her he grabbed the sugar dispenser and vigorously polished it with his new sweater, which had taken the whole of the previous day to choose. He wondered if she would like it, as he sat in his final choice of attire. He rubbed his foot up and down the back of his leg, feeling his shoes had to be cleaned again. He began to feel annoyed, observing the staff who happily chatted among themselves, they didn't seem to care at all. How dare they? he thought. Being in such a fluster kept his mind from the forthcoming meeting. As the door opened he heard the bell interrupting his frantic behaviour. He sat up trying to look poised as he admired the perfect young woman whose name was Eve standing in the doorway. She could change her mind, he nervously thought. She wasn't in arm's reach, he wouldn't be able to pull her in quickly and shut the door behind whilst trying to glue her to the empty seat opposite. The anticipation inside him built as fast as her steps brought her closer.

"Hello again, I'm sorry if I'm a little late, I had to get the smell of fish from me. Oh, you haven't asked me what my job is yet have you? Never mind, we can get to that later." Eve arrived in a total fluster as she had been rushing all morning after visiting her friend.

She knew it would have been sensible to stay at home and get organised. She had to give herself at least an hour to look respectable for her coffee and bagel. Her stomach filled with nerves. She knew she was already waffling on. She wanted to kick herself. In fact she did, tripping up as she went to sit, her hand grabbing at the table. Matthew leapt forward to help, knocking over the sugar dispenser as he did so. Sugar fell upon his gleaming shoes and stuck to his lovely sweater.

"Are you all right?" Matthew just managed to steady her.

"Um, OK, yes, OK," Eve responded with difficulty because of the burning sensation in her ankle. She wished her accident could have happened at home – at least she could have shouted out bugger, or something even more offensive. But there was a place and time, well for most things.

"You're only five minutes late – you can have a nice cup of coffee now."

Matthew felt a great concern for Eve, but was slightly relieved her panic had taken any attention from his.

Eve sat down. The last thing she wanted was a nice coffee; she needed a stiff gin after such an escapade.

Dusting sugar grains from his sticky jumper, Matthew stood at the counter, looking at his table with pride.

"Can I have two coffees and a bagel please?" Even while placing his order his thoughts were filled with her. How had he ever managed to be in the company of such heavenliness? She was sitting waiting for him, the perfect amazing her.

"Change sir!" He was rudely interrupted in his admiration by the scruffy lady serving. To Matthew she needed a good haircut and a manicure as her fingernails were not well kept. She needed a total once over, and then once over again in a major beauty salon. She certainly wasn't to his satisfaction. Returning proudly to his table he sat down opposite Eve, allowing her space but also giving him full view of her beauty, while not wanting to be covered in sugar again.

"Smell, you said?" Matthew held the previously polished and newly refilled sugar dispenser in his hand and generously shared spoonfuls of sugar between both cups.

"Smell? Oh yes, The fish market. It's not very interesting but you know what it's like, once you start working in a place you kind of get used to it, and by the way, I don't take sugar."

Matthew was unable to hear her as he was completely captured by her appearance and continued to fill her cup. He gave Eve a very hot over-sweetened drink which would take her all day to swallow. As she felt quite nervous too, she kindly drank it, trying not to pull a face as the sweet taste went down the back of her throat. There was something about him she couldn't quite put her finger on. Feeling like he had caught her in a fish net, but she didn't want to get away. Each time she looked into his eyes she felt her stomach churn with excitement.

"How have you come to work with fish? I take it you are at the local market?"

Eve tried to hold back her nerves – a direct question deserves a direct answer, her father always told her. She took a deep breath.

"It wasn't by choice believe me. I have an apartment which of course needs paying for and on my doorstep was money waiting to be earned. So I gave it a go. Five years ago mind you. The thing is, Matthew, I have great friends and my own little place. I'm only a fledgling on a branch so there is plenty of time to do something else when the time calls."

"Fledgling?" Matthew interrupted, sounding confused.

"You know, young. Anyway enough about me, do you have an amazing nine to five career?"

"I'm a mechanic."

Eve couldn't hold back her giggles, nearly giving the game away and spitting out her coffee. He certainly didn't look like someone who would ever get dirty.

"It wasn't my ideal career move either, but my father passed away six years ago leaving a family business. As I'm the eldest I was next in line. My brother Harry helps me a lot, in fact he could teach me a thing or two." Matthew hoped Eve wouldn't leave at that moment. Surely a woman of her beauty could choose to be with any man with a top-paying salary.

"I am sorry to hear about your father." Eve began to feel uncomfortable, the throbbing in her ankle was worsening by the minute.

"That's OK thank you. He was a hard man to live with, nothing

21

was ever good enough for him. Nothing we did or said. So even though I'm sorry he's gone I can relax now he's not looking over my shoulder, watching every move I make or don't make."

Matthew never imagined he would ever be able to speak so freely, especially to a stranger even if she was completely adorable. It had been the first time Matthew had spoken about his father since his death.

"How old is your brother?" Eve changed the subject rapidly.

"He's twenty-eight, and a total contrast to me. He didn't seem to care what our father thought, he never takes care of himself, and he doesn't care at all about his appearance. But his rugged unshaven look certainly goes down well with the ladies. He has broken many a young heart."

"You don't take after him in that do you?" A sense of desperation rushed through her. Why did she ask him such a question? She dreaded she might have blown it with him.

"Oh no, you don't have to worry about me." Matthew knew she was the only woman for him. It was crazy and ludicrous. Love at first sight, whatever it was she had got him.

Eve began to feel more relaxed by the minute and wanted to share her family with him also.

"I wish I had a brother or sister, being an only child mum and dad are forever fussing over me. They are always doing things to help, secretly slipping money into my pocket every time I go to see them. I keep telling them I'm not going to starve, I work in a fish market for heaven's sake. But I want to show them I can stand on my own two feet. Well sometimes." Eve's thoughts went back to her grand entrance. "So if I have to smell of fish and sit in my place for a hundred years, I know I can make them proud."

Taking a sip of her coffee, she found her cup was nearly empty and the suffering would soon be over.

"I can kind of see your point, Eve." Deep down Matthew couldn't understand why someone would choose to live in such a way, if another option could be so much better. If her parents were willing to help then surely she could leave the fish market and have a better place to live. She didn't have anything to prove, she was perfect already.

"Would you like another coffee?" Matthew hoped she would stay for as long as possible.

Did Eve want another drink? The thought of saying no and ending the date was something she didn't want to do. Another coffee was a must even if the sugar contents could have her whizzing around later. She would need more than a bagel to absorb it, but there was no way she was leaving.

"That sounds lovely thank you. I'll get this one." Eve rummaged through her handbag, trying to find her purse hidden among old hankies and sweet wrappers. She knew it had to be cleaned out later, another job she would get around to.

"Oh, um, no Eve, I'm getting them. Please put your bag down." Matthew made his way to the counter, feeling mortified. He could never allow her to pay for anything. She was a beautiful woman, he wanted to give her everything, even if it was only a cup of coffee. He certainly wasn't going to behave as his brother did. Harry had been bought dinner many a time and still managed to woo them back to his place.

Eve was unsuccessful in her search. She felt relieved he had offered to buy another. Feeling happy she waited for him to join her again. They chatted slowly, managing to consume another two drinks, and time moved fast.

Taking her eyes from his for a brief moment, Eve looked at her watch. It was time to go, there was no way out of it. She had to be at work within the next hour.

"Matthew, I must be off now, fish call. Get it? Fish off?" Eve laughed aloud at her own joke, really wanting Matthew to respond or at least pretend to laugh before she left. "Thank you for a very nice time Matthew." She was full of anticipation.

Matthew couldn't let the moment pass. "Wednesday, I could cook you dinner. We could meet here before if you wish. About four?" Matthew waited for her answer that would decide his forthcoming days. He would certainly have to get organised.

"As long as it's not fish." They both laughed, to the relief of Eve. She was beginning to wonder if any jokes she made were funny. "See you in the same 'plaice' Wednesday at four. You didn't get that one either did you?" Hovering over the table with a belly full of sweet fluid and a very sore ankle, she waited for the usual

23

embarrassing moment which normally occurred after a first meeting with a handsome man. Matthew just sat still, staring at her in admiration. Eve began looking around and cleared her throat, hoping he would come out of the trance he seemed to be in. Finally she decided to take matters into her own hands as she couldn't stand for too long. Quickly she leant forward and kissed his soft cheek.

"Bye Matthew." He smelt lovely she thought.

"See you Wednesday, Eve." Matthew remained in bewilderment.

Eve, made her way to the door with her eyebrows raised.

"Eve wait!" Matthew jumped from the red leather seat, which clashed with his brown sweater, and followed her. "Eve, goodbye."

As she turned he kissed her with all his force on her glossy red lips. A quick kiss, but on the lips all the same. Their lips were like magnets, his whole body felt alive. An intense feeling of arousal consumed her, something she had never felt before. Surely it wasn't real?

5

They stood in the hall watching their mother closing the door, shutting their father out from their crazy world inside, and waited for her anger to show as it always did after their father left. Thoughts of what was going to happen next rushed through their minds.

"Happy birthday my dear Natty. You must all be tired. It's time for bed now girls, it's school tomorrow." She spoke softly. This time however their mother walked past them as though they were invisible, making her way back to the dining room and closing the door. Natty, Ruth and Glenn stood in complete silence, unsettled by their mother's behaviour. They were now being shut out of her crazy world. Normally they were used to getting a beating before bed. But not tonight – she didn't care enough. She was allowing them to be free. Never having felt so alone and lost they made their way to their bedrooms.

Natty lay on her bed, creasing her dress, thinking about her birthday. She'd had a lovely time. She wondered if there were any other fifteen-year-old girls lying alone in their bedrooms, wishing they could feel happy all of the time. Hoping their parents could one day be together. Did her parents love each other at all? Would they ever love each other again? She got up, untying her purple sash. She undressed and hid the dress away, letting out a huge breath with a sense of relief that she could finally take it off.

Realising her fantastic gift was still in the dining room, she covered her thin body with her yellow nightgown and rushed to get it, feeling the soft carpet on her bare toes as she went down the stairs. The house had an unusual silence to it – normally she could hear their mother pottering around somewhere. As she left the last step she stood outside the closed door. Should she go in, as she knew her mother was inside? Would she get the beating she'd missed out on earlier? Would she be acceptable in her nightgown and with bushy hair? As she turned the handle she could hear her mother's cries.

Pushing the door open slightly she peered through the gap. Her mother was curled up on the floor, her arms firmly around her waist, holding her stomach as if in pain beyond belief. Her tears were falling like a waterfall. Natty couldn't believe her eyes. She could see an open drawer, its contents displayed on the top of the unit. Four bottles of pills, not empty. But why did her mum have them? Natty knew all medicines were kept in the kitchen, clearly labelled. Why did her mother have her own little hiding place? Natty felt a deep need to understand more clearly what was going on. Being the eldest she would have to work it out for herself. She couldn't share it, she knew she couldn't, although the thought of rushing upstairs and waking Glenn did go through her mind.

"Mum what's happening?" Natty felt sick with fear as she walked slowly towards her mother, holding the edge of her nightgown with her shaking hands.

Her mother stayed in the same position, almost frozen, her tears still falling and her cries more intense. As Natty drew nearer her mother's cries filled her with more fear.

Natty held her hand out and placed it upon her mother's shoulder. Her mother didn't feel her touch at all at first.

"Mother, please, Mother. Why are you so sad, have we done something to upset you?"

All of a sudden the blue silk dress seemed unimportant. Her mother sat up slowly, moving her arms away from her stomach. She wiped her tears away. The bottom of her apron had more than one use. She looked into Natty's eyes with shame.

"What's the matter darling? Why are you not in bed?" Her mother spoke to her softly.

"Mother, why are you crying?" Natty felt a sudden moment of courage, she wasn't scared any more and felt that her mother wasn't going to be cruel, not that night.

"I'm OK, you don't have to worry about me. It's my job to look after *you*. You are my beautiful little girl. Now stop worrying and get yourself off to bed. It has been an exciting day for us all. Don't

26

forget your present my angel. It will look wonderful on you, such a lovely gift."

"Goodnight Mother, will you please go to bed too?" Natty kissed her mother on her wet cheek and turned away. She grabbed her gift and fled. She wanted to know why their mother was so sad. She couldn't remember the last time she had spoken to her so kindly. Natty returned to her bedroom. Any excitement she felt from the day had been washed away. She felt alone.

"What's going on?" Glenn called. She could rarely ignore what was happening.

"Nothing. Go to sleep will you?" Natty slowly pulled her new dress from the box and hung it with her school uniform – a pleated grey skirt, below the knee of course, a black blazer which held a white folded glove in each pocket, and a beautiful white blouse. They always had to look their best at school. Natty wasn't worried about anything, just her mother downstairs in her own little existence. In her own sadness. Why did she have those pills? Natty would have to take a look for herself.

Natty was the first up on Monday morning, at least an hour before they needed to be ready for school. School was a place where they all felt safe for a few hours. Natty and Glenn went to the seniors across the road from Ruth. They felt lucky they were not kept too far apart, as it meant they could all walk together and chat. They looked forward to this, but today Natty was distracted. She had to find out what her mother's pills were for and why she was so secretive about them. The fear of finding them made her feel sick inside. As she crept down the hall she saw her mother still asleep, alone in the large bed. It almost swallowed her small body. She looked beautiful as she slept, her soft face on the over-sized pillow. How could someone be so cruel but so gentle and at peace when they slept? Natty held on tightly to the banisters, taking every step with great care. If anyone was to wake how would she explain what she was doing? She would have to share her discovery with her sisters. She pushed the idea to the back of her mind. The consequences of her mother finding her did not bear thinking about. She had made it to the dining room, now for the hardest part of her mission. She knew what she was aiming for and tried to concentrate on that. As she stood at the drawer, her sweaty fingers wrapped around the small brass handle, she closed her eyes tight.

"Please don't catch me, please God don't let me be caught," Natty whispered softly to herself. The opened drawer revealed nothing, absolutely nothing. Not even a piece of fluff lay within. Where were they? She knew she was looking in the right place, she just knew it. Why had her mother taken them? Natty knew her mother's behaviour could not have been normal. She wanted to fit the pieces together.

Natty had to give up on her search. Once again she walked past her mother's room, her heart beating hard, desperate to reach her own bedroom. Natty closed her door inhaling deeply. She began to wash in her little basin. With sinks fitted in all bedrooms there was no excuse for not washing. The warm water dripping from her face, she glanced at herself in the small mirror. She looked at her face with unhappiness. She thought she wasn't as pretty as her sisters and wondered if that was why she managed to get all the blame. She started to dress for school, taking her underclothes from the well-organised drawer. She could hear her sisters moving about in their rooms and her mother going down to the kitchen. The girls were not allowed downstairs until their ties were straight, their hair had been brushed thoroughly and everything was in its place. Glenn definitely had the right idea by keeping her hair short. Glenn was always ready first, except today.

They stood smartly, immaculately dressed for school. They descended the dreaded stairs to await their mother's wrath.

Their mother served egg and bacon. She had turned nearly a whole loaf of bread into toast. "Eat your breakfast and get on your way." She wanted to be kind that morning and turned away from them, knowing she couldn't look at them for too long. They had to be out of her way quickly. It seemed too easy for them as they cautiously sat down. They sat around the table, looking at the breakfast which could have lasted them the whole week. Did this mean they weren't going to get fed later? Natty bit into her freshly made toast, thinking hard to herself. They hadn't been checked again, their mother had said nothing at all. Why was she behaving so strangely? They waited for her to pounce, but she just kept serving more breakfast. Was she finally regretting how she had treated them for such a very long time? Natty kept her secret deep inside, her eyes quickly scanning the kitchen for the bottles. They finished the feast of fried food, grabbed their satchels and left.

"Goodbye Mother!" All their young voices were raised as they went to the front door.

There was no answer from the cluttered kitchen.

Their mother heard the door slam and let out a huge sigh of relief. She had done it, she had been kind.

6

"**G**o on then, you can ask me." Matthew felt the need to visit his brother after his wonderful afternoon with Eve.

His brother Harry was laid out on the sofa, consuming beer. The belt to his jeans was undone, his shirt had been thrown across the room scrunched up like a piece of paper. Harry hadn't heard Matthew come in and was showing no interest to him at all. Matthew stood silently, waiting for a response so he could share his exciting day.

"Harry, I said you can ask me." Matthew was standing over him by this time, the eagerness to share nearly killing him.

"What on earth are you talking about?" Harry managed to glance at his over-excited brother.

"My date! I had a date with the most gorgeous girl and you didn't know about it? I told you I was going to meet her today. At least you can act like you're bothered." Matthew slumped in the chair, disheartened.

"What's the point Matt? You can never keep them. How long will this one last? I'm pleased for you, I really am, but talk to me in a month when you're still dating her. It's a shame you weren't born with your brother's charm." After his lecture Harry walked to the fridge for another beer, rubbing his hands over his unshaven chin.

Matthew watched every move his brother made. Harry had a good body and he knew it. But how he looked really didn't seem to matter – he would get the girl all the same. "Harry's charm" he would call it.

Matthew sat in his chair, perfectly handsome, but not so rugged as his brother. Harry was right, he couldn't hold down a relationship for more than a month. Matthew knew he spent longer looking for the woman of his dreams than actually dating them.

Feeling a little resentful of Harry's honesty, he decided to make his point heard. "At least I don't disrespect them. I treat them well, make sure I look my best and like them for who they are." Matthew certainly felt better.

Once Harry had returned to his favourite position on the sofa the ring was set and the gloves were off. He leant forward. "Now look, I know you do nice things for them, but you are a freak – you can't take a breath without making sure everything is done right. And that goes for your small number of women. You've got to let them breathe. Relax now and then, stop trying to make them – what is it you call it? Oh yes, the woman of your dreams. At least take them to bed first before they happily leave." Harry lay back again, knowing every word he had just spoken was hated by his elder brother.

"Sorry Harry, but that's not the way I do things." Matthew stood up abruptly. He decided to leave – the mess and his brother were driving him crazy.

"It doesn't change my life my dear man." Harry always had to get in the last word before he saw his brother leave. Not a second had passed before he leapt from the sofa, and running outside half-dressed he called his brother back.

"Matt, Matt, OK, I was out of order, come and have a beer with me before I drink them all myself. Let me know about this new girl in your life." Harry moved his head left and right with a child-like look, trying to persuade his brother to return.

Matthew was halfway up the path by now and took a huge sigh pausing for a while in his own thoughts. He stopped, turned slowly, then returned inside with Harry, muttering under his breath.

Two beers were taken from the fridge. Harry gently threw one at Matthew.

"Sit and tell." After giving his orders he sat and waited for his lovesick brother to start.

"She's really lovely. She's the most beautiful, perfect woman you could ever see."

"You can't always tell a book by its cover, Matt. I can't believe you haven't found fault in her yet, not even an incy weenie bit?"

"I have just told you, she is beautiful and intelligent, even if she works in a fish market, and she wants to see me again. She was waiting for me to ask her out on another date. She can't wait until Wednesday, I know she can't. I'm going to make everything so great for her."

"Take a breath Matthew, you look like you're going to burst a blood vessel." Harry laughed. "No seriously, you have to give her time. Anyway, what have you got planned for this amazing feline?"

"Dinner, I'm going to cook a meal she will never forget." Matthew spoke with excitement.

"Bad move." Harry felt like banging his brother's head on the brown cladding walls that surrounded them.

"You can't cook her dinner. You're going to make yourself look desperate. Take her out and let someone else do the worrying for you. You know what you're like – how many dinners have you cooked for those other wonderful women? And how many have been actually finished?"

"I can cook." Matthew was getting even more offended. Why had he bothered going back in?

"I'm not saying you can't cook, what I'm trying to say is don't let her see you cook."

"OK Harry, I'll just blindfold her on her way in, that way she can trip up, break her neck and never get to dessert. I'm going Harry, you're not taken me seriously at all."

Matthew left once again.

"I can't wait to meet her Matt, she sounds very lovely." Harry shook his head and chuckled as he took another sip of his beer.

Matthew hadn't heard what his brother had said. He had slammed the door, only hearing mumbles in the background.

7

Natty still admired the dress her beloved father had given her for her birthday weeks ago. When would she ever get to wear it? Every night before the ritual of getting ready for bed, she would take it from the wardrobe and hold it up against herself in front of the mirror, just imagining. Then she would carefully put it back where it belonged.

"Natty, Ruth's gone again." Glenn came into Natty's room, school tie in place and hair combed in a boyish style, short back and sides.

"Not before school surely! Where's Mother?" Natty became downhearted, taking a deep breath.

"Where do you think? Doing breakfast of course. I don't know how but it seems she doesn't know yet, so hurry, we have to find her. How are we meant to get past Mother? I haven't got any invisible powder, have you?" Glenn wanted her elder sister to hurry. She didn't want a beating before school as had happened so often. She was tired of having to sit in class with an aching heart and stomach.

"Glenn, I don't know. Maybe we can tell her we're going for a run in the garden in our best school shoes."

"I never knew they were best – how wonderful. I would love to run around the garden in mine, really muck them up, how fantastic would that be?" Glenn smiled to herself.

"Dare you!" Natty giggled as she passed Glenn who stood aside, allowing her to go in front.

"I take it I'm following you?" Glenn's smile became wider.

"Thank you so very much Glenn, how kind you are becoming," Natty said sarcastically.

Grinning together knowing they had to find their sister, aware of the trouble little Ruth had caused, they slowly walked past their mother hoping she wouldn't notice them. No such luck.

"Girls, where are you going?" Their mother's voice was slow, you could hear her anger surfacing

"Mother, Ruth's in the garden again." Glenn looked down at her gleaming black school shoes. The thought of covering them in mud quickly rushed through her mind. Then she began to feel nervous once more as she waited for their mother's response.

"Well, Natty you go, it doesn't take both of you." As she turned her back to them she hoped Ruth wouldn't be too cold.

Glenn made her way to the table. She didn't sit down, she wouldn't dare. She stood still and waited for her sisters so they all could have the ritual check.

It was a crisp sunny morning, but very cold. Natty could hear the crunching of the grass under her shoes which were not to be shiny for long. Her thoughts went back to Glenn – getting their shoes messy would be lots of fun.

"Ruth, where are you? We have to get moving or we will be late for school."

Natty folded her arms in an effort to keep warm. She gazed into the branches of every tree she passed imagining Ruth hanging upside down from them, not caring if she showed her knickers off to all and sundry. The bushes were sprayed white by the early morning frost. It did look very pretty, something Natty would have appreciated more under better circumstances. But today she didn't want to be there.

"Ruth, if you don't come out now I will really lose my temper, you're just being a pain!" Natty weaved her way through the maze of trees.

"BOO!" Ruth pounced on Natty, giggling.

"I'll give you 'Boo!' What are you doing out here? Are you mad? It's freezing and Mother is going to go crazy at the both of us!"

"Natty, I would rather be out here than in there any day. See, I have given you a moment away from Mother." Ruth hadn't wanted to be found. She would make her escape one day, she knew it, she would be rescued from it all.

"Look Ruth, just hurry up or I'll bury you out here!" Natty was definitely starting to lose her cool.

34

"But please Natty, a little longer, I'm not doing any harm am I?" Ruth's eyes filled with tears.

"You can't stay out here Ruth."

"Why, Natty? Who says?"

"I say, Now come on." Natty grabbed Ruth's arm roughly, dragging her back into the house. Natty felt sorry for having to take her small sister back. Two pairs of shoes were dirty, two bodies were cold.

They went back to the kitchen. Glenn was standing in the same spot. They both rushed to join her.

"Well done Ruth," Glenn whispered in annoyance.

"Leave it Glenn." Natty felt in complete control that morning. She looked down at her shoes with dread, knowing exactly what was about to happen.

Mother had finished placing breakfast on the table but it wouldn't get eaten now. She hadn't completed her ritual. All three girls knew they were going to school hungry again.

"Why did you go outside, Ruth? Put your hands out all of you." Their mother spoke sternly.

Again in unison they all raised their trembling hands. Natty and Ruth's hands were bright pink from the cold. Ruth's words would not leave her mouth, as if they were as frozen as her fingers. Her long blonde pigtail was tugged spitefully.

"Messy hair, dirty shoes, dirty hands. Well done Ruth, you are improving." Their mother's voice was now full of ridicule.

Ruth was quickly swung around by her arm. The force of her mother's slaps against her cold legs became unbearable.

"Please Mother, stop!" Ruth found the only words she needed, but the slaps just got more intense. Her mother didn't stop, she never did, not until she was ready. Their mother would never be told to do anything.

"MOTHER!" Natty couldn't stand it any more and her urgent shout disturbed her mother, finally causing her to stop.

Inhaling deeply, she stared at Natty in disbelief.

"Get upstairs and clean yourself up Ruth, there's no time for breakfast. So you should have more time to get it right." Their mother was talking to Ruth while staring intensely into Natty's eyes. Her eyes were full of hatred for her daughter.

Natty fell to the floor as the blow from her mother's fist plunged into her stomach. Images of the desperate woman crying in the dining room overtook her mind.

Glenn still stood in the same place. She hadn't moved an inch, not a hair, not even a button. Her heart was beating fast, her breathing was heavy.

"Go to school, all of you!" Their wonderful mother left the kitchen, as if disgusted to be in their company, leaving the uneaten breakfast and her heartbroken girls. She wondered to herself how silly they had been for not doing what she had asked. Daft things she thought.

Natty felt Glenn's soft hands wrap around her arm pulling her to her feet.

"Come on Natty, let's get out of here. Are you OK?"

Glenn helped her sisters get ready and they very quietly left for school. As they walked together in the cold air Natty could feel her aching stomach. Ruth cried the whole way. Their bellies were empty and their hearts were filled with sadness. All the satchels were held by Glenn, trying to help. The feeling of guilt overwhelmed her as she hadn't got a beating that morning. Suddenly Ruth came to a halt.

"I'm so sorry for what I made Mother do to you. I know I stood there like a perfect little angel when I should have spoken up, I should have. What are we going to do?" Ruth managed to speak through her tears. It had been the first time she had spoken since she was sent to her bedroom,

"I don't know darling, I simply don't." Natty's voice was gentle.

"But you're the eldest, you're meant to know what to do. Please, please, don't let this happen." Ruth continued to cry.

Natty felt fearful of her sister's request. She felt her own pain and wished by all the stars in the sky it could end for them all. Her stomach seemed to ache more. The usual hunger pains filled her stomach as well, but concentrating on her sister meant she had to forget about herself.

They all finally arrived at school. Glenn ran across the road to the junior school, handing her sister's satchel back and lovingly wiping her face clean. All the tears Ruth had cried that morning had stained her pretty face.

36

"There you go little one, as good as new." Glenn put the wet hanky back into her pocket.

"Thank you Glenn." Ruth managed a small smile.

They both watched as other girls were saying goodbye to their parents. They wondered how it would be to have a goodbye kiss, a hug or even a small wave.

"Have a good day, you will be safe here. And don't worry, Natty will sort it out, she won't let us down I promise." Glenn knew she was wrong to say such a thing but it was all such a mess that a little white lie wouldn't hurt.

Ruth turned and entered the playground. She disappeared into the mass of small black blazers. She looked like all the other girls but she wasn't.

Glenn walked back to Nattty.

"It's all madness, what are we going to do? Shall we tell Dad?

"No Glenn, don't be silly." What had happened didn't seem important. The image of their mother crying in despair couldn't be taken from her. It was the nearest thing to reality Natty had.

"We won't say anything to Dad, not yet, not until we're sure."

"Sure about what?"Glenn sounded confused.

"Just sure, it really doesn't matter now."

They heard the bell ringing. It was time again for them to play their part. To pretend to their friends that everything was all right. Behind their smiles and lunch-time chatting they were just like them, happy. They walked in together. Scene one was about to commence.

8

"What time are you meeting this new gentleman? I do hope he's respectable." Miriam always worried for her daughter Eve. It was Wednesday, the day Matthew had promised to cook dinner. Eve had finished her day early at the fish market and decided to visit her parents before she set off.

"He seems respectable, Mum." Eve sat at the kitchen table and began fiddling with the tassel on the checked tablecloth.

"I don't feel happy with the way you said that my dear." Miriam was making teas for them. Eve's father was in the living room watching a documentary on the TV about animal behaviour. The volume was set on the highest point as usual.

"Eve!" Donald shouted from the noisy room.

"Yes Dad." Rolling her eyes she waited for her father to be overly concerned about the new gentleman. He had always interrogated her in the past.

"He's OK isn't he? Would you like me to come with you? I can drop you off if you like?" Donald's eyes didn't move from the television.

"It's all right Dad, I don't need a chaperone." Eve laughed with her mother.

"Your tea is ready my darling!" Eve's mother had never served her husband hand and foot. She wanted to be a good example for her daughter.

Donald walked into the kitchen to retrieve his tea, quickly picking up two custard creams on the way. He kissed Eve on the cheek as she sat at the table.

"Love you sweetheart." Her father's stubbly face rubbed against her soft perfumed skin. Eve couldn't remember a day when he hadn't stopped in his tracks to kiss her. He was a terrific dad and had always had time to speak to Eve whenever she wanted. He would never miss a play in which she was involved at school, even if she was behind the scenes. He had never let her down in his promise to take her to the seaside each and every weekend come rain or shine. Eve had had a fantastic upbringing and her father was her hero. He returned to his favourite cosy place in front of the TV.

Eve began to chat quietly to her mother, hoping she could let her know as much as she could about her new acquaintance. As they talked, she glanced repeatedly at her watch.

"Don't worry my sweetheart. I'm sure you won't leave it too late. You really do look wonderful. I hope he deserves you." Miriam swept the falling hair from her daughter's face.

"He seems really nice Mum, totally different to anyone I have ever met before. He reminds me of the typical English gentleman. He's just up your street Mum." She laughed while gently pushing her mum on her shoulder.

"I've got enough to keep myself busy, your dear father for instance."

"Dad's still got it in him then?"

"Don't push it dear." They laughed aloud together. They were always laughing, enjoying every moment in each other's company.

"What's so funny in there?" Donald liked to be involved in almost everything when it came to his wife and daughter.

"Never mind, Dad, you just watch your animals." Eve placed her cup into the sink, glanced one more time at her watch, and finally decided it was time to leave.

"OK Mum, I'm going. Are you going to wish me luck?" Eve kissed her mother on her head.

"I was hoping you didn't need any luck. Have a wonderful time and be careful." Miriam took her daughter's hand and led her into the living room to join Donald.

"Bye Dad, going to meet the man of my dreams." Eve leaned over the arm of the chair, kissing him before she turned to leave.

"Don't forget you're still my little girl, anyway I thought I was the man of your dreams?" Donald rose from his armchair, biscuit crumbs sticking to the jumper which stretched over his large belly.

Her parents stood side by side and watched their beautiful daughter leave. She had grown into a woman they were very proud of, independent, caring and definitely the pettiest on the street. Their only wish was that she'd come home.

Matthew arrived at the coffee bar at ten to four. He was never late for anything, and for the first time neither was Eve. Matthew quickly kissed her on the lips. They stood with their eyes transfixed on each other. Neither of them wanted to move. They could have stayed looking into each other's eyes for ever. Matthew finally broke the silence.

"No need for coffee today, let's go straight to mine." He placed his strong arm around her waist. Eve was somewhat relieved coffee was not on the menu, she had enough sugar in her system to last her a lifetime. She felt safe with Matthew although a little apprehensive. Even though she wanted to be there she was definitely nervous, and wondered if she should have stayed at her parents and stuffed custard creams all afternoon. Before she knew it they were outside a beautifully painted door, with a very shiny brass handle placed perfectly in the centre. Number thirteen – unlucky for some, she thought.

"Here it is, my humble abode." Being such a gentleman he moved to the side to let her in first.

"Humble abode? I don't think so, do you?" Her words were out before her brain was in gear as usual.

She was getting used to the feeling of wanting the whole world to swallow her up every time she opened her mouth. Matthew didn't find it funny at all.

"Take a seat and I'll make you a nice cup of tea first." Matthew proudly showed her to the sofa. She was almost scared to sit, she didn't want to ruffle it in any way. Maybe he watched television standing up. Matthew went into the kitchen and began making the tea while Eve tried to prepare herself for the over-sweetened drink she would be served. With the gorgeous gentleman out of her sights it gave her a chance to be nosey. In front of her was a small coffee table, highly polished, with magazines placed on it like playing cards in a pile – cars and more cars, he obviously liked reading about them. Seats around her held beautiful cushions. He'd obviously never had a pillow fight in his life. The red carpet had been thoroughly hoovered. The record player looked like his pride and joy. It filled the corner of the room. She couldn't see the other corners for green plants. Wonderful plants which had taken years to grow. They wouldn't last very long if she watered them. Everything was kept exceptionally tidy. She was a little confused at how tidy it was but nevertheless very pleased how he could manage on his own. He didn't want a maid, she wouldn't have to wait on him hand and foot, and wouldn't her mum be pleased?

A tray of drinks was placed in front of her.

"Thank you Matthew." Here we go again she thought. If she started jumping around the room she would be sure to knock something over, one of the twenty plants maybe. She almost felt like a small child in a large china store, afraid in case she moved too quickly and smashed everything around her.

"How's your week been, Eve?" Matthew sat back and admired her, waiting for her soft red lips to move.

"Not much really, smelling a lot, drinking a lot."

"Drinking?" Matthew frowned.

"At the coffee bar. You are funny, you did look serious when I said that. Drinking coffee, without sugar shall I say, with my friends, I'm sure you'd love to meet them one day, they're smashing. We have such great times." Taking a moment's breath, Eve thought to herself how she wished she could be quiet for more than a few minutes. What was it about him she liked so much? For some reason she felt the need to say everything right.

An hour had passed and they spoke constantly. Eve still felt cautious at making a sudden move. Matthew went and laid a clean white cloth over the small round table next to the window, then added posh cutlery and even a small vase of daisies. It did look very quaint. He was getting better by the minute. She couldn't believe her luck.

"Can I use your bathroom please Matthew?" As she made her way to the bathroom a sense of relief raced through her, knowing she could relax for a while. As she went in she took a huge sigh as she closed her eyes, and then she opened them again.

"Oh heavens, heavens." Quickly placing her hand over her mouth, praying she hadn't been overheard, the feeling of the china shop rushed through her again. Lifting the lid of the toilet she sat down slowly. He actually placed the seat down, she couldn't believe it. Once again everything shone and gleamed. There wasn't a fingerprint showing anywhere, not even a smear from an old splash. There would be no place in his bathroom to hang stockings. She was wondering if he could come and do her apartment. She would pay him the going rate. Eve chuckled to herself. She finished her duty and pulled up her black trousers – they were far too tight for her around the waist, but her bum always looked good in them – washed her hands and then wiped them dry on the perfectly folded towel. Being taught you should always leave things as you find them, she took the towel to the wet sink, quickly dried away any sign of water from it and left it gleaming once more. Turning around she checked everything was satisfactory, before she returned to the museum of order.

Matthew stood proudly at the table, on which were placed two china plates filled with beef and vegetables and warm gravy poured over the top.

"That looks fabulous. It looks like you can cook very well." Eve spoke with delight.

She sat down opposite him as he poured her a glass of white wine. He couldn't keep his eyes from her. Eve thought he would spill it over the edge of the long-stemmed glass. She wished he would allow her to eat without watching her every move, she normally gulped her food down while lying on her sofa in her apartment. This could be one of her most embarrassing moments – perhaps she could ask him to close his eyes? Matthew put his napkin on his lap. Eve's was still placed neatly untouched on the table, if alone she would have wiped her mouth with the back of her hand. With her mouth already full she followed him in his table manners, trying to slide the napkin off the table, hoping she wouldn't be seen. This was of course impossible.

"Oh my God, oh my God! I can't believe I've done that," Matthew yelled out, dropping his knife and fork as though they had just reached boiling point.

Nearly choking with the shock, Eve gulped some wine to wash down the stuck beef in her throat. Matthew went into the kitchen.

"Oh my God I can't believe I've done that!" Matthew kept repeating it to himself.

Eve needed the whole moment to be rewound. What was actually going on? Were her eating habits that bad? Matthew returned holding a lit candle, calmly placed it between them and then continued to eat. Great, Eve thought, now he can see up my nostrils while I chew. The food tasted wonderful, she was very impressed as she laughed and chatted freely putting all the commotion behind her. Sometimes Eve would laugh out loud, extremely loud, when she relayed to him her most treasured jokes. Her friends would always become hysterical but Matthew didn't find them funny at all.

"Will you get married Eve?" Matthew felt a sense of pride, it had been a fantastic evening so far, and his feelings for his stunning guest continued to become more intense, being completely and unmistakably smitten by her.

"Married! I've only just eaten my dinner."

"I didn't mean on a full stomach, I meant in the future."

Another joke which went straight over Matthew's head – he had definitely been stuck in a time machine somewhere.

"I haven't really thought about it." Eve placed her knife and fork together on her empty plate, feeling indigestion coming on suddenly.

Matthew took hold of her hand.

"You are very beautiful Eve."

"Oh thank you Matthew, it's very kind of you to say so." Eve wanted to giggle and burp at that very moment. He was extremely romantic, looking into her eyes and telling her how beautiful she was. The feeling of excitement and nerves was making her blush. Who was worried about eating after this? Eve wasn't sure what he was going to do next. She hoped he would lean across and place his soft lips onto hers again. He stood up and let go of her hand.

"I'll put some music on. You take a seat while I clean up."

Apart from not getting her wish, Eve thought he was far too good to be true. An awful racket bellowed from the record player. Eve quickly topped up her wine glass before heading for the sofa, thinking how awful the music was.

"Would you like some help Matthew?"

"No thank you, I know how I like things done." Matthew's raised voice came from the kitchen where he was busy getting organised.

She certainly didn't want to hear this music ever again, and she thought he could stick her help up his tight gorgeous behind, if it wasn't going to be good enough.

He was very efficient, and was back in no time at all. Back on the sofa before the song had finished.

"Are you OK, Eve?" He leant forward so she could feel his breath on her face.

"Yes Matthew I am, I am very much OK." She knew it was finally going to happen.

Their lips touched, their kiss lingered. Eve knew Matthew would have to take his lips away at some point, but wished it could last for ever.

9

The Christmas tree stood tall, lights gleaming through the dining room, every branch filled with multicoloured decorations. The prettiest tree you could ever see, it must have taken hours of organising. It was their home's main focus at Christmas, and their mother liked it to be immaculate. Tidy tree, tidy Christmas she would always say.

A year had passed. All their birthdays being in the Christmas month made it extra special as they would see their father more times in December than the whole year. Natty had turned a big sixteen, Ruth had turned a big eleven and Glenn was due to be fourteen at the end of the month.

The previous months had passed slowly. A lot of tears had fallen, three hearts had been broken into tiny pieces, but there was still more laughter in the house than ever before. They liked their mother for more than a split second and a feeling of warmth would fill them. Natty would stand up for her sisters and would even take a lot more beatings herself, just so they could have it a little easier. Another punch couldn't hurt her, another tear wasn't hard to wipe away, she felt it her duty. She was the grown-up one after all, she had to show an example. Their mother seemed a little weaker for a while which gave Natty a chance to relax, even talk to her about the weather. She would have to wait until her mother wasn't so angry, when she was being nice, but it gave Natty a chance to chat, just for a while. Their mother always denied her actions towards them. Sometimes the only resolution to the brief discussion was that Natty would get it harder in the stomach or harder around her legs and face than she could ever imagine.

"Why can't you come today? You know how I need you here today of all days. The girls are all ready and waiting for you. Why are you making this so difficult for me? You said you would take them out for a Christmas treat, you promised me but worst of all you promised them. I can't take them with me, you know that. You're being cruel just like always." Their mother was on the phone to their father, he was due to take them out so they could pick their gifts. They stood in the hall, praying he wasn't going to let them down. Natty had her fingers crossed behind her back, hoping he would come. They couldn't wait to see him. It had been a very hard week at home, not a moment's rest from their mother. They all felt in that moment that nobody wanted them; they were like three lost souls, with nowhere to settle.

They could hear the muffled voice on the end of the phone. Their father was speaking very loudly.

"Look Eve, you're going to have to take them with you, I simply can't make it today. I know it's risky but you'll be fine, just let them wait outside. No one will see them!"

"I can't believe it, if someone sees them with me you are going to be in real trouble. Some father you've turned out to be."

"Stop overreacting Eve. I am really sorry. I've told you I can't make it."

"You're not sorry. If you were then you'd come and get them. You're being selfish."

"Eve calm down, it's not ladylike."

"I'll give you ladylike up your backside." Their mother ended the phone call, standing and breathing heavily for a while, not taking her hand from the receiver. As she turned she realised her girls had overheard the whole conversation.

"We're not seeing Dad today Mother, are we?" Natty took off her hat, messing her hair, and Glenn and Ruth followed feeling downhearted.

"No, you're not seeing your father today. I can't understand why I thought you were precious to him."

"We can't get our presents today Mother, can we?" Ruth already knew what she wanted for Christmas. It was a princess castle to put on top of her wardrobe, so she could always see it. So she could lie down on her bed and imagine living inside with her prince. It was going to be her escape.

"Put your hats on girls, I will take you." Their mother had never spoken in such a way before. The girls could see the fear in her face as they stood totally amazed at the thought of a day out of the house with their mother. She had never wanted to take them out before. She seemed to do nothing else but hurt them within their beautiful home. It was always either their father who had to be with them or they had to all go out together. Even though they could see how scared she was, excitement rushed through them all.

"What about Dad, Natty?" Ruth suddenly felt as though she was letting her father down. He was the one who took them, he'd told her once before that if she needed to go anywhere, he was the one to ask. Now what was she to do?

"I won't be a minute." Their mother grabbed her bag and gloves and quickly pulled on her coat.

"Let's go." She couldn't get out of the door quick enough, she hadn't checked herself in the mirror or even given the girls a once over.

They all froze as they watched their mother pace down the garden path.

"It's a beautiful morning, come on girls, what are you waiting for?"

They were waiting for the stranger to leave and their mother to come back.

She was quite a way in front of them. All they had to do was catch her up – it had never been so simple for them.

"Natty what's going on?"

"Don't ask me Glenn."

"Maybe Mother's taken funny pills."

"Be quiet will you. Why can't you just leave it?"

"I was only joking, keep your hair on will you, and anyway when did you become all loyal?"

"I didn't. Let's catch Mother up shall we?"

Natty slammed the door behind her. They were all outside together with their mother. It had been such a long time for them all, they could finally share the sunshine and feel the cold wind on their young faces.

"Where are we going Mother?" Ruth was the first one to speak as she strolled next to her.

"We are going for coffee and then to the best department store in town. And if we get time we can go and visit your dear grandmother."

Ruth's hand was being held by their mother. Her woolly glove kept it extra warm. Their fingers clasped together. Glenn kept looking and wondered why her hand hadn't been taken.

"How have you been my dear? I haven't had the chance to ask you lately." She was looking down at Ruth.

Their mother walked tall, almost stretching her small body, as though she wanted the entire world to see her out with her girls.

"Everything is OK Mother." Ruth gripped her mother's hand tighter. Was this really the wicked witch she had desperately wanted to escape from?

"Natty, how's school?"

"Yes, it's fine Mother." Natty trailed behind a little trying to absorb the whole situation.

"Glenn, what about you?"

"Yes I'm fine." Glenn spoke a little nervously but subconsciously still waited for their mother to take her hand.

In no time at all the journey was over. Their mother requested for the bus to stop before the town centre. She was full of excitement.

"It's still here, I can't believe it." She came to a sudden halt without any warning. The coffee bar was still as busy as she remembered.

"Come on girls, we're going to stop here first."

As the door was pushed open by Natty the bell rang clearly. The lady who'd served there years ago was nowhere to be seen, and a very clean and respectable-looking gentleman was now serving.

Natty, Glenn and Ruth found an empty booth and sat down excitedly.

"Four coffees and four bagels please, with extra milk in one of the coffees." Their mother looked as though she was in a total dream. She walked over to the place where her daughters sat.

"Here we are."

"Thank you Mother!" They all spoke at once, feeling comfortable for seeing their mother happier than ever before. As they all sat drinking and eating, the sugar dispenser remained untouched. Their mother drank her coffee just how she liked it.

"Have you ever been to the department store in town?"

"But Mother, it's really expensive." Natty spoke with her mouth slightly full.

"Hey, I think we shouldn't care today girls." Their mother didn't work but her house had been paid for and their father provided for them all. She had begun the habit of putting savings away when she was young. Whatever happened in her life she always remembered to save. It was something her parents had always taught her. They had been right. But she had always looked for a good enough reason to dip into her savings.

"Have you been here before, Mother?" Glenn wanted to know how she knew of the place. It was obvious she had a life before them, it was just that none of them knew anything about it at all.

Their mother stopped sipping her drink and gently placed it down on her empty plate, smiling softly, almost becoming coy.

"This wonderful place is where your father and I met."

"You met in here? No way."

"Yes way dear Glenn. Your father and I were young once, you know."

The girls all laughed aloud. They felt relaxed and happy, having found a connection with their mother they had never managed to find before. It felt great, it felt scary.

Leaving four empty cups and plates on the table, they made their way out of the coffee bar. Their mother stopped and looked before she closed the door behind her, as if it was to be last time she would ever go in the place. She slowly closed the glass door and turned towards her girls.

After a long cold walk they finally reached the store. "Anything you want girls."

"Anything, Mother? We can choose anything?" Ruth knew exactly where she was heading. There was only one thing she could ever possibly want.

Glenn strolled away from her mother's side, touching the make-up stands and cautiously spraying all different types of perfume. It was making her nose itch. She loved anything pretty and scented. She grabbed at a huge powder puff, and dusted it onto her cold cheeks, white dust going everywhere. Natty stayed close to their mother's side. She couldn't understand the day, she didn't really want to. The wonderful surroundings took her breath away. Decorations hung around the glorious building, and sweet fragrances filled the lobby. Natty thought most of them had probably been sprayed by Glenn, which bought a smile to her face. Noises from the happy Christmas shoppers filled the air. The shiny marble floors seemed to go on for ever, the escalators looking like they were going to touch the ceiling. It was a magical sight, it was Christmas. Natty thought if she were to hide, then she could get locked in all night, and when everyone was asleep she'd help herself to all the treats. She could have her own little Christmas, whatever she wanted.

"Natty, what are you looking for?"

"I'm not sure what I would like, Mother."

"I know my dear, I know exactly what you mean. If we all knew what we wanted our lives would be so much easier. Sometimes you just have to live with the things you believe you want."

OK Mother, I'll go and have a look thank you." Natty dashed off quickly – the thought of her mother starting to preach in the middle of the store was too much for her to contemplate.

An exciting thirty minutes passed. Ruth ran back to her mother with her Princess Castle and Glenn had chosen a rather peculiar-style handbag. Natty decided on a beautiful brown leather diary. Taking her cheque book from her bag their mother walked with the girls to pay. They all followed in delight. A cheque was written with ease and handed over to the lady at the cluttered counter. Her make-up looked as though it could have taken the most of the morning to apply.

Their mother picked up the large glossy red bag, thanking and gently smirking at the over-dressed cashier. They all turned around, bursting into laughter, and left.

"We have time to visit your grandmother if you wish girls."

Missing their grandmother and her home-made cakes was something else they had to live with. They were thrilled to be given the chance to see her again. They all waited together wrapped up warm at the bus stop. They had forgotten how long it took to get there, being very small the last time they went.

Ruth sat next to their mother in front of Natty and Glenn. As the bus travelled they all took in the world around them. The busy shoppers, the large buildings, they were all part of it today. It only took six stops on the bus and they were there.

Their mother rang the doorbell. It felt like they had been waiting for ever as the cold air began to bite into their faces. The front garden was overgrown, but their grandmother's house still looked the same as they remembered it.

They almost didn't recognise the old lady who opened the door, she seemed slower and her hair was very grey. Her wrinkled faced looked sad. But they still knew it was their dear grandmother under the blanket of age, hoping to get to know her again.

"How wonderful, how absolutely wonderful, hello my darling Eve. What a lovely surprise. Please don't tell me these are my beautiful granddaughters? You have all grown so." The tears gently left her old eyes. Miriam didn't give any of them a chance to enter the hallway properly before she was kissing them all over their cold faces.

"I've only just put the kettle on." With cold and now damp faces they followed their grandmother. Her house was very quiet, not even the sound of a radio or television to disturb it, no background noise to keep her company. They threw their coats on the sofa – it was lovely for them not to worry at all.

"Stay in here girls for a moment, I have to speak to your mother alone."

Miriam left them in the quiet living room and went to join her daughter.

Their mother and their grandmother were finally alone. They hugged each other and all the strength Miriam had in her old arms was used up in that one hug.

"How are you darling?"

"We're doing our best Mum, we really are."

"Eve, you haven't got to prove anything to me, I am always on your side."

"I know Mum, I just find it so hard sometimes, but I can't let them go. I only need to get on my feet again. It won't take long."

"Why are you hurting yourself so much and those beautiful girls?"

"Mum, I don't know. I would rather have them this way than not at all. I know that it's really selfish of me, but I know I can do it.

51

I know I can get better. Matt said he would keep an eye on me, but he doesn't seem to care."

"He would be in real trouble Eve." The tears left their eyes, they cried together. Miriam would have cried more if she really knew what was happening to her beautiful granddaughters waiting in the other room.

"Right, anyway, let's get them girls a warm drink – they must be frozen." Miriam and Eve took a deep breath in unison and carried on the visit.

"I haven't come to upset you, Mum."

"I know sweetheart, it's not your fault." Miriam carried drinks on a small tray into the living room. The girls told her about of school and what they enjoyed doing there, which was really all they could share with her. Apart from the great day with their mother, and the gifts they had all been able to choose. Natty still felt unsure as she sat in a large chair in front of the television. The evening was drawing in and it was time to leave. As they left their grandmother slipped some money into each of their coat pockets.

"Buy yourself something nice for Christmas. But don't forget to put a little away." Her voice was slower as she was becoming tired. "Bye Ruth, goodbye Glenn, goodbye Natasha."

"Grandma, it's Natty."

"Sorry dear, it's my age. I love you whatever you're called."

Another journey on the bus home, as amazing but just the other way. It really was going to be the end of their day soon. They wanted it to go on for ever, and their mother to stay kind for ever. Surely when the day ended then her kindness would too. The warmth of the house hit them it as they all stood in the hall, waiting for their mother's orders. She just walked passed them to the kitchen, placing the large bag on the table. Their bag full of the wonderful things they had all chosen. Their mother took off her gloves.

"Girls, come here."

"Oh no, here we go." Glenn sighed.

They all walked slowly into the kitchen and waited.

"Thank you girls, for a very nice day, thank you for letting me share it with you."

Their mother turned away and started getting pans out to begin dinner.

Natty responded first.

"Mother, we really enjoyed today with you too."

"Yes Mother, it was great." Ruth pulled her coat off in eagerness, everything was finally OK. She knew it, she could feel it inside.

"Thank you too Mother." Glenn glared at Natty in disbelief.

They all stood, not quite knowing what to do next.

"Go on girls, don't fuss, go and clean up for tea." Their mother didn't look at them.

On their gentle orders they scampered upstairs to talk about the day's events. Natty found it quite strange that she hadn't thought of her father once. They finally felt relaxed in their mother's company and all it took was one wonderful day out. As they sat in Glenn's bedroom the smell of burning began to fill the house, taking their attention away from their excited discussion.

Natty stood up and looked out on to the landing. The smell wasn't from inside, it was coming from the garden. She ran back to Glenn's bedroom and pulled the net curtain to one side. A fire had been started in the garden bin. Natty could see a glossy red bag full of gifts melting away.

10

"Eve, I have a question to ask you. I know we've only been seeing each other for six months, but I was wondering if you would like to help me out at my place?"

Matthew sat in Eve's small apartment surrounded by mess – clothes hanging over the chairs, stockings drying around the bathroom, pegged onto string. Every time Matthew wanted to use the toilet he had to work his way through them. He always found it hard to tolerate and usually only stayed as long as he needed. Depending on what Eve was doing, sometimes he would choose to wait outside while Eve went in quickly to change.

Eve pushed herself from his chest where she had only just got comfortable.

"What do you mean, Matthew?" Her heart jumped a beat, was this to be the question she thought he was going to ask over their first dinner together?

"You know what I mean, to move in with me. You can't live in this mess for ever."

"But I like this mess, it's my mess." Nitwit, she thought, rather offended by his comment. She had hoped the moment a man asked her to move in with him would have been a little more romantic and a slight anger stirred in her.

"But you deserve better."

"This is great for me." Her anger was beginning to build even more. Eve could feel her lips tightening.

"Yes, I know Eve, but I'm not here am I?" Matthew smiled a cheeky smile that could never be refused, his gorgeous eyes shining.

Eve thought for a moment. Matthew did have a point. She couldn't bear to be away from him for more than a day, and there would be one set of bills. She knew how much she already loved him, but she also loved her little place. She had worked so hard to keep it, how could she just give it away? But she would have to move on some day, and now was as good a time as any.

"I would love to Matt!" She jumped on top of him and threw her arms around his neck, trying to forget her anger, having to push it deep into her stomach."

"That's great Eve, I can't wait. Now I have things to do." Matthew pushed her away, quickly kissed her on the cheek and left.

Eve just sat there dumbstruck yet again. There had been quite a few times in their six months together that he had left her lost for words, and that was saying a lot. Flopping back on the sofa, she decided to call her friends, she couldn't wait until the morning when she would see them at work. It had to be done now, especially now, due to the huge fact there was nothing else to do. Now her handsome man had done a leap. She imagined him running into the nearest phone box and changing into an action hero and then probably saving the world. She sat for a while with the handset to her ear, tapping her fingers on her knees.

"Hello."

"Hi Mary, it's me."

"Hello Eve my dear, and to what do I owe the pleasure of this wonderful evening call?"

"I'm not sure really. I was sitting here about five minutes ago with Matthew, he asked me to move in with him, I said yes and now he's left me just sitting here, romantic wouldn't you say"?

"You said yes! No way, oh Jesus, you're moving in with coffee boy? You're moving in with him?"

Eve had to take the phone away from her ear, while her screaming, over-excited friend calmed down. Thinking maybe Matthew had extra sensory hearing and could hear too.

"Mary, he's only just asked me, my slippers aren't there yet. Relax will you." Eve was starting to feel a little flustered.

"So why's he vanished? Didn't you tidy for inspection?"

"That's not fair, he just likes to be tidy that's all, you know what he's like."

"Only by what you've told me. I wouldn't want to live with him."

"So are you happy for me then?" Eve was slightly sarcastic – she wanted a little faith from her friend.

"Eve, if you're happy then I'm happy"

"Stop trying to be philosophical Mary, it doesn't suit you."

"No darling, I'm pleased for you, only thinking you couldn't leave your pubic hairs in his soap. Joke, I'm pleased for you. Look after yourself, got to go, see you tomorrow. Bye sweetie."

"Bye Mary." Eve placed the receiver down in relief. The whole idea of calling the others seemed far too unbearable for the time being. They had all met him at the coffee bar and she didn't want a repercussion of the same call. She would have pulled all her hair out by the end, ended up with a bald head, and knowing Matthew he would polish that too. She imagined him polishing her head till it shone and laughed to herself.

She began flicking through the newspaper, then looked around at her apartment which desperately needed cleaning. Throwing the paper down Eve promptly jumped from the sofa. Pulling her sleeves up, she stood for a while with her hands on her hips wondering where to start. She began to clean, after all she wouldn't be able to let Matthew's house get this way, not in a million years. As she cleaned she thought of her parents. What would they say to her now? They hadn't even met him.

As she closed the door to her apartment for the last time, Eve thought of all the happy days and nights she'd had there and of course the lonely times. She would miss every little thing about it. Waking up some mornings finding old plates from supper and empty bottles of wine scattered on the floor, where her friends had chatted for England the previous nights. Her friends would fill ashtrays high, the smell of company would enthral her. Sometimes she could just, sit and sob for no reason at all. But whatever she felt it belonged to her. She didn't have to let anyone see how mad she got. Would she ever be able to dance around the kitchen and jump all over the sofa, holding her hairbrush imagining herself as a star? Sit on the sofa with a blanket and a huge bowl of salted popcorn? And sometimes not even change her pants for a couple of days! She didn't have to answer to anyone.

She closed her front door slowly. There was no turning the key again to all her little singular pleasures. She stood holding a box containing some books and a withering plant. As she looked at its poor brown leaves she knew Matthew would bring it back to full glory with no trouble at all.

"Come on Eve, let's get you home." Matthew was waiting for her, and took the box and placed it in the van. It wasn't any ordinary one, but a great big yellow one. If her friends could see her now, she would never live it down.

Matthew made himself very busy when they arrived at his house, placing her belongings where he thought they should go.

"Oh dear, you don't want this do you?"

"Yes Matthew I do, I've had it since I was small." Eve went to grab her china doll from Matthew. He was holding it by one arm as if almost too ashamed to look at such a thing. To him it just looked like something you would pick up at an old flea market. To Eve it looked like her past was being intruded upon. She didn't get to Matthew in time, and before her eyes he had put it in a rubbish sack. She felt uneasy seeing the man she loved shuffling through her belongings, almost as if trying to erase her life before she met him. She didn't want to seem childish – she hadn't even spent an afternoon with him yet as a cohabiting couple. It was only a silly doll anyway. It had always taken up too much space on her bed so it really didn't matter.

The whole job was done very quickly. Very well organised as usual. Matthew would not sit down once until there was not a scrap of paper or a box put in its rightful place. Eve felt a mixture of feelings but all the same couldn't wait for her future with him to begin. She knew one thing only as she sat with him. She did love him very much but knew his standards would be very hard to meet.

11

They had enjoyed Glenn's birthday but whatever happened they were all still hurting, feeling let down and betrayed, and trying to forget their shopping trip which had ended in tragedy. They hadn't dared question their mother about it or even show any form of anger towards her. Glenn hadn't received the dress from her father she had been eagerly waiting for and Ruth continued to lie on her bed dreaming about her princess castle. Their mother seemed to be getting worse. Natty would find her crying nearly every day and was told strongly not to share her findings with her sisters, or else. The months passed but their father didn't come to see them as much and they couldn't work out why. Everything was becoming unbearable, but somehow they managed to hide their sadness from their school friends. Natty's efforts to be in control of her mother's actions had been truly wasted. She had bowed down to her yet again; this was the way it was going to be and they just had to live with it.

As they all sat in the garden they wondered if the pain would ever end, each girl lost in her own thoughts, hoping to work it out enough to give the others the answer.

"Natty, we can't go on like this." Glenn was stroking Ruth's hair as her head rested on her lap. It was the only affection either of them had had all week.

"Why do you always ask me for the answer? Maybe we should tell Dad. He will put a stop to it and then it will all be all right and you won't have to ask me any more." Deep down Natty did want to tell him.

"But you can't tell Dad, you can't upset him." Ruth sat up quickly with Glenn's fingers still caught in her hair. She was near to tears.

"Upset him? How do you think he would feel? He would go crazy if he knew we had kept it from him. I wasn't sure if it was a good idea at first, but there seems to be no other way. I have tried to be strong for you both, hoped I could make Mother be kind so she could stop hurting you but it's just a waste of time. And our hopes." Natty still remembered those pills which had been hidden from them all, choosing to keep her discovery secret. They must be their mother's only help.

"Why hasn't Dad come? Why? Is he leaving us?" Ruth started to cry. She had cried so many tears already in her young life, she had cried more than her whole life should have allowed. Once she became a woman there would be no tears left inside her.

"He hasn't left us Ruthi, I'm sure of it." Deep inside Natty felt he had, how could a father not see their pain? To Natty he had left them physically and emotionally already. It was another thing they had to accept.

"Come on, let's try and cheer up now, at least make the most of a good day. Let's talk about Natty's leaving party. You're going to look great. Can you believe you are finally leaving school? You can wear your beautiful dress at last, even though I would have loved to have worn it first." Glenn's face lit up as she imagined her sister in her beautiful silk dress. She was full of enthusiasm, bouncing up and down on her knees, but then stopping hastily, fearful of looking at her trousers. Please don't let there be grass stains, she thought.

Natty looked very pleased.

"I've been waiting so long to wear it. The feeling's almost unreal, but looking at things in our crazy world, what's real?" Whatever Natty had to look forward to, it would be overtaken by the sadness and burden of her family.

"You're going to look like a princess, Natty. I have a real princess for a sister."

"Ruth, you're already a princess and don't you forget it." Touching her sister on the arm Natty smiled reassuringly.

"Girls! It's time to come in now!" their mother called from the back door.

They all stood to attention without any hesitation.

"Oh yes, your father is coming tomorrow!" She went back inside and slammed the door.

"Yes I knew it! I knew he hadn't really left us." Ruth was jumping up and down clapping her hands together. Her sisters gazed on as they saw their sister doing a perfect seal impression.

"See Ruth, I told you." Natty looked at her sister with a very smug but relieved smile.

Natty knew she would feel a little better at the school leaving party that evening. All was not lost, they still had their father.

They all walked back into the kitchen, vigorously wiping their feet, making sure they took as much time as needed and not giving themselves any reason to get into trouble. Their mother was sitting at the dinner table, with her head in her hands. They were all able to witness her crying.

"Are you all right Mother?" Glenn finished wiping her feet and walked over to her. She was looking at Natty, jeering her on with her head movements and tightened lips, hoping she could make sense for her.

"Mother, what is the matter?" Natty spoke with a gentle tone, wishing Glenn could have sorted it out for them all just this once. If only she hadn't been born first then she could be the one standing back behind the others.

"Glenn, Ruth upstairs." Natty gave the orders just as her mother would have.

They both looked at her in complete bewilderment.

"Now, will you!" Her voice raised, Natty felt something inside which made her nervous.

Glenn took Ruth's hand, taking her away from the kitchen. Without any doubt she would be intending to peer through the banisters. There was no way she was missing this one.

Natty sat down beside her mother. She was daring – she hadn't washed her hands or even asked permission to sit.

"Natty, please don't look at me, just don't, I—" Their mother was unable to make eye contact with her beautiful daughter, she felt too ashamed. She was praying she would be forgiven.

"Mother, please, why are you crying again?" Feeling brave again she pulled her mother's hands away from her face. Fear overwhelmed her, but maybe now she could finally find out what was going on.

"Natasha, I have asked you politely not to look at me!" Her

mother's hands were wet from her tears; she was still unable to look at Natty even for a second.

"Mother, please stop this, we can't go on like it any more. We want to be a proper family Mother, please!" Natty was becoming upset but knew she had to be strong.

"How do I know Natty, what I'm meant to do, could you help me, let me know?" Her mother spoke softly, sounding childlike.

"Please just stop." Natty became the adult, feeling she was finally getting somewhere.

"I have always wanted to Natty, I really have!" Her face was still shadowed by her hands she hadn't looked up at all. Her petite body was full of pain.

"Mother, we all love you very much, we really want you to let us love you Mother, to show you just how much. It's as though you don't seem to love any of us. We try so hard to please you all the time." Before she knew it Nattty felt the sting from her mother's hand. She thought she had managed to break her mother's silence, but as usual it had been a waste of time. Hearing her sisters at the top of the stairs she felt foolish. Her mother placed her head in her hands again, as though nothing had happened. She had slapped Natty's face with sheer force, but didn't seem to recognise the fact at all.

The situation could never be solved by Natty. She began to believe it couldn't be solved by anyone. Natty wanted her night to begin as soon as possible. She was going to her ball, but once the clock struck twelve everything in Natty's life would go back to normal.

"If only you knew how much you all mean to me. I have ruined it for you I know." Their mother sat alone, crying. Watching her daughter leaving her alone, desperately wanting to run after her and hold her close.

Walking past her sisters at the top of the stairs Natty stood and shrugged her shoulders. "It's always going to be rubbish." Natty planned to stay in her bedroom until her party. Closing the door behind her she took a deep breath. The world outside, the other side of the door, seemed to be unreal. She heard her sisters entering their bedrooms too. Everyone in the house was alone, all in their own worlds. How can a home feel so lonely, each one escaping from the other? Natty wondered what they were all thinking in their hideaways. Were they as lonely as she was? Did they all want to stay hidden away for ever as well? Feeling unloved, each soul in her own pain, in her own silence.

Natty gave up on her thoughts and moved away from the door. When should she start getting ready? The sooner the better.

Opening her wardrobe she could see her uniform and slid the hangers across to reach for her dress. She kept sliding them; maybe it was in between the neatly hanging clothes. Suddenly all she heard was herself breathing heavily. She scraped the metal hangers across the pole frantically from left to right, the panic rushing through her.

"Please God, where is it?" she said over and over – hoping that if she kept talking it would reappear as if by magic. It wasn't there, her blue silk dress which had hung for so long. Waiting for the day it would finally be worn. She stood frozen, trying to convince herself that she must have missed it in her search. Her thoughts went to her mother. Surely she wouldn't have it. The night out was allowed. The tears in the stomach were about to come out if she liked it or not. She didn't want to cry, not tonight. Natty left her bedroom, knocking on Glenn's door with all of her energy.

"Glenn it isn't funny, give it back or I will come in and get it!" Natty was still furiously knocking.

Glenn's door flew open.

"WHAT!"

"Give my dress back Glenn, I need to get ready. It's not funny!"

"I haven't got your stupid dress."

"Glenn, please let me have it?"

"What are you? Mad or something? What would I do with it anyway?" Glenn's voice was hostile.

Glenn shut the door in her sister's face.

Natty's anger was building up with every second; every moment her dress didn't appear was another knot in her stomach.

Ruth came out on hearing all the noise.

"Nat, what's the matter?"

"As if you didn't know, you must have heard me. Ruth have you seen my dress?"

"No I haven't. The last time I did was on your birthday." Ruth opened Glenn's door and went inside. The door was shut on Natty yet again.

It was a conspiracy, Natty knew it. They all hated her. Why did they? What had she done to them that had been so bad?

Standing on the landing alone she turned her head to see the long journey down to her mother. Slowly but hesitantly she made her way down to her dear mother again.

She didn't seem to be as sad as before. She had stopped crying and was flicking the pages of a glossy magazine, sitting perfectly poised with a smug look on her face.

"Mother, I can't find my dress." Natty stood at the door, her voice a little shaky. Wishing she could scream.

Their mother slowly turned around and looked up at her.

"Dress Natty? Oh yes dear, it's in the trash." She wanted to tell Natty how she had tried to stop herself, but there wouldn't be any point now, it was done; it was only a silly dress anyway.

Natty's heart almost stopped in shock on hearing the statement spoken so coolly by her mother. In complete disbelief she ran to the rubbish bin. Slowly lifting the lid she could finally see her dress. It resembled blue seaweed, shreds of soft blue silk lay on old cartons of broken egg shells. Finally discovering the whereabouts of her dress was a waste of time; it couldn't be worn, it wasn't her dress any more.

"Why Mother?" Natty looked to see her mother going up the stairs. A large pair of kitchen scissors lay on top of the cupboard, while walking proudly up the stairs was the woman who took them in her hand. Grabbing a handful of silk and filled with rage Natty ran after her.

"Mother, what have you done?" Don't ignore me you fucking mad woman!" Natty had no fear at that very second. Screaming, she rushed after her her mother. She was nearly at the top. Natty grabbed at her arm.

"Mother, will you listen to me? Natty held her mother's arm with all her strength, her fingers pushing into her skin. Suddenly she felt the force of her mother's body falling past her. Standing on the stairs, her hands sweating on the blue silk, she watched her mother plunge to the bottom. The thud from each step as she fell went through Natty's body like a lead weight. It all went quiet.

63

Natty just wanted to wake from the nightmare she was having. She could never wake, her mother was lying at the bottom. It was really happening. She turned to see her sisters. The blood had drained from their faces too.

"Is Mother dead?" Ruth moved forward very slowly.

Glenn stood with her arms folded. They were whispering as if they didn't want to wake her from her sleep.

"Glenn, please will you help me?" It was Natty's turn to feel like a small child, who needed help even to walk a few steps.

"I'm not touching her. No way, I'm not getting the blame!"

"Thanks a lot. You wouldn't care if she was dead, what kind of person are you?" Fear consumed Natty; she could barely breathe through her panic.

"The person I am my dear sister is what that wonderful woman has made me. Stop being so dramatic, she'll get up in a minute and beat you up again." Glenn spoke sternly, her voice emotionless.

All their whispers were getting louder through the despair.

"Please help her, Natty. You pushed her, you have to help her now." Ruth wanted to escape to her castle more than ever before.

"I didn't push her, OK? The mad woman cut up my dress."

Their mother's bruised body was as still as could be. Natty started to walk down each step. Her hands wrapped around the banisters, pushing her fingers hard around the wood, making her fingers feel sore. As she stood over the petite powerless body a tear left her eye. Natty could hear a slight groaning.

"She's not dead!" Natty raised her voice slightly to her onlookers. They hadn't moved an inch. It wouldn't matter if she cried now. Their mother would have had her in tears before she went to her party anyhow.

"What are all the tears for?" Glenn's behaviour remained uncaring.

"Mother, Mother, we need you to wake up now. I didn't mean it." Natty's tears fell onto her mother's blouse as she knelt down next to her.

Their mother wouldn't move, not an inch. Their god damn stubborn mother was still hurting them, but this time she wasn't aware of it.

"Natty, you will have to call Dad." Ruth finally found the bravery to move, and went down to join her trembling sister.

64

"Don't call Dad, he'll be upset, I don't want to see him like that over a crazy woman." Glenn followed Ruth, stepping over their mother's body as if she was a pile of dirty laundry.

"Ambulance please!" Glenn was on the phone in no time at all. Her sisters didn't get any say in the matter.

"No Glenn." Natty tried to pull the receiver from her. The raising of Glenn's fist made her retreat promptly. She returned to where their mother lay.

Glenn's voice was almost robotic. Placing the receiver down hard, she stepped over the dirty laundry again.

"She said keep her warm." Glenn went back to her bedroom and yanked a blanket from her bed. She threw it down the stairs where it landed hard on their mother.

"Glenn, what's wrong with you? You can be so cruel sometimes."

"I wasn't the one who pushed her." Glenn left the commotion and her sisters to find her own hiding place. The others needed to be together more than ever before but Glenn didn't want to be a part of them. Natty held Ruth, kissing the top of her head. "She's going to be OK Ruth." Natty couldn't understand why she hoped her mother would survive. Their life could be so much better if she wasn't around. She quickly put the thought out of her head. They went to stand in the cool breeze. Waiting outside the house of sadness. The minutes passed until the ambulance arrived, lighting up the whole street. The two handsome ambulance men took control. Natty felt relieved, finally standing back to watch someone take the pressure from her. Natty, Glenn and Ruth all watched as the two strong men took their mother outside. Glenn from the top of the stairs, Natty and Ruth standing side by side. For once their mother was not in control. She was being fussed over, pulled around without any say. She would go mad if she knew.

"Can we come?" Ruth's voice was soft.

Three girls together, with loneliness and confusion filling their young hearts and minds.

12

Over two years had already passed. Eve's life with Matthew had grown into a beautiful flower. The love she felt for him exceeded anything ever written in the best romantic novel. When she was younger she would always read romance, imagining one day she would be the shy elegant woman swept off her feet. This was better – it wasn't false words put together. This was real. Matthew worshipped the ground she walked on, he couldn't do enough for her. Everything around her had to be meticulous. If he couldn't manage it, he would make sure she achieved it for herself. Even when Eve felt she achieved her best he was constantly telling her it wasn't good enough. He wouldn't allow her from his sight, if it could be helped, other than the hours in a working day. Matthew requested that Eve should leave her job at the fish market, which for one thing gave her a chance to get her chores finished, but mainly freed her to give all her attention to him. As she wasn't seeing her friends at all it gave Matthew a chance to control her every move. Eve would be alone all day wondering if her friends would like to hear from her. They had tried to keep in touch, but Matthew informed them how busy she was so meeting up would be a no go. She hoped they would have ignored him and one of them could knock on her door and come in for a quick tea, and a laugh, when he wasn't there.

Being indoors all day made her feel suffocated, the walls around her seeming to move in closer and closer. Some days, when all her jobs were done, she would sit and stare at the walls for hours, Looking for an answer to why she loved this man so much, but at the same time felt a slave to him. The only reason to move from the chair was when she heard Matthew putting the key in the lock. Matthew wanted to move home for more space. It would mean more rooms to clean and keep immaculate and less time thinking for herself.

Eve had missed a period, but had not yet informed the man of her dreams. She wanted to make the moment wonderful for him, hoping he would be happy about the news. Would it fit in with his ideal perception of life? Eve found herself behaving differently in front of Matthew, as he wanted her to be more and more like his perfect image. He would correct her in her grammar and attire. He would argue the point constantly with his brother that Eve was perfect, and the more he argued the more he had to prove. Through all his efforts to make everything fantastic and deserving for her, Matthew never knew the pain Eve felt. She would talk to herself every day, and fight with herself – the young happy-go-lucky, messy woman she used to be. And loved being. Against this false image of perfection for the man she loved so very much.

"Eve, where are you? I've seen a beautiful house, you'll love living there." How pleased Eve will be with me, Matthew thought, hurrying through the door, too excited to wash grease from himself. He wanted Eve's attention and he wanted it right then.

"Hi Matthew, I'm in here." Eve was lying on the sofa. She needed to rest, she had worked her fingers to the bone all day. Her hands were stinging from all her efforts.

"What are you lying down for? It's only early evening. Sit up and let me show you." Matthew spoke with eagerness.

He waited for Eve to move her legs and then he sat down, but only on the edge so as not to make too much mess.

"I don't want to leave here Matthew, I really love living here." Eve hoped he would listen to her.

"This place isn't good enough for you now, you deserve so much better. You must be bored with it – you have to have ambition you know, set your sights higher."

Matthew decided to leave the papers on Eve's lap and then left the room, feeling on top of the world.

"I'll give you ambition right up your hairy backside."

"What did you say Eve?" The force from the shower that Matthew turned on drowned Eve's words.

"Nothing my truly loving creature." Finding the whole moment rather amusing, she thought she would make the most of it. "You clean freak, pain in the arse, piece of poo at the bottom of my shoe, you nutty yucky globby mother fucker, fuck head."

"Eve, have you gone mad?" Matthew stood in confusion.

As she looked up Matthew was standing over her behind the sofa, rubbing the towel over his hair. She wanted to die at that very moment. How was she going to tell him now? The mother of his first born was a foul-mouthed fruit cake.

"I don't know Eve; I try my best for you, I really do." Matthew shook his head and went to get dressed as if having a damp towel wrapped around his waist for longer than necessary would have him growing two heads.

"Do you want tea darling?" Eve chuckled to herself and entered her extremely clean kitchen. She wanted to get the tub of flour and throw the whole lot everywhere, especially over her dear boyfriend's head. The moment of madness turned into sadness for Eve; she started to cry. She found her emotions hard to deal with. One day she could take on the world, another she would cower into the corner like a lost soul. Why did she feel so sad and angry? When did she start feeling that the whole world was out to hurt her? With two drinks in her hands, she went to read the paperwork Matthew had been so excited about.

"Looks nice don't you think? We're going to look at it tomorrow." Matthew took the papers from her and folded them neatly.

"I don't want to Matthew." Eve tried once more, if only he would listen to her.

"I've booked it now, three thirty OK?" Matthew said excitedly.

"OK Matthew, whatever you say." Eve felt sick, her stomach feeling heavy.

"Now come and give me a kiss Eve, I've missed you so very much." He held out his arms to her.

Taking a deep breath and realising that her boyfriend only wanted the best for her she held his arms and kissed his lips as hard as she could. The thought of "mother fucker" came to her, sincerely of course.

Eve loved the company of Matthew, and they would always sit cuddled up on the sofa. Often her eyes would gently close and she would fall asleep on his lap. When she woke she could always feel his strong hands stroking her hair. The evenings always drew in quickly, one because she loved him so much and two because she spent so many days alone. But the thought of feeling his body near her each and every evening also gave her the feeling of excitement when she waited for him.

"Matthew, would you like to be a father one day?" Eve lay on his bare chest.

"Eve, could you stop calling me Matthew? It feels rather formal. And to your question, yes I would love to be a father. But everything would have to be sorted first, new house, new car. I would have to work more hours to make sure our child had the best, I would want it to be perfect in every way."

"Have you quite finished Matt?" Eve wished she'd never asked him.

"Well I could find out about names, maybe go to the library – they have books on baby names and everything you would ever need to know about bringing up children."

"I didn't mean have you finished your speech, I meant let me tell you something. I think you will be going to the library sooner than you think." Eve paused, waiting for Matthew's screams.

"I don't know what you mean." Matthew raised his eyebrows.

"Baby names, Matthew. You may have to visit the library sooner than you think." Eve was shaking her head and wondering why he just wasn't getting what she was trying to say.

"Yes Eve, that's where I'll go when I need to get information."

Eve was almost bursting with annoyance.

"Matthew I am trying to say something to you. I am trying to say that I have missed a period."

There was a silence: Matthew looked up and down, frowning, trying to make sense of the whole situation.

"Eve, are you going to have a baby, are you going to have another perfect you?"

"Thank goodness the light's finally been switched on. I'm not sure yet but I'm never late." Feeling relieved her dear boyfriend had taken the news calmly, Eve went to lie back on his chest.

Matthew jumped from the bed, pulled ironed trousers from the wardrobe, a smart shirt and clean socks and quickly dressed, not forgetting polished shoes. "I'm going to go, I have things to do." He was gone again.

69

As Eve heard his car engine starting she took a huge sigh. She felt very excited but suffocated at the same time.

Her thoughts were disturbed by the phone ringing.

"I'm OK Matthew. I haven't lifted anything too heavy." As she spoke out loud she pulled herself from the bed. She could imagine him on the other end of the phone enquiring if she was all right, or if she had any pains.

"Hello!" As Eve stood naked with the phone against her ear, she waited to hear him. There was a long silence.

"Hello Eve." The voice on the other end was soft and shaky.

"Oh, hello how are you? How are things going?" Eve was so happy to hear from her mum: she was busting to tell her she might be pregnant. She hadn't spoken to her in such a long time. And the mood she had been in lately she could do with some good advice from her dear old mum.

"Eve, hello darling, I'm sorry to call so late, I wouldn't normally you know with how things are, but I don't know how to tell you." Miriam sounded very upset. Eve sat down, her bare bottom touching the sofa. Matthew wouldn't have been happy.

"What is the matter Mum, are you ill?"

"I'm OK, I'm sorry my sweetheart, but your father has had a heart attack, he's not doing very well at all." Miriam started to cry.

Eve's heart felt like it was about to stop, her body as if it were becoming paralysed. She wanted to reach down the phone line and hold her mother close, she wanted to touch her. Eve's world would end if anything ever happened to either of her parents. Whenever she felt alone, which was often, she knew they were somewhere near, always under the same sky.

"But Mum, he's only fifty-nine."

"Can you come to him sweetheart, come to see him? I don't think he's going to see the sun rise. You know how he loves the sun on his garden."

"Oh Mum, please don't say those things, please don't cry, try to be strong. I'm on my way. Where are you both?" Eve's voice sounded broken, she held her tears back as much as she could.

"We're at the hospital where you were born my darling."

Eve slowly placed the handset down; she couldn't believe what her mother had told her. What was she to do? Her parents had

70

always been so strong together. They were like a walnut shell. Not letting anyone or anything break them. It felt like someone had just found a huge hammer and smashed their shell to pieces. Eve dragged her feet as she started to dress, feeling as though she was in another time and place, unable to be in the moment. Not sure how to feel, all of a sudden she couldn't feel. The pain would be too hard to bear. With all the fear building up inside of her she almost forgot how to dress. She tried anyway.

"I'm back Eve!" Matthew found Eve on the floor with her skirt held in her hands, crying like a little baby.

"Eve, my Eve, what's wrong?"

"My father is going to die Matthew, he is going to leave me." Her tears couldn't be stopped, her heart was breaking in half. Her parents were the only ones who could make it whole again.

"What are you saying, Eve? Come on, I'll take you to see him. You can't go out like this, sort yourself out and we'll go straight away. I've bought you some fizzy drink. I'll put it in a safe place."

"My fizzy drink? You selfish man, you bastard, Matthew. My father isn't going to be here to see his first grandchild, you make me sick." She began to scream, lunging for the first thing she could reach. The bottle of red fluid splattered across the wall, glass smashing everywhere. She grabbed at the lamp by its shade and banged it onto the floor; everything her small shaking hands could lift was thrown into the air. Naked and trembling, Eve jumped onto the bed and began ripping at the pillows, screaming. The pain wouldn't leave her body. Suddenly without warning she stopped and breathed hard, gasping as she tried to get her breathing back into rhythm. The walls were bare. Debris from broken pictures made the perfect collage, all thrown and ripped lying around her. She wanted only to rip her heart out, clenching her fist near her breast.

"I hate you! I hate this house! I hate myself! Everyone hates me! I want to die Matthew, please let me die and not my father, please?" Eve sat curled up on the mattress, her hands now holding her knees tightly to her chin. She rocked to and fro.

"Eve, let me help you, I'm so sorry." Matthew felt numb and slowly held her arm, taking her from the bed. He began helping her to dress, and as he brushed her hair and wiped a warm flannel over her swollen face, he began thinking to himself, unable to understand what he had done to upset her so.

"Let's go." Matthew took her hand as if she were a small girl and led her to the car.

"She said he wasn't going to see the sun, my father loves the sunshine, he said I was his sunshine." With her face sore and her legs weak, she held Matthew's hand tightly.

"He will be fine Eve, I promise you."

13

The lights seemed to make the huge building like a fantasy, sparkling on the white walls. Was the building full of people who were horrible to their children? Is that why they were all there?

Putting on a performance, pretending their accidents happened another way. All wicked parents in one place together. Natty's mind was in turmoil, she couldn't think rationally at all. She opened her hand, and as she looked down she saw she still had hold of the blue silk shreds. Through all the sweat and fear they had stuck to her palm. Was the dress trying to mould itself together? She wanted it to, and then all the chaos wouldn't have happened. She would have her dress back and her mother would still be sitting in the kitchen.

"Dr Peters, this lady had a fall down the stairs, her daughters say she hasn't moved at all since the incident." The ambulance man passed their mother's information over to the doctor. As if they were playing pass the parcel. The ambulance man left promptly to save another parent from their fate. The doctor leant over her.

"Come on Eve, you can wake up now. Everything is OK. You will be safe here." Speaking with complete compassion, he was very sensitive. Natty felt he and their mother were not strangers. To the doctor she didn't seem to be another person on a trolley. He wrapped his hand around hers and whispered in her ear.

Their mother lay still as all the tests were completed efficiently. The doctor kept talking to her over and over. She started to move, her hand started to tighten around his. The doctor took his attention from their mother for a moment and faced all three girls.

"I take it your father is behind you somewhere?" The doctor's voice was full of assumption.

"He's on his way," Ruth muttered almost under her breath. She just wanted to go home.

"I don't understand why you are here without him, most of all alone with your mother." The doctor looked and sounded extremely concerned.

"He doesn't know, OK? And he doesn't live with us." For some reason Glenn felt the need to tell the truth, the whole truth and nothing but the damn truth.

The doctor seemed a very caring man, soft grey hair which complemented his soft but serious face. He went over to another colleague. In between their whispers he was pointing at them. Natty, Ruth and Glenn stood still, it was their turn to perform. It was at that moment they knew they had to get their father.

They had been separated from their mother. They sat patiently in the relatives' room where warm orange juice was served, while their father was contacted. Natty was imagining her evening out. What would it have been like? It was all she could do, imagine. The white blinds which covered the glass doors kept them shut out from the real world again. Where was their father? Why was he taking so long?

"Well done Natty, you've really done it now, all because of your stupid dress." Glenn was still being cruel.

"I can't believe you, you opened your mouth. You don't care about anyone but yourself. If Mother had done that to your dress, how would you react?" Natty raised her eyebrows, waiting for Glenn's reply.

"Get it right Nat, she didn't do it to your dress, she did it to you." Glenn gave her sister a smug grin.

"Please stop fighting, we have to be nice to each other, we need to be strong." Ruth sat right in the middle of her quarrelling sisters, behaving in a far more grown-up way by far.

"Ruth, you're too young to understand anything, so for the first time act your age will you."

"You're not much older than me Glenn; I hope you're proud of yourself. I hope you can live with what you say to Natty."

Natty saw the door open. Dr Peters entered, followed by their father.

"Daddy!" Ruth ran to him wrapping her arms around his waist.

"Hi Dad, thank God you're here." Natty couldn't bring herself to go anywhere near him, she was off parents for one night.

"It's all Natty's fault Dad, she put mother here." Still feeling the need to make her sister endure more pain than necessary, Glenn sat with her arms folded.

"It's not anyone's fault girls, your mother is fine now." Their father seemed to be embarrassed, they had never seen him like it before. The immaculate appearance they had always seen was not there, his clothes were not as tidy. Natty noticed how unpolished his shoes were and she couldn't believe that for the first time her father was not showing any attention to detail.

"What's going to happen to Mother, Dad?" Ruth wouldn't let her father go.

"She will be coming home tomorrow." Their father's voice was stern.

"So where are we to go?" Ruth's voice was muffled as she spoke into her father's chest.

"With me, you are coming home with me."

"Not a bad job after all Nat, at least we can stay with Dad." Glenn got up and kissed her father on the cheek.

"Let's go girls." Their father led the way.

Natty felt as if her nightmare was finally at an end.

"Sir, please don't forget we will be in touch," the doctor said quickly as he passed them in the corridor, before going to carry on with his duties.

"Dad, can we see Mother before we go?" Natty stood twisting the blue silk in her hands, praying her father would say yes.

"I'm not sure Natty; I don't think it's a good idea."

"Dad what are you saying? Please?" Natty just had to make sure their mother was still alive and they were not all pretending she was all right.

Their father spoke to the doctor briefly and called Natty over.

"Girls you can all go to see her."

"No thank you Dad." Glenn wasn't going anywhere; she made sure Ruth was to stay at her side, yanking at her arm.

"We just want to go with Dad, don't we Ruth?"

"Um, yes, we just want to go now."

"We'll wait outside, Natty, don't be too long." Their father smiled softly at Natty, feeling full of uncertainty.

14

Eve and Matthew had lived in their new house for only six months. Eve found the house beautiful, and she loved the large garden which was full of apple trees. There was more space than could ever possibly be dealt with, but it was a family home, and she intended on making it wonderful. Heavily pregnant, she found keeping the house clean harder than ever before, Matthew was never at home; living in a larger house meant more hours of work. Eve was still alone each day, each hour passing slowly. She would climb onto a chair every day and polish the large clock in the dining room. She loved the old clock which had been a gift from her father. She had made a promise to him that she would always treasure it and pass it down to his first grandchild one day. Matthew hated it; he found it an eyesore. He thought it made the room look cluttered. This was the only thing she got away with. She made the point very clear, if the clock went, then she went with it. He found her rather silly – after all it was only a stupid clock.

Her mother had been right her father didn't see the sun shine again. The lights in the room had been dimmed too much for Eve's liking when she was taken in to see him. She asked if all the lights could be turned on, she didn't want her father to die in the dark. He held her hand as he passed away.

Just before he went, he pulled her down to his lips and whispered, "You will always be my beautiful sunshine." Then he fell asleep for ever.

His words would go through Eve's mind again and again. He was the one who shone in her day, but he was gone. She knew there would never be anyone in her world who could ever replace him. She rubbed her well-manicured hands over her bump, hoping she would feel differently once her baby was born. She would cry every night. She hated everything in her life. She did love Matthew very much, but he had made a promise to her, after all. He'd said her father would be fine; he'd lied. How could she ever trust him after that?

"I knew you would love living here Eve – how fabulous it is!" Matthew was still as enthusiastic about the house as he'd been from the very first viewing. He'd managed to be there at three thirty exactly, not a second later. Eve's father had died the night before and he still put his priorities to the test.

Eve was cleaning as she normally did, even though she had already cleaned that morning.

"Eve, stop for a moment, I'd like to ask you something. Come and take a minute's rest."

"I need more than a minute's rest Matthew, I need a lifetime." Eve sighed, rolling her eyes.

"Don't be silly Eve; I want to be serious, for your sake." Matthew couldn't understand why his perfect Eve seemed to be so unhappy. He had given her everything and more.

"Heaven's more like." Eve rolled her eyes and sat opposite him.

"No Eve, I want to ask you to be my wife, my beautiful wife. We couldn't get married now, obviously, because of your fat stomach, you wouldn't look right. So as soon as you have given birth we will get the wheels in motion. I love you Eve, you are the most amazing person I have ever met, you are everything to me and more, I am so lucky to have you. I don't know what I must have done to deserve you, but thank you Eve, thank you for coming into my life. Will you marry me Eve? Will you make me the happiest man that has ever lived?" Matthew was full of excitement. He was certain what Eve's response would be. Holding her hand he looked into her eyes and waited for her to answer.

"Well, apart from the fat comment, I never thought you were going to ask. Of course I would love to become your wife." They kissed and held each other so very close. Eve's thoughts quickly went back to their first dinner together when she was sure he was going to ask her. It was definitely about time. She had a heavy feeling welling up in her stomach again – it must have been excitement, surely.

"Don't squeeze me too tight Eve, your stomach is getting squashed."

Eve took the cloth and continued to clean. She wasn't sure what she was going to clean, but knowing that at any minute Matthew was going to leave her again for more work made her worry; she found it totally unbearable. Eve smiled as she cleaned, not wanting Matthew to see her unhappiness. It was a feeling she didn't understand, a feeling she didn't want to feel. There was no reason why anyone who had so much could want so little. She couldn't upset him – he had asked her to be his wife. She had to smile, until he left, anyway. Matthew kissed her on the cheek and left her alone. After making sure he had gone she began to punch the worktop over and over again, until her fingers felt as if they were going to break.

"Help me!" she began to scream. Unexpected tears left her eyes. She felt fuelled with anger. She stopped and breathed heavily, slowly composing herself once more, her mood changing to her normal calm self in a blink of an eye.

Taking the cloth from the floor she wrapped it around her aching sore knuckles and continued cleaning.

"Pull your gown down Eve, everyone can see you." Matthew blushed as he felt the nurse could see more than he thought she really needed to.

"Matt I'm giving birth, for goodness' sake." Eve spoke through gritted teeth. She felt like punching him.

"I know darling, but is there really any need for all and sundry to see?"

"Will you shut up? I can't do it, I just can't. Please make the pain go away!" Eve screamed, looking at her calm husband. She was going to punch him afterwards, she had decided. Standing there telling her not to show off her fanny to anyone; the way she felt she didn't care if all the people in the hospital came in for a look.

She was pushing as hard as she could, her hand squeezing the life from Matthew's arm. Wanting to stop hurting, praying it would be over soon.

"Push Eve, you're doing it. My beautiful Eve, you are doing it, one more push and they said it will be over!" Matthew couldn't believe what was happening. His perfect Eve was having his child. He stood as if in a dream, unflustered.

"Matt, this is your entire fault you shit! You lie here and push something the size of a melon out of something the size of a lemon. Fuck sake!" Eve yelled at him with anger.

"Language Eve, please don't speak in such a way."

"Fuck off!" Eve screamed like she'd never before.

It all went silent. The beautiful sound of their baby's soft cry filled the over-heated room, as the most beautiful baby in the world came into their lives.

"You have a perfect baby girl." The young nurse wrapped their new daughter in a clean white towel and passed her gently to Eve. She had been given a gift. Eve knew she had been sent from the angels – her father had asked them to. Now Eve had her.

"She's the most wonderful thing I have ever seen. She is just like you, Eve." Leaning over Eve and his new daughter, Matthew's tears fell upon the white towel that was holding his daughter safe.

"Hello little one, how are you? You've had a busy day." Eve touched her perfect puffy face, the feeling of love and protection overwhelming her tired body.

"You have made her as perfect as you are, Eve. She is going to be called Natasha."

Matthew had already decided – he had spent hours sifting through baby names, but he had kept his choice to himself until the time mattered.

Eve looked up at him, scrunching up her face and frowning, only taking her attention from her baby for a few seconds.

"Matthew she doesn't look like a Natasha." What a horrible name, Eve thought.

"No Eve, she is going to be called Natasha. It's a beautiful name, surely you can see that?"

They both sat transfixed, looking at their amazing new daughter. If they had wings they would be flying like birds, free in the blue sky. They were going to feel like it for ever.

When they arrived home, Natasha was placed in her nursery; there wasn't one thing out of order. The best baby products money could buy. She lay in her crib, her skin untouched, her little eyes sparkling like stars. Her little mind as innocent as could be. Like a clean sponge it would absorb the water of life.

Matthew left the nursery where he had sat for some time. Eve stayed behind, she wanted to say a few words to her father's angel before Matthew came back. She hadn't seemed to get a moment alone with her, with Matthew fussing and nurses rushing back and forward to her bed at the hospital most of the time.

Eve placed her finger into Natasha's pink palm.

"Hello again little one, thank you so much for coming to me, I'm so gloriously happy you are here. Your grandad has made the most fabulous choice. I pray with all my aching heart I will make you as happy as my father made me." Eve leant over, kissing her baby's head.

Leaving her to rest, Eve realised what she had said. How could such a thing ever come true? She knew she would be no good. No one could make anyone as happy as her father had.

15

Natty, Glenn and Ruth had been living with their father for nearly four months. They hadn't had a chance to see their mother since the hospital and even though they were very relieved and happy to be with their father, they wondered what was happening. She was only meant to be in for the evening, after all. "She will be coming home tomorrow," that's what their father had said, but where was she? Why did their father not discuss her at all? Natty would lie in the bedroom which she shared with her two sisters; she hated every minute of it. Only a little while back she would have given anything for them all to be together when they slept. But now she disliked them both. She longed to see her mother. Their father's house was better kept than home. Their mother could never have produced such organisation, even when she had scrubbed the floors and skirting boards all day long. Even though he worked everything was in total order. He seemed different to them. When they only saw him for a day he had time to show them affection and was much more relaxed around them. Now he seemed to have a lot on his mind. Ruth was in complete happiness now that her dear father was looking after her. She had been rescued from the wicked witch and didn't care much if she never saw her again. She didn't want another spell ever to be cast upon her that would make her life so very unhappy again. She was always by her father's side, before school, after school and when he read the Sunday papers. He would feel uncomfortable sometimes at how she wanted constant attention.

Glenn was being smug about the whole thing and kept reminding Natty that if she hadn't thrown their mother down the stairs then they would still be living with the crazy woman. She strolled around their father's home as if she owned the place, trying to be the one in charge, correcting her sisters on what their father occasionally missed. In only four months she had grown stronger than ever before. It must have been a false strength, it must have been. Their mother wasn't there to put her in her place.

The only difference that Natty could see between living with her mother and her father was that he was not to beat them; he never raised his voice and wouldn't go out of his way to cause them unnecessary pain. But he was strict and maybe as finicky as her.

"Dad, when can we go and see Mother? It has been a really long time." Natty stood at the ironing board, pressing down hard on her blouse, her fingers gripping the iron as her nerves welled up inside her.

"Natty, why do you keep asking me? I said when she is ready." Their father spoke with dread, knowing one of them would speak of her sooner or later, turning the pages of his evening newspaper in front of his face and trying to avoid any form of eye contact and confrontation.

"I don't understand, Dad. Why should she not be ready?" Natty sounded almost cocky. She didn't look up from pressing her blouse thoroughly – she wanted to make her mother proud.

Her father looked very serious and placed the newspaper onto his lap.

"Natty, I thought you liked it here. I can't work out what all the fuss and worrying is about. I have told you, you will see her soon. Things have to be sorted first. Now just leave it. Your mother has obviously made you like this." Feeling vulnerable, he continued to read.

"But sort what out? OK Dad, I'm sorry, whatever you say." Natty huffed and continued with her chores.

It seemed that their father had received a very important phone call that morning. He would always close the door and keep his voice low, giving it away when he didn't want them to hear him, which made the girls want to know more. He received these calls regularly since they had lived with him. Natty knew he was already agitated, and wondered if she was being too persistent, but she thought she would throw caution to the winds, he was her father after all. She should be able to ask him anything.

"Dad, I was just going to ask one more thing. Can I call her then?" Natty waited for a confident *no*.

"You can do what you wish Natty, I'm sure your crazy mother would love to hear from you." He left the living room very quickly. Natty was alone trying to figure out why her father would make such a statement. What was really going on? All of a sudden the pills Natty had found resurfaced in her mind. They had been pushed to the back for so long. That was it, it must be. Their mother was unwell. Surely it was as simple as that. Natty planned to be home late. She hung her blouse on the back of the door and smiled.

16

Their new home was finally up to the standard of Matthew, gleaming like a new pin. Everything in its place, and if there wasn't one he wouldn't rest until there was. It all had been chosen by him, the furniture, carpets, even down to the teapot. Matthew hadn't even asked for Eve's opinion. At least she had got her own way with the clock. Eve would pick up every toy Natasha left on her trail around their large home and place it neatly back into the toy box.

Every now and then Eve would stop for a moment and twist her wedding ring. She would let out a deep sigh and then begin to cry again. All she had ever wanted was for her father to walk her down the aisle. She longed to put her arm in his. To walk with the most important man she had ever known. She had to make do with Harry. Of course it was Matthew's idea. She found his brother rather handsome as she made her way to her husband-to-be, who seemed to be missing out on such allure. Eve had been able to finally get hold of her old work friends, happily knowing she could spend longer than five minutes with them. They'd spent most of their precious time together hoping to talk her out of it. Marrying the coffee man just wasn't on. She hadn't seen them since. But she was glad they came to share her special day all the same, just as her mother desperately wished her husband could have done. Miriam cried throughout the entire day for her precious child who, through her own choices, would be leaving her for ever. Also for her husband Donald who had had to leave her without any choice of his own. She also spent a little time informing Eve in a gentle motherly way that it wasn't too late to change her mind. Eve couldn't understand why they were all against Matthew so much; all he wanted was the very best for her – surely they could see.

Eve's nerves switched from the feeling of excitement to panic, praying everything would be exceptional for Matthew. But then again she would quickly remember that he had organised it all. So it would of course have been arranged with complete precision. Her dress was very plain but beautiful, a long white silk gown which flowed to the floor with elegance displaying her petite frame, and she held a small picking of sunflowers, bright and fresh against her dress. The plainness of her attire brought out even more of her natural beauty. She thought hard to relive the day as if it were only yesterday, but the sorrow which now consumed her tired body diminished it.

Natasha now had the company of her new sister Glenn, her name chosen by Matthew of course, along with everything else including the nursery colours. Eve didn't care much for colour schemes. In fact she didn't care much for anything.

"Eve, the girls are crying, why don't you pick them up?" Matthew bent down to comfort them as they sat on the floor in the dining room. Intense fear overwhelmed him. He didn't want Eve to cry again, not over simply feeding their children.

"They're fine Matthew, they really are." Eve wiped a tear from her eye. She wanted her tears to go, she simply didn't know how to do it alone.

"You're calling me Matthew again."

"That's your name isn't it, or shall I call you 'meet a woman and totally shit her life up'?"

"What on earth is wrong with you? Please don't use language in front of the girls," Matthew pleaded with Eve. "Come here Natty." Picking up Natty he left Glenn to fend for herself.

"Matt, I don't know. In fact you seem to be so in control of it all, I'm surprised you can't tell me." Eve was very angry by this time, an anger she couldn't understand.

"Eve please don't be like this, where has my beautiful Eve gone? Will you feed the girls?" Matthew put Natasha in her chair and went back to get Glenn. He was like a little boy lost. He didn't know what to do.

"No Matt, I will not feed the girls, and in answer to your question, I have gone mad Matt, Matthew whatever you name is.

Has that made you feel a little better?" Eve began to raise her voice, she sounded full of arrogance.

"Why are you saying these things? You're just tired that's all. Feed the girls and then you can rest."

"Oh thank you very kind sir. Matthew you're not listening to me, you spend so much time telling me what to do, you haven't got time to see how I am. I think I need some help Matt. I'm sure of it. I don't want to feel this angry any more. I desperately have to see Dr Peters. I have an appointment with him at the hospital tomorrow. You will have to stay home just for one day, please Matthew, please can you do that for me? I don't want to take the girls to such a place." Eve began to cry in desperation.

"No I can't take a day off from work. You must simply stop being so dramatic and snap out of it. You can stay home and take care of the girls! That's how it's done." Walking into the kitchen Matthew took some food from the cupboard, placed it on the side and then left; he had to. He didn't know what to do or say to her any more. Eve stood and looked at the uncooked food she would have to prepare whether she liked it or not. An awful thought rushed through her – if she didn't feed them, he would finally have to. As promptly as the thought came it left her.

Eve looked into the girls' nurseries, each child in their own space. They were full from dinner and were sleeping peacefully. She had to use the phone.

"Hello, is that Dr Peters?" Eve spoke quietly, feeling a sense of worry that someone might hear her.

"Yes, how can I help you?"

"This is Eve Hopkins. I would like to cancel an appointment I have with you tomorrow. I'm far too busy you see. I have managed to make too many plans for the same morning. There is no possible way I could make it even if I were to rush through everything. There never seem to be enough hours in the day at the moment. My family keeps me busy all the time, so you see I simply cannot be there." Eve's voice was almost squeaky. She took a long deep breath.

"My dear, I hope you don't mind me saying this to you, but no! It isn't OK for you to miss tomorrow. By the sound of it, you need to see me today." The doctor sounded stern.

"No Doctor, I can't come. I feel OK honestly." Eve began to feel anxious.

"I will see you tomorrow; you can tell me how great you feel when we meet."

"Bugger!" She was in complete confusion. Matthew had said she couldn't go but deep down she was too scared to miss it.

17

Their mother stood at each door of their quiet, untouched bedrooms. Glaring in from the edge, too afraid to go in, knowing deep down that if she were to enter the realisation of her loneliness would be too hard to bear. How she wanted them, how she wanted to hear them. She missed their presence terribly. She had always felt comfort when they returned home from school. Their beds had not been slept in for so long. She closed her eyes and then opened them as if they would appear by magic. She could only pray they would be home soon. Their mother returned to her own bedroom, the only room that had had constant use in the previous four months.

She had to have a weekly visit from the persistent Dr Peters and a panic would fill her body, but with God willing the visit from her father would not clash with his. The doctor said it was all in her imagination. But what would he know? She liked seeing her father and if he wanted to come to see her for a while it was his prerogative. And what would the over-paid doctor know anyway? He read everything from books. Her father was real. The doctor couldn't convince her otherwise. She lay on her bed staring at the white ceiling, visually making patterns with the Artex; some days she would see evil faces, some days she could only see angels. She looked over to the bottle of pills on the side and realised they were the only things that could somehow make her forget. The feeling would confuse her. The pills made her forget things she desperately needed to remember; sometimes she would sit and stare in the bedroom mirror trying to recognise who it was in her reflection, desperately knowing she had to belong in her family. Their mother lay quietly. The ringing of the doorbell disturbed her. She leapt from the bed and eagerly ran to let the long awaited guest in.

"Hold on Dad, I'm coming! Forgot your key again?" Opening the door briskly their mother stood frozen.

"Hello Mother!" Natty's voice was full of apprehension, the nerves she felt almost making her want to be sick. It was only when she pushed the bell that she realised it was too late to run away. Natty stood optimistically waiting to be invited in. The appearance of their mother took her by surprise. It was the craziest thing she had ever seen: her mother's hair was not brushed very well, and it was as though her real beauty was being protected by a layer of make-up. Natty could barely recognise the woman who stood in front of her, her lips bright red. The thick glossy lipstick had been smudged all around her mouth, thick red circles of colour, and any remaining lipstick was used to make her cheeks rosy. A bright blue eye shadow had been rubbed into her eyebrows and on her eyelids. Her black eyelashes were thick and gloopy. She was a mess – it couldn't have been their mother.

"Oh, hello Natty, I thought it was you. Come in and I will make us a nice cup of tea." She felt a little disappointed that it wasn't her father. He'd said he was going to come so she knew he would be arriving soon.

Following her mother into the kitchen, Natty wondered if she had made the right decision in returning to their home without her sisters. She wished she had followed her mother into the bathroom so she could help her wash the mess from her face. She was waiting for her mother to seem bothered that she hadn't seen her for so long. She wasn't asking for the world, just a small hug. Or even a smile.

"I can't believe you have come to see me, what did your father say? Where are your sisters? Come here and give me a hug? I haven't held you for such a long time. You can all come home now; I am feeling so much better. Has your father told you?"

Natty went to hold her mother, although the thought of becoming covered in her make-up didn't really appeal to her.

"Mum I am so sorry for hurting you, it was an accident, and I really didn't mean it. I was just so cross that you'd done what you did. I am so happy that you feel better now."

"That's OK Natty, I know it wasn't your fault, your grandad made the whole thing clear for me."

89

"Eh? Mum, Grandad died before I was born."

Natty was pushed away by her mother. "Why would you say that, Natty? Why have you come here just to hurt me? I knew it was too good to be true. Why do you all want to hurt me so much? Your father has put you up to this, hasn't he? I thought you all wanted me to get better." Their mother's belly filled with fury.

"No Mum, I haven't come here to hurt you, let me help you wash your face and then I can make a hot drink. I wanted to see you. No one knows that I'm here. I would be strangled if they knew. Please Mum, don't get upset. I'm glad Grandad put it straight for you." Natty broke down in tears. She just wanted to see her mother, just to see her. Yet again she was full of fear and sadness, in complete bewilderment as to why her mother was acting so strangely.

"Natty I think you should leave, before I get cross. Why have you made me get cross Natty?"

"But Mum, I can't leave yet, I've only just got here, I don't want to leave, not until you are fine."

"Natty, do as I ask! Please now just go!" Feeling irritated their mother pointed to the door.

Before Natty could make another attempt at calming her mother down, she felt the crack of her mother's fist against her cheek.

"Please Mum stop, I don't want to do this any more!" Natty was not going to run away, this was her mother, she wanted to love her, she wanted to help her love them. She ran to the corner of the kitchen. Her mother stood silently, smudging her lipstick further across her face. Natty felt scared, she was uncertain who she was in the kitchen with.

"Mum, are you OK?"

"No Natty I am not OK. Shall we have that drink now?" She spoke softly again.

Walking cautiously to the kitchen table in fear of getting another blow to her face, Natty quietly pulled out the wooden chair, so as not to disturb her mother in her chore.

"I would like tea very much, thank you Mum."

A hot cup of tea was placed in front of her and a small plate put in the centre of the table. Her mother filled it high with custard creams.

18

The doctor's waiting room was crowded with people in need. Eve knew her reason for being there and she just wanted to keep it to herself. Eve wanted to remain the same private person, only sharing her deepest feelings with her mum and dad. Why should she have to break the habit of a lifetime now? Natty and Glenn played in their pram. Eve stood waiting for her name to be called. Her father would have given up his chair for a young lady; her hope would be in vain. She new they would all hear her name being called, she would have to share who she was with the strangers who surrounded her, whether she liked it or not. She couldn't understand how such a busy place could be so quiet. You were automatically programmed as you entered the large glass doors. Hearing her name echo through the waiting room, she let out a huge sighed as she pushed the pram to the doctor's door, trying to avoid the maze of legs in her way. She knocked on the heavy door, slowly entered and sat on the soft chair. Waiting for a miracle. She felt uneasy in his company, and even though he was seated opposite, he still seemed to tower over her, as though he were a giant invading all of her space. Rocking the pram, she waited for him to begin interrogating her. Would she answer him honestly? Only time would tell.

"Hello, Mrs Hopkins how are you feeling today?" The doctor had a very posh pen in his hand and was eager to write down whatever she revealed.

"I'm feeling fine. I still get a little upset now and then. But it does tend to pass rather quickly." Eve rocked the pram harder. The girls would probably bring up their lunch at any moment. Her belly started to feel a little heavy.

"When you say upset and pass quickly, what do you mean?" The doctor wasn't looking at her. His eyes were firmly fixed on his small notebook.

"Quicker, I'm not angry for long. I just think about my father and then I feel all right again. That's good isn't it?"

"Are you saying he is the only thing that could possibly help you to feel better? You have lots of other beautiful things in your life to be happy about."

"I know Doctor, it's just that I miss my father so very much, and I don't feel there is anything or anyone that could ever replace him. Not even my children. You see if their grandfather was here then he would make everything seem so much more manageable. He had a way of making everything OK, all of the time." Eve's thoughts quickly moved to her hair, wishing she had left it down that day.

"I am sure he would be upset if he could see how upset you were – they are his grandchildren remember. He wouldn't want you to say such a thing now would he?"

"I'm sure you know what I mean Doctor, of course I do love them very much, but cannot help feeling I should be with my dear father."

"You don't want to be here, Eve?" The doctor stopped writing and looked straight into Eve's watering eyes.

"No, Doctor, I don't. Matthew said I should stay at home where I belong. I will never be able to go anywhere. Could you ever imagine me trying to disappear from the face of the earth without him making a god damn fuss about the whole thing? My dear father was allowed to go peacefully, why can't I, Doctor?" Eve's voice was raised.

"Eve, are you starting to feel angry again?"

"If I want to be with my father, I will be. He has asked me to go to him, I have always been a good girl and I have always done as he asked. I can't let him down now can I?" Still rocking the pram Eve couldn't remember what she had spoken about, nor did she really care. She needed to get home before Matthew and was starting to feel a little anxious.

"Do you want to hurt yourself Eve?"

"What kind of silly question is that? Why would I hurt myself? Why should I hurt anyone?" Eve's anger began to churn in her stomach; she was thinking how Matthew was right in saying doctors mess with your head. She should have listened to him and stayed at home. She was going to leave and no one was going to stop her. She wanted to shove the doctor's gold pen right up his arse. The same gold pen was used to write out a prescription for her. She snatched it from him and began to walk to the door.

"Eve, one more question, when you said your father has asked you to go to him, what did you mean by this?"

"I mean, Doctor, he asked me. He came to see me and hoped I would join him soon. Now can I go?"

"Would you do everything your father asked, Eve?"

"Well of course."

With the last question out of the way she left abruptly. Dr Peters simultaneously picked up the phone and ordered the receptionist to make another appointment for her the following week without fail.

Arriving home before Matthew, Eve felt a huge sense of relief. She could now get tidy and put the dinner on, bathe the girls and look pretty and he would be none the wiser.

Going to see the doctor seemed such a waste of time anyway. She had far more important things to be getting on with. Eve prepared food, and for the second time that day she washed the girls from head to toe. It was a pattern she had got into and liked to keep it that way. What would her dear father say if he knew she had gone to someone else for advice? Especially an over-paid gentleman with a gold pen sticking out his arse.

Everything was sorted in no time at all. She felt calm again and was ready for her husband to arrive home. Her little day out would be a secret. Her girls were too young to let him know, and if one day she felt brave enough she could tell her father. Placing Matthew's wonderful dinner on the table, she sat opposite the empty chair and waited, each sigh and puff in rhythm to the tapping of her fingers on the table.

Her eyes repeatedly glanced at her watch with each minute passing, the minutes turning into hours. Her tapping became louder as she could feel the anger fuelling her small, tired body. Why hadn't he called her to say he was going to be late? What had she done to make him treat her this way? Her father was

93

always on time for dinner. What made Matthew so different? Ignoring the cries of Natty, she sat in her own misery. Natty's cries became louder; Eve didn't move. She was going to sit there until he arrived, even if it meant all night. As she felt a rush of energy she grabbed the full plate of dinner, held it high and hurtled it across the room. Everything she had placed neatly on the table hours ago followed.

"Where are you Matthew?! Where the hell are you?! Eve screamed as loud as she could, waking Glenn who was now crying in unison with her sister.

"Will you both shut up?" Not wanting to leave her anger at the dinner table, everything in her reach was taken from its place, the walls being a blank target.

Eve had left herself panting and tired, sitting weeping, trying to absorb all of the mayhem around her. What on earth had happened? She felt a slight tap on her shoulder.

"Eve, let me help you clean up."

"Thanks Dad. I don't know what came over me." Inhaling deeply, she was extremely relieved to see her father again. Feeling at ease now, she was happy to put everything right.

"Eve, Eve."

"Yes Dad."

"The little ones are crying."

"Oh yes, I'll go and see them right now." In a daze she went to see her girls, knowing that everything would finally be OK. As she turned she gave a smile to her dad.

"I love you Dad."

"I love you too Eve."

Comforting her girls and laying them back to rest, she went to help her father. Entering the kitchen, which resembled World War Two, she hummed to herself. The man who now stood among the mess was not her father, but a very cross Matthew.

"What has happened here? Are you and the girls OK?"

"Where's my father, Matthew?" Eve stood with her lips tight and her hands on her hips.

"Sorry Eve, your father?"

"Don't tease me Matthew, where is he?"

"Calm down, he's not here. What's got into you?" Matthew

94

began to pick up the glass which had been broken on the table. He felt unsettled.

"Got into me, how dare you? Where the hell have you been? You couldn't call me could you, just doing as you damn well please!"

"You'll wake the girls if you keep shouting Eve. I called you earlier. I thought you were bathing the girls or something when you didn't answer. Why are you acting so crazy? Your father is six foot under, Eve, how many times have I got to tell you? Stop hurting yourself."

"Oh, I suppose you telling me he's six foot under somewhere isn't hurting me."

"Eve, I really don't know, how come everything is such a mess?"

"Unhappy, Matthew that's what I call it, why don't you take a long look?" Eve turned away from him and went to clean up alone, trying to compose herself. She felt embarrassed. Maybe she did overreact a little.

"The phone's ringing Matthew – do something useful and answer it will you?"

"Maybe it's your father."

"Not funny Matthew, really not funny!" Eve looked up at him, her long hair falling around her face.

Matthew went to answer the phone, wishing he had never come home.

"Hello."

"Hello, this is Dr Peters' surgery. Your wife forgot to pick up her card; we have made her an appointment next Tuesday at the same time as today. Would you please let her know?"

"Yes I will." Matthew stood dejectedly.

"Thank you ever so much."

Matthew put the phone down. Eve was on the carpet; she was on her hands and knees scrubbing stains that remained from her terrible evening.

"That was the doctor; they have made you another appointment, same time as today. Eve, I thought I told you not to go; all they do is mess with your head. Now I can see why you're acting so strange."

Eve's heart stopped, she had been found out, caught like a child stealing a one-penny chew from the sweetshop. An action so small could have huge consequences.

95

"Matthew it's not like that, I can assure you."

"What is it like? All you need to do is what you do best, and stay away from places like that. If your leg's not hanging off then there is no need to go."

"OK Matthew." With her head lowered and feeling relieved Eve continued to clean. She hadn't been sent for execution this time, and she wondered why she didn't listen to him in the first place. He did make sense most of the time, and he only had her interests at heart.

Matthew walked up to see his girls, kissing them on their soft cheeks as they slept.

"Goodnight girls."

19

As Natty walked up to their father's house, she tried to push through her mind all the excuses she could use for being home so late without permission, and for why she had left her sisters to walk home alone. From the time she had finished the biscuits until she reached her front door she had thought of her mother constantly. She didn't want to leave her alone, simply looking into space. Natty had said goodbye to her but she hadn't heard. Being used to her mother's rejection, Natty brushed it off.

Why couldn't her sisters and father give her mother a chance? There must have been love inside her somewhere. Then she realised that she hadn't seen her mother for the last four months but had still managed to gain another slap to her face. It was just another one to add to the list. Their mother had made her cry again. Maybe her sisters weren't as silly after all, not putting themselves through unnecessary pain. Natty wondered to herself if she could also pretend their mother had never existed. As she walked to her new home she knew everything was far from normal. Their living with their father was only a stopgap.

"Natty, where have you been?" Their father sat engulfed in paperwork – it was scattered all over the table and floor. He was sifting through it as though his life depended on it. He was relieved Natty was finally home. She could get supper started.

"Oh hi Dad, I'm sorry I'm so late. I went to see a friend."

Natty automatically waited for a beating, but slowly remembered their father would never have laid a finger on them, and was thankful she was lying in his company.

"Natty, what on earth made you just run off like that? Without letting anyone know where you were going?"

"Sorry Dad, I'll let you know next time, I promise. Can I be excused Dad?" Natty swallowed hard – the saliva in her mouth had built up through her nerves. Glenn and Ruth as usual were listening to every word from the landing.

"Yes, for a while. I would like you to start supper soon as I have lots to get through. But please do not believe I am very happy with you, because there will not be a next time you run off without any warning. You have to stick together, you are the eldest, Natty. How can I relax knowing your sisters may be left alone when you feel like running off? I know Glenn isn't much younger than you but all the same she is younger."

With a huge sense of relief, and thinking her father had gone on just a little longer than necessary, she promptly dismissed herself from her father and went to relax for the first time that day. It hadn't seemed like ten minutes had passed when she heard their father's command from the hall to come and help in the kitchen. As she lay on her bed she thought hard about the next visit to her mother. Perhaps she could share her secret with her sisters. As she looked up she suddenly changed her mind. They were together as usual, stuck like glue. Laughing and sniggering through their whispers, as if they were the only two in the room.

"What friend did you suddenly feel the urge to visit?" Glenn looked as though she already knew the answer.

"Just a friend, that's all you need to know. Anyway, what have you two got to be so happy about?"

"You don't know, Natty?" Ruth spoke with happiness in her voice.

"Know what, Ruth?"

"Dads going to keep us, we never have to go back there again."

"What do you mean, keep us? He can't just keep us, what about Mother?" Natty felt full of guilt, her heart almost skipped a beat. How could they be so carefree about it all? She was their mother.

"Surely Nat, you don't want to go back there, do you?" Glenn was brushing Ruth's hair and looking completely satisfied.

"No, but all our things are there." Natty began to leave the overcrowded bedroom. She felt as though she was going to lose her patience with them; she wanted to scream at the top of her voice at them both. She grabbed at the door handle to leave.

"Natty, I don't understand you, I really don't." Glenn felt happy – at that very moment she never wanted to go back again.

"How do you know about Mother?" Natty turned around slightly with a puzzled look.

"You should know me by now, I don't like to miss a trick. Dad had a visit from the old doctor from the hospital. He was really cross with Dad. Something about we shouldn't have been with her all along. She's not very well or something like that. But then again I didn't need to earwig to work that one out." Glenn spoke with excitement.

"Glenn, what are you saying?" Natty stood with her mouth wide open.

"I'm saying, if you listened the first time, Dad's in trouble for letting us stay with her. He has to keep us until she gets better and by the sounds of it, it will be never." The anticipation nearly burst from her body.

"Does Mother know?" Natty felt angry.

"Not yet, I wish I could be a fly on the wall to see her face when they tell her. All those beatings for nothing, can you believe it? The old cow deserves it." Glenn didn't look up at Natty, her attentions were on Ruth's hair.

"I can't believe you. How can you say such things? Why would you speak in such a way? Mother isn't well and all you can do is worry about how you are feeling in all this. Stop thinking of yourself. I know it has been really hard living with her but now we can see why. It's obvious. She must love us, truly she must." The sinking feeling in her stomach overwhelmed Natty as she was fuelled with fear yet again for the uncertainty in their lives.

Their father's voice became louder. She knew she had to get downstairs at that very moment.

"Hard? How hard could it have been? You must be on another planet if you think I want to live with our mother ever again. Stop being so humble. What about how we all feel about it, instead of how you feel about it? Why do you have to stop us feeling bad? It's not up to you." Glenn had become furious, staring directly at Natty.

"Glenn, calm down. Dad will hear you." Natty leant into the bedroom, glaring at her sister.

"I don't want to be scared any more Nat." Ruth looked up.

"I know Ruth, we are all scared, we have been for such a long time. All I am saying is, she is our mother, that's all."

"Look Nat, if you're happy living in such a way then go ahead. But I am damn sure you won't get me back there in a hurry, and I am sure I can speak for Ruth too, isn't that right Ruthi?" Glenn finally gave up on her sister's pampering, and sat back on her bed leaving Ruth's hair in a tangled mess.

"Don't worry Ruth, I'll finish it for you after I've helped Dad." Natty went and stroked her little sister's face, smiling at her reassuringly and desperately trying to ignore Glenn's tuts.

"Are you happy that we can live here Natty?" Ruth looked up with her soft eyes.

"I don't know, I really don't."

As Natty walked down to her father she could remember a time when their mother would sit with them quietly and brush through their hair until every strand lay in place.

Their father had given up on his wait for her and begun to cook supper. He didn't look very happy as he started to peel potatoes with his lips tightened.

"Sorry Dad." Natty quickly grabbed a knife to help him.

"Yes young lady, I know." Their father looked up at her and smiled.

20

Eve walked slowly around her large garden. Natty and Glenn were playing on the freshly cut grass, their giggles filling the open spaces. To Eve no one was around as she slowly walked barefoot, each step pressing on the blades, entwining them into one small mass. She loved the feeling of the coolness of the grass. It was the warmest spring Eve could remember for a very long time. Sunbeams reflected on the flowers, bringing light to the petals. Blankets of colour filled every edge and corner, with the apple trees providing the only form of shade. Eve smelt the fragrance in the air as a soft breeze ruffled her hair, pushing her thin lemon dress onto her legs. She did not look acceptable barefooted with messy hair; Matthew would not have liked to see her this way, so free. Natty and Glenn played alone, without her guidance. Both heads were covered, socks and shoes too. Eve couldn't chance them getting burnt; even the slightest hint of colour she would have found unbearable.

Eve stopped in the centre of her vast garden and inhaled deeply.

"Hi Dad, how are you doing today? It is lovely, isn't it?" Eve spoke softly as she touched the grass with her long fingers.

Her father's ashes were scattered there. Her mother had agreed to Eve's request, anything for Eve her mother would say. One reason was that he had never seen her garden; he would have loved it there, sparing his Sunday afternoons to help Eve maintain it. It would have been transformed to the masterpiece it now resembled in no time at all. This way he was always going to be there, with every flower that bloomed, every bird that sang, and feeling each drop of rain.

"A beautiful day, don't you think?"

"Dad, you made me jump, what are you doing here?" Eve felt her heart skip a beat.

"I thought I would come to see you, it's such a glorious afternoon and it would be a shame to miss it. We can sit for a while and talk about things – you know, things which have been bothering you."

"Oh Dad, I miss you so much, I wish you could come and visit more often. I am so happy when you can share all of this with me." Eve spoke softly. She could see her father's face was glowing with the rays from the sun as he knelt beside her on the grass. She could only see him faintly at first but he was there, she was sure of it.

"My sunshine, I am here sharing everything with you, but don't forget you can come to see me when you are ready."

"But what about my family, what will they do without me? I don't know how to let them go Dad, even if they don't like me very much."

"I am sure they will understand, Eve."

"Matthew would never let me go, Dad, never would he understand. Who would take care of my beautiful girls?" Eve frowned as she glanced over at Natty and Glenn.

"We could watch over them forever, sharing them with each other. No one can ever hurt you Eve, not when you're with me."

"I don't know how to let them go, Dad."

"Just leave it up to them, let them help you, Eve. You will find a way, trust me, my beautiful sunshine."

"Bye Dad, will you come back soon? I will see you in a while, yes?" Eve felt scared and vulnerable.

"Goodbye, my sunshine."

Eve fell to the grass as if all the energy had been sucked from her, looking around not quite sure where her father had gone. She quickly got herself together and walked into the kitchen to make her girls some fresh orange juice, brushing any dirt from her dress. Her bare feet now on the cold tiles, she felt the warmth of the sun tingling her face. She smiled as she began to feel comfort from her father's visit.

"Girls, I have some lovely juice for you." As she placed two pink beakers in front of them she heard the doorbell. Patting her hair down and pulling her straps back onto her shoulders, she quickened her steps and went to receive the visitor. Matthew was not due home for another hour or so and thoughts of who it could be rushed through her.

Opening the door she felt the warm air fill the hall.

102

"Hello Harry, what are you doing here?" Eve felt a sudden rush of excitement in her stomach.

Matthew's brother stood handsome and strong in her doorway.

"I thought I would pay my beautiful sister-in-law a visit. How are those girls of yours? I thought it would be nice for us to spend a little time together." Harry invited himself in, kissed Eve on the cheek and walked confidently into the kitchen.

"You're such a charmer Harry." Eve liked his forcefulness, she had not seen him in such a long time. Harry was such a contrast from Matthew, he was like the fresh air that surrounded her.

"Would you like some orange juice? I have only just made some for the girls."

"That would be lovely Eve. Thanks."

"Matthew won't be home for a while, Harry, I hope you didn't think he was going to be here."

"I see him every day, Eve."

The reality hit Eve; Harry knew his brother wouldn't be home, he had probably just left him at the garage.

"Eve, may I say how wonderful you look. Matthew says you have not been very well. In my eyes I have never seen you looking so lovely."

As Harry took his orange juice, they caught each other's stares, and held them transfixed for just a moment. Eve felt herself blush, it had been such a long time since her appearance had been complimented and not criticised.

"Right, let's go and see those girls." Harry walked with his shoulders back and spoke louder than was really needed.

They both went out into the garden. Remembering she was nearly half naked and feeling Harry wouldn't mind brought a feeling of sexual arousal in Eve. She began to feel beautiful and enjoyed pretending she was unaware of her body. Her nipples were pushing onto the soft fabric – she wanted him to want her. She watched his lips and thought of how they would feel touching her breast. Harry went to play with the girls. She sat and admired her husband's handsome brother as he rolled on the grass with them. It was such a wonderful sight, such fun and happiness filled her garden for the first time. She couldn't recall the last time she or Matthew was prepared to get dirty for the benefit of Natty and

Glenn. Eve wanted to freeze frame the whole moment and put it on a shelf, and when she felt sad she could take it down and have a look at it, to prove to herself life outside her own misery really did exist. Harry picked both girls up in his strong arms and walked inside. His muscles protruded trough his T-shirt.

"I'll help you freshen them up Eve, if you like?"

"Thank you Harry, that will be great." Finding it hard to keep her eyes from him Eve followed Harry to the bathroom.

Did Harry know his brother so well, knowing what he would expect when he arrived home – clean children, clean house and a hot dinner waiting?

They knelt side by side watching Natty and Glenn splash in the bath, as they all laughed together. Eve could feel the force of Harry's knee touching her as she knelt. Splashes of water went onto Eve's dress making it almost transparent.

"Eve, you look wonderful."

"Thanks Harry, best we get them out now." Eve felt overwhelmed with passion and deliberately allowed her firm breasts to show as she bent down to pick up the towel. She could feel him looking at her. Absorbing every moment of the attention made her arousal and need for his touch greater.

Eve knew she should push the compliments from her brother-in-law to the back of her mind but it was difficult as she thrived on the attention. Natty and Glenn were washed, dried and laid down for an afternoon nap before they knew it. Two happy girls lay asleep, red faced and clean.

"I think you need a nice hot drink, Eve."

"Thank you Harry for all your help, you have been great."

"Eve, I would just like to say one thing to you. I think you have been great to be with my brother for as long as you have. I can honestly say, I thought he would always be a bachelor, but hey presto, he's a dad and a husband. I only wish I went to buy a cup of coffee that morning."

"Sorry Harry, what did you say?"

Harry brought the drinks into the dining room. Eve sat and waited for him to repeat what she knew he'd said. Her damp dress revealed the outline of her breasts, and as Harry sat down next to her he tried to focus on her face.

104

"I think you heard what I said Eve."

"What do you mean Harry?" Eve's enjoyment was nearly bursting from her stimulated body.

"Eve, I have to hear about you every day, how wonderful you are, how sad you are becoming. How you make my brother so very happy, and how you make him so very sad. He rarely talks about your 'moments' that you sometimes have."

"My moments? I don't know what you're talking about." Eve's response was sharp.

"Eve, you haven't got to lie to me. I am only here because I care."

"Look, I sometimes get a little down, but that's all. Everyone can have a bad day Harry, can't they?" Eve began to feel a little cross. She just needed to be touched by him.

"Eve, are you happy with my brother? Is he the one making you so unwell?"

"No Harry, I love your brother very much." Eve became confused, her head felt full suddenly.

"Are you sure Eve?"

Eve sat and stared into his gorgeous eyes.

"He is a good man, he loves me and his girls and that is all I ever need. There is no other man who could make me feel like he does. I love him very much."

"This isn't about Matthew. This is about you. Stop thinking about him for a moment and think of yourself."

"I am Harry. He's your brother, how can you say such things?"

"OK, you win Eve."

"For goodness' sake Harry, I thought you were coming to have a nice time. Not to give me the third degree." Inhaling deeply, Eve concentrated hard to keep her anger under control.

"I am having a nice time."

"Well I am not, so please go." Eve stood up and pointed to the front door, hoping Harry would follow her orders. "Now Harry, before I do something I regret."

Harry stood up and looked deep into her eyes.

"The only thing you could do, Eve, is kiss me goodbye. I am sure you wouldn't regret that."

"Harry, now!" Her voice was raised.

"OK I am going." Gently, he touched her arm.

The energy ran through her; she thought about how she had felt earlier around him and what he had said, she wanted more than anything to kiss him, to feel his tongue in her mouth. The feeling which engulfed her small body was intense. Everything and everyone at that moment didn't matter. There was a silence as they both looked at each other, both knowing what to do next, but each one as scared and excited as the other. Harry pulled her near him, their lips barely touching, only an inch away. Eve's wet lips were waiting to feel his soft touch. As his lips touched hers, her body felt as if it was going to burn. Their tongues entwined. Eve slowly moved her hands away from her sides and felt the softness of his hair with her fingers. She felt his hands gently touching her skin, making her hair stand on end with exhilaration. The straps to her dress were pushed down her arm. She pushed herself firmly onto his strong chest, his warm mouth now embracing her neck. His kissing became firmer as he pushed his mouth into her shoulder, grabbing at her, moving his hand hard on her breast, squeezing at her nipples, bringing his head down sucking and biting at the tenderness. Holding the back of her hair he kissed her again with force. Her dress was pushed up revealing her knickers. He pulled at them, pushing his fingers into her own wetness, pushing his fingers harder and harder into her. The feeling was intense, she felt alive, she wanted to surrender her whole body to him and allow him to do as he pleased. Her body throbbing with passion, wanting his whole body to go inside of her, the firmness of his penis pressing onto her. Unbuckling his belt and zip she pushed her hand onto him, moving it up and down. His penis was now uncovered, waiting to feel inside her to absorb her completely. Harry pulled Eve onto the floor, protecting her. He pushed her dress over her shoulder again, revealing her bare skin. He began to kiss her face, working down to her breast. Her stomach tingled as his tongue moved slowly down onto her wetness, pushing her legs apart and pressing down onto them as he licked her inside pushing his tongue inside her openness as far as he could, tasting her. As she climaxed bringing more wetness onto his lips, she felt inside herself and felt how ready she was for him, pushing her finger into his mouth for him to suck onto it as she would him. Her lips kissing and sucking his large firm penis, she moved in rhythm pushing it to the back of her throat, licking and sucking it hard as she pushed it in and out. Suddenly he pushed her from him and grabbed her arms, slamming her onto the sofa. He entered her hard and thrust himself back and forward into her fulfilled body, each movement bringing them self-stimulation. As he went into her harder and harder the force and pain overwhelmed her. She grabbed at his hair and their fingers locked as he released himself into her, her moans allowing him to hear her satisfaction with him. They lay breathing heavily; she could feel his warmth in her. Their moment of being completely free as two adults had come to an end. Harry slowly slid himself from her, rose to his feet and began to dress. Picking up Eve's dress he slowly passed it to her.

"Eve, you had better get dressed before Matt gets home." Harry was trying to catch his breath.

Harry pulled her to her feet, held her to his chest and kissed her, his tongue pushing into her mouth once again. As they stopped, Eve looked at his hot flushed face.

"What will Matthew say, Harry? Why did we do this?" Eve's body was trembling both with fear and adrenaline.

"Eve, this isn't about Matt, we wanted to. Your tea has gone cold now."

Eve laughed and Harry joined in. Dressing slowly Eve felt wet and fulfilled. They held each other close once again; Eve wanted him to touch her again, to put his strong fingers inside her, just for one last time. He had read her mind and she felt the pressure of his hand between her legs, pushing his fingers into her once more, moving them, rubbing her, allowing her to feel alive just as before. They kissed, everything had been wonderful.

The only thing that broke the silence was the turning of Matthew's key in the lock. Moving apart, as they sat they were careful not to show any form of contact.

Matthew walked into the kitchen and realising that his wife was not there, went into the room where only moments earlier he would have been the last person welcome.

"Hello Eve, what are you doing in here?"

"Hello Matthew, Harry just popped in to see the girls." He must know, she thought.

"Harry, why didn't you tell me you were coming over? We could have left together. Where are the girls anyway?"

"In their rooms Matthew, they're having a little nap."

Matthew kissed Eve on the cheek as though she were a stranger and left.

"Just going to get cleaned up. Staying for dinner Harry?"

"No thanks Matt, better get on my way."

"I'm sure Eve won't mind doing an extra serving. She's a whiz in the kitchen."

"OK Matt, just for a while." Harry quickly squeezed Eve's hand. And then quickly let it go. Eve felt it would be the last time they would ever touch.

21

Another year passed as quickly as ever. Their father was rarely at home with them, working all the hours he could to make sure his girls had everything they needed. They were not to go without, even if it meant sacrificing spending time with them. And even though the girls were living with him, he would still send money to their mother. Their father wanted their mother to have nice things too. It was all he had ever longed for, to provide for them all and make them happy.

Natty decided to stay on at school, having finally chosen her future career. She thought becoming a nurse would be fulfilling and she would also make her parents very proud. Her studying was continuous, every night books were piled high for her to work through. Natty didn't mind – it kept her mind focused on something other than how she felt inside. She visited her mother whenever she could. Each visit revealed her mother looking worse, every departure bringing more sadness to both of them. But Natty couldn't stay away and her mother didn't seem to want her to, either. She had placed a door key into Natty's hand and held it tight as she looked into Natty's eyes and smiled. Natty was allowed to enter her mother's home whenever she wanted to and felt she had finally managed to make a small friendship with her. Glenn and Ruth would never have understood. Natty and her mother would sit opposite each other, chatting about all the silly things they could think of, the weather being the most important topic. It didn't matter what was said, they were together. On a rare occasion Natty would take a blow to her face, or her wrist would be squeezed for no reason at all. Natty would attempt to prise her mother's hand from her wrist. Her mother's eyes would fill with tears as she pushed her pretty fingers into Natty's skinny arm. She would stare

109

into Natty's eyes as if she was trying to say sorry. But Natty would still keep visiting. Sometimes when everything had calmed down Natty would sit with a warm flannel and gently wipe her mother's face, removing the mess little by little, hoping to recognise her again.

There was one visit which Natty knew she wouldn't forget. It was on the dreadful day when their father had gone to see her mother in the company of the famous Dr Peters. They let her mother know quite sternly that her girls were not going to come home any more. Natty had waited for her father to arrive home that day before she made her excuse to leave. The library was the familiar lie. As Natty went into her mother's home she was the only witness as she watched the woman who she prayed one day she could look up to, rocking to and fro sitting on the bottom step of the stairs. Repeating the same words over and over, "You're not coming back." Natty went to sit next to her full of dread and uncertainty. She sat with her for almost two hours as she continued to chant and cry. The screeches from her mother went through Natty's whole body, making it shiver. Her mother hadn't realised she was even there, but she sat next to her all the same. Her face was covered by her hands; they looked old and her nails were unpainted. She was so tired and frail. Her body completely bent over, she was finally exhausted. When her mother's screams and chants slowly diminished and only sobs could be heard, Natty wet her face with a flannel and covered her shoulders with a soft blanket. She stood at the door for a while, watching her in pain, wishing she could take it all away for her. Then she quietly left. There wasn't anything in the world she could ever do to change it.

Natty stopped visiting for a while, fearing she would have to sit on the stairs again. When she did finally pluck up the courage their mother didn't say a word about it, but found the courage to stroke Natty's face and kiss her on the cheek. Natty felt alone; she chose to be alone. Their mother had treated them destructively for so long, Natty now blamed her father and over-friendly sisters for not helping her; they could have given their mother one more chance. They would never ask of her, or ever wonder if she was sorry for what she had done. They would never have understood their mother wasn't OK, she was never OK. If Natty could now tell them she was unwell, maybe then they would love her, just as she did. She could feel their mother longed for all of them to love her, she was sure of it.

"Natty, dinner's ready!" Glenn stood at the door of the bedroom, still as neat and groomed as ever, but with a smile that went from one side of her face to another.

"OK Glenn, I'll finish up soon." Natty lay on her cluttered bed, all her books open, thousands of words displayed.

"It's on the table, Dad's waiting." Glenn became impatient.

"OK Glenn, I'm coming. Do you think mother is eating enough?"

"Don't know and I don't care. Come on, it's your favourite." Glenn sounded abrupt. She turned away from Natty with her nose stuck in the air.

Natty's favourite was a huge plate of sausage and mash, with lashings of thick gravy and onions. Following her sister down to the wonderful smells, she almost felt guilty that she was going to be filled to the brim. Automatically sitting down when she entered the kitchen, Natty could see there were three eager people waiting to tuck in to what lay before them. They began grabbing spoonfuls of mash, filling their plates high.

"Have you washed your hands, Natty?"

"Yes Dad." Natty hadn't washed her hands, she was sick of washing. She wasn't going to get herself cleaned up for anyone else's approval ever again.

"Come on then girls, eat up." Their father had changed considerably. Now he was out of the house more he seemed relaxed when he was there. He knew he was only just popping in either to eat, bring in groceries or to complete all the other adult chores. The girls' only responsibilities were cooking, doing the dishes and pressing a few items now and then. And of course keeping their overcrowded bedroom tidy. Their father believed that everyone should do a little, just to keep it going. It would produce outstanding results. The girls were all happy to share dinner with him as always. Natty sat next to Ruth. As they ate together her sisters would discuss the day's events. Their father listened eagerly to every word Glenn and Ruth said, watching Ruth's lips moving and absorbing every expression on her gentle young face. He was filled with admiration. Between each mouthful they would grab the chance to get his attention. Natty sat and watched the noisy table.

"How was your day Natty? You haven't let us all know yet," their father asked. There was a sudden silence. Natty now became the focus, her sisters staring at her intently, both smirking.

"It was fine, how was yours?" Natty mumbled, speaking with a mouthful of mashed potato.

"My day was fine, how is all your studying going?" Their father's eyebrows were raised – he wasn't happy to see his daughter speak with her mouth full.

Natty quickly swallowed her food before she responded.

"It's going well Dad. I have plenty of reading to keep me going. I may have to go to the library later."

"The library again? I'll be taking your dinner down there soon. It must be hard going for you? But it is lovely to see you working so hard. You are going to have a great future young lady."

"It is hard Dad, but I know I will get there in the end. What job did Mother have? You know before you both met, before you got married?" Natty knew she was asking an unacceptable question. She wanted to know, and why shouldn't she? After all she was their mother. She felt nervous as she waited for the answer.

Their father placed his knife and fork down, resting them on the side of his half-empty plate.

"Why do you need to know?" His voice was stern.

"I just thought it would be nice to know." Natty knew she had to carry on.

"Natty, is there a reason why we have to discuss your mother over dinner?" The emotions began to stir in him. His stomach felt heavy again. For a moment earlier he was relaxed watching his girls, but the feeling wasn't to last.

"I just want to know, that's all." Natty could see he was getting angry, but there was sadness in his eyes and she began to feel unsettled.

"You're beginning to sound like your mother, Natty. She was very good at saying the wrong thing. She worked in a fish market, now eat up!"

112

"She worked in a what? A smelly fish market? Stink!" Glenn felt the need to join in.

"Glenn, it's not funny." Natty gave her a stare that could kill.

Ruth sat and held her nose. She didn't have to utter a word to make her point.

The sniggering from her sisters turned into loud laughter. Natty felt it best to ignore them – pretend they weren't there, just as they did their mother.

"Did she like it, Dad?" Natty thought it a good idea to try to make the situation as normal as possible.

"I am sure she did Natty, she was quite highly spirited." Emotions which had been suppressed for so long began to emerge inside of him. He felt a sense of endearment for their mother mixed with bitterness. He wanted to cry, but he had to push the feelings inside himself again; he couldn't be weak. It would be unforgivable in front of his girls.

"Did she leave to have us, Dad?"

"Natty, I really can't see the purpose of this." He spoke more softly hoping his daughter would stop asking him and let it be.

"Oh Dad please tell me, I really want to know." Natty was full eagerness.

"Oh Dad, please let us know, please." Glenn began mocking Natty.

Ruth sat smiling, cheekily looking around at each member of her family as they spoke.

"Did you love her, Dad?" Natty asked.

"Of course I loved her; we loved each other very much. I am sure you three sitting here is the answer to such a ridiculous question. Things happen sometimes, they don't turn out how you think they will. People change sometimes and there is nothing anyone can ever do about it. It doesn't matter how much you try. We all belong together now."

Their father covered Ruth's hand with his; he looked into her eyes and smiled. It felt as though time stood still as he wondered if things could have been different.

"But Dad, I don't understand why it all went wrong."

"Enough is enough, Natty. Eat your dinner, it's getting cold. All you need to know is we loved each other once. Life changes, people also. But I will say your mother was and still is the most beautiful woman I have ever seen. Or shall ever see again." Their father conveniently finished his dinner and left them alone. He had a pain in his throat as he tried to hold back the tears. He swallowed hard, as if trying to push the tears and feelings back into his stomach. As he left the kitchen he wiped a small tear from his eye.

"Well done Nat, opened your mouth as usual." Glenn stood up with her empty plate in her hand.

"Glenn, I think you should take a good look at yourself." Natty wished Glenn could vanish into thin air.

"Please stop it, I can't take it any more, everyone is always so sad in this house and in that house." Ruth dismissed herself from the table. To the exact pattern of their father, as she left she also wiped away tears.

"You've made Ruth cry now. Well done Nat. If you're so bothered why don't you go and live with her, after all you're sounding more like her, making everyone cry." Glenn followed Ruth.

Natty sat alone among the empty plates, flicking her mashed potato with her fork, thinking that if the pile of mash had been big enough, she would have buried herself in it. She sat eating alone, slowly gulping down her cold food, tears of her own now falling onto her plate.

The dishes had been put away; they had been scrubbed and dried. She worked slowly hoping one of her sisters might finally decide to come in and help. They could say sorry to her for being unkind and get back to chatting again. Natty threw the tea towel onto the clean side and thought about leaving for her mother's. She wasn't sure if she felt up to it. The feeling of leaving her mother alone in her large home helped her make the decision.

She quietly grabbed a bag which lay on the floor under the coat rack, where a large selection of coats and scarves blocked most of the sunlight from the glass in the front door.

"I won't be long." Stepping outside, Natty stopped and looked up at the large window of the living room; she knew they were all in there together, their own little family. Her sisters and her Dad all as one. Natty continued to walk to the other part of her life.

22

Each room became a reflection of Eve's sadness; it seemed to be in each corner, every inch of space that surrounded her. She cleaned to try to stop her pain. To try to forget how she felt. And sometimes she would clean simply because she had nothing else to do. She wept whenever her father left her. Having to tell him she was pregnant again made him upset and she watched as he left in haste. She kept calling him but he didn't turn around. Between tears and cleaning she would take a pill, it felt like it was the only break of the day. It was the only time she wanted to stop. Stopping meant thinking and it was too hard to contemplate.

Glenn would always follow Natty around, every step Natty took Glenn would become her shadow, tugging on her dress, never leaving her side. Dreading being alone, at such a tender age fear was a part of their tiny existence. They never complained, never let out a tiny murmur. They were too young, unable to understand how things could be different. The only person who knew was Eve. Whose wonderful exterior hid pain only she could live with. Sometimes it would come out without any warning at all. She could become out of control in seconds. Afterwards she would cry with guilt and condemnation, only to despise herself more.

"Eve, I have to go to work for a while, will you be OK?" Matthew stood anxiously, waiting to leave. Something deep inside him seemed to be telling him not to go. He glanced down at his girls, holding hands, their small fingers gripping onto each other. He looked into their eyes and sensed their sadness. But if they were sad surely they would cry? Eve tapped the girls on the head and they instantly walked away from their father, almost as if it had been a silent command. Natty looked back briefly as she walked into the dining room. She was crying out for help without any

115

voice, how could he hear her? How could someone so small ever be able to let someone so big understand? To Natty and Glenn their father was like a giant, a big friendly giant; their mother, even though smaller than he, seemed to tower further than their eyes could see.

"Will you be OK, Eve?" Deep down Matthew prayed she would be.

"Of course, I'll be fine, you can't stay here for ever." Eve's voice was soft and unsettled. "I will be fine Matthew, go on." Inside she needed him to stay, she couldn't quite understand why but she wanted him there all the same. He would have seen it as a sign of weakness if she had told him.

"Let me just kiss the girls." Matthew walked into the dining room to say goodbye to the other most important girls in his life. He bent down, slowly kissing Glenn then gently wiping her cheek. Her skin was so soft. Natty managed to unclasp her sister's hand from her dress and moved across quickly to kiss him goodbye. She didn't want to let go of him. Matthew had said his goodbyes. Just before he turned to leave he pulled Natty's hair away from her face and placed it neatly onto her shoulders.

"Hey, where did you get that mark my little angel?" A round bruise shadowed a part of her small neck. Matthew touched it gently with his finger, he could see it had been there for some time. Why had he not noticed it before? And why did Eve not inform him? He composed himself and rose again, becoming the giant once more.

"Be careful little one." He turned away once again, the most awful thought rushing through him like electricity. He turned and took one long look at his girls before finally leaving them. He pushed the thought away. As he walked through the hall full of worry he kissed Eve on the forehead. Eve quickly shut the door, shutting out the world. She pressed her face against the wood, breathing heavily. Almost afraid to move away, she was desperate to feel OK, running through in her mind what she was going to do, how she had her day planned.

Matthew's journey to work seemed to take for ever. Being part of the everyday build-up of traffic out of town gave him a chance to think but he wanted more than anything to get the thought out of his head. It was already too full – he didn't know what to think about first. He couldn't possibly make room for another worry. He could see all the traffic in front of him and behind, he was trapped between the day's workforce. He gave out a huge sigh, wishing at that moment that he was a smoker, at least he would have something to do. He tapped his hands on the steering wheel half-heartedly to the music, trying to pretend as Eve had done that morning that everything was all right. Any onlookers could never guess he was full of anguish, he was just a handsome young man on his way to work with no cares in the world. He felt as if he was being squashed between two slices of bread. He was trying to convince himself not to make a quick call to Dr Peters. Surely the doctor would blow things out of proportion again; there was no way his beautiful wife, his perfect Eve, could have been as ill as the doctor kept saying. No way, not my Eve, he kept repeating over and over again in his head. Matthew's perfect vision was being scrutinised by Dr Peters. He didn't know her, not like Matthew did. A feeling of self blame came over him for a short moment. He knew he had always expected a lot from her, just as his father had from him. There was nothing Matthew did that was ever good enough, so could he blame his father for making him this way? If his father was alive he would be looking at him in disgust for choosing such a woman.

"Damn you, Dad!" Matthew found himself speaking out loud as he took a look at the other frustrated drivers, each in their own little world, thinking hard about their own lives behind the safety of their car doors. Probably feeling they had the biggest problem out of all the drivers in front and behind, in fact anywhere. He was hoping they hadn't seen his outburst. There was surely only room for one crazy person in his daughters' lives. He glanced across at the driver next to him, also having to wait for the traffic to clear whether she liked it or not. Her passenger seat was covered with enough sweet wrappers to refill the sweet aisles; by the time she got to her destination she would have to stop off at the nearest dentist. Matthew chuckled in his thoughts. The movement of the traffic became steady. Maybe once he reached the garage he could have a good honest chat with his brother. He was always good at listening, especially when it came to Eve. Matthew knew only one thing for sure that day, amongst all the thoughts overpowering him: he loved his wife with every part of his being. His soul belonged to her, everything he wanted to achieve was for her, his heart would beat for her, and that was all he knew.

Eve had been left alone with Glenn and Natty. She slowly walked around each room in her spacious house, each beautiful room unable to fulfil her needs. If you were to play hide-and-seek there would have been lots of great places to hide. She never managed to find any. She needed somewhere to go where no one could find her, not until she was ready to be found. Natty and Glenn roamed around together, managing to find the odd toy to play with, those which were only allowed because they didn't leave too much mess. They played happily in their child world, the only place where two young children should be allowed to go, a world full of love and care and warmth, a world where they could discover who they were and be free. This was a place they never knew in reality. Eve made sure of it. Whatever good could have been given to them, she would take it away in a blink of an eye. Their tiny minds had adapted to the dialogue which surrounded them and their tiny bodies were already becoming immune to the pain. Their hearts would beat only for themselves and their father, waiting and hoping for their mother's love. To Natty and Glenn it was what being small was all about. They weren't allowed to speak – whatever words Natty had learnt she was unable to express. She was too scared already to call for help from her mother. Glenn was simply a shadow of her sister; every move Natty made was mimicked by her. Her hand constantly clutching at Natty's clothing, in Glenn's young mind Natty was already her strength and protector. But Natty didn't even know it. They would sit and kiss each other, holding each other's small hands; nothing was going to separate them.

As Eve walked into the dining room to see her girls playing under the clock, she smiled gently; she absorbed their presence for a while and felt warmth pass through her. She wondered why she would ever want to leave them. She knew it was going to be a hard thing to do; the hardest thing ever, especially now she was expecting another. As she looked at them she felt a sense of pride in how pretty they were. Her third pregnancy certainly wasn't planned, it was not her intention at all to cause any more mess around the house. She thought hard about her moment with Harry and felt an excitement stirring in her body. It was madness, Matthew would break down if he knew. The fear and anticipation of what her husband would feel were taken over by the reality of how wonderful Harry had made her feel. She was the sexy, daring woman she had always aspired to be. A smile came to her face. Eve sat beside her tiny girls, her legs tucked up near her chin. She pulled her blue woollen jumper over her knees. She began to build the bricks up high, knocking them down on purpose and bringing laughter to them all. As she happily repeated her actions Natty and Glenn would push the bricks down with all their force and the bricks were scattered around the soft, red carpet.

They were to be found under the sofa near the fireplace, and all three of them went scurrying around like hungry little rabbits. Retrieving the bricks, they continued to play the game. Eve touched their heads, pushing her fingers through their hair, gently sliding the back of her hand down the side of their faces and stroking their rosy cheeks. She knew how special they were, she had just never told them. All her love and affection was focused on them for the very first time – she felt it from deep inside.

Suddenly she felt a tap on her shoulder and turning her head slowly, she felt her father's hand now upon her head. As he stroked her hair Eve closed her eyes and embraced the moment. She felt like the happy child she had always been. Her attention had been quickly taken from Natty and Glenn who were holding the bricks in their hands, waiting for her to continue the game.

"Hello Dad, I have missed you. Have you seen how your wonderful grandchildren are playing?" Eve's voice was shaky but full of pride.

Her hair wasn't being stroked any more. As she admired her father she could see his hair was still soft and grey, he looked strong and still had his large belly.

"Eve, I can't visit any more, I have waited too long, I'm tired and I need to rest now. Your girls are here now, you must not forget."

"But Dad you can't go for ever, you just can't. I won't let you."

Instantly Eve was on her knees praying at her father's legs, pleading with him to listen to her. Her tears were flowing. Her voice was full of desperation. Her tightly clenched knuckles were becoming wet from her tears.

"Eve, my little girl, my dear sunshine girl, you cannot be expected to let go of your family. I couldn't allow it. You have to stay with them. They need you as once you did me. I will always watch you from my place. I'm happy Eve; you have to let me sleep now."

"Dad, I will come with you, just wait a little longer. I'm scared that's all, don't give up on me. You have never given up on me, not now, please don't do it now. I'm coming, hold on!" Eve was full of anguish and fear. Her voice was soft but she could feel an overwhelming anger building up, just like the bricks earlier.

"Eve, please, you have to remember how much I love you and that I will always love you. Goodbye my little girl."

Eve wiped her tears from her face with her hands. When she looked up her father had gone.

"Father, please come back!" Her screaming echoed through the girls' tiny bodies. They began to cry. Eve turned to them and stared in disbelief, her face evolving into a face of hatred.

"Shut up, will you just shut up, both of you, it's your fault I can't be with him!" Her surge of anger became out of control. As she grabbed at Natty's arm and pulled her up the brick Natty was holding dropped to the floor. Eve slapped her tiny cheek to try to quieten her. She pushed her shaking hands into Natty's small arms. Natty was thrown with force onto the sofa and as she rolled off she fell to the floor with a thud. Next, Glenn was grabbed. Eve's fingers dug harder into her soft skin. She was thrown on top of her sister. Glenn mimicked her sister yet again, but this time without wanting to.

Eve looked at her girls sobbing on the floor. Picking up a handful of colourful bricks she threw them with all her force at their unprotected bodies. Their screams filled Eve's head as she frantically scurried up the stairs to the bathroom, her head pounding with the panic rushing through her.

"Quick, I've got to be quick, can't waste time, haven't got time, Dad please wait, I'm coming!" She pulled sachets and bottles from

120

the cabinet in rhythm to her chanting. She couldn't hear Natty and Glenn crying from the room below. She had found what she was looking for, swiping up Matthew's razor as though she had discovered buried treasure.

Gripping it in her hand with precision, she took the shining metal to her wrist and felt a glimmer of hope from what she saw before her. This was it, she was now ready. Her soft white wrist joined the razor like a magnet. She cut deep inside, desperately wanting to get it right. She inhaled deeply as she slumped onto the toilet seat, her wrist now a bright red. The damp, warm moisture filled her lap; she became relaxed. It was the first time her mind felt clear, the first time she was finally doing something right. She closed her eyes and waited to see her father once more.

"Harry, I've got to go home!" Matthew felt a sudden urge to leave. He hadn't wanted to be at the garage that day, he'd known from the moment he left his home. Every minute away would bring a knot to his stomach; he had watched the clock all morning and as the hours ticked by the need to make a move home concerned him deeply.

"Matt, we've got loads to do." Harry spoke sharply.

"Harry, I'm going, I've got to go to them." Matthew let out a sigh, glad he had finally made the decision. He threw everything down as though his life depended on it. Or, as he thought, his family's. Harry was confused to see his brother in such a state, leaving his tools all over the floor for one thing and rushing out of the garage as though he had burst into flames.

"Matt, I'm coming with you!" Harry hastily wiped his hands on a cloth, grabbed his jacket and followed his brother. Matthew drove fast now as the traffic was clear.

"Matt, everything is going to be fine." Harry tried to sound reassuring.

"I don't know, Harry. I have a really bad feeling she's getting worse. I shouldn't have left her today, I shouldn't have."

"But you did, Matt."

"I know, god damn it. What will I do without them? I can't survive without my beautiful Eve. It doesn't matter how sick she is."

"Matt, I think you're jumping the gun a little, aren't you?"

They both became silent, thinking alone. Matthew screeched to a halt outside his wonderful family home. As he sat and inhaled deeply, he saw that everything looked normal. He glanced over at Harry who was also becoming tense, his oily fingers tightly crossed in his pockets. All of a sudden they had forgotten their sense of urgency and sat in the van for a moment, as if hoping to wake from a bad dream. Suddenly Matthew leapt into action.

"Oh shit, Harry, we're wasting time. Hurry!" They both rushed up the path; there were no obstacles for them to overcome as not a toy or small trike lay in their way.

"Can you hear anything Harry?" Matthew was scuffling through his keys.

"No Matt, I can't."

Matthew finally opened the door. The sound of his keys being thrown down on the hall table would have gained anyone's attention. But there was not a movement from anywhere. Nothing could be heard. Normally, Natty and Glenn would run to him when they heard his keys.

"Eve, are you here?" Matthew's voice echoed through the house.

"Listen Matt." Harry placed his hand onto his brother's arm. The sobs from the dining room gently filled the hall. Matthew knew his thoughts were becoming a reality. Each second after each cry, he knew his children were waiting for him.

Harry rushed into the dining room.

"Oh my God!" He went forward and knelt down by their sides. Natty and Glenn lay heartbroken and weak. Harry pulled them both to him.

"Harry, what is it?" Matthew stood frozen as he watched his brother gripping on to both his daughters.

"Matthew, I don't know what's happened." Harry's voice was full of tears.

Matthew couldn't move.

"Call the hospital Matt, now!"

"My babies, what's happened to my babies?"

As Harry lay them down gently on the sofa, a sudden flash of his moment with Eve rushed through him. He looked up at his brother. "Come on Matt, get it together." Harry began to search for Eve, taking a long look at the top of the stairs. He stood apprehensively on the first step before he made his dreaded way up, terrified of what he might or might not find.

"Eve, where are you Eve, are you OK?" He didn't need to search for long – the sudden glimpse of red caught his eye. He felt like he was going to collapse.

"Eve, what have you done, you stupid, stupid woman!"

Eve's weak and slowly emptying body now lay on the floor. Harry grabbed as many towels as he could, wrapping them tightly around her open wrists. Her blood quickly absorbed each towel, turning Harry's jeans to deep red as he knelt.

"Matt, hurry up, oh fuck!" He gently held Eve's nearly lifeless body over his strong arms, just as he had her daughters earlier, pulling her up high with all the strength he could find in his scared body. He made his way down the stairs. Matthew had just put the receiver down. He turned, only to stand frozen once again. This could not be happening. Eve was being held by his brother as though he were a wolf and she were his prey. She seemed soulless in his arms. A faint steady dripping sound was all Matthew could hear as her blood went onto the carpet.

"My Eve, my beautiful Eve!" Matthew moved slowly towards them. Harry, tired, now sat on the stairs holding Eve. Her small body lay over his lap. Matthew went down to Harry's feet, kissing Eve's face he now became drenched in her blood. They had once said they would share everything: he held her head and kissed her face once more.

"Please don't leave me Eve, please. Oh God, please let her stay with us. We can make her better, please." Matthew pressed his head into Eve's chest, he cried hard, as he should have cried when he lost his father.

Harry placed his blooded hand upon his brother's head. "Shh Bro, she's going to be fine, they all are." Harry looked up to the ceiling and closed his eyes; he prayed.

23

Natty strolled slowly away from her father's house; the other three people in her life didn't seem to care much for anyone or anything but themselves. How could they? she thought. Their mother was the other part of their stupid messy lives. Natty looked down at her shoes as she walked. They were slightly dusty, so she stopped, quickly licked her fingers and wiped them clean. She couldn't let her mother down, always wanting to look her best.

"Hey Natty, where are you going?"

As Natty placed her foot onto the floor it was as if time had just stood still. Her stomach felt as though it had sunk as she heard Glenn running up behind her. Natty began walking at a quicker pace, wishing she could begin running.

"Slow down will you? Where are you off to? Have you got a secret boyfriend or something?" Glenn wouldn't give in, walking with a bounce as she kept stepping in front of Natty to get her full attention.

"Come on Natty, who is it?"

"Don't be so ridiculous. Go home and take care of Ruth will you?"

"Natty's got a secret admirer, wait till Dad finds out," Glenn sang mockingly.

"You are being an arse. Mind your own business." Natty pulled her coat together at the front as she was feeling chilly. Being so slim didn't help, she was always cold.

"Natty, what are you being so cross for? Are you hoping to hide his spotty face and greasy hair? I bet he wears huge glasses." Glenn laughed so hard it made her double over.

Natty found herself laughing too. She could imagine the sort of boyfriend she would end up with – he sounded like the exact one.

Natty stopped walking for a while, hoping to take control of her sister's frantic movements. She was getting on her nerves.

"Look you nut, I'm not going to meet the man of my dreams OK? I felt like a walk – it's a free country isn't it?" she said impatiently.

"It depends if you're in Mother's country or not." Glenn's so-called jokes continued; she couldn't shut up.

"Not funny Glenn. Really, you do amaze me more every day. Anyway stop being so horrible about Mother, you don't have to keep being cruel."

"Protecting Mother again, Natty?"

"How could I ever possibly protect her? Dad will be wondering where you are and Ruth will be looking for you too."

"Oh, so I'm responsible for Ruth now am I?"

"Well you're always together." Natty raised her eyebrows.

"It's not my fault she won't leave my side. Gets on your nerves after a while."

"I know what you mean Glenn." Her thoughts rushed back to when they were small.

"What did you say?"

"I didn't say."

Glenn was still jumping around excitedly.

"Glenn, have you got ants in your pants? Will you stay still?"

"Depends what you're going to get in your frilly pants later."

"Piss off." Natty wanted to laugh.

"Natty, where has your sense of humour gone?"

"I didn't have one, remember."

"I am so excited for you Nat, seventeen and never been kissed."

"Excited about what Glenn? You tell me what I have ever to be excited about?"

"I'm excited, dear Natty, for you putting your tongue down the poor boy's throat for the first time." Glenn spoke through her chuckles, nearly in song.

"And may I ask how you know it's my first time?" Natty began walking with haste again, hoping Glenn was finally bored and would make her way home.

"All right sweet pie, you can't pull the wool over my eyes."

Natty finally grabbed hold of her sister's arm forcefully.

"Shut up will you? It will be you who does that and anyone will do." There was a pause. Natty's anger turned to laughter. The thought of it all made her finally chuckle. Natty and Glenn stood out in the street laughing together. It had been such a long time since they had shared joy. Stopping suddnely, they stared at each other, realising how deeply unhappy the other looked. They gave each other a reassuring smile.

"Are you all right, Natty?"

"Yes fine," Natty replied, rubbing the top of Glenn's head.

At that moment she knew how much she loved her sister, even though she would spend most of every day trying to irritate her.

"Where are you going? You didn't say." Glenn continued in her quest to find out as much as she could.

"You don't give up, do you?"

"You know me." Glenn smiled at Natty, scrunching her face up.

"Look, I can't tell you."

"Why can't you trust me for once, Natty?"

"Look if I tell you, you will go mad, tell Dad and everything. I will be locked away for eternity in Ruth's castle, and never get rescued, which would mean I would never get the chance to put my tongue down anyone's throat." Natty began walking yet again; the journey to their mother's house was taking longer than expected.

"Please Nat, trust me, eh?"

Natty took a huge sigh and considered quickly. She was never going to get rid of Glenn unless a confession was put in place. Her thoughts were interrupted yet again.

"Well Nat, I am coming anyway, going to follow you if you like it or not. You will have to get there sooner or later."

"OK Glenn, you win, don't say I didn't warn you." Natty took a deep sigh. They continued walking only a slight distance away from each other. Natty could almost feel her sister breathing down her neck. Inside Natty felt a sudden sense of relief; she could release herself from the burden and finally share her secret. As Glenn followed Natty remembered again the days when her sister was always close behind.

"Hold on, this is Mother's road. Why are we going down here? She will see us Nat. Is there no other way we can go?" Glenn came to a sudden halt. "Nat, you're not doing what I think you are? I'd

126

rather watch you kiss your boyfriend or lock you away and throw away the key, for Christ's sake!"

"The whole point is for her to see us, stupid." Natty watched her sister as she stood full of fear.

"You're the stupid one, wait till Dad finds out."

"He's not going to find out though, is he Glenn?"

"All the things she has done, I can't believe you can just turn up like this."

"It's where I go, OK? Do you want to come or not? Or are you going to stand there like a stupid arse all night? My goodness, anyone would think we're going to the ends of the earth, never to return."

"Oh, now I see, you're trying to be the funny one, that's funny, very funny, almost cracked six ribs."

"Saves Mother doing it. Joke, Glenn, just a joke." Natty put her arm out to Glenn, moving her hand back and forward, silently commanding her to hold it tightly.

"Come on Glenn, she will be pleased to see you." Natty felt calm and in control.

"Needs to punch me I suppose. Anyway, I look a mess."

"She isn't going to punch you, break your ribs or wash you all over. She doesn't care if you look a mess."

"So you're saying I do?" Glenn put her arm out to take her sister's hand.

"Come on!" Natty took her hand and started leading the way.

"But Nat, I'm scared, scared to see her." Glenn felt herself being slowly dragged.

"I know you're scared, that's what makes you human."

"But what if she still hates me?"

"She doesn't still hate you, she never has hated you. Don't be scared. No one is going to hurt you any more while I'm around, I promised you didn't I?"

"She did hurt me, and you couldn't do anything about it then so what makes you think you can now?"

"Nothing, remember I'm human too."

"OK, just don't leave me."

"OK Glenn I will," Natty teased. She glanced at Glenn and smiled.

24

Matthew didn't know which room to visit first, all his life hidden away by two white doors. The beating of his heart echoed in his head. As they made their way to the hospital it had felt like longest journey of their lives. His beautiful Eve and his susceptible girls were taken away from him. He had finally managed to sit down after Harry successfully found a couple of plastic chairs, putting them near the ward entrance. Matthew put his head in his hands. He thought hard, wondering what he had done to make his perfect Eve behave as she did. All his family were in danger and it was all down to him; surely it was the only answer to it all.

"They will be looked after, Matt They're in a safe place now." Harry's voice was soft as he placed his bloodstained hand on Matthew's shoulder.

"Safe! How safe can they be at home in the middle of the day? I can't believe it Harry, why has she done this to me?" His eyes began to glisten with tears. He wouldn't cry; he held them back again. For the first time Harry saw his elder brother, who was always the one in control, organised and sensible, in more pain than ever before. He was only a man after all. Matthew constantly informed Harry that he was only human, it was a shame he didn't listen to his own words. He never did.

"Go and see them Matt, I will wait here for the doctor."

Matthew looked up at his brother.

"But—"

"Just go Matt, and see Eve." Harry helped Matthew to his feet. He couldn't have found the strength to do it himself.

"You're a great brother Harry; I really don't know what I would do without you in my life." As Matthew stood up he felt lost in the world, desperately wanting someone to help him, tell him how to make it all better. He remembered feeling the same as he watched his father's coffin being placed into the ground, seeing his father's name on a highly polished plaque. He couldn't see the point of it being polished or even being there at all. It would never be seen. He did think maybe it was the only time when anyone could have their true identity, the only time when their father was allowed to be recognised as the person he was born to be. He wondered if he would ever belong in his family. Harry was always the favourite; their father loved him more, he was sure. It wasn't until he had met his perfect Eve, that he finally felt part of the world. But she was now lying in a bed, wrist-bound and hanging on to every breath. She had put herself there; she had put their children there. Matthew could hear the echoing of footsteps becoming louder, surrounding the corridor, taking him away from his thoughts. They came to a stop behind him.

Harry leapt up to give his brother support, holding onto his arm.

Dr Peters shook Matthew's hand and then Harry's. He seemed to look a lot smaller than when Matthew saw him at home. It's funny how surroundings make people look different. The doctor was the only one who knew what was going on.

"Matthew, how are you?"

Matthew just shrugged to the doctor's question, wanting Harry to think and feel for him.

"I have been taking care of Eve and those wonderful girls of yours."

"Are they OK? Please tell me they are." Matthew felt his body race with fear.

"Matthew, try to be calm. I'm very pleased to say they are fine."

"Fine, you say?" Harry couldn't help but speak up, knowing how relieved his brother would be.

"They are a little shaken and confused. But I am sure you can take your girls home in a short while. They will be running you ragged and having fun in no time."

Matthew's thought of fun never really existed. Matthew and Harry gave out a huge sigh of relief exactly in unison.

"I told you they would be all right." Harry rubbed both his hands together.

129

"My Eve, Doctor, how is she?" Matthew's voice was soft. He didn't hear Harry talking.

"She is stable but she hurt herself quite badly. She was very lucky you were there."

"But I wasn't there was I? She wouldn't have done those things if I were."

"I think you'll find she would have Matthew, it was just a matter of time. Please don't blame yourself, it is no one's fault. Not even Eve's. I am so pleased to tell you the baby is safe." The doctor smiled.

"Sorry, how do you mean, safe?" There was a thundering in his head and he felt like he couldn't take any more.

Matthew went down in a slump on the chair and held his head in his hands.

"Matt, she's having another baby, that's great isn't it?" Harry said, rubbing his hands harder together.

Matthew jumped off his chair, the adrenaline inside now at boiling point. He began to pace up and down.

"Yes Harry, it's great. You didn't think Immaculate Conception really existed did you? Or am I missing a major life fact here?" Matthew was furious.

"Matthew, I think you should be happy your family are well. You must try to keep strong, your wife needs you desperately at the moment, more than ever before. She is very sick." Dr Peters stood calmly gently tapping his notes on his side.

"I just don't understand, Doctor, I just don't. Can I see my girls? I need to see them to make sense of the whole thing." Matthew became calm instantly. He knew he had to stay calm.

"I think you should see Eve, Matt. Go and see her first."

"Can I?" Matthew had to ask permission to see the people he loved more than life.

"Of course, please don't expect too much from her. She has managed to talk about a few important things to me, but she needs to keep her strength. Especially after her ordeal." The doctor pointed at the door where Matthew was to enter.

Matthew walked quickly. "Ordeal, I'll give her ordeal." Sadness and anger engulfed his body.

"I am sorry, but only next of kin allowed." The doctor put his hand in front of Harry.

130

Harry stood back and left a clear path for his brother to enter.

Matthew's beautiful Eve could not do any more harm to herself. She had bandages around each wrist, almost as though she had been tied to the bed, just in case. She seemed so small. Matthew still found her as pretty. His breathing felt heavy, he could hear his heartbeat thumping in his head, echoing just like the footsteps from the doctor earlier. Slowly he walked to her bed, his fingers gently brushing over the clean, crisp sheets which covered her perfect body. Standing over her, trying to understand where she had gone, if she would ever come back to him. She was extremely pale and her eyes were puffy even as she slept. He imagined the inside of her – the tears filling her body; if she were to cry now she would never stop, he was sure of it. She must have been sad for such a long time, longer than he could ever imagine. He touched her finger and then let it go, watching it flop back onto the bed. With his strong hand he gently entwined his fingers into hers, placing them onto his so they lay just right. He longed for everything to be wonderful for her. He never wanted to ever let her down. He hadn't held her hand in such a long time. He'd longed to, and wished with all his heart she could wake at that very moment and feel him touching her. He quietly dragged the chair from behind him with one hand while still holding her with the other He was never going to let her go again. Should he try to talk to her? Would she listen? Would she understand? Matthew read once that people can hear you talking while they sleep. Something about the subconscious mind. He'd thought till that moment that it was a load of old poppycock. But for once in his life he wanted to be proved wrong.

"Hello Eve. My darling, Eve, I pray you can hear me. Please, if you can, I am only asking you to listen for a while. I won't keep you too long. Why did you hurt yourself? Why did you? I am here for you Eve, I always have been. You only have to talk to me. I can't ask you to explain yourself now, it wouldn't be fair. I will have to one day Eve, and I am sorry for that." His hands became sweaty, he could feel them damp on her fingers. His voice was gentle and unsettled, he was rushing his words.

"I knew you were acting strangely but I simply ignored it like I do everything in my life. Why, Eve? Why didn't you tell me you were hurting so much? I thought I gave you everything you ever wanted. I hope you can hear me, don't go deaf on me now please. I know how stubborn you can be. Our beautiful girls, why did you hurt them? How could you? I will try to understand, Eve, I promise I will, but I am only human after all. Don't give up on me, don't sleep for ever. We have to go home some time, wake up Eve and I'll take you home today, what do you say?" Matthew began to cry, feeling desperate.

"Sorry but you need to let her rest now, your girls are waiting to see you."

"Sorry Doctor." Matthew slowly unclasped his hand from Eve's fingers, wiped the tears from his face with his cuff and stood up. Leaning over her he kissed her gently on the forehead, inhaling the scent from the perfume she had put on that very day.

"I love you Eve. I love you more than you know." As Matthew left her side the feeling of emptiness overwhelmed him. He had to push away any thought of failure; he couldn't fail her – he never wanted anyone to feel the same way he did when his father was alive.

25

Their mother was still, her two daughters standing in front of the overgrown garden. Glenn was still standing behind Natty, holding on to every inch of Natty's shirt she could. Time stood still for a moment, not a movement or word from anyone; they all just looked at each other.

"Has Ruth come also?" As their mother spoke her eyes moved on to the garden. She frowned, thinking how beautiful her daughters looked, and not wanting to look for too long, afraid she may find fault in them. They had come to see her and she felt extremely thankful.

"No Mother, only us." Natty pulled her sister into the hallway.

Glenn stood for a while and focused on the stairs that led to the safety of their rooms.

"Glenn, I am so glad you wanted to see me. What did your father say?" Their mother walked slowly into the kitchen. Natty had already sat down. The kitchen didn't seem as shiny, everything was out of place and it was a mess, it was something Glenn had never seen before. It looked like their mother had dressed herself in less than a minute that day. She wore an old greying sweatshirt with black jeans which were far too tight for her.

"What the hell has happened to her face?" Glenn whispered to Natty.

"Shh."

They hadn't been checked before they sat; the fruit bowl in the middle of the table had old fruit mixed with fresh. Glenn tried to make eye contact with Natty so she could see for herself, but Natty had spotted it.

"Shall I get rid of this old stuff for you Mother?" Natty picked out the old from the fresh and returned it to its normal standard.

Glenn felt a sense of dread, thinking her sister would get a blow to her face for being so impertinent.

"Oh, thank you dear, I haven't got round to it."

Glenn froze for only a moment, thinking she was dreaming. She couldn't even begin to understand what was happening.

Their mother placed two glasses of cold lemonade on the table; once she sat she put her hands on her chin and smiled.

"How are you Glenn? What have you been doing?" she asked, realising just how pretty her daughter was becoming. A little plump but pretty all the same.

"I haven't got up to much Mother, same old stuff." Glenn spoke quietly, transfixed on her mother's blue eye shadow covering most of her unplucked eyebrows, and feeling cautious just in case she answered her incorrectly.

"Stuff? What do you mean?" Their mother wondered why her daughter couldn't answer a question clearly and she began to feel agitated.

"School stuff, nothing much really."

"I see." Their mother left her chair inhaling a long breath.

Natty sat and drank her lemonade, watching Glenn, hoping she would get fully involved in speaking to their mother.

"How's your father? Is he all right?" Her voice was gentle.

"He is great, yes I would say since we have lived with him it has been kind of catch-up time." Glenn began to wiggle her toes with nerves.

Glenn felt a sharp pain on her ankle from Natty's foot. Natty was giving her a look which could kill normal weak folk.

"Oh I see, you like living there, do you?" They were happy to live without her. They wanted their father. The thought went over and over in her head.

Glenn didn't want to answer the question. As always curiosity would get the better of her. She wanted to ask a question.

"What are all those tablets for, Mother? You don't take them, do you?"

"It's lovely to have you both home." Their mother pretended she hadn't heard, just as Glenn did earlier.

"We haven't come home Mother, you know how it is?"

"No Glenn, I am afraid I don't." A feeling of uncertainty and anger consumed her instantly. She didn't want to hurt Glenn, but she wanted her to stop saying such hurtful things. Who did she think she was with her nose stuck up in the air?

Natty could not hold back any more as she could see her mother's face changing. She remembered it well, and was surprised how quickly Glenn had forgotten.

"Thank you for the drink, Mother. We will see you again soon." Natty yanked Glenn from her chair.

"You've spilt my lemonade now."

"Glenn, move it!"

They left their mother alone in the kitchen.

As the fresh air filled the hall, their mother realised they had gone. She had been left alone once more. She tried to make sense of the visit – they didn't seem to want to stay for long. She walked slowly to shut the door, taking her clip from her hair and feeling it fall around her shoulders.

"Bye girls," she said seeing them rush off down the road away from her, away from their home.

"What the hell were you playing at Glenn? One minute you were terrified and grabbing my shirt and then you go all cocky-bollocks on me." Natty's voice was raised.

"I only asked her a question. I suppose you haven't asked her any such as why she cut up your dress and beat the crap out of us, and why we were scrubbed until we fucking shone. If I had ever felt the urgent need to look at your arse long enough I would have seen my reflection in it. For Christ's sake Nat, what kind of world are you living in? You're the one who threw her down the flaming stairs, so stop being so innocent in all this!" Glenn's voice was louder.

"*I did not throw her down the stairs!*" Natty felt outraged.

"OK Nat, you've made your point, I don't think anyone heard you."

"Look Glenn, I do ask her things or I guess. She was taking tablets before we went to live with Dad, she is obviously very sick, give her a chance will you. You don't have to be bloody Einstein to work that one out do you? Look at her face, have you ever seen anyone so sad?" Natty's anger overwhelmed her, she wanted to contain it. She didn't want any more conflict with anyone ever

135

again. The emotions would have to stay inside of her like they always did.

"Oh so that explains it, dear Mother has been unwell and decides to purchase all of the make-up any woman can fit in their bag and plaster it all over her face, and look a little scruffy and good old Nat thinks that the sun shines out of her petite hairy arse!" Glenn smirked at Natty, a smirk which could anger anyone enough to gain a small slap, especially in the given situation.

Natty clenched her fist and she scrunched her face.

"Glenn you amaze me, you always have and I am sure you will continue to until you reach the age of maturity, which shall I say for you will be ninety."

"So we've all suffered for nothing, if I'm not going to change, who's going to give our nut of a mother a miracle cure, little miss forgiving?" Glenn's voice became louder.

As their mother pulled the curtain away from the dining room window, she could see her girls in the street, at each other's faces pulling pain from each other. Trying to hurt each other and forgetting they both come from the same place.

"Silly things." Their mother closed the curtain and began shaking her head and tutting. She made her way to the bathroom to wash her hair, as she was expecting a visit from her father later and wanted to look her best. She continued to shake her head as she went up the stairs.

Natty sat down on the kerb. Glenn watched her and decided to sit by her side.

"Nat, sorry for shouting, but I'm not much younger than you, how comes you know everything, how comes you seem to know what to do?"

"I don't know everything. But sometimes it feels things aren't always as straightforward as they look." Natty was watching the leaves blowing across her feet and into the drain.

"Straightforward, how un-straightforward can you get? We have a pill-pushing mother, who for some reason has turned into Coco the Clown. We can't see her even if we wanted to, let alone begin forgiving her. She can't see Dad because well, I don't know why that one is. You've probably got more chance stepping on the moon

136

than getting them holding hands again, the only place Dad wants his hands is around her neck.

"We have a sister living in fairyland waiting for some Prince Charming to come and rescue her – the luck we've had the horse will probably break its leg in the process, throwing Prince Charming head over tit. Ruth will be lying there for all eternity while he drags himself to her, and that's just the good points of it, oh yeah not forgetting your boyfriend." Glenn inhaled deeply.

They both roared with laughter, but then again what else could they do? Two sisters together sitting on a damp kerb, not knowing where to go, not even knowing where they wanted to be.

"Oh what a mess, Glenn."

They laughed harder than ever before.

26

Matthew lay Glenn in her bed and slowly pulled her pristine covers over her, kissing her gently and stroking her face. Harry lay Natty down to sleep in exactly the same way. At home in their beds was the only place Matthew could feel his children were finally safe. Natty and Glenn were allowed to be taken home; it was a huge relief and Matthew felt he at least had part of his family with him. He wouldn't have to ask permission to see them – he could pop his head around the door whenever he wanted to.

"Good to have them home Matthew, isn't it?" Harry went to make a cup of tea. He would have preferred beer of course, but there wasn't anything else to drink. They could maybe wet the baby's head when he became an uncle for the third time. Wondering if he would ever become a father, he poured the water into the cups.

Matthew was sitting in the dining room just listening to the ticking of the clock as the seconds passed. He picked up a play brick and rolled it between his fingers to see what animal was on each side.

"Tea's up Matt." Harry came in, placing the cup next to his brother. The last time Harry had sat there was with Eve. He remembered it well, very well. He hadn't got it out of his head ever since. He looked at his brother and felt a sense of guilt; it was the first time he had felt this way, but it was too late to make amends now.

"Thank you Harry, thank you for everything, being here I mean and the tea." Matthew gently rolled the brick on the coffee table and began to drink.

"What did the doctor say before you left, Matt?"

"He needs to talk to me about Eve. Something or other she is not allowed to hear, as he doesn't want to upset her any more. Can you believe it, he doesn't want her upset; she's allowed to upset everyone else though. Sorry, you know I don't mean it about her, I feel unsettled, that's all. He has given me an appointment card to go and see him." Matthew reached into his pocket and flung the card on the table. It was folded tightly together, as if Matthew wanted to make the problem smaller by making it into a tiny cube. Harry unfolded it and read.

"It's tomorrow."

"I don't know, I told Eve to stay away from the doctors. They make you out to be what you're not; give you illnesses if you haven't got one." Matthew had another sip of his tea. He voice was heavy. He hadn't looked at Harry at all, he wanted to feel sorry for himself, even if it was only to last a short while.

"I don't understand."

"Look Harry, it's quite obvious Eve's not right in the head, doing something like that. Selfish or what? Look around you Harry, what else could a woman want? Just look, not bad for starting off in a fish market, eh?"

"Matthew, that has nothing to do with it, you've got a funny side to you sometimes, you kind of don't see the clear picture. It goes deeper than material things, don't you think?"

"Like how deep do you mean, are we talking drown deep or feet touching the bottom deep?"

Harry didn't like his brother's tone of voice.

"I don't know Matt; I don't suppose I am the one to really ask, being single still and everything. I only hope you haven't been too hard on her that's all. You know how you like things just so, but extremely just so."

"Oh, so because I like things to be the best, or as you say just so, she cuts her wrists. Well, let's work that one out shall we? She wouldn't have done it if her precious father was alive." Matthew made eye contact with Harry finally, wishing he had kept his mouth shut.

"What has her father got to do with anything?"

"Nothing Harry, forget I ever mentioned him."

"Matt, come on, just say."

"I can't explain it to you, but Eve's been on medicine for a little while, well actually since her father died. It's all to do with the

139

stupid Dr Peters bloke. He's the one who stuffed her full with pills. For her nerves, for heaven's sake, they've made her more nervous than ever. Look I don't mean to have a go at the medical profession and I don't knock the help that anyone truly needs, in whatever means they find it, but not my Eve. It begins to drive a man wild. Harry I don't know why she has done this truly I don't."

"Maybe you'll find out tomorrow." Harry drank the last dregs of his tea.

"Probably attention seeking. I can't think about the situation or her father any more."

"Because of our dad Matt?"

"Dad? What, our dad?" Matthew sounded confused.

"Yes Matt, our dad."

Matthew began to feel angry again.

"My wife's problem has absolutely nothing to do with our father. For God's sake, what are you trying to do to me? I have enough to worry about without thinking of him!"

Matthew sat back on the sofa, legs sprawled, rubbing his hands up and down his stained jeans.

"Have you cried, Matt, have you cried for him? Like Eve cried for her father?"

"No I haven't, if that is OK with you and Eve. I'm not sure your sense of timing is OK with me either. While we are on the subject have you, my dear brother, cried for him?" Matthew's stomach was churning with nerves.

"Yes Matthew, I have cried lots of times."

"Oh well, bully for you." Matthew couldn't believe his brother would ever cry or, even worse, actually admit to it. He always looked so strong and rugged to him.

"Matt, come on now."

"He made me cry all the time when he was alive. Nothing I ever did was good enough. Everything I tried to do was for his approval, for his love, so I could feel some kind of meaning for being his son. But he left, Harry, so it didn't matter did it? He would be disapproving now if he were alive. Why should I cry now he's dead and buried? And I still don't understand how Eve's problem has anything to do with our father." Speaking steadily and in control, Matthew felt as though he was going to burst with anger. He was

140

full of adrenaline, feeling as though he wanted to run away, but he knew he would never have stopped.

"It's what I am trying to say, Matt. You don't have to keep trying so hard to please her all the time. She fell in love with you for you, not for all the things you can provide for her, and you fell in love with her. I am sure she wouldn't disapprove in any way, whatever you were to do. So stop trying so hard and start enjoying her and your girls before it's too late."

"It was too late for our father, wasn't it Harry? He didn't enjoy us too much, did he?"

"We didn't get the chance to enjoy him either. So we all missed out. Don't let it happen to you, Matt."

Matthew put his hands over his eyes and began to cry, cry like a little boy. Like his own children earlier. The tears came from so deep inside, pushing their way out; they had waited so long to come away from his body, they were not going to stop. His tears had been buried with his father. They were now set free.

Harry reached forward and held his brother tightly, his muscly arms wrapped strong around his back. Matthew's head lay on his brother's shoulder.

"Don't leave me Harry, please don't, like Dad did, please. I don't ever want to be alone."

"I won't, Matthew, ever."

27

All the girls woke together the following morning, and as Glenn leapt from her bed she smiled over at Natty, approving of their time together the previous evening. Their bedroom was small, too small for three single beds, two overfilled wardrobes and a dressing table. This was a place for Natty to put all her books, to the annoyance of her sisters. Ruth would have liked to sit at it each evening to brush her long hair. Having no idea of her sisters' new-found friendship, Ruth jumped onto Glenn's bed with her brush in hand so her hair could be straightened yet again.

"I don't feel like doing your hair today, you can do it yourself." Glenn went to wash and get ready for school.

"But you always do my hair for me in the morning." Ruth sat on the edge of the bed feeling sorry for herself. Natty began packing the enormous books into her bag – trying to make room for them was a huge job in itself everyday.

"Girls, I'll be late home tonight, make yourselves something will you, and stay indoors." Their father's voice bellowed from the bottom of the stairs.

An excited and nervous feeling came over Natty – she could quickly visit her mother, even bake a cake. She promptly pushed the idea from her head, taking a glance over at Ruth. She was still the eldest and knew she had to show responsibility. Ruth needed to be taken care of. And then again, so did Glenn.

They were all ready to leave, grabbing their umbrellas. Glenn had broken hers and was trying to pinch Ruth's, but to no avail.

Ruth walked in protest in front of her two sisters, but also trying to grasp what they were saying.

"When are you seeing Mother again, Nat?"

"I don't know. Why?"

"I was going to come, that's all. Oh, this umbrella's driving me mad, let me get under your one with you." Glenn threw it away in the nearest bin, running back to safety, grabbing Natty's arm to stay dry.

"Glenn, you're going to confuse everything." Natty stood still as she spoke – she wanted her sister to understand fully. "Look, I know you want to come with me, but what if Dad was to find out? You've never been to the library in your life."

"What's the library about then?" Glenn looked shocked.

"Because I always see her when I go."

"What, at the library?" Glenn looked even more shocked.

"No, stupid, that's my excuse for leaving the house."

"Nat, that's all the time. Do you ever do any studying or are you going to be thick? You've been seeing her behind our backs for ever, I can't believe it, I never had you down for a liar." Glenn let go of her sister's arm in a sulk and began to get slightly wet.

"Oh well thanks, at least there is a compliment in there somewhere."

"Nat, you're really being out of order!"

"It ended up becoming a habit." Natty let out a huge sigh.

"Habit, my arse, picking your nose is a habit, and I don't see any of us doing such a thing nearly every day of the week."

"It's not every day, I couldn't stand it."

Ruth was way in front by this time. Any chance of her overhearing her sisters was impossible. They both saw her alone.

"Ruthi, wait!" They shouted together. Deep down within each of them they always knew they wanted to do everything together. They started running, two sisters trying to reach the other part of them. They needed to reach Ruth, to feel complete; with each other they felt whole and apart they were lost and scared. United they were a strength which could never be broken by anything or anyone. They finally caught her up, the backs of their legs wet from splashing in the puddles as they ran.

"Sorry Ruth, we got chatting, you know what girls are like." Natty placed her hand firmly on Ruth's shoulder, to comfort her and to keep still for a moment after her swift sprint.

"That's cool, what were you chatting about anyway?"

"We were only talking about Mother." Glenn was trying to catch her breath.

"Mother? Why Mother? Please say we're not going back." Ruth stood frozen with fear as she did once in their mother's kitchen.

28

Two months had passed, slowly, since the awful ordeal. Matthew kept running through his mind what the doctor had said to him. He had tried to let it go, hoping to forget, but it was still uppermost in his thoughts. Matthew sat on the chilly wooden bench in the park and watched his children play in the grass, laughing, the air fresh and clean. His intense thoughts took him away for a moment, remembering and hearing the conversation in his head again, every word which had been spoken.

"Your wife has a very serious illness, Matthew."

"Doctor, you must tell me what is happening to her, please."

"She has a very severe brain disease. It can affect women in their twenties or early thirties, she hears internal voices not heard by others and can believe other people are reading her mind, plotting to harm her. She will become frightening to others. The first signs appear shocking, changes in behaviour for instance, hallucinations, finding it hard to separate real from unreal experiences. She will not see anything as you do, being confused and living in a distorted world. It will be frightening for her. You may have noticed, Matthew, that sometimes Eve will sit for ages as rigid as a stone. And other times she may not rest, showing severe reduction in emotional expressiveness. It's an obvious explanation for your wife trying to take her life, as suicide is extremely high in these circumstances. Has she become violent?"

"No, absolutely not."

"This can occur mostly on family members and more often takes place in the home. She can believe people are out to hurt her. She will have to be monitored and take medication. I suggest you stay with your children as much as you can, it's really important you try to not leave them alone with her, for her sake and theirs."

"Sorry, Doctor, but I think you're talking out of turn. Not my Eve, she is OK. She had a bad time but she will get better."

"Matthew, you have to face reality."

"I am facing reality. I think what you're saying is completely unacceptable. What makes this happen?"

"We are not sure of all the factors, but with research hopefully we can understand the illness more fully. Eve will need a lot of care, you must let her know that she is doing things right. Criticism in this case is not very helpful in the long run. She may refuse medication straight away due to being in denial; remember it is reality to her. Your love and your life will be tested, Matthew, like you have never been tested before. Take care of her and we will help her too."

"I can imagine this thing has some kind of gobbledegook name, but please don't tell me – I refuse to have her labelled by the profession."

"Just take care Matthew, we are here, remember."

Through the whole conversation the doctor tapped his gold pen on the table, which irritated Matthew even more.

"Dad, Daddy!" Natty's cold nose pressed against his face, bringing him back to the present moment in the park with his girls.

"Hello little one, let's get you both home, what does he know, eh?" Matthew just looked into his daughters' red flustered faces.

They walked slowly together, each step taking them nearer home. The light in a shop window caught his eye.

"Shall we buy mummy a present, girls? I think it will cheer her up." The most immaculately sewn apron was placed beautifully in the shop window, embroidered flowers and butterflies covering the front with elegance. Matthew left the shop with a small brown bag and inside was Eve's gift.

As soon as Matthew opened the front door, Natty and Glenn rushed inside.

"Daddy will give you a nice bath in a minute, I'm just going to find Mummy." He had left her in the armchair in the dining room, with the pillows puffed up around her. He could hear a mumbled voice; Eve was obviously speaking to someone, but as

146

he crept nearer he glanced back into the hall. The phone was still there. He stood in the doorway holding his girls' small cold hands even tighter than before. He couldn't see Eve's face, just the edge of the blanket scrunched on the floor where it had previously covered her. He put his fingers to his lips, requesting the girls to be quiet as they looked up at him. They knew if they were home then they had to be quiet. Matthew listened carefully, his eyes piercing Eve's chair.

"Dad, I didn't mean to hurt anyone, please don't be cross with me. I don't want to be without any of them Dad, I don't know what to do. You have to help me."

Matthew stood in complete shock, he couldn't move. She had to be joking.

"Eve, what are you doing?" He quickly let go of the girls and walked over to her.

He stood over his perfect Eve. She didn't look at him straightaway, almost as if she was waiting for someone to leave. When she was ready she gave her Matthew full attention.

"Hello sweetheart, back so soon? Everything has been fine, you didn't have to rush back so quickly." Eve pulled the blanket back onto her lap and folded it neatly, pressing her hands over it. "That looks better doesn't it?" She smiled slightly as she looked up at Matthew once again.

Matthews eyes widened in disbelief.

"What looks better Eve? Tell me for Christ's sake!"

"Matthew what's wrong, have the girls played you up?" She sounded almost childlike.

"No, the girls are fine, nothing is wrong, nothing at all."

Matthew didn't want to make a scene, he was trying to be strong like the doctor had asked him; the thing was he didn't want to be strong at that very moment.

"You're a mess, Eve. Look at you, you're untidy, the girls are always filthy, the house is turning into a complete tip. Maybe you could try being a mother instead of living in your own stupid fantasy world. And you haven't even said sorry for what you did to me, not even a murmur of such a word."

"What have I done to you Matthew, please tell me?"

"What have you done to me? You always do this, don't you?"

147

Matthew's hands were pulling at his hair, he was furious.

"Matthew, you are starting to sound a little crazy." Eve gave out a little giggle.

"Can you let me know, Eve, who it is you are talking to?"

"You Matt. See? Gone crazy."

"No, before I came home, or I suppose you have a new talent of springing up conversations with the drapes."

"Sorry Matthew, I don't know what you are talking about."

Eve just stroked the blanket. She wouldn't look at Matthew, and she couldn't look at those grey eyes, they always made her melt.

Natty and Glenn sat and waited for their parents to finish. Matthew bent down over Eve.

"I'm sorry for getting cross. Just one more thing. The baby, Eve, I need to know, I don't think it is mine."

There was a silence, Eve could feel Matthew's heavy breath near her.

"No Matthew, I don't think it is either."

Matthew didn't even have the strength to speak. His beautiful perfect Eve had suddenly drained him of any feeling he had. He felt at that very moment that his heart had been ripped out. Everything he'd ever felt about anything had been washed away; he couldn't feel any purpose of caring and loving any more. He stood, shattered and betrayed.

"I bought you a present with the girls, I will get it." He walked away from the stranger she had become.

The thought of speaking to her that day became a punishment he could not endure. He placed the small brown bag upon her lap. She opened it slowly. She didn't say thank you or even look up at him. Matthew stood waiting for some response; he wasn't quite sure why but he waited all the same. Nothing came. Matthew went to leave the dining room again.

"Thank you, Matthew, it's really pretty."

He recognised her again; it was the voice of his beautiful Eve. The one he loved so very much. He sat on the stairs and cried. The same step Harry had been sitting only months ago with his Eve. He cried for her, for his girls and himself. He cried for not knowing who the father of her child could be. The only thing certain in his life was his two little girls, and the pain he felt which diseased his body.

29

Their mother sat quietly, the sound of the clock vibrating through her. She was alone. She had always felt alone. Her petite arms were wrapped around her knees, holding them up to her chin. The hours passed; the hands on the clock moved slowly, unlike her. She hadn't moved an inch, not a hair. Sitting in her own world too scared to face another moment. Moving would mean doing something like taking another tablet, having another doctor's visit. Every day the same, every day except when Natty came. Even though she never stayed for long, she came all the same. Thoughts of her beautiful girls came to her, how she loved them so very much. She pined to be with them, to have them near her. If only she could bathe them and brush through their shiny hair. Kiss them all goodnight. Their mother knew it would never happen, she could only imagine having her time with them again. She had had her chance to get it right. To do what she should, to be the mother they all deserved her to be. Her over-spacious house held her like a prisoner. She felt small and fragile, like a tiny china thimble amongst mounds of clutter, trying to break free without getting damaged. Biting onto her knee she sobbed like a child who had fallen and grazed herself in a playground. There would be masses of children around her, but she would sit crying on the cold concrete. No one was going to pick her up; no one was going to wrap their arms around her.

"Eve my little girl, why are you so sad?"

She suddenly saw her father kneeling down in front of her; he would be the one to take her from the cold. He gently lifted her face, holding her chin with his hand. Eve lost herself deep in his eyes. She didn't have to say anything at all. He understood her, he knew how she was feeling, she was sure.

149

"Daddy, I feel so lost, I don't know how to find my way home again. Please show me the way." Eve cried in her own world, where everything she felt and knew belonged only to her. All she wanted to do was to feel safe, but every time she did her father would leave again. She realised she would never feel all right again if he kept running away.

30

Matthew pottered around Eve, who was now heavily pregnant, serving drinks and sandwiches. Natty and Glenn sat quietly and ate, swinging their small legs under the chair while enjoying every mouthful. It had been an extremely hard few months for Matthew; he was desperate to hold his Eve, to gain some kind of eye contact with her, to love as once before. He watched each day as she grew larger, knowing the baby was not his. He left the water running as a dreadful thought came to him. He stood still at the sink, the steam making him almost disappear. Slowly he reached up on to the shelf and took her tablets from their place. The small plastic lid popped open with ease, the contents now lay in the bottom of the steel basin. The hot sink becoming white, the tablets melting like snow. He breathed a sigh of relief, turned off the tap and turned slowly to his family.

"Guess where we are going today girls?" His voice was full of commitment.

Natty and Glenn carried on eating while looking up with excited expressions.

"We are all going to the seaside. Eat up, we don't want to miss the rides now do we? Mummy is coming too. We are all going to have a family day out." Panic filled him; he just had to keep the enthusiasm going. It was madness, he knew. It was also an extremely cold day.

Matthew packed some towels, buckets and spades, and checked his wallet quickly to make sure he could give them everything they wanted.

"Come on, Eve. Let's get ready."

"Oh Matthew, please, you must go without me. I'm very tired, I would rather stay here." Eve sat at the kitchen table, staring into space. She could hear Matthew flitting around her.

151

Matthew knelt down beside her. "Eve, let us be together for one day. We can forget everything. Just us. How we should be." Matthew hung on to hope she would agree. She could pretend if she wanted to, he thought.

Eve looked into his eyes. She pushed herself away from the chair and left Matthew kneeling down in the middle of the kitchen clutching onto a large bag.

"Matthew, you already know what my answer is. I can't come, you know I can't. I don't think I should anyway. You're only playing with me, I know you don't want me there really, any of you."

Matthew wasn't going to feel beaten by her any more. He went to follow her. Natty and Glenn were playing near his feet with the empty buckets, banging the spades on top making imaginary sandcastles.

"Excuse me girls. Eve, wait a moment."

Eve turned to face him. He wanted to hold her, he wanted to shake her too.

"We can beat this together, we can do it Eve, you have to let me help you."

"Help me, Matthew? The problem is I'm not sure what you are trying to help me with. What is going on Matthew? What's happening? Why don't any of you understand?"

"We are trying to." Matthew held her arms with his hands. It was the closes they had been for a very long time.

"I'm scared, Matthew. I don't want to take tablets. I don't want everybody thinking I am sick. Why do I have to be? Why do you all want me to be?" Eve spoke softly, her voice shaky. She sounded like she wanted to cry.

"Eve, you are sick, but I am here for you." Matthew wanted to take her pain away. He could feel himself holding back his own tears.

"Matthew, I don't know how to be sick." Eve slowly fell to her knees. Matthew went to the floor gently with her. They were together just like their children. Matthew bravely held her. He couldn't let her go, he didn't want to. Even though she was hurting and needed his comfort Matthew found the whole situation exhilarating. He was able to touch the woman he loved more than

152

life. He knew he was being selfish, but didn't care. He wrapped his strong arms softly around her not to hurt her in any way.

"You don't have to be anything Eve."

Eve lay upon his lap. Matthew touched her forehead gently, pushing his fingers through her soft hair.

"Shh Eve, it will be all right. Shh, shh."

Tears fell from her eyes, and Matthew wiped them away one by one.

"I am lost, so very lost."

"Eve, I need you to do something for me. I want you to take a look at our beautiful little girls, take a look Eve, look what you have done. You have made two wonderful gentle children. You don't have to feel lost, you must realise we all want you back and we need you to come back to us. Please, Eve, even if it's for one day." Matthew was now resting his chin on her head, his tears falling with each plea. Glenn and Natty looked at their parents sitting on the cold lino as they cried together and held each other tight.

"The seaside you say?" Eve spoke through her sobs.

"Only the seaside Eve."

Looking in the rear view mirror Matthew could see his two girls safely in the back seat, smiling. He grinned with pleasure to see them so happy. Looking over at Eve he felt complete. He hadn't felt this way in ages, his family with him, waiting for an exciting day, anticipation running through them all.

"OK Eve?"

"I am very fine Matthew, thank you for this." Eve felt an attraction for the handsome man who sat next to her.

The music on the radio played softly; giggles could be heard from the back seat. The scent of Eve's perfume was in the air. Matthew drove steadily, absorbing the moment. He felt in control. He was taking his family out; he was going to give them a day they would never forget.

Natty and Glenn dug through the sand as though they wanted to reach the bottom. They were placing their small feet in the large holes, pushing the soft damp sand onto them and pulling them up

153

hard again to feel the sensation of the sand falling from their legs. How they laughed. How free they felt. Matthew wrapped a blanket around Eve as they leant on the wall together watching their children's new discovery. He held Eve close, protecting her from any sense of fear. Eve held small shoes and socks in her hands, tapping them together. Hearing the laughter was wonderful, it was all they could hear. It was all they wanted to hear. They were away from everything they had ever known, all the pain their elegant home seemed to contain.

"Shall we help them build the biggest sandcastle in the world?" Matthew suggested with excitement.

"I haven't built a sandcastle since I was small, Matthew."

"Even more reason for us to join in, wouldn't you say?" He held his hand out for Eve to grab, praying she would agree.

"Let's give it a go then." Eve and Matthew joined Natty and Glenn. They began pushing the sand into huge piles with their hands, mounds of sand being gathered around them. They were kneeling down almost mimicking Natty and Glenn. The wind blew through their hair. Eve piled sand onto her skirt, Natty and Glenn imitated her, covering their little pink matching trousers. They all sat immersed in cold, damp sand, laughing together. Matthew stopped for a moment and looked at his beautiful wife. She was glowing with happiness, she was glad to be with them. He loved to see her smile. He wished she could stay like it for ever.

"I love you."

"Sorry Matthew, what did you say?" Eve looked up, trying to wipe her hair from face.

"Never mind, shall we take these girls to the funfair?"

"Girls, how about a few rides before we get an ice cream?" Eve slowly pushed the sand from her lap.

The music from the fair was everywhere, the smell of candy floss and sticky toffee apples made them all hungry, the warmth of excitement filled them all.

Natty and Glenn cheered each time they went past on the merry-go-round. Matthew was dragged happily from one small ride to another so he could witness their fun. Eve slowly guided the pram behind them. Four ice creams, candy floss and a hot dog was the dinner of the day. It had been the most amazing day he had ever had. Matthew held both his girls in his tired arms.

"Let's wait for Mummy, little ones." Matthew turned suddenly, realising his day was coming to an end. Wondering why he had turned around at that very moment, he wanted to believe he hadn't seen anything, but he had. Eve had stopped in the middle of the fairground. Yet again he was left wondering who she was speaking to.

Matthew put the girls back on to their feet, taking hold of their cold sticky hands.

"Girls, I think it's time we got you both home." Matthew felt sick as the realisation overwhelmed him.

31

"You look tired Dad, are you OK?" Ruth sat on the edge of the armchair, where her father had been sitting for the last hour. Memories and emotions consumed him. He sat and thought of his perfect Eve, his beautiful children, but his not so wonderful life. He had never stopped loving his Eve. He found it hard to admit it even to himself. He could never tell her how he felt; he was too scared, it would mean looking into her eyes for longer than necessary. Could he tell his girls what happened? Was there a time and a place for such a conversation? They had a right to know the truth. They should be allowed to feel whatever they wanted; decide things for themselves. Would they understand at such young ages?

"Dad, why are you sitting in the dark? Shall I put a lamp on?"

"Sorry Ruth, what did you say?" As he looked at Ruth he felt another pang in his stomach.

"Lamp Dad, you know the things that make you see more clearly."

"Oh, yes please." The one thing their father did not need at that very moment was to see anything else in his life more clearly.

"Where are the others Ruthi?"

"I think they have gone to the library again."

"What, again? I didn't have Glenn down as a bookworm."

"Tell me about it, I never see her with any books, so maybe she reads them all when she's there. Drink, Dad?"

Ruth slowly walked away from her father.

As Ruth made two cups of warm chocolate, she heard the front door open and laughter echoed through the hall. The new partners in crime had finally arrived home.

"Hi Dad, hi Ruth, one sugar please."

"Glenn, don't push it. What did your last slave die of?" Ruth

156

stared at Glenn as she stood at the kitchen door, smirking.

"Nothing, she's still alive." Glenn laughed out loud.

"Oh very funny, how many books did you need to read to become so comical?"

Glenn walked up slowly behind Ruth, almost breathing into her ear. "Ruth, what's the matter, I thought you wouldn't mind making your big sis a drink."

"I'm making you one, aren't I. Ask Nat if she wants one can you?"

"So what's the problem then? We're older, we can go out a little more than you."

"Did I say I had a problem?"

"No, Ruth, you didn't." Glenn decided to leave and join her father and Natty in the just lit sitting room.

"Hi Dad, what you up to?" Glenn sat next to Natty who had already made herself comfortable on the sofa. She had taken her shoes off and was already using up most of the space.

"Budge up, big bum."

"I wish." Natty still hated her slim figure, she still wished she could have had a little more shape.

Ruth placed a large tray on the table.

"Any biscuits Ruthi?"

"I don't know, I'll check shall I?" Ruth left the room as slowly as she'd entered.

"Custard creams if we've got some," Natty bellowed.

"What? Sorry ..." Their father looked up quickly, something else had disturbed his train of thought.

"We haven't got any, not that we ever buy them," Ruth bellowed as she rummaged through the kitchen cupboards.

"Chocolate then, please slave." Glenn laughed in her wind-up.

"Ruth come and sit down, your sisters can get the biscuits if they want any."

"Are you OK Dad?" Natty felt the need to show concern for her father at that moment.

"I am fine, why are you all asking me if I am OK?"

Natty sat forward, taking her feet from the sofa. "You just seem to be a little quiet, that's all."

"Sometimes we mere humans are."

157

Natty glanced at both her sisters and raised her eyebrows; maybe they were all thinking the same thing, it was their father's turn to go a little loopy.

"Can we put the TV on Dad? There's something we wanted to watch." Natty took a sip of her hot chocolate.

"Wait a while – I wanted to have a chat with you." He didn't understand why he had even said such a thing. They were all quite happy to relax in front of the television. He didn't have to confuse anything. But he couldn't go back now.

Their father placed his cup on the tray and sat back again. He didn't look as comfortable as earlier. He resembled a very young school leaver waiting patiently for his first interview. His held his hands together tightly, as if all his secrets were held inside of them, and if a small gap appeared surely one would slip out. He wouldn't have been ready to let one go. He wanted to feel free from all of the pain and secrets inside. He needed to talk about his life and how it had moulded the three beautiful young ladies who were waiting in anticipation. They were all holding cups, all holding on to hope. He looked at Ruth a little longer than the others, feeling her pain prematurely. Inside his body he could feel all of their sorrow. He had always covered it with his own. He hated himself for it.

"I love you all so very much. I have always loved you from the second you were born. I have never stopped, and I never shall, any of you." The tears were beginning to appear in his eyes, his eyes being mirrored by his three girls.

They sat and waited for him once again like they always had, waiting for him to begin speaking about his life. They wanted him to hurry.

32

Matthew intended to visit the garage for an hour or so, which of course wasn't allowed so it made the need almost greater. He was taking a risk not only for himself but also for his family. He placed the girls in the dining room surrounded by the few toys they were allowed to enjoy, building a wall of protection with multicoloured items. Eve had been sitting staring into space, with a blanket over her. Matthew tucked it in at the edges of the chair, pushing down firmly, subconsciously not wanting her to move.

"I won't be long, Eve. Everything is OK, you don't have to worry about anything." Pushing the soft grey blanket up to her chest, he gazed at her – she was still as beautiful as he remembered from the coffee bar. It wasn't often he gained the courage to look into her eyes for long. He couldn't hurt himself any more, he wouldn't let himself fall in love with her again.

"Not anything Matthew? I don't have to worry about anything?" Eve's voice was soft.

"No Eve, just wait for me to come home." The room felt cold; maybe he should get her another blanket. Dismissing the thought, Matthew shook with nerves – he was leaving his family vulnerable. He wanted to feel fabulous again, like the day when he met her; he could have taken on the world. He stood for a moment remembering how he loved her from the moment he set his eyes upon her, how she smiled. He still loved her. He turned to take one more look at them all before he left.

As he sat in his van, he let out a huge sigh, not through lack of love but one for the sheer intensity of it. He knew he was doing wrong, being irresponsible, selfish, whatever he wanted to call himself. He should have stayed home or taken the girls with him,

159

but the urge to release himself from the dreadful reality made him drive away.

Driving steadily humming, pretending everything in his life was well, he blasted the heater. The hot air smothering his face took his thoughts back to home and how cold they all must have been. He could have put the fire on for them before he left. He decided to turn the heater off as he began to feel guilty for being warm. He would be with his dear brother soon. Harry had always been an important part of Matthew's life; they rarely saw eye to eye but they would always be there for one another. If only there was time to crack open a few beers now and then. Matthew chuckled slightly and wondered how it was, that when he could do things like have a simple beer he never would, and now he couldn't do things he wished he had. Twenty minutes had passed – twenty minutes of freedom. Arriving at the garage Matthew was greeted by his brother's backside sticking out from underneath a bonnet, his foot tapping to the tune on the radio.

Harry heard the van door slam. "I'll be with you in a minute!" His muffled voice echoed through the garage. He was still concentrating on the engine.

"Harry, it's me!"

CRACK . . . on hearing his brother's voice Harry jolted from the car quicker than intended, having to rub his head while making his way to his brother.

"Come here Matt, how are you? Are the girls and Eve doing well?" Harry squeezed Matthew as hard as he could.

"They are doing all right Harry. How have you been?" Matthew didn't want Harry to let him go. He needed to be held, he had waited for ages for someone to reach out and hold him. He pulled away quickly, not wanting his brother to see him weak.

"Apart from nearly giving myself brain damage, I'm absolutely fine," Harry replied, thinking to himself how tired his brother looked.

"You've always had brain damage."

"Oh yeah, I forgot." They both laughed together. "Come on Matt, I'll make us a coffee."

"Just came down to see how things were going. I do have an interest in this place." Matt followed Harry into the small office

160

where the smell of his half-eaten hamburger filled the air. Matthew sat at the cluttered desk scrunching up his nose. "I see you are organised as ever, Harry." Picking up the cold burger in disgust he tossed it into the nearest bin.

"As I always am. As long as the job gets done I can sort all that out later. I have work coming in from everywhere. Anyway you have better things to be worrying about, stop thinking about the chaos I'm good at dealing with."

Matthew received his coffee with grace, wishing for the first time he was in his brother's shoes eating hamburgers for lunch and taking it all with ease.

"Thank you Harry, awfully kind of you."

"Don't push it, you're not getting another." Winking at Matthew Harry sat on the desk opposite, covering papers with his greasy overalls. "How is she Matt?"

Matthew took a huge sigh, rolling his eyes. He wanted to talk to his brother but it would always be about Eve. He was unable to feel he had managed to escape her for a while.

"I don't know any more Harry, I keep praying she will get better. I want to help her so much but I don't know how to. I feel so lost in it all. I get to a point when I feel I have got it under control, and then something awful happens. The baby will be coming any time now. I don't seem to be waking up from this nightmare. I don't know who the father is, Harry. How can I do it? She isn't having my child, she isn't." Again he wondered how she could have ever behaved in such a way.

"Matthew, you have to be the father, who else could there be? I can't understand how you could believe any different."

"Harry, I have always loved her. She will always be my beautiful perfect Eve. But I can't seem to get my head around it all. I'll kill him, I swear I will. I'm not even meant to be here. I am not meant to be anywhere. I can't be there twenty-four hours a day, it's impossible, Doctors' checks, medication. I got rid of them Harry, I threw her tablets away. Thinking maybe if she didn't have them she would get better. I was a complete idiot. She has been worse. Talking into the air, she speaks to her father all the flaming time. I can't see what about, it's too much. She can be like a blank page sometimes you know. Other times whizzing around the house like she will never stop. I am so grateful the girls are too young to understand." Matthew began to feel confused again, it was all becoming a blur, there seemed to be so many problems he wasn't sure which one to deal with first.

"Matt, take a breath. You are doing your best. Come on, you left them alone just for a while. Think about all the hours you spend with them. What's an hour, sixty small minutes?"

"Harry, an hour can change someone's life for ever, as you say sixty small minutes. She's going to have the baby soon and I don't even know who the father is." Matthew placed his head into his hands. He felt exhausted.

Harry shuffled on the desk uncomfortably.

"Look, the baby has to be yours, it has to be. Just get it out of your head."

"Why's that Harry, why are you so certain, if I'm not?

"I am certain because you are talking about your Eve." Harry's voice was low, their father had always taught them to be honourable.

"I know, you're right."

"Matt, be there, that's all you can do, love her like you always have, live each day with them all, whatever it brings." Harry grabbed his brother's cup to give him a well deserved refill. He started feeling a little unsettled. How could he be honest? Was he able to share the secret, the secret he had with his brother's perfect Eve? The words were inside of him ever since it happened. They had to be kept safe. The truth needed to be protected – his brother couldn't survive with betrayal as well. Harry had kept another thing to himself. The fact that he also fell in love with her from the first moment Matthew introduced her to him. He remembered vividly how she sat on his sofa like a porcelain statue, untouched and flawless. Harry remembered how the intense emotion ran through him instantly. He had never felt the same way about anyone he had ever met since and knew he wasn't going to. Eve could never be his, she was part of his brother.

"Harry I've got to get back, please don't make me another. Thank you for always being there, you do know I couldn't do it without you."

"I'm not doing anything." Harry spoke with a high pitch,

162

desperately needing to cover up how guilty and lonely he felt.

"Yes you are, I know whatever happens I have you." Matthew smiled, unaware of Harry's trauma. His voice was soft. He stared at Harry and realised how much he loved him.

"You'll always have me, Matt always."

"See you later." Matthew walked to his van, nerves and tension built up again inside. After his time with Harry a new surge of energy rushed through him. How he loved them so. He was going to do it, he was going to get Eve well, she was going to be even more perfect. If that was possible. Not ask any more questions, take it for what it was. They were going to have another child. An unnatural feeling of determination and excitement surged through him. They all needed him. He took a look at himself in the car mirror. "You can do this Matthew, you know you can!"

Driving away from the garage he was unaware of his brother watching. He knew Harry was the only person in his life he didn't have to worry about, which made him thankful.

The view of his house became nearer. The ambulance outside his house became real.

33

"Who would like another drink?"

"No thank you Dad, but if we do then Ruth can make it."

"Thanks Glenn, a whole bunch."

"Oh keep your wig on, I'm only messing." Glenn wobbled her head, jeering Ruth on even more.

"I don't see you doing much." Ruth sat with her arms folded, leaning back deep into the chair.

"Girls, girls! Just be nice eh? You may find that you'll all enjoy it. I will have a talk with you another time; I can see you're not in the mood to listen to me tonight." Their father went to take his cup into the kitchen.

"Dad, we will stop now, promise. Stay and speak to us, please."

"Another night Glenn, I have told you." Their father left them all sitting together in the dimmed sitting room.

"Well done you two, flipping typical. You manage to ruin everything." Natty felt extremely angry, desperately needing to hear what her father had to say.

"Nat, be quiet will you, it isn't our fault."

"Glenn you can't keep your mouth shut for a second. Dad said he was going to talk to us and you didn't take it seriously."

"If Dad was going to he would have, stupid." Glenn began to raise her voice.

"You're the stupid one."

"You are." Glenn was standing by this time.

"You are, stupid stupid stupid cow." Natty was in front of her sister, their faces nearly touching.

"On second thoughts you couldn't be a cow because a cow is too fat, you're more like a giraffe. Ha ha." Glenn began smirking.

164

"Idiot. You sound like a two-year-old." Natty wanted to punch her right in her pretty face.

Ruth sat with her arms still folded, looking up at her two elder sisters. The feeling of desperation began to fill her – where was her prince? When was she going to be taken from all the sadness around her?

Their father stood in the kitchen listening to his daughters' hurtful comments. Putting more pain inside themselves. He knew he had to go in to them, stop them. The talk was long overdue. With a huge sigh he placed his cup into the sink; he had held it tightly while listening through the door, peeling small flecks of paint off with the other hand.

"Pig face." Natty couldn't let her sister win. Whoever ran out of things to say first would be the loser. It was a game they would all play when they were smaller; the only thing different was the words. As they all became older, the words became more wicked.

"Duck's crap."

"Natasha and Glenn sit down!" Their father gave them an instruction they followed instantly. He didn't even need to raise his voice or point at them.

"Smelly bum." Natty whispered her last insult to her sister and sat. She had won.

"Girls, I am going to tell you something you may find upsetting. I feel you need some questions answered. My intentions are not to hurt any of you." Inside he felt sick. Wishing he had stayed in the kitchen and completely finished defacing the kitchen door.

"It's about Mother, Dad, isn't it?" Glenn rudely interrupted.

"Yes Glenn." There was a pause. "You know she is sick, don't you? She has been for a very long time."

Natty felt in a daze, she knew she hadn't been wrong. Their mother did love them.

"What's wrong with her, Dad?"

Their father sat, quiet and overwhelmed, unable to answer Ruth. Realising how loyal he was to their mother, he couldn't give them what they needed. He didn't want them to think badly about her. Tears began to well up in his eyes. His head began to throb as he looked at his wedding ring, turning it again and again. Quiet with his own thoughts. What was he doing? What was he thinking?

"Girls I am so very sorry, I can't, not yet." Their father looked at Ruth. Smiled at her with his teary eyes. Knowing he had started something he one day had a duty to finish, he left them once again, wishing he could have let the whole thing be. Natty and Glenn sat at each end of the sofa. Ruth was perched on the edge of the chair, confused and lost for words. Their eyes fixed on each other in disbelief, hoping their questions would one day be answered. They all feared they wouldn't have the guts to ask any.

"I knew she was sick, I just knew it." Natty had the last words yet again.

34

Pulling up quickly behind the ambulance Matthew felt as if his heart had stopped suddenly, he could barely move feeling as though he had been glued to the seat of the van. Finding it hard to breathe, trying to inhale deeply, should he go in? He could always drive away and pretend he hadn't seen anything, anything which would cause him any concern. Surely he had a choice, who said he had to go in and deal with such nonsense? He realised he had been longer with Harry than intended. He had been away from his family for nearly two hours, the small clock in the dashboard was telling him. It made him sigh in frustration – it seemed that everything in his life was always trying to tell him something or another, even when he wasn't asking. Knowing the situation he was about to endure would be inescapable, Matthew didn't rush, he didn't need too. He recognised the feeling where he knew only pain and sorrow waited for him. For the first time in his life Matthew didn't feel the urge to be the one who would try to wave the magic wand and simply make it all OK. He couldn't watch his family dejected any more. Getting out of his van and walking steadily to the house he always wanted to call home, he heard a baby's soft cry. Going on further Matthew realised it had finally happened, the day he was dreading. He wanted to look into his own child's glistening eyes for the first time and smile into them, sending a father's message of love and protection. He knew he would be unable to, or worse still not allowed to.

He stood outside the dining room leaning on the door frame, seeing his family, his beautiful family. His girls sat on the floor, beside them were blankets and towels used for their mother and for their new little baby sibling. Eve sat on the floor, embracing her new child, their new child. The ambulance man prepared a wheelchair to take his Eve away from him. Matthew stood in silence and wondered why people just couldn't leave them alone to be together. He knew how to sort everything out, wanting to help her with anything she needed him to. Eve's face was flushed – she seemed to glow, filling the whole room with radiance. How he longed to rush over and kiss her, to take the new child into his arms.

"Matthew, we have another little girl, as amazing as our others, how lucky we are! Come over here please, don't stand so far away, come and see her, take her Matthew, take your beautiful daughter." How Matthew would love her so, she thought, speaking gently, tiredness slowing her words.

"Sir we have to take your wife and child to the hospital. We need to check them and we will have them back to you in no time at all. You are a very lucky man, what a wonderful family you have." The unknown ambulance man spoke of their great joy almost in admiration. If only he knew. Maybe he would wonder to himself later why the father of the newborn child looked as though his world was about to end abruptly.

Eve tugged onto Matthew's shirt as she was slowly pushed past.

"Matthew, I think Ruth is a wonderful name, don't you?" How lucky she felt to have such a wonderful husband who was so caring and understanding. How she loved them all.

"Yes Eve, I think it is too." Catching a glimpse of the beautiful child, he could see her little face peeping through the hospital blanket. A blanket which held a multitude of sins, just as their life had for so long. Matthew wished he could wash his life clean also and start over again. She was beautiful, the little miracle. Matthew felt tears in his throat, he felt as if someone had hold of his neck, placing pressure on his Adam's apple. He found it hard to swallow. He pushed the greying blanket a little more to one side, revealing how beautiful the new addition to their family really was.

"Eve, she is so lovely, so pure. I just don't . . ."

His wife was pushed past him. Could he pluck up the courage to follow her? Natty and Glenn were his priority now. They sat side by side playing together as always. Never causing any trouble. They seemed to fit in with the furniture. They kept quiet and clean. It wasn't fair for them. They glanced at their confused father and smiled. Almost with reassurance, trying to tell him it was all going to be fine, one day it would.

35

All three girls sat alone once again, left by their father in the sitting room. Why had he gone again after speaking briefly of their mother? What were they to do? Sitting slumped on the sofa, each one was making up stories with their own ideas.

"What do you think is really wrong with Mother? Was she sick when she hurt me so much? When she hurt us?" Ruth spoke while looking up at the ceiling.

"She must have been unwell, wouldn't you say Glenn?"

"Nat, for the first time in my life I really don't know what to think about anything, if Dad had said a lot more then things could be clearer. He kind of put the carrot in front of the donkey. Why didn't he tell us before? I don't know, I really don't." Grabbing the cups in the middle of the table, Glenn went to make another drink, consumed with anticipation and out of questions. As she stood in the kitchen listening to the slowly boiling water a tear fell from her eye. She could hear her sisters' muffled voices and decided quickly to rush making the hot drinks, unhappy that she was missing what they were saying. Wiping away the tears from her face, mess from her nose stuck to the back of her hand.

"Yuck, that's yucky." Pacing around the kitchen trying to spot something she could wipe it on she grabbed at a tea towel and thankfully made the yellowy mess disappear. Finding the whole moment quite funny she decided to fold the tea towel back up and placed it neatly on the shelf, waiting in suspense for someone else to pick it up and get it on them. Chuckling to herself she finished making the teas and quickly went into her sisters.

"Thanks Glenn."

"That's OK don't ever say I don't do anything for you Nat."

"You do always do something for me dear Glenn, like piss me

off." Chuckling, Natty took the hot under-brewed tea from her sister.

"Come on then, what are we to do?" Ruth ignored the jibes between her two elder sisters and went to put another lamp on. The shades were brown so it was hard to get any benefit from them. The atmosphere in the room was heavy.

"As I am the eldest, I feel we need to ask Dad to come out of his bedroom so we can ask him a few more questions. Do we have a right to do such a thing? Surely we do? Something must have gone desperately wrong, and it's surely understanding why it did that will help us. We didn't have a choice in any of it, how unfair is that? I don't know about you two but it hurts all the time, you know, not knowing. I remember a time when I saw some pills Mother must have been taking, so she has been unwell for such a long time. Maybe we can help her now. It's a good thing then that I see her." Natty paused to take a sip of her tea.

Ruth finally caught on to what Nat had said.

"Who was it you said you see? Mother? How come you have been seeing her Nat, why wouldn't you tell us? How could you do such a thing? Dad will be really upset. I'm her daughter too, why didn't you think I had a right to know? Christ, being the eldest doesn't consist of taking advantage of me. Glenn, do you not think you should be saying something to our big sister? Looks like I am never going to escape from her. You're just bringing her back into our lives every day." Ruth was in dismay.

"Ruth don't forget she's never going to be out of our lives, she is our mother, remember. Anyway stop getting so big for your boots. You always have been. Daddy's little Ruthi. That's you, Daddy's little girl waiting for your imaginary Prince Charming to come down, kiss you on your lips and take you off out of here." Natty felt embarrassed as she knew Ruth looked up to her and she wasn't showing a very good example or even any consideration for her feelings.

"Some sister you have turned out to be Nat, going behind our backs. Now you're just being cruel like Mother – why would you do it, see her like you do?"

"Will you two shut up? This isn't about us arguing or hurting each other, this is about our mother and father and not Prince Charming as

170

you say Nat." Glenn for the first time showed complete maturity. Natty and Ruth sat back in shock, almost lost for words.

"What are you both looking at me like that for? Cats got your tongues all of a sudden? Ruth, I knew about Nat going to see Mother. Natty took me there, it takes some getting used to, she looks like Coco the clown – she has make-up all over her face. I suppose Nat was trying to protect you, being the smallest and all." Glenn tried to reassure Ruth.

"I am fine with that, of course I am. Not only do I feel betrayed by one sister but the bloody pair of you are treating me like I'm two. I'm not stupid you know, I have been part of this mad family as well. I feel different as it is, why do you two have to make it worse?" Ruth began to cry.

"Look Ruth, I am sorry for speaking to you in such a way. I find it hard too, just because I'm the eldest doesn't mean I can't feel, or I know everything."

"Nat I know. I know more than you and I'm prettier." Ruth chuckled while crying.

"Ruth you are prettier than me and Glenn of course, I would never dispute it. But thanks for reminding me. What makes you feel different?" The conversation switched from their mother instantly.

"I know it's mad, I can't really put my finger on it, I wish I could. I think I've always been treated different by Dad."

"Yeah, tell us about it, always at his side, what do you think, Nat?"

"Maybe, maybe not, he does seem over concerned about you; I don't know who really knows how it's meant to be. Ruthi don't you think we have got enough to think about without all this feeling different emotion going through your head?" Natty smiled.

"Maybe you're not his." Glenn's moment of maturity didn't seem to last long. She had left her sisters in the same gobsmacked pose as earlier.

"Why are you two looking at me like that again? God damn free country isn't it?" Glenn huffed.

"Very funny Glenn, thanks for making me feel so much better. Of course I'm Dad's."

"What makes you think you're his? He might have adopted all of us." Glen spoke sharply, shaking her head in disbelief.

Natty raised her eyebrows at Glenn wishing she would shut up.

"Actually come to think of it, I think Glenn was knitted at birth."
Ruth laughed aloud, her tears suddenly beginning to slow.

Each one was lost for words again waiting for someone to say
something, anything. Hearing their father's footsteps on the stairs
they all sat up to promptly, eager for him to come in to join them
and hoping he hadn't overheard what they had been speaking about.

"Are you OK girls?" Their father stood in the doorway and
leaned forward slightly.

"Yes Dad." They all answered in unison, a unit of three whatever
happened. Anything they said or had ever done to each other really
didn't matter. They had something very important in common
coming from the same family, understanding the same emotions,
hearing and seeing the same things. It was now up to them to find
out why they had their lives, to look after their future. Nobody else
was going to do it for them.

"I'm glad; you make me very proud, all of you." Their father's
strong body nearly filled every inch of the doorway.

"Dad, please can you tell us, please can you try? We really need
to know."

"Ruth, I have said maybe this isn't the time, maybe you aren't
ready. I don't even know if I should be telling you." He wished he
could hide behind the heavy blue curtains, feeling like a child under
pressure.

"But Dad it has to so much to do with us, please, and I think we
are all ready."

Natty and Glenn sat and looked in admiration at their younger
sister, wondering how she had grown up so very quickly. She had
a unique way about her, she wasn't like them. She had a certain
charm.

Their father let out a huge sigh and pushed his hands up through
his hair, taking the time to look at each one of his girls in need.
He slowly moved over to the corner of the sofa and sat, knowing
he had to become the adult once again.

"I said your mother was sick and she is, very. She has been since
before you were born. Before any of you were. You know all the
things she has subjected you to she has not meant any of it. It must
be so hard for her, not to know what she is doing, or even who you
are sometimes. And worst of all, who she is. There must have been

172

lots of times you saw her looking at you as though she hates you. Your mother thinks you hate her. She hears your grandad, talks to him now and then. It's hard for her to know what is real and what isn't. There is no cure for her but she has been taking tablets." Their father's voice sounded unsettled as though he was holding back a bucketful of tears.

"I don't understand Dad, I really don't. Why didn't you tell us?" Glenn felt empty of any emotion.

"There are lots of people who are unwell, lots who you would never expect, Glenn."

"That's what those pills were for, wasn't it Dad? On my birthday I found some, she was sick on my fifteenth birthday wasn't she? Mother cried so very much. I had never seen anyone cry as much before then."

"Natty you knew something was wrong for a long time. I know it has been hard for all of you. I have lots of things I need to sort out, everything is a bit up in the air at the moment." He wanted to stop speaking. Looking at his girls he knew he was hurting them with every breath.

"Dad, she hurt us most of the time, she was always hurting us." Ruth broke down in tears. Their father fell to his knees, pulled her to his chest and cried with her, holding her tighter and closer than ever before, as he always wished he had from the moment she was born.

Her two elder sisters watched their vulnerable father and sister.

"Ruth I am so very sorry, I am so sorry for everything." Turning around to his other girls he gestured with his arms for them to come and join him. In an instant Natty and Glenn held Ruth and their father, all their hearts beating stronger than ever before. Sobbing like four children. They all were innocent in different ways. The part missing from them couldn't be seen or heard.

She sat alone in her own world only a mile away. Crying to herself, wrapping her small arms around her waist for her only comfort. No other heartbeat could ever be heard by her.

Gently moving away from them, their father wiped tears from their faces.

Sniffling through each breath, Natty thought she would ask the ultimate question.

173

"Dad, if you knew she was so sick why did we stay with her, why did you leave us?"

Their father glanced at Ruth and stood up slowly, wiping his face.

"I am sorry girls but I have to go somewhere."

He had left them once again; their tears hadn't finished falling and he wasn't there to wipe them away yet again.

"Are you two OK?"

"As good as we can be Glenn. Are you OK?" Natty went to stand.

"Load of rubbish." Glenn took a deep sigh, wiped her face quickly with the sleeve of her jumper.

"Ruth are you all right? it is going to be all right now. We will all sort it out. Next time we go and see her you come too, what do think Glenn?"

"I'm not sure if we should now we know how mad she is." Glenn wanted to end the drama and run upstairs to cry alone.

"I think I would like to come with you. Please Glenn, come with us. We have to stay together," Ruth pleaded.

"OK Ruth. You win, I'm out of here." Glenn started to walk out of the living room with her head held high.

"I'm going to wash the cups up and make us all another drink. I think we need it." Natty took her turn to go into the kitchen and do the tea duties.

Ruth began to cry again. Glenn turned and watched her and decided against leaving. She sat down next to Ruth and took her hand.

Washing the cups quickly under the warm flowing water, Natty was thinking hard to herself. She grabbed at a tea towel she found neatly folded on the side and the cups were dried.

Three hot drinks were placed on the table. Glenn glanced at the damp tea towel over Natty's shoulder.

"Oh pants," Glenn said in shock.

"What?"

"Nothing Nat, you carry on." Glenn chuckled to herself. She suddenly didn't feel thirsty.

36

A year had passed since the birth of little Ruth. Matthew barely spent any time with her at all, just glancing at her briefly as he passed her playing on the floor. Natty had started school which was the only sanctuary the little one had. Glenn was to follow in a year. Eve had more visits from her father than ever before. She constantly sat alone with the mess piling up around her, talking to him, telling him how she felt and how much he was still terribly missed. She very rarely washed the girls; they would have to stay dirty unless Matthew took control. Some days he would wake to find her cleaning like her life depended on it, everything how he remembered shining like a new pin. But most of the time the once beautiful house they shared became a prison of sadness, a place which held pain and heartache. Matthew would try to see if he could gain a small smile from his Eve, but he never could unless she was with her father. There was nothing he could do other than to stay inside the four walls, worrying fuelling him just in case his family were hurt like before. Tablet after tablet his perfect Eve would take. He had to watch her every day in complete pain and confusion. He knew she was in there somewhere behind the sadness that covered her like her blanket did every day.

Matthew was always stuck for words, not knowing what to say to her. They rarely exchanged words. They seemed to be each in their own world, and even though Matthew was in the real world he felt sometimes it would have been easier not to know what was happening, like his perfect Eve. The only time Matthew felt the courage to speak was when he would fill her a glass of cool water and give her tablets to her, each time hoping the one he gave would make her miraculously better.

Eve would grab the girls by their small arms and drag them

up the stairs, her fingers pushing into them. Matthew would hear the screams and run after them, trying to save them all. Eve would hit them quickly as she passed. Each time he held Eve, trying to make her understand that what she was doing was wrong, saying to her over and over again how she really didn't want to be doing such things. How they loved her, they were her babies. She was too far in her own world, there was no way she could understand. Her father was the only one who could help her. Matthew often heard her speaking to him; she spoke as though he was cross with her, saying how sorry she was for hurting them so much. Matthew never heard his name mentioned, she was never sorry for hurting him. He wished he could be crazy enough to ask her father for advice. He knew he wasn't ever going to have a day off from life, a day in the fantasy world of Eve. When his family were in bed, he would call his brother on the phone. Harry understood him, and he seemed to really care for Eve which made Matthew happy. Harry never really visited much; if he did manage it would be extremely brief. His tea would never be finished before he left. Matthew would feel a little cross at his manner at first, then would try to put himself in his brother's shoes, realising how hard it was for anyone to sit in their home for longer than twenty minutes if they didn't need to.

Matthew knelt down on the floor with dustpan and brush in hand, clearing away the broken plate that Eve had decide to throw at him because he hadn't washed his hands before dinner. The dinner he would always cook, the house he would always clean, the nappies he would have to change. He hadn't had time that day to wash his hands, he was normally good. As he pushed the small broken pieces onto the pan, he spoke out loud to himself.

"Eve I don't know how much more—" Throwing the dustpan down he quickly rushed to the screaming coming from the dining room.

"EVE, LET GO OF HER!" He had to prise his wife's hands from Ruth's arms, they were being squeezed as tight as could be. "EVE, NOW LET GO!"

In a second Eve released her daughter from her grasp.

176

"I was talking and she wouldn't stop crying." Eve's voice was gentle. How rude of her little girl to interrupt her and her father talking.

"It's OK Ruth, come here. Glenn, upstairs please." Matthew took both the girls from Eve's sight. She couldn't hurt them. She could sit and talk to her father without any interruption.

Dr Peters was due to visit them soon anyway, so he could calm the situation down quickly, and hopefully look as if he was doing a good job.

Placing Glenn and Ruth on the bed he sat and began to get them ready for a bath. Pulling their small grubby T-shirts over their heads, he revealed more bruising, especially on Ruth's tiny shoulders. When had it happened? How come he hadn't seen it? Looking over at Glenn he could see identical proof of the pain that had been inflicted upon his little angels.

He was exhausted, filled with despair. He couldn't do any more. With all the things happening every day, all of the pain he allowed his perfect Eve to serve upon himself and his children, it finally was enough. He was with them every day and she still managed to hurt them. Looking at the clock at the side of the bed he realised he would have enough time to pack a small number of things and still collect Natty from school.

"No more, no more, girls, she is not going to hurt you any more." He wanted to run in the bathroom and be sick, as he crept into each bedroom taking a couple of outfits from the drawers, picking up a few small toys, gripping onto them for dear life. He couldn't take the girls and leave without a small part of home, for what it was worth. Putting their T-shirts back on, he covered their arms with a cardigan. He stood with a full bag and two small girls desperately waiting to reach the other part of them. Could he go without telling Eve? Could he disappear into the world without ever telling her? Looking over at their wedding picture on the side, he knew he still loved her, he always had, and the thought of losing her was too hard to bear. The fear of not seeing her again, knowing fear could only hurt you if you were to surrender to it. Taking a deep breath he picked up the bag and took his girls and belongings down to freedom. He didn't know where he was going, maybe Harry would put them up. The thought went out of his head – he didn't want his brother to see he had failed. It didn't matter, going was enough. Quietly taking each step, the guilt and anguish filled him more and more, waiting to be caught like a child who had stolen a sweet from the shop. His head was thumping, his heart breaking for the loss of his beautiful wife. Opening the door he slowly pushed the girls out into the free world.

"Where are you going Matthew?" Eve spoke with anger.

Matthew stood as if frozen, feeling as though someone was going to stab him from behind.

"Just out, for a while." Matthew didn't turn around, he couldn't look at his beautiful wife, the beautiful lady he had fallen so deeply in love with, he couldn't let her see him walking away. He held the bag tight, his girls waiting for him on the doorstep. Glenn and Ruth looked at him, unsure, sensing Eve staring at him from behind.

"What's in the bag?" Why is he doing such a thing? Eve thought.

"Nothing, Eve."

"Surely you don't think you can take my girls away from me. I would only kill myself if you did Matthew." Eve had spoken firmly. She walked back into the dining room and sat down, ready to continue her conversation with her father.

Matthew gave directions for Glenn and Ruth to come inside, placed the bag in the hall and closed the door behind him.

"Daddy will be with you in a minute." As he went into the dining room he sat down opposite Eve. He looked at her in her own world, her eyes piercing at him.

"As I said Matthew, I would kill myself if you took my girls from me. If you don't believe me you can always put me to the test." Silly man, why does he want to keep playing games? she thought.

Matthew couldn't stand it any more. Getting up from his chair he went upstairs to clean the girls. As he picked up the bag on the way he let out a huge sigh. He knew being part of her mad world was the only way forward for them, if they liked it or not.

37

Christmas 1971 was approaching. The girls had decorated the most spectacular tree, without a hurtful word being exchanged. All of their birthdays were near; another year had brought something new for them all to learn – they had been given another understanding of life, a different challenge they would have to accept. Their bodies were like walls: one brick at a time building upon the other. Some bricks were made of sadness, some happiness, others confusion. Thoughts of their mother ran through them all as they placed each small angel on the fresh branches. It had to be a real Christmas tree, the smell was always so wonderful. White lights and sparkling stars, which use to belong to their Nan and Grandfather. Red and white candy sticks, and all the little things which were made by them when they were very small. Their mother would always take extra care with them when it was time to pack away. The hand-made items would always bring a smile to her face. Their mother's tree was always the best in town. They wanted to make her proud, wondering if she was going to have a tree as pretty.

They had only made a few visits to see her. Ruth would always chicken out at the last minute, standing outside the door. She'd then run all the way home, crying and alone, it was too much for her. Natty and Glenn would make their way up the concrete steps to the front door, take a deep breath and knock. Hoping one day they wouldn't be welcomed with the same over-made-up face. Everything around their mother seemed to gleam – the pots and pans were so shiny they could almost imagine her standing alone scrubbing at them all day. Her hands were always red from far too much bubbly water. She would always wear the same old grey sweatshirt, and over it her favourite apron. It needed a good soak.

179

Her black trousers were damp on the bum as she would always wipe her wet hands there. When Natty and Glenn talked to her they would sit in the kitchen, plates of custard creams on the table in front of them, and as their mother sat she would stare at the spare chair for a while, subconsciously waiting for all of her girls to sit around her. It was never a good idea to stay for too long, only long enough to have a quick drink and nearly a whole packet of custard creams, timing it just so they had enough time to leave without a punch to the stomach or a slap to the face. She would look at them, trying to make sense of their visit, becoming agitated. This would always be their cue, as they saw her getting angry, recognising it on her colourful face. Their cups would be placed down in a hurry, they would kiss her goodbye quickly and would depart.

Sometimes she would manage to keep them hanging around too long. Natty had received a punch to her face on their last visit and they'd ended up running back to safety at their father's. All they wanted was to try and make it all OK, to learn to feel close to her. To help her feel close to them. But they knew it was never going to happen. Maybe they were wasting their time. The hardest part was trying to explain to their father where they had been – the library excuse was wearing a little thin. If Natty had a mark on her face she would have to say that her sisters were play-fighting. Thinking about it hard Natty wondered why he had never noticed anything before. Maybe he pretended he never saw anything. Overwhelming guilt would consume them if they thought harshly of their father. A birthday card never arrived from their mother on each of their special days, but their father never made an excuse for her to help them feel better. Should he have written cards and pretended they were from her? Would they have respected him for doing such a thing? Neither would have been OK; they wanted their mother to sit up proudly and write each card with meaning and love, hold her head high and post it. A Christmas card had never been sent either.

As they sat at the table on Christmas day, food piping hot, fresh and colourful, they all thought of their mother. Their father raised his glass for a toast and held a small thought for himself. He asked for good health and happiness and all the other poppycock. All they really wanted was for them to be together as one family. Wherever

180

they were there was always someone missing. If they were at their father's their mother wasn't there, if they were at their mother's, Ruth and their father weren't there. And when they lay in their beds they were all alone, completely. They knew another year would quickly come and go, feeling it would all be the same, grabbing on to false hope, and working through everything that was to be put in their way.

The girls always did their homework together. Natty had more studying than the others by far, but she would sail through it. Glenn would spend the whole time huffing and they would always say to her, if she spent as much time on homework than making an impression of the big bad wolf then it would be done in no time at all. Ruth always sat quietly and worked it all out for herself. Papers and books on all different subjects were scattered all over the bedroom floor.

Glenn stopped her impression for a moment and looked up at Ruth.

"Why don't you want to come with us, Ruth? It is OK you know, we don't stay for too long."

"I suppose I don't want to add to my confusion. Best left with the memories I have of her, and I don't want a mark on my face like Natty got."

"It's only very rarely she does it, we normally scarper before then." Glenn realised how crazy the whole thing sounded.

"Rarely too much I think." Ruth started to doodle on the side of her neat work; she didn't look up at Glenn.

"Glenn, she will come when she is ready. Just don't hassle her." Natty looked up from her huge book on medicine, having to pull her hair up with her hands as it constantly fell in front of her face when she read.

"OK, we'll leave it up to you then Ruth." Glenn threw Natty a hair grip.

"Thank you Glenn. I'm not ready, that's all. Anyway, changing the subject on to Dad, have you noticed how quiet he has been? Since he spoke to us, he isn't the same. He looks so very sad." Ruth's voice was soft.

"It must have been really hard for him to say things to us." Natty spoke while she sifted through her pages; she didn't look up.

"Do you think Dad has caught on that we go to see Mother?" Glenn continued to throw hair grips at Natty as she spoke, finding the action comical.

"I have a funny feeling he does. Will you get lost, throwing them?" Natty was ducking from the missiles and beginning to feel agitated.

"Girls, dinner is ready!" Their father's voice bellowed from the bottom of the stairs.

They could smell eggs and bacon. Throwing papers into the air they all rushed to eat. After rinsing their hands under the tap in the bathroom and wiping them on their trousers they rushed down the stairs, each one pushing in front of the other, pulling at their jumpers, laughing, excited to reach the bottom. Grabbing at the cutlery, helping themselves to the fresh bread piled high in the centre of the table, happy to enjoy their dinner together.

"Thanks Dad!" They all spoke together and smiled at their father.

Their mother sat with Dr Peters at her kitchen table. He was helping her take her medication, all different shapes and sizes, the colours of the rainbow. She took them slowly, washing each one down with a sip of cool water.

38

Even though Matthew felt like a prisoner in his own home, he would do the best he possibly could for Eve, attending every appointment with her and giving her all the support she needed, talking to the doctor. He hoped she was being treated right and things were being done the way he assumed they should be.

Matthew often said to Harry on the phone that he'd come home one day and find the doctor on his side of the bed, false teeth in a glass. They would laugh together until their bellies were left aching from the moment's joy. As soon as Matthew placed the receiver down reality would always hit him again.

Although Eve had become a little chattier the medication was consuming her body, but Matthew didn't mind having to wait on her. Natty, Glenn and Ruth were growing up. Natty always looked wonderful in her uniform; prancing up and down the long hall looking at her black shiny shoes. How she loved them so. She would do this nearly every morning. It was another sense of freedom for her. As it was also for Matthew: helping all three girls get ready, taking his time as he walked with them in the fresh air, picking up some groceries and often stopping to pay bills. As they all waved goodbye to Natty in the playground he certainly felt a sense of pride for how smart she looked. He was doing a good job and he knew it. Always having to be efficient came to him easily. Loving Eve was still as natural, though he would try to fight it, make the whole thing wrong, desperately wanting to be angry with her for being so unwell, for making such a threat. How could she think of hurting herself again? Matthew couldn't bear the thought of ever losing her.

Each morning when he woke, his head often hurting from panic, he would make his way up the stairs to see her. He would lean over their large bed to check if she was still breathing. Every day since it had happened. His makeshift bed on the sofa seemed to be the best place for him; its oversized cushions were soft and being dark green it was hard to get dirty so it was ideal. He would find it unbearable to lie with her and be unable to touch her. He longed to embrace her small body with his strong arms. Every night Matthew paced up and down the hall believing he could manage it. His final decision would lead him always to the sofa. He would lie on the cushions, plumping them up with his fist. He wondered if his perfect Eve wished he would lie by her side as she slept.

"Daddy, I don't like apple." Natty stood close to Matthew while he prepared her little packed lunch.

"It's good for you." Placing the unwanted fruit in her lunch bag he put it on her shoulder. Wrapping the peel in newspaper ready to throw it away, his eye glanced at the date. 3 March 1961. He couldn't believe how quickly the years were passing. He held on to hope that things would one day get easier.

Glenn sat on the stairs waiting for the rest of her family to be ready, tapping her foot against the banisters. Ruth sat patiently in her pushchair, watching her sister's new game.

"Come on girls, let's get going." Matthew wanted to leave the house quickly that morning. It had been a hard night with Eve, she had cried for hours and hours he had been ordered not to comfort her or touch or speak to her in any way. She told him her father would give her a cuddle later, so he chose to sit with her until she was calm. He wanted to understand.

Pretending to be a daredevil Glenn jumped from the third step, landing steadily. Ruth clapped and laughed at her sister's bravery.

Matthew went in to say goodbye to Eve. She was polishing the clock in the dining room. As she turned she smiled at him slightly. She looked so very tired, so confused.

Looking at her puffy eyes he shook his head gently.

"I won't be long, Eve; I'm only going to the greengrocers after school. Would you like me to pick you up anything?"

"No thank you Matthew, I have everything I need." How kind of him she thought.

184

Matthew gave her a quick smile and left. He didn't think she had anything she needed.

The school trip didn't take too long. Matthew and the two younger girls were back in no time at all. As Matthew walked with part of his life a courageous thought had gone through him. Staying with Harry for a few days sounded like something he could have a go at. Glenn dancing through the leaves kept convincing him that maybe the whole idea of going away could be too much. But if he gave Eve the responsibility of the girls then maybe she would have something else to think about. She was too sick, deep down he knew it, but deep down he needed to be alone for a while, to sacrifice his girls for a few days, so he could be a better father, and could take another look at everything. As soon as he tried to justify it to himself guilt would overwhelm him. Guilt was a wasted emotion, his father would always say. But he wasn't his father; he would have to think about the idea a little bit more.

"Hello Matthew, did little Natty go into school all right?" Still polishing the clock, Eve felt very happy to have her family home.

"Yes Eve, she loves to go." Matthew's voice was soft and unsettled, the earlier idea still going around in his head.

"I know she likes school, I am really pleased, she's so much like you, and she can put her hand to anything." Looking at Matthew, Eve knew how much she admired him.

Eve's compliment overwhelmed Matthew. It suddenly gave him unexplained courage. He inhaled deeply.

"Eve, I was thinking of staying at Harry's for a couple of days, do you think you could handle everything here?" He had done it, said the ultimate words to her.

"I think it would be very good for you to see him. I can handle as much as you, don't worry." Eve gave Matthew a grouchy look, not quite sure why he would be so worried about doing something for himself. After all she was their mother.

The doctor wasn't coming for another couple of days so Matthew could go and return without anyone else knowing. He took his opportunity, rushed upstairs and put a few things in the bag. His stomach was churning with excitement, but deep down he knew he was being outrageously irresponsible. His three girls rushed through his mind, again and again. Who was he running away from? Was it himself? Being away from his home, away from his wife and children, meant part of his life didn't exist. That meant part of him didn't either. He grabbed items which needed a desperate press – he never managed to get around to the ironing, just got it all washed and dried and shoved it under the stairs until they were completely out of garments. As he steadily made his way back to the kitchen he kissed Glenn and Ruth on their heads.

"Eve, Natty comes out of school at three fifteen, don't forget will you? Give her a kiss for me. Will you be all right? I will only be a couple of days." Matthew was almost out of breath, behaving like a robot and not allowing one feeling to get in his way. Pretending in his mind he didn't have any feelings, he had to push the fear and guilt away as far as possible.

"Matthew, just go and have a good time." Eve finally stopped polishing. Looking over her shoulder she smirked at him standing emotionless at the door. She couldn't wait to spend time with her amazing little angels. She never seemed to have a chance to because Matthew was always doing everything and he was always there. She couldn't work out what he was waiting for.

"Goodbye then." Matthew stood outside the front door and inhaled the deepest breath he could. He instantly thought, what had he done? How could he go and leave them? It was his family for God's sake, what gave him the right to leave them when he felt like it? How the hell was she able to remember the school? How was she going to bathe them, and lock the doors at night? And the rubbish, how was she going to manage it all? Why had he been so impulsive? He couldn't go back in, he wasn't going to make himself. He knew how horrendous his next few days were going to be as he made the journey to his brother's.

Eve looked at her girls. She was going to take care of them; she was going to do it, and if it couldn't be managed then she knew asking her father for help was the next move. Her girls were like shooting stars who she would feel rushing past her each day. How she saw them sparkle. She was going be all right. How Matthew must have trusted her so.

"Hello girls, would you like Mummy to make you both a nice

drink? Then we can have some sandwiches and play. What do you think?" Eve bent down to their eye level. She hadn't looked into their eyes for such a long time. Their little glistening eyes. They both stared at her in bewilderment, how were they to answer? The house seemed to have a sudden silence.

"Right girls, we mustn't forget your sister. She will be surprised to have us pick her up don't you think?" Eve took her time pouring two glasses of milk. Her hands a little shaky, milk overflowing the glasses, splashing the work surface.

The girls drank their milk with happiness. Playing with toys, they were going to be busy waiting for their father, he would be back soon.

"Matthew, what are you doing here?"

"Don't ask, wondered if I could stay with you for a couple of days." Matthew stood on his brother's doorstep, clutching his bag. He could almost read his brother's mind, he knew what he was thinking. He would have thought the same if it were Harry.

"Course you can. I'm off to work now anyway, make yourself at home."

"Thanks Harry." Matthew walked passed his brother as he left for work.

He sat on the cluttered sofa, newspapers and beer cans scattered on the cushions.

Placing his head in his hands he cried hard, feeling more lost and alone than ever before.

"Please God forgive me for doing this." Matthew fell back onto the sofa, newspapers crumpling behind him. His eyes still wet from his tears, he fell asleep; he hadn't slept properly in such a long time.

39

Natty sat on the stairs, gazing at the letter box. Feeling chilly, she grabbed Glenn's cardigan from the coat hook. She had studied hard for nearly a year, surely she would the results she wanted? It would give her the opportunity to follow her path and discover for herself the world outside her secluded home.

"Hurry up post, hurry." She tapped her foot frantically, wanting the letter more than anything, but wishing it could remain unseen as the feeling of being let down was beginning to worry her.

"Not come yet Natty? I am sure you will have done fine." Her father slowly walked up to her, resting his hand on the knob of the banister.

"Dad I hope so. The post seems to be taking for ever today."

"If you wait for something, Natty, it will never come. Let it happen." His voice was soft and reassuring.

"I feel like I'm going to have a nervous breakdown any minute."

"I'm sure you're not going to have one of them. Trust me on that. Come and get some breakfast."

"OK." Natty rose from the stairs and followed her father into the kitchen. Hearing the letter box clang, she stopped in her tracks.

"Oh my God, it's come." Natty held her breath as anguish rushed through her.

"Well go and get it then, you've been waiting all morning." Putting on a brave face for her, he felt sick and hoped his eldest daughter would achieve the results she had worked so hard for.

"No, you get it." Natty found it hard to move from the cold, tiled floor.

"Natty, you've been waiting for it."

"Dad, please go and get it, I can't look, honestly. Don't tell me what it says."

"You lot make me wonder more and more each day." Their father picked up the long awaited brown envelope.

"Come on, let's get it over with." He tapped the letter on his hand, making his way into the kitchen, praying Natty would read it and not give him the responsibility. He couldn't bear to see her let down any more.

Natty joined him and her sisters at the table. Most of the breakfast had gone but it really didn't matter, she had suddenly lost the will to live, let alone eat anything.

"Come on Dad, open it for her." Ruth bit into her toast, peanut butter dripping onto her skirt.

"Natty, are you sure you want me to do it?" He looked at his daughter for confirmation with his eyebrows raised.

"I'll do it." Glenn looked on.

"Yes Dad, now will you, actually no, OK, oh shit." Natty placed her hand over her mouth and blushed because of her unacceptable language.

"Do you mind young lady?" His eyebrows rose once more.

"I am sorry Dad, now can you open it?" Natty composed herself her voice slightly raised.

Their father slid his fingers through the sealed envelope to reveal a simple A4 piece of paper which held the key to his daughter's future.

Ruth continued gulping down her breakfast. Glenn stared at their father and Natty with her fingers crossed.

Their father held the paper in front of him, prolonging the result.

"Dad will you come on?" Natty raised her voice again while scrunching her nose, she did look a sight.

"Natty, take your fingers out of your ears."

"What?"

"Well I'm not reading it to you if you don't." He spoke sternly.

"God, everything is so difficult." Natty released her fingers.

"What did you need?"

"Three Cs or above would help me get in Dad."

"Looks like you have finally got what you've been waiting for." Their father handed Natty the paper and let her see for herself.

"What are they?" Glenn was leaning across the table, her sleeve touching the butter which would leave a permanent stain.

"I don't believe it, two Bs and an A. Surely this isn't mine. Oh my God I have only gone and done it." The sheer relief and excitement filled Natty as she glanced at her family around the messy table, looking at her sisters' stained clothes and their smiling faces; it had all been such a drama but a wonderful one.

"Well done my darling, I am so very proud of you," her father said in sheer relief.

"Good on you girl. Girl power." Ruth spoke with her mouth full.

"Yes, well done Nat." Glenn felt a sense of pride to have a sister so clever, feeling sincerely happy for Natty took her by surprise. Glenn also wondered if there was ever going to be the time when she could maybe borrow her sister's notes.

Natty stopped and thought for just a moment. There was only one person who wasn't sharing her joy. She knew she would have to write the whole momentous occasion in her diary. It was a gift from her mother. It had been wrapped up in silver foil; Natty's name had been scored on the front with something sharp. When she had walked into her mother's kitchen with Glenn it had been placed in the middle of the table, perhaps it had been there for a few days waiting for its retrieval. Glenn was a little fed up that Natty had been given something. It was the most wonderful thing Natty had had from her mother, the pages were not dated so she could write anything on any day and it wouldn't matter.

"We can all have a special dinner tonight Natty." Their father tapped the table with his fingers.

"Sorry Dad?" Natty was interrupted from her thoughts.

"What would you like for dinner? Anything you want."

"What I'd really like, Dad, is for Mother to come to dinner tonight. We could all have dinner as a proper family." Natty felt instantly deflated, knowing what the answer would be.

"Natty we can't, you know that." He spoke softly, almost in shock.

"Who says Dad? Who says there is a rule what you should do, why can't we?" Natty became assertive, still hanging on to false hope. "I think she would be really pleased, even Ruth and Glenn would like it."

"Come on Dad, who says?" Ruth and Glenn spoke together.

"I say." Responding in a high pitched tone, their father was overwhelmed by the request from his girls, but also felt a deep urge to grant it. Wouldn't it be nice? he thought, if only.

190

40

Matthew's thoughts for the past two days had consisted only of his family; he couldn't manage to find any room in his mind to help himself. Guilt and fear consumed him the whole time – surely remaining at home would have been easier. What a joke, he thought, he couldn't even escape in peace. Harry was driving him mad making a mess all the time, admittedly it was his house but Matthew always liked certain standards. The weekend's meals consisted of Chinese takeaways and burgers, washed down with more than the week's quota of beer. They talked mainly of Eve and the girls. Harry would talk briefly about all the women in his life, not sure which one to take out for dinner. Matthew knew that while his brother spoke of other women, he would always choose Eve. For everything that had happened and what was going to happen, she would always be the one for him. If only he could meet her again, buy her coffee one more time and start right at the beginning.

Matthew packed his bag slowly, throwing in dirty washing, wondering how it was going to be when he arrived home. With the biggest miracle everything would be fine. He imagined how the girls would run to him with their small arms held out. They would be happy – their faces wouldn't show any sadness which could have been caused while he was away. Eve would greet him with the smile he remembered from the coffee bar, she would hold him close and be the happiest woman alive because he was home. She would want him to make love to her, as they had before.

"Never in a million years. Anyway, thanks for everything Harry, it's been great." Matthew huffed as he picked up his bag from the bed where he had tried to sleep all weekend.

"Been great? Liar. Do you want me to come with you?" Harry

stood with his hand down the front of his unzipped jeans, scratching his groin.

"No, I'll be fine. Nothing I can't handle." Matthew left, deeply inhaling the fresh air.

The drive home was filled with uncertain excitement. What if everything was all right? What if it had miraculously turned back to normal?

He was finally home; he was back to his family. Standing at his van door he looked at the front of his house with pride. It was beautiful. The best in the street.

"Hello, I'm home, girls it's Daddy!" Matthew placed down his bag. He could see three pairs of little shoes neatly lined up. It made him smile. His stomach filled with nerves.

"Hello Eve, it's me!" His voice was slightly shaky. Entering the kitchen he could see the garden door was open. The echoes of laughter became more apparent as he walked closer to the open door. Eve didn't hear him. How could someone look so elegant when they were hanging out washing? Matthew was mesmerised by her beauty. Natty and Glenn were playing, running through the freshly hung white sheets. Everything was normal again, he couldn't believe it. Admiring his family, he walked into the garden to await their greetings. Natty and Glenn ran to him as he'd imagined. He grabbed them and twisted them around again and again.

"Daddy, Daddy."

"Hello my girls." He squeezed them tight. How he loved them. He made a promise to himself he would never leave them again. He put the girls down again so they could continue their game – he had never seen them playing like it before.

"Daddy, Daddy." The girls chanted as they ran.

"Hello Eve, how are you?" Matthew spoke softly, stepping forward to see her fully.

Eve didn't respond. Pushing the pegs harder on to each garment, she wouldn't even look at him.

"I'm home now, thank you for understanding." The sense of dread overwhelmed him again; it was only for a few minutes that he could pretend his life was different. The moment his girls greeted him, that would be something he could always hold on to.

192

"Understanding! Understanding! Understanding!" Eve spoke as if she were a scratched record.

"Where is Ruth?"Matthew looked around for her.

"Ruth? Ruth? I don't know." Eve had finished her chore and began walking into the kitchen, her apron filled with unwanted pegs.

"What do you mean, you don't know?" Matthew instantly felt suffocated, as though as someone was squashing his head within their strong hands.

"EVE!! Will you listen to me?" Guilt from the weekend had instantly vanished.

"Matthew, I am listening to you, I said I don't know. What I mean is I haven't seen her for a couple of days." Eve undid her apron and hung it carefully behind the door. She was trying to understand what all the fuss was about.

"This is mad, you're making me go mad. I'll go and get her myself. Why do you have to keep playing silly games with me?" Matthew rushed in and out of each room. She wasn't there. Running up the stairs praying he'd find the last piece of his family. Feeling almost faint, everything around him a blur. Pushing the door open quickly and beginning to fill with rage he could finally see her. He looked at her for a few seconds to make sure he wasn't seeing things. Relief rushed through him to see her asleep in her cot. As he walked slowly towards her his legs were still shaky. The smell of urine made him shudder. His little Ruth lay upon her damp, stained, sheet, the stain larger than her small body, wearing only a dirty nappy. No baby grow or vest to keep her warm. Her pale sore body managed a few small gasps. Without any hesitation Matthew pulled her weak body up to his chest, his heart about to explode. She weighed barely anything, he could have held her with one hand. Her nappy fell to the floor, the sound revealing how wet it had been. He held her bottom in his strong hand. The dampness and sores could be felt on his palm. Grabbing a blanket he wrapped her as tightly as he dared, fearful of wrapping her too tight in case he stopped her breathing. Ruth was being punished because of him; he went away and his little princess had to suffer. Matthew didn't know what to do first. Taking his broken child down the stairs he picked up the phone and called for Dr Peters to come immediately. It could only be him – no one else would understand.

"Look at her Eve, look, what you have done? You've left her alone. Why, Eve? Why have you done this to her? She is our beautiful little girl!" Matthew screamed at Eve, longing for the stranger to answer.

"She isn't our little girl, she is my little girl." Eve spoke with sarcasm.

"So why are you doing this to her? The doctor is coming in a minute."

"Best not let him know you left, Matthew, eh?"

"Eve, look what you've done; please tell me why you left her so very alone." Matthew wanted to scream louder than ever before. He could feel himself wanting to run to Eve and hurt her. He clenched his fist and then released it. He clung to Ruth he wanted to protect her. He wasn't going to let her go until the doctor arrived. He held her, knowing from deep inside she was his.

"Matthew, what should it matter to you?"

"Eve, she is mine and she will always be, whatever you say." Fucking mental bitch, he thought and suddenly felt guilty for thinking so badly of her.

Eve stood calmly. Her power engulfed the whole room.

"You'd better ask Harry about that," she said turning away from him and smirking.

"Why should I be asking Harry about anything?"

"She belongs to him Matthew, your wonderful helpful, can't-live-without brother."

Eve turned around and walked up to Matthew's face, making sure he heard every single word.

"Eve, what are you saying?" He's my brother, he would never do anything like that to me, not ever, no way. Matthew wanted to understand why he was being punished by Eve; he had only ever wanted to love her, to look after her. Had he not been good enough for her, had he hurt her in some way?

"You can explain it all to the doctor when he arrives, Matthew. By the looks of it he is here now."

A sudden fear consumed him again; it must be a nightmare, all of it, it couldn't be happening. It wasn't his fault, he kept on telling himself. He rushed and opened the door. He could have run away with his child in a second, but he requested the doctor to follow him upstairs.

"We are going to the bedroom, Doctor, please come up." Matthew needed this man to save his daughter. He couldn't seem to help his wife but surely he couldn't fail with little Ruth.

Her body seemed even smaller as Matthew lay her on the bed. The doctor looked stern as he slowly began to check her over. Ruth lay naked, an innocent child looking uncertainly into the air.

"Matthew, she is very dehydrated. she has not been looked after very well. What on earth has happened? What were you thinking of, letting her get in such a way?"

Matthew's head fell in shame, wishing it was he who was lying frightened and hurt.

"I went away. I left them for a couple of days. Only to get my head together. It's really hard, watching the people you love so heartbroken. I was thinking about myself. I'm so sorry, please don't take her away. I can get her better, I can make it right again." His head was still low. He remembered the emotion as a small boy standing outside the headmaster's office, waiting for his father to arrive. He was scared and full uncertainty of what was going to happen next, keeping his head down in shame.

Placing his hand on Matthew's shoulder, Dr Peters sat beside him.

"We should take her to be checked, to make sure. She will be fine with plenty of fluids. She has to be cleaned up a little because of those sores. And then she will come straight back to you. Do you understand what I am saying to you?"

"Yes, I understand, everyone else can take care of her but me, I understand. Please allow me to have the medication she needs and I promise I won't let you down." Matthew was becoming angry and vulnerable. Why had he been so stupid?

"I said how hard it was going to be for you Matthew, we spoke in depth. We can take Eve to let her rest as well. She will be safe."

"NO! I don't want them to go anywhere. I know they won't come back to me, ever."

A silence filled the room as Ruth was wrapped in a blanket by the doctor. He had grown fond of Matthew. He had faith in him. How could he let such a man down? The doctor knew Matthew was willing to sacrifice everything, that he wanted and needed to get it right so desperately. He wanted to look after them all. The doctor had never witnessed such love and determination from anyone he had ever met before.

"Matthew, the love one person can hold for another can either be a saviour or a destroyer. You have to be careful you're not getting your emotions mixed up. Letting people go is also a form of love. I do trust you Matthew; I know you won't leave them again. The nurse will come and give Ruth the fluids she requires here. She will not be taken away from you. Please understand, you cannot expect me to be so willing to behave unprofessionally again. I know Ruth will be OK; otherwise she would be coming with me right now. I'm still a little unsure about Eve's progress. Keep Ruth warm Matthew, keep them all safe, remember this is your choice." The doctor left Matthew and Ruth alone. Before he went to the front door he spoke to Eve. Once the doctor had gone, Matthew realised he was the man who could put an end to all of the pain, only if he wanted him to.

Matthew could take control once again. Eve was sitting on the sofa reading Natty and Glenn a story, all huddled together, seeming content. Eve looked around at him standing near the sofa.

"Where's little Ruth? She would like to listen to the story. How I love reading to them." Eve's voice was gentle. She gave Matthew a reassuring smile and continued with the book of fairytales, thinking to herself how handsome he still was.

Matthew shook his head at her; he was in turmoil. He went into the kitchen and poured himself a glass of water. The tears flowed on his face as easily as the cool water touched the back of his dry throat. There was a knock at the door which stopped him filling his glass again. The pretty nurse stood outside with a couple of bags. She was young and by the way her eyes sparkled she had only just started her life in the big world. She must have still been filled with anticipation for what her life could hold. Would she also change? Is it possible for life to suck all of your ambitions and dreams away? Their home was beginning to look like a chemist's. It was starting to feel like a mental institution. What a joke, Matthew thought. As he led the pretty nurse up to Ruth, Matthew felt like a patient, knowing what he was trying do was crazy.

As the night drew in everyone was asleep. Eve was safely tucked up in bed, to the relief of Matthew as she couldn't cause anyone any more harm. Ruth had been given her fluids, surely more than a small body could possibly take. Matthew watched over her as she slept. She was finally safe now he was home. She had already been bathed before she was put to bed. Matthew couldn't bear not holding her, he wanted to look at her until the morning, to feel her breathing in his hands, so he began to run the bath for her again. The thought of his brother rushed through him while he watched the water filling the bath, and poured the bubbles into his hands, swishing them up and down in the warm water.

"Come on darling, Daddy is going to take care of you." Matthew held little Ruth in his arms and began to undress her. Gently he placed her in the soft bubbles, taking a handful of water and covering each part of her sore skin, warming her tired body. He took her in his strong arms and touched her wet face. Her hair was soft, her cheeks had a slight glow of pink. She returned his gentleness with a small smile, her eyes beginning to shine again. Kneeling on the bathroom floor he lifted her wet body to him and cried, warmth from his clothes drying her body as he rocked to and fro.

"I am so sorry I left you, so, so sorry. I love you my darling, I am sorry, please forgive me. You are part of me, I know you are." As he wrapped her in the soft towel the pain he felt was immense but taking a deep breath he vowed that he would always protect her from now on. He dried her gently and dressed her. She was so tiny, he had never really noticed before. He was trying to push to the back of his mind the terrible ordeal she had been put through all because of him. He felt overwhelmed with an intense love he wished he'd had the day she was born. She was his, he knew it. It didn't matter what Eve said, it was all crazy. Kissing her on her forehead he lay her back into her clean cot and covered her with a soft pink blanket. She could sleep the pain away. She would be smiling again soon, Matthew hoped as he looked at her once more.

*

The big house was dark and quiet there and was a chill in the air. Matthew wandered around helplessly, praying for a miracle again, desperately not wanting to call Harry. Waiting for the confession from a man who had always been there for him, the only person he ever felt he could trust, apart from his perfect Eve. Going into the dining room he put the fire on, moving his shoulders up and down trying to get warm, rubbing his hands together as he was coming out in a cold sweat. His clothes were still slightly damp from Ruth's wet body. He kept looking at the phone in the hall, going in and out of the room, not sure whether to believe what Eve was saying. If she was messing with his head again, he would surely lose Harry for even considering he could do something so awful. Could he really take any more that evening?

Seven small numbers away from the truth, the ring tone seemed to go on and on.

"Hello?"

41

A few months had passed since Natty had received her results, and she was going to go to medical school – after everything that had happened in the past, her future was going to be bright. The thought hadn't left their father's mind about the dinner invitation to their mother. Their eldest daughter had achieved so very much under such ludicrous circumstances. All the girls were going to be a year older in a very short while. It didn't seem possible, how quickly they were growing up. Maybe they could all get together on Natty's eighteenth birthday. Have a little supper and maybe even open a bottle of their mother's favourite wine. What harm could it really do? Glenn had left school and Ruth was at the secondary school. Surely there couldn't be more to drink to? The thought of their mother not wanting to come crept in and out of their father's mind. He had been so selfish, why would she want to be around him? It was one thing his girls saying they wanted to see her, but, really, how would they deal with it? It was something he could possibly consider. Their father had found himself in a lot of trouble for allowing them to stay with their mother as he had. Yet again it had been agreed that the girls were never to be allowed to live with her unless he was living with them too. He was curious whether his girls ever thought of her, were they missing her in anyway?

As their father scoured through paper work he had brought home, the house remained silent. He hadn't put the radio on or the television. It was satisfying to have peace. Saturdays were often calm as he spent them alone most of the time. The girls would get up early, and spend ages getting dressed to look their very best. Natty would always put make up on her favourite pink lipstick and wear her best black trousers. As she was starting to plump out a

199

little her slim figure had finally taken a presentable womanly shape. She would stand in front of the long mirror in their bedroom and move round and round to really get a good look, her hands sitting on her bum to feel how wonderful. Glenn wore her casual red jumper over a white blouse, the collar showing slightly. Whatever her attire Glenn was always so beautiful. She could have gone out in a brown paper bag and still all the boys' heads would have turned. Ruth was constantly trying to catch up with her elder sisters, Glenn especially. Ruth would check her bust size each day before she put her clothes on, the clothes she took from Glenn's drawer, before using some of Natty's glossy pink lipstick.

They all walked together towards their mother's house; due to not visiting in a while their nerves resurfaced as though it was their first time, putting themselves through confusion and anticipation, craving for her to put her arms around them and hold them close as they all wished she had so long ago. A sense of guilt rushed through them, as being disloyal to their father seemed to be getting harder and harder. He had always put them first. Each weekend he handed money to each of them in case they saw something pretty in the shops. None of them ever come back with anything. But he never asked for an explanation of where his generosity was going.

When they were nearly at their mother's house they watched Dr Peters leave. The good old doctor had been around their lives for so long, he'd never be replaced. Being part of the family history he knew more about their own mother and father than they ever would.

"Don't let him see us or he will tell Dad." Natty sounded full of concern, imagining their father's reaction.

"Nat, we do know." Glenn made a tutting noise. "Where would you like us to hide? Any space in that huge handbag of yours?"

"Behind this car!" Ruth gave the command to her sisters to follow as she knelt down behind a beautiful red Mercedes.

"Posh choice, don't you think? I'm going to have one of these when I'm older, you wait and see." Ruth began to chuckle.

"Are you going to park it outside your castle?" Glenn was now at eye level to Ruth, trying not to laugh out loud while sticking her tongue out.

"You can laugh, you wait and see." Ruth gave a smug look, sticking two fingers up. Realising the laces were coming undone on her blue velvet pumps she had to do them up.

"Will you two just shut it. I don't want him hearing you both." Natty squeezed behind the car with them in a panic.

"Nat, I don't suppose the old man's got supersonic hearing, he can barely walk for Christ's sake." Glenn continued sticking her tongue out at Ruth.

"See your point." Natty gave Glenn a gentle nudge on her arm.

All three girls huddled behind the car, laughing.

"Oh God, hurry up old man, I need the loo." Natty began swaying quickly to and fro on the spot.

They became hysterical. Nat had her legs crossed in case she wet herself, feeling the warmth gently going into her knickers.

"I've wet myself a little, I don't believe it!" Natty laughed aloud. Her black trousers were going to be ruined. If only their father could see them all hiding. Not only hiding in front of their mother's house but Natty with wet knickers too.

"Quick, let's make the escape, he's gone." Ruth became sergeant major ordering her troops out from the trenches.

"Wait, if I move too quickly it's going to come out. I haven't got any spare knickers obviously have I?" Natty looked like she was in agony, trying to hold back the rest of her wee and clutching onto Glenn's arm for strength. Desperately trying to stop laughing, this made them laugh harder. They finally stood up slowly. Giggles automatically substituted by nerves. Natty didn't want to go to the toilet any more. Ruth became more nervous than ever, the whole idea of going in there for punishment was too much.

"I'll wait outside for you both again, what do you say?" Ruth began picking at her nails, chipping the pink nail varnish, the one she had taken again from Natty. She had sat on the steps outside the front door on the last visit, hoping to find the ability to forget what had happened, as it seemed her sisters had. Only becoming thirteen soon Ruth still needed guiding.

"Are you OK Ruth?" Natty's voice was soft, as she tidied Ruth's fringe with her fingers.

"Yes thanks Natty. I've changed my mind, I'll be OK this time

I promise. I won't let you down." Ruth continued biting her nails.

"You're not letting anyone down. Let's knock, eh? I've got to change my knickers."

Chuckling and giving her a reassuring look Natty led Ruth by her arm to their mother's front door. Glenn wasn't far behind. The front steps, wet from the rain that had fallen earlier in the morning, still were really shiny as the sun shone on them.

"Mother's taking ages again, did you knock hard enough?" Glenn stood behind Natty, huffing.

For whatever reason their mother always took her time answering the door. Finally their anticipation came to an end as the front door was opened.

"Hello Mother, we have come to see you." Natty spoke with assertiveness even though her stomach was churning with fear

"Natty, hello dear, are you all here?" Her voice was shaky, she was different. She had hardly any make-up on, her clothes were clean and she had a smile they'd never seen before. Holding onto a cigarette, she inhaled on it, blowing the smoke into their faces.

"Come in girls, don't stand out in the cold." She saw how wonderful her girls looked, and felt a slight panic in case she hadn't bought any chocolate cake or special biscuits, eager to treat them to something delightful while they had a lovely chat. Their mother flicked her ash on to the carpet as she walked past them and went into the kitchen.

"Come in girls, go into the dining room, shut the cold out and the rest of the world." She spoke sharply, sounding demanding as she began making a pot of tea. She was scurrying through the cupboards to find all the lovely things her girls deserved. I must give them a special treat. It will make them so happy, she mumbled under her breath. Finally their mother found some wonderful chocolate sponge and a half-eaten packet of cookies; how they would love them, she thought, tipping them onto a plate and slicing the sponge.

"How yummy it all looks, now for tea! This will warm them up. I hope they're OK in there," their mother said to herself.

Natty, Glenn and a very scared Ruth sat in the dining room. The smell of stale smoke overwhelmed them. There was a plate on the small coffee table piled high with old butts. Used cigarette packets

202

were scrunched up on the floor. It was obvious to them where her favourite seat was – ash covered the floor at the base of the armchair.

"Does she ever clean this pit, and when did she start such a thing? Oh how exemplary of her, silly cow." Glenn picked up the plate while whispering how annoyed she was, tipping the contents in the overflowing bin.

"Glenn, there's another one over there." Natty pointed at another plate immersed in ash and butts with bright red lipstick on the tips.

"God's sake woman, do you want to kill yourself?" Glenn began to raise her voice slightly.

"Glenn, why do you have to say such things?" Ruth voice was full of fear; she sat on her hands looking around in complete disbelief. It wasn't her mother's home, it couldn't have been.

"Ruth, she must be doing at least a hundred a day." Glenn was stunned to see her mother standing behind her holding a tray with three teas on and a plate of plain biscuits and another packet of cigarettes. The plates were only ever used on special occasions now they were makeshift ashtrays. As their mother sat opposite them they all waited for her to start talking, waited for her to have another smoke. Without hesitation she did as they wanted, and with her hand shaking she lit the cigarette, inhaled, then sat back into the chair and started flicking the ash onto the floor.

"How have you all been? I haven't seen you for such a while. Ruth, how are you my dear, my dear Ruth?" She couldn't believe how much Ruth looked like her father and was looking at her for longer than necessary.

"Fine Mother, I'm OK, as long as you are." Ruth felt herself blush, wishing her mother would take her eyes from her, otherwise she would be running for sanctuary on the outside step again.

"I got the results I needed, Mother. I can study to be a nurse now," Natty said, trying to take the attention from Ruth as she could see how uncomfortable the whole situation was for her.

"That's great Natty; I'm very pleased for you." Inhaling another lungful of poison. "And what about you, Glenn? What are you going to do? She wondered why her daughter's hair was so short. Not understanding why such a pretty thing would want to look like a boy, she knew her face was showing disapproval.

An hour passed quite quickly under the circumstances as they all spoke briefly of school and career choices. And of course a conversation about the weather when there was an awkward silence, watching as their mother inhaled one cigarette after the other; she had fed her body nearly a whole packet.

"Shall we go now? We have to do some bits in town." Glenn stood quickly. Not wanting to stay in the smoky atmosphere any more she spoke quite abruptly. Natty and Ruth looked at each other and followed her out of the room.

They stood in the hall as they all did long ago, waiting for her to punish them. It didn't come.

"Goodbye girls, please come again." Their mother sounded like she was going to cry. My girls have to go again. I wish they could stay for a little bit longer. I have chocolate cake for them, she thought.

"Went well, don't you think?" Natty held both her sisters by an arm.

"Please don't speak to me, I want to get as much fresh air as I can. My lungs – I can't breathe." Glenn held her hands to her throat and pretended to collapse, as if she had been overcome by fumes.

"Glenn, you're mad." Natty laughed, feeling happy they were going home. It was hard seeing their mother damaging herself so badly.

"I know. I'm mad like Mother and I am now dying from lack of oxygen." Glenn still had her hands to her throat.

"Glenn, it will take more than twenty cigarettes to kill you." Natty pulled out mints from her handbag. A bag that held everything special to her, where she kept her diary close at all times.

"Mint Ruth? Glenn?"

"Thanks Nat. Did go OK, didn't it? Why does Mother live in such a mess? The house stinks."

Ruth took the mint from its packet and passed it to Glenn. She was still holding her throat while swaying on the pavement.

"Will it help me breathe? I don't know what a flaming mint's going to do, we flaming stink, stink of it."

"And the Oscar goes to Glenn for playing bollocks." Laughter filled Natty again. She made her sisters laugh with her.

"You are so kind. My thanks go out to our dear nutty mother who is now a chain-smoking nutter, who is now going to get us in the shit with our father. As we don't smoke and the shops in town don't smell of smoke. Only our mother's dump of a house does, so thank you for the award. I hope we all don't get found out."

"Oh no, I didn't think of that." Natty placed the mints back into her bag.

"Look you dimwits, Dad surely doesn't know she smokes. Blimey, you're nearly eighteen Nat, you can experiment can't you?" Ruth spoke over her noisy sisters.

"That, young Ruth, is a great idea." Glenn stood still and turned around.

"Oh thanks you two, I'll be the one who gets in trouble."

"We can say that you forced us to smoke."

"Glenn, you sounded better when you were choking." Natty was bewildered in what they were saying.

"Let's go home, Dad's all alone!" Natty walked briskly feeling really fed up.

Glenn and Ruth walked together behind her, laughing about the whole situation.

"All right pissy pants." Glenn continued to be the comedian.

"I forgot to go, can you believe it?" Natty began to walk quicker as the sudden urge to do a wee rushed through her, remembering and feeling how damp her knickers were.

"Pissy pants, pissy pants." Glenn spoke louder and louder.

It began to rain slightly. None of them had an umbrella so they decided to hurry.

In the kitchen their mother put the cups in the sink and filled up the kettle to make herself another drink. She took the chocolate cake and cookies from the plates and put them into the bin.

"Fucking ungrateful girls. See Dad, I told you they didn't deserve nice cake."

42

"Hello? Who is it? It's midnight for God's sake."
"Have you ever made angels in the snow?" Matthew sat in the dark.

"I'm sorry? Matt is that you? Are you OK?"

"Just lying down, not worrying what anyone thinks. The freezing ice biting into the back of your legs. As you move your arms up and down the snow gathers under you and you find it hard to move. As you look up into the greying sky the snowflakes fall onto your cold face. Watching each flake as it becomes nearer. You can see your breath in the air, all you can hear is your heartbeat. You know what you feel, Harry, you feel you are the only one in the world."

"Matt, you haven't had a drink have you? Get some sleep, it's late."

"No Harry, I haven't had a drink. I wanted to let you know how I felt, that was all, you know, as brothers should." Matthew was stern.

"Matt, you're starting to freak me, what the fuck is it with you?"

"Harry."

"Yes Matt!"

"Did you have sex with my wife?" Matthew felt a shooting pain in his head, he felt like he was going to be sick.

"I'm sorry, what did you say?"

"I'm asking you if you if you had sex with my wife?"

There was a pause. Matthew could hear his brother breathing heavily.

"No Matthew. Christ no, I wouldn't."

"Harry I need to know, you have to tell me right this second." His mouth was becoming sore from biting the inside again and again.

206

"No, Matt. I would never be so dishonourable."

"You wouldn't?" He could taste blood as he bit the inside of his mouth too hard.

"No fucking way. Look mate, do you honestly think she'd want to sleep with someone like me anyway?"

"Funnily enough Harry, yes I do." Matthew's knuckles were nearly white as he held the receiver with force.

"Well you're wrong. Look Matt, she is beautiful, but she idolises you."

"Harry, she says Ruth is your little girl. She says she doesn't belong to me, apparently it looks like something I thought was mine is actually yours."

"Matt, she doesn't look anything like me, she is you all over."

"Thinking about it Harry, she does look like you. But hey, that's obviously impossible because you didn't have sex with my wife." Matthew squeezed his eyes shut as the intolerable words came out of his mouth.

"Matt, she's on pills, you know she isn't well, she's going to say crazy things."

"Don't speak of her so flippantly!" He was shouting into the phone, becoming fuelled with anger.

"Matt, Matt. Go to bed mate. Sorry for being rude. Stop saying crazy things. OK, it's just really hard for you at the moment."

"Harry, I need you to tell me, I can't live like this any more, she made Ruth unwell. And if she's your daughter you would want her to be OK wouldn't you?"

"Is she OK? Ruth, I mean?"

"Harry!" Matthew felt rage stirring in his stomach again. He wasn't going to give up.

There was another long pause.

"Look Matt, I don't know, I'm so sorry. She is very beautiful. And, you know, she looked so sad. I wanted to comfort her. I'm so sorry Matt, it was one time. It never happened again. I felt so bad for ages. I don't know what to say. Fuck, man, I don't know what to say to you. Ruth can't be mine, no way. I don't need all this right now. I'm so sorry, I hope you can understand. I didn't mean to hurt you."

Tears fell onto Matthew's lips, falling onto his jumper. Trying to stop the tears with his cuff pulled over his hand, wiping his face vigorously. Matthew took a deep breath. His body was full of pain, every part of him aching, he was struggling to breathe, feeling as though his lungs were being crushed.

"Understand, you want me to understand? I understand you didn't mean to fuck my wife. I also understand you didn't want to gain a daughter. And I understand how you didn't mean to hurt me. And I hope YOU understand I will never give up my Ruth to you. Go and join our father, you belong with him, rotting away. I don't want to remember you, ever." Matthew found the strength to speak calmly, pausing for small breaths to compose himself.

Placing the phone down Matthew sat silently, hearing the ticking of the clock. The moon glistened through the window revealing the clock face in the dark. He watched as the second hand moved. He was fully aware he'd remember his brother always, every time he looked into Ruth's beautiful blue eyes. It was all happening because he was such a useless husband and father. He knew it; he was unable to help the most pivotal people in his life. They were his life.

Consumed with fear for himself, Matthew couldn't move from the chair all night, his eyes full of tears. Full of confusion, he felt almost numb with shock. Checking Eve came to the forefront of his mind. Waiting in a moonlit room for the first sound of small footsteps in the morning, praying they'd call for him, needing to hear it more than anything in the world. He simply waited.

"Daddy!"

43

"HAPPY BIRTHDAY!" banners covered every space their father could find. As if this wasn't enough, he'd also filled the kitchen with balloons, and so throughout breakfast Natty's feet kept getting tangled between the colourful rubber underneath the table.

"Dad, it looks great, thanks so much." Natty buttered her toast feeling happy, admiring the end result her father had spent all night preparing.

Glenn thought it highly hilarious to kick the balloons up into the air as she entered the kitchen.

"Weeeee! Happy birthday old girl." Glenn was almost singing at the top of her voice, and as she sat balloons landed on the table between her and Natty.

"Is there really any need for that Glenn?" Natty giggled, hitting the balloon away.

"Is there any need for that?" Glenn pulled a silly face.

"Don't worry, thanks for my card its lovely. Such captivating beautiful words, it must have taken you ages to choose. I didn't think you cared so much." Natty continued giggling.

"But I didn't get you one." Glenn sounded confused.

"Oh no, you didn't did you?" Natty began to laugh with a mouthful of toast and marmalade, pretending to be OK with it.

Glenn screwed her face up and winked at her. It wasn't deliberate that she'd forgotten such a special occasion. She had never been the sort of person to buy cards and presents – her sisters often said she was as tight as arses. In her mind Glenn knew she could have managed this one. It was her sister's eighteenth, after all.

"I'll get you one later, sorry Nat." Glenn's head suddenly fell with embarrassment, as she gazed into her cornflakes.

Their father gently kicked the balloons in the air and sat down to join his two girls.

"I heard Ruth, she should be coming down in a minute."

As their father finished his sentence in came Ruth. She stepped over the balloons to sit down opposite Natty.

"Happy birthday Natty, have a lovely day." Ruth handed her sister a small present and a card.

"Arse lick." Glenn continued to eat her breakfast, tapping her spoon on the side of her bowl, trying to take the attention away from what Ruth had managed to achieve.

"Thanks Ruth, it's really kind of you, thank you." Natty put her perfume and card at the side of her plate, leant over the table and kissed her younger sister on the cheek, finally feeling appreciated.

"Would you like a kiss, Glenn? You know, simply for being my crazy sister?"

"Well, if you put it like that." Glenn stood and kissed Natty.

Their father felt intense pride as he watched his three beautiful daughters cuddle and kiss each other so freely. He felt a lump building in his throat as he held his tears back. It was finally his turn to acknowledge his daughter's coming of age.

"Happy birthday to you Natty, I hope you have a wonderful day." He handed her a little rectangular box, wrapped in silky pink paper. A small pink bow had been placed in the centre. Natty already knew she would keep it in her purse.

"Thank you Dad, it is wonderful." Natty pulled out a beautiful gold necklace; clasped onto it was a heart-shaped locket. As she opened it, she realised it had taken all her father's strength and love. He had placed a picture of himself on one side and their mother on the other.

"Dad, Mother was so beautiful; then again you weren't bad either!" Natty eagerly allowed her sisters to see it.

"See Dad, you did have more hair once." Glenn looked at the necklace with envy.

"Thanks Glenn, how kind of you to remind me." Their father smiled at her.

"It's really beautiful, really." Ruth passed the locket back to Natty.

As Natty closed the gold heart it looked as if her parents were going to kiss, she opened it once again, and watched slowly one more time their faces moving closer.

Kissing her father she realised that for some reason or other he had finally found the courage to display them as a couple. He had united them, making them part of Natty's life. The subject of their mother had always been pushed away; somehow trying to pretend it never happened. Or that she didn't even exist. But it was them and it had always been. This proved it, this was his life. Their father and mother started it all simply by falling in love. It was such a wonderful gift, something she'd always have around her neck, whatever happened. Natty felt she finally belonged somehow to people whom she'd never really understood.

"Could you do it up for me Dad, please? I can't wait to put it on." Natty leant over to him and handed the necklace to him gently.

"Of course I can." Their father stood and placed his arms around his daughter, moving her hair to one side and placing the elegant chain around her neck.

Natty touched it, checking it was there and tapping it a couple of times, feeling completely happy.

"What are you girls up to today? Are you going shopping again?"

"I think we will, not sure what we will buy yet." As she spoke to their father Glenn cleared the table, admiring her sister's gift once more.

"What are you up to today, Dad?" Overwhelmed with pride, Natty held onto her necklace and smiled at him.

"I have to get things for your birthday dinner. You're going to be back in time aren't you?"

"What are we having, Dad? I hope it's beef and roast spuds, lashing of gravy and a huge Yorkshire pudding." Ruth sat licking her lips.

"Well I wasn't going to but it does sound rather great. I think we should let Natty choose, as long as it isn't beans on toast." Their father left the table and grabbed his coat from the well-organised rack above the stairs where Natty had sat in anticipation not too long ago, before making his way back to the kitchen again.

"Egg and beans on toast then. I don't mind, honestly it will be great whatever you do and we will be back if we have to run all the way home." Natty's voice was getting louder, her finger and thumb on the necklace holding her parents in place. Near to her, not far from her heart. She could never thank her father enough for such a thoughtful gift. It was more than a gift, her parents together again. Now and then she would remember seeing them in the garden together; her father would sit with her and play sometimes, and their mother always sat alone, watching.

"Natty, Natty, anyone home?" Glenn stood behind her waiting for her plate.

"Oh sorry Glenn, what's the matter?"

"Nothing old girl, did you want to go out or not? I know you're getting old and your bones are brittle, but today would be handy," she said, finally taking the plate and shaking her head.

"OK, I'm coming." Natty went to get ready. Going into their bedroom she placed her small pink bow in her purse. She had a quick glance in the mirror and smiled to herself. "Happy birthday Natty Hopkins, have a wonderful day."

"Bye Natty, have a great day and I will see you later!"

"Bye Dad." Rushing to the top of the stairs, she wanted to say thank you one more time. She was too late, he had already gone. The door slammed and she stood at the top of the stairs. If only she could let him know how much she loved him, how much she loved both of them.

"Will you move your arse?" Glenn was behind her again, tapping her foot impatiently.

"Glenn, that's no way to speak to your elders. I was thinking, shall we go?" Natty raised her eyebrows in shock as Glenn pushed past her.

"Well yeah, that is the bloody plan."

"No, you know, *go*." Natty spoke slowly and clearly.

"No way, you've gone mad too. Ruth will you get over here and talk some sense into this sister of yours. I'm getting my coat."

"Glenn, you know the coffee bar where Mother took us, where they both met?" Natty sat on the top of the stairs, her head filled with anticipation.

"Dear God what have I done to deserve this, why the bloody hell are you talking of the place, please don't say you want to go there?

212

But then again it is a bonus, I thought you wanted to go and see her, and I really wasn't in the mood for her today. I really would like to shop." Glenn's voice was raised and slightly aggressive.

"I can't remember the way; I think it was the number five. I'm almost certain of it. Yes it was." As she sat on the stair Natty followed the square pattern on the wallpaper with her finger; she didn't dare look at Glenn.

"What's she saying?" Ruth came out of the cleaned kitchen.

"She wants to get flipping coffee in our parents' old coffee bar."

"Cool." Ruth turned to Natty and smiled, nodding her head.

"Oh, mother of Jesus, get me out of here." Glenn huffed and puffed and left the house. She stood with her arms folded outside, tapping her foot in annoyance.

"Glenn, what's so terrible about it?"

"Ruth, can we have a day off from our flaming parents? Actually go shopping and have fun."

"Yes we can, but let's go to the coffee bar first, eh?" Ruth joined her upset sister outside. They stood silently as the culprit of the stupid idea joined them.

"Blimey, it's cold." Natty slammed the door shut.

"Don't worry Nat, you'll warm up with a nice drink of psycho coffee inside you." Glenn would remain stubborn until they reached the bus stop.

They all waited as they had with their mother. Three sisters alone, Natty and Ruth standing at one end and Glenn at the other, arms still folded and tapping her foot.

Their father walked slowly around the store, glancing at shelves of food. More than could ever feed a nation. For some reason food was the furthest thing from his mind, as he gazed at the special offers and the different kinds of people around him. Strangers grabbing handfuls of groceries, their trolleys piled high with enough food for the next month. Their father began to feel suffocated. He needed to hurry, picking up Chinese ingredients and a bottle of dry white wine. The queue went on nearly all the way down one aisle. Preparing himself for a long wait, he joined the irritated strangers. He wished the stupid idea out of his head, if only it wasn't put in there by his girls. What was he to do? Did he really want their mother to join in the birthday celebration? Or did he simply want to be in the presence of his perfect Eve again, for his sake and not his girls? He desperately wanted to convince himself it was only because his girls had asked him. Hoping the answer would come to him before he reached the check-out.

Their father finally left the store in a daze. He placed the unplanned Chinese feast in the boot. By the time he had slammed it shut his mind was made up.

"This is definitely it, I'm certain of it." Natty came to a sudden halt and wanting to look inside she pressed her face against the large window.

"I think you're right Nat. Well go in then, we haven't come all this way to stand outside in the cold." Glenn's voice was sharp but she began to sound almost comical. She forcefully opened the door for her sisters to enter, hearing the bell once more.

"Over there's free." Ruth began to rush, swerving through busy tables.

"Is this where we sat with Mother?" Ruth sat down excitedly, rubbing her hands on top of the table, sugar grains sticking to her palm.

"Yes Ruth, it was. Glenn would you like to order?" Natty squeezed up to a happy Ruth.

"I feel you should, considering it was your idea." Glenn sat opposite them, her arms folded.

"What are we having?" Natty finally took the responsibility to order. As she took the money out of her pocket that their father had given her the week earlier, she thought that Glenn was just being selfish. It was her birthday after all; there was no reason why Glenn should be so upset. Natty held her necklace again, looking around at her sisters.

"Coffee, Nat, it's a coffee bar remember." Glenn tapped the menu.

Natty returned quickly with three coffees. She was feeling content, so far it had been the best day ever, whatever Glenn felt.

"Nat, if that boy stares at you any more you'll have holes in your back," Ruth informed her sister.

"What boy?" Natty looked quickly around the coffee bar.

"The blind one with a dog and walking stick." Glenn laughed at last.

"Glenn, if you say anything nice to me today it might actually be a miracle."

"We could have two miracles in one day if that boy's looking at you. I'm only joking Natty, really I am. Actually come to think of it he's really looking now. How embarrassing – where's his dignity?" Glenn picked up the menu and put it near her face.

"Will you two stop it; he's not looking at me, drink your coffee and we will go."

"We've only just got here, make your mind up. Now we're here I actually like the place. I don't want to make things worse for you Nat, but he is one sexy mother. Anyway he's coming over so you can see for yourself." Glenn's voice was soft, almost a whisper, as she spoke from behind the menu.

"Piss off, Glenn," Natty whispered.

"Hello."

"Sorry?" Natty turned to the gorgeous stranger. He was exactly as Glenn described, one sexy mother. But she thought he must be having a laugh.

"I said hello." The young man's voice was gentle.

"Hello." Natty felt as though her blushes were filling her body, not only her face. She looked at him red faced while her sisters were trying not to giggle. She was being kicked by Glenn under the table and she wanted to tell her politely to piss off again, but it wouldn't have made a very good impression. So she chose to endure it until the gorgeous stranger went back to his table. Then she planned to punch her.

"My name is Ben. I haven't seen you in here before."

"Hi, I'm Natty; this is my sister Glenn and my sister Ruth."

"Hi." Glenn and Ruth spoke in unison. They found it hard not to chuckle out loud, as Ruth pinched Glenn's leg. Natty's legs were still being gently kicked.

"We have only been here once before, only popped in." Natty wanted to go at that very moment; she knew her sisters were savouring every minute. Cows, she thought.

"I know this is extremely forward of me, but would you mind if I gave you my number maybe we could meet up sometime?"

"OK, that would be nice." Natty was impressed – he spoke very well. She was amazed at her quick response.

Without hesitation her new-found friend wrote his number on a serviette.

"Be seeing you again soon I hope." Leaving the coffee bar the young stud looked back again at her.

"Oh my God, oh my God, what the hell just happened?" Speaking in shock Natty quickly grabbed the serviette and with both hands held it to her heart.

"Well Nat, he looked at you, you looked at him, introduction, introduction, number, kiss, sex, marriage, lots of children and divorce." Glenn roared with laughter, hitting Natty on the head with the menu she had used as a shield only moments ago.

"Thanks Glenn, you really have such a way about you. He was a little forward don't you think? Shall I ring him?" Natty raised her eyebrows.

"Natty, calm down, he was asking you out on a date, that's not forward. He was cute." Ruth nudged her.

"He was more than cute. I can't believe Mother and Dad met here too." Ruth took a sip of her drink. It was still too hot.

"Oh my God Ruth, you and Natty are so desperate. I don't think the luck our parents have had meeting here is really a start to your future."

"Don't talk rubbish. What has our parents' life got to do with that sexy young man?" Natty spoke sharply, suddenly feeling fed up for the first time that day.

"Look my dear elder, I don't want to take you off your bubble. You couldn't wait to take his number, talk about needy." Glenn tapped the menu on the edge of the table.

"What? So you wouldn't have taken his number then? Give me the menu will you?" Natty felt agitated, snatching it from her and trying to push it back among the other menus all squashed together in the smallest piece of plastic.

"You haven't got to get so stressed. And no, I wouldn't have taken his number."

"I don't believe that." Ruth joined in again.

"Ruth, you're too young to understand." Glenn dismissed her comment.

216

"Oh that doesn't surprise me. I'm nearly thirteen, get it into your head Glenn." Ruth gently poked at her sister's temple, and decided to sit back again and observe the whole situation.

"As I was saying, I wouldn't have taken his number, I would have given him mine after taking my tongue out of his throat." Glenn roared with laughter, and they all followed.

"That's horrible!" Ruth joined her sister once again, leaning forward.

"We have just popped in young man. Oh, how very posh." Glenn held her stomach as it ached through laughing.

They all sat laughing and drinking coffee. To any passer-by who took the time to look through the window, they portrayed happiness and maturity. They were so lost and confused, but they didn't even realise.

Their father stood at the familiar front door. Memories came flooding back. Was he in a dream? Why was he standing there? Feelings of excitement and fear entwined within his stomach. His eyes glanced slowly around the door, it needed another coat of green paint. He remembered the day when they had entered the house for the first time; it was everything he had ever wanted – a perfect wife and a marvellous house to protect her. His fingers were sweating in his coat pocket; they had been crossed since his arrival. He needed this to go as smoothly as possible.

The door had been opened slowly. He felt hopeless as he once again glanced into the eyes of his wife. His beautiful perfect Eve looked back into his. He felt lost for words again. After everything he had been through he still couldn't manage the thought of making a fool of him self. Their mother looked deeper into his eyes.

"Hello Matthew, would you like to come in?" As she stood at the door he looked at the front of her apron, it was the same one her had bought her all those years ago. The butterflies were faded and most of the wings had diminished in the wash, soft threads hung around her legs. Their father followed her. She still looked as beautiful. She was like a cord to him, she could always pull him back, and she had for years; however hard he tried to forget he couldn't. It was as if they shared the same heart. Whenever she took a breath he would take the other for her.

Their father knew he had to be firm and do what he had come to do.

There were bottles of tablets everywhere, but no sign of the doctor's teeth, which brought a smirk to his face. The room seemed to be quite organised. There was a huge bowlful of mixture which she began to stir vigorously. It was splattering everywhere.

He wished he could see her face, but her back was to him. Her black hair, shining as it always did, looked wonderful tied back. Her bottom wiggled as she stirred the contents of the bowl. Their father couldn't keep his eyes from her petite figure. He knew he had to compose himself. He closed his eyes, inhaled deeply and began.

"Natty was wondering if you would like to come for her eighteenth dinner." His stomach ached.

There was a silence – all you could hear was the bashing of the wooden spoon on the side of the huge bowl. It looked like enough mixture to feed a whole neighbourhood.

"What are you making?" Matthew hoped he would get an answer if he asked another question. There was still a silence.

"Eve, could you turn around please? I am starting to get a little fed up. I haven't come to be ignored." Matthew fingers were uncrossed by this time.

"I got you."

"I am sorry." Their father raised his voice and eyebrows in shock.

"That's the man I knew and loved." She turned around quickly and winked at him.

Matthew had now filled the room with silence; it seemed that everything had been frozen in time. They stood at opposite sides of the room and stared. Noticing each other's chest moving in and out, their breathing was heavy. They were each lost in their own world – they were only a few feet away from one another but it was still an unreachable place.

Eve turned her back to him once again.

"Sugar, Matthew? Do you still take sugar?"

"Yes please, Eve."

"Are you going to stand all day or are you going to take a seat?" Eve moved with ease as she added sugar to a cup and reached for a tablet, taking one with some water.

A sense of guilt filled their father as the reality crawled around him; his wife and the mother of his daughters was still unwell. Feeling angry with himself he felt he could have tried harder. He hadn't made it all OK. He should have put his pride behind him and stayed, for her, and not for how she was behaving.

Eve placed two hot cups of tea on the table accompanied by a huge plate of biscuits.

"You look quite well Eve, how have you been?" Their father felt more settled and smiled.

"Quite well Matthew, not beautiful to you any more." Their mother tried to stop their glances meeting.

Matthew had never thought of her any other way. She was still a picture of perfection. Behind all of her confusion and sorrow she was simply beautiful.

She had gone away for a while, but she was going to come back one day, he knew it. Deep down he'd longed for it from the day he'd left, prayed that even for one small moment she would hold his face with her small hands, look into his eyes, and know who he was. She would remember how much he loved her, she could tell him, and know what she was saying. He would wait a lifetime, he knew, as he took a sip of his over-sweetened tea.

"Dinner, you say?" She sounded inquisitive.

"Yes, Natty would like it very much if you could join us. It would be a total surprise."

"I think it would be. How about you Matthew, would you like very much for me to join you?"

"It would really make the girls happy, I'm sure" Their father took a huge gulp as if something was stuck in his throat.

"Matthew, please answer my question, please let me know how you feel if I were to join you."

"It would be fine Eve, I would like for you to join us. So are you saying you will?"

"No Matthew, I'm not saying." Eve sat in front of him, her hands clasped around her cup.

Matthew suddenly felt tense again, fearing the whole idea of even considering it was ridiculous.

"Eve, don't worry, I'm truly sorry I bothered you." He felt it was time to leave, but stopped at the kitchen door and looked back just once. Then he walked to the front door in haste.

"Please wait Matthew; please don't leave, not like this." Her voice full of desperation, she rushed after him, pressing her hands together praying for him to turn around; she had seen so many people walk away from her.

"Eve, there's no point. I thought I would try and do something for our little girl."

"Natasha isn't little any more."

"You haven't called her that since she was born." He thought Eve was being sarcastic.

"I hated it, that's why I kept quiet Matthew. I was so used to keeping quiet."

"But Eve, I thought you liked it. I thought I made you happy, I have only ever tried to make you happy, get everything perfect for you just as you used to be."

"Matthew I have never been perfect from the minute we met. I only wanted to be me, to be left as me." Eve's hands were still pressed together and there was a softness in her voice which hadn't been heard for such a long time, by him or their daughters.

"Eve I am sorry, sorry for making you upset and intruding upon your home." Matthew held the door handle, waiting to leave. Had his wife just woken from her sleep? Was she finally back? The thought left him quickly. He was going to stop kidding himself, stop living in a dream, at least until the next time he wanted to believe.

"Bye Eve." His back was turned to hers.

"I would very much like to come, I would like very much to see you all together, how you are as a family. Please let me join you. I am just so very scared that I will mess up, that they will all hate me. I always leave people hating me." Tears fell from her eyes.

"Just come eh? No pressures."

"Only if you pick me up." Eve managed the smallest of grins.

He felt as if he was thirty again and was going to take her on their first date. Remembering as if it was only yesterday, excitement rushed through him.

"I'll be back around six to collect you, if that's OK with you."

"It is OK, truly OK."

Eve was left alone in her large hall, glancing up at the ceiling.

"Dad, you're not going to believe where I am going."

The birthday girl glided around the glittering shops with her head held high, and a very valuable serviette in her pocket. Her dear Glenn had decided to continually mimic her from the moment they had left the coffee bar, as she had managed to succeed in her quest with sheer ease. Deep down Glenn wondered why she hadn't been given the number; she assumed it would be her getting the attention. She stared at Natty for a brief moment, noticing just how pretty she was becoming, she may become even prettier. The cold air was starting to bite, and the Christmas lights seemed dimmed through the slowly falling fog. The parades of wonderful shops and Christmas stalls, the smell of chestnuts roasting, families dashing to and fro, excited children laughing and skipping past them – they could have been characters on the perfect Christmas card. It seemed like another world.

As they made their way to the bus stop they were all looking forward to returning home. Glenn was busting to tell their father of her sister's new friend, over their feast which would be fit for kings as long as they all remembered to save room for birthday cake.

The heavy bags of Chinese products pressed into his fingers as he walked nervously to the front door, the home he now shared with his beautiful daughters. Each time he pushed the key into the lock he wished his wife would be waiting for him on the other side, standing looking as beautiful as she always had all those years ago. Excitement would pump through him, he desperately wanted to hold her, confirming to him that she was really his. As he pushed the door shut with his foot the familiar sense of loneliness consumed him, as it had for so many years, from the very first turning of the key.

"Girls, are you home?" There was the usual silence. As he stood alone the hall would echo his pleas.

"Eve I'm home, Eve it's me, its all OK, I'm home now!" he called, just as he always did. Shaking his head in disbelief he made his way to the kitchen. He knew it would be a wonderful dinner; they were all to be together. It had been such a long time. Praying he had done the right thing he began to wash his hands before cooking. He proudly glanced over at the fabulous birthday cake – pale yellow flowers skilfully iced and small petals falling onto the beautiful writing. It read HAPPY 18TH BIRTHDAY NATASHA xxx. She would be happy, he was certain of it.

The door slammed; his girls were home.

"Shit, shit, shit!" Running and shaking water from his hands he grabbed at the masterpiece, rushing around looking for a hiding place.

"Hi Dad we're home." Natty looked at her father standing in the centre of the kitchen looking flustered.

"Hello Natty, did you have a nice day shopping?"

"Yes thanks Dad, how was your day?" Natty moved forward to kiss him. Both his hands were behind his back. She was followed by Ruth and then Glenn who were smirking, waiting to inform their dear father that Natty would soon be bringing a sexy man home. They all grabbed at the ingredients sprawled out on the worktops.

"Dad, this looks great!" Ruth's voice was raised as her father suddenly disappeared.

"Your dinner isn't the only thing that looks great, eh Nat?"

"What's that girls? I got plenty of grub, you look as if you're all rummaging at a jumble sale."

"Let us help cook, Dad. It will be fun."

"Glenn, I have it all under control." If only they all realised how out of control he really felt. When should he tell them about the guest?

He knew he couldn't finish cooking the meal until everyone was seated. It had to be served hot and everyone needed to be seated together. It had to be flawless.

"Natty, could you place the knives and forks out for me please? Girls, you can go and get cleaned up."

"OK Dad." Glenn and Ruth hurried up the stairs, laughing.

"Could you set five places please Natty?" Their father began making himself busy so as not to make eye contact.

"Five; Dad? Who is the fifth place for? Is it Mother, she's coming for dinner?" Holding on tightly to her necklace, she was hoping her father would make it the best birthday ever.

"Yes Natty, I'll go and get her at six, once I've got this prepared."

As she began to lay the table with a huge grin on her face, they didn't say a word, they just communicated through silence. They each knew what the other was thinking and simply allowed each other to flow in their own thoughts.

"Happy birthday to you, squashed— blimey, who's died? Is everyone OK?"

"Um, yes Glenn, fine, come and help will you? I would like the table to look great."

"It's only your birthday young lady, stop fussing. Your boyfriend isn't coming over yet you know." Glenn grabbed at the forks.

"Boyfriend, girls? What kind of talk is that?"

"It's nothing Dad." They spoke together.

Glenn sat at the table, getting in the way of the organisation, placing each fork down.

"Excuse me, pain, I need to place another setting."

"You've done enough, mad woman."

"Glenn, you need to budge over. Dad will ask you to shift."

"Out of your sister's way please Glenn."

"Oh for heaven's sake, she's done enough, I'll show you. Your place has been set Dad, me of course, Natty unfortunately and Ruth. Oh my God, Mother's not coming is she? Oh my God I can't believe it, Dad, what's going on? How come she's coming for dinner? I mean, I'm not saying it's not OK with me, I know it wouldn't matter if it wasn't but I'm just saying, oh my God, have I got it wrong? She's really coming isn't she? She is. I've got to let Ruth know, oh my God." Glenn leapt out of her chair finally out of her sister's way, moving frantically and very much out of breath.

"Do you think she's guessed, Dad?" They laughed together like they hadn't for such a long time, really laughed.

"How do you think she took it? I feel that she was pretty calm."

"I've never seen her move so quickly Dad." The laughter continued.

"Dad, Glenn just said that Mother's coming for Chinese food."

"Yes Ruth." Their father was trying to hold back, chuckling, being interrupted by Ruth who was behaving hysterically, almost charging at him as if he were to be in a jousting match. At any moment he was sure to be thrown into the air.

"Girls, calm down will you? You'll bust a vessel. She's just

223

coming for a while. Only for a short while. I thought it would be nice for Natty's birthday. I'm going to get her soon. Going to have a quick clean up, you know how she likes things just so."

There was a sudden change of mood as an unusual sense of fear filled them all. They stared at each other, waiting for each other to show some reassurance. Their father took a huge breath, pulled all his girls to him and gently kissed each of their heads.

"It's just dinner."

44

A week had passed since Matthew had made the awful call to him. Harry paced the floor, picking things up, placing them down again. What was he to do? Where was he to go? How was he ever going to mend the damage? He felt alone – more than ever before. He had always felt alone but had never let anyone know. It was something he could never do. How could he share with anyone how lonely he had always felt? Sitting on the sofa, grabbing at his hair, he knew the reason he had made the terrible mistake. He had wanted to feel as his brother did, even if it was only once. Matthew spoke so much of how much in love he was, and how wonderful his life was. Harry had always been jealous of Matthew. How could he let Matthew know how much he wished he was in his shoes? Harry wanted to be loved, to feel secure and have someone to come home to, as it was he never had anyone to share each and every moment of his life with. The only girls Harry managed to attract would never be there waiting for him when he arrived home; they were happy with one night in his bedroom, or sometimes they wouldn't even wait until they reached the front porch before they were ripping his clothes off. It began to hurt after a while, the more he put his guard up the more one-night girls he would attract.

He sat and thought hard about the first time he saw Eve. She had sat in the very spot his heavy body was covering. She was beautiful, it was all he could think of. He tried hard to make interesting conversation but couldn't clear her from his mind, wishing she was his. He wanted to get to know her, wished he could be planning a future with her. He knew Matthew wouldn't really appreciate her, not show her respect and love like he could if allowed the chance. Harry felt convinced he wouldn't have let her get so sick. It had been a moment of sheer madness, a time he would never forget, he didn't really want to forget. He had never meant to hurt his brother. He simply couldn't resist her, he had to be part of her life in some way or another; she surely would remember his touch.

"Bollocks, bollocks, bollocks! Ruth can't be mine. Eve would have said, surely. Bollocks, bollocks, and bollocks." Harry grabbed his keys and left his messy house. Seeing Matthew was the only thing he could do, the only way forward. Whatever the outcome, he wanted to explain. Matthew was always forgiving. Harry's mind was full of stuff, feelings which had surfaced from deep inside of him. Emotions he only remembered feeling as a child: to be brave, to be invincible, to conquer the world. He felt a sudden strength from knowing he had a right to be free from whatever was causing him pain. Why did people have to permanently suffer because someone else wouldn't like what they have to say? He had the right to be honest with himself. He pulled up slowly outside his brother's house, feeling unsure again, what would Matthew say on seeing him at his front door? Harry walked to the window and looked in; a blanket covered Eve as she sat quietly. Matthew joined her in the room. He was bringing in a small bowl and placing it in front of the most beautiful child. Harry had never really noticed how beautiful and amazing little Ruth was. His brother sat her on his lap close to his chest. Was Harry to claim her back if she really was his? Would he do it to Matthew? He wouldn't be any good with something so precious; sometimes he couldn't really take care of himself. He could have been looking at the happiest little family. He felt he was at the window for ages, nearly forgetting the reason for being there. But it was too late, Matthew had seen him. Harry didn't run like a scared child; he waited at the door, wanting his big brother to have his chance to be angry, to let him know everything he thought. Maybe even get a punch in the mouth, if he was lucky.

"What are you here for Harry? Did you forget something?" Matthew stood in the doorway like a protecting lion; he wasn't going to let any animal get to his lioness and cubs. He stood tall and stern, his lips tight. His chest seemed to fill the whole doorway. He spoke calmly but abruptly. His face looked flushed and sore, with the aftermath of the tears which had fallen all night.

"Matthew, please let me talk to you – if you would let me

226

explain." Harry was like a little mouse in the lion's claws as he pleaded with him.

"You don't need to explain anything to me Harry. You never have to explain anything ever again. I'm so sad for us all, and I can't take it any more. Each day I'm hoping my wife will get better. Every day I'm hoping my children will laugh, dance and skip like other children. But I know while things are the way they are and Eve is so unhappy they won't. I feel too guilty. I have to look after them, do it for them. Keep them safe from people who are going to hurt them, hurt me. Like you, Harry. I need to keep them away from people like you. So if you don't mind I need you to leave now, and never return." Matthew remained calm, trying to recognise the young man who stood in front of him. He wanted to see him as his loyal brother, but couldn't. Harry would never have hurt his family this way.

"But Matt, I want to be OK with you. I've come to say sorry. Forgive me Matt, please why can't you just punch me or something, do something instead of being all calm and typically you about the whole thing!"

"Harry, can you hear little Ruth crying? Why don't you ask for her forgiveness? All her life she will be different from her sisters. I'm going to have to lie to her forever. You have given such a thing to her. You fucking well ask for her to forgive you. A quick punch on the nose and it's all over, is that what you're saying? Harry, pain is temporary, pride is for ever. I'm not going to punch you." Matthew was finding it difficult holding his tears back, his throat was aching. He wasn't going to let Harry see him cry, not ever again.

"I don't want to take her Matt. I want us to be cool." Harry's voice was full of desperation.

"Of course you do, you always want just what you want. And that's how it's always been. You haven't got to tell me you're not going to take her, good old Harry doing me a fucking favour again. You're not taking her. So get the thought out of your head. I'm not coming back to the garage – you can have it. I'm going to shut the door now and I will never open it to you again." Matthew took a step back, pulling the door slightly in front of his body.

"Mate, I don't want you to forget me!"

"My wife, you fucked my wife – how the hell am I going to forget you? Every time I look into Ruth's eyes I see you, every birthday she has, everything she does I will see you, you Harry, I will see you, but guess what, brother? I love her, I have her and you will never see me again, so that means you will never see my family again."

Matthew went back inside, closing the door quietly. Leaning on the door he began to sob, his body sliding to the floor. It felt as if his insides were shaking as well. He heard tapping on the door above his head,

"Please leave Harry, please leave." Matthew cried so hard he didn't have the strength to comfort Ruth, who had been crying the whole time. He hoped Eve would have picked her up for a while.

"Who was that Matthew, are we having company?"

"No, Eve not ever." His words could barely be heard through his tears.

45

All the girls were now another year older and their father could see the change in them all; they were all growing up to be wonderful young ladies, certainly with the looks to match. He knew where their obvious beauty had come from.

Since that day when Natty turned eighteen, their father would roam around the house feeling lost and unsettled. His days seemed to roll into one, each day resembling the next and the next. The following week would be the same.

"Girls, I'm off now, don't be late, I'll do dinner and maybe we could go for a walk together." Wondering if they had all heard him, he left for his day at the office.

"Bye Dad! Bugger, I missed him." Ruth rushed to the top of the stairs with a mouthful of toothpaste.

"Excuse me dear Ruthi, have to get to college, first day and all. Have a good day. What did Dad say before he left?" Natty shuffled passed her sister at the top of the stairs. She looked fabulous; her black high heels looked wonderful with her very skinny blue jeans. She was full of anticipation for her day ahead.

"Something about going for a walk after dinner. Got to go, mouth burning." Ruth dashed to the bathroom.

"Glenn, open the door, I haven't finished. Glenn!" Ruth knocked frantically to no avail. Saliva building up in her mouth, she was dribbling white fluid down her school shirt.

"I'm in here; you've had your turn."

"Glenn, you're such a—"

"Ruth, come and rinse in the sink down here, you'll be late."

"Hot, hot, hot." Ruth ran past Natty as she was putting her coat on.

Natty heard the water gushing from the kitchen tap.

"See you later, don't argue!" Natty went to leave, shaking her head and laughing to herself.

"Nat!" Ruth quickly made her way to Natty before she left, wiping her mouth on a tea towel, looking relieved.

"What is it Ruth? I have to go."

"Are you upset Mother didn't come to dinner for your birthday?"

"Why are you asking me now? I think we all are, don't you?" Natty wanted to forget her birthday.

"Kind of. It would have been OK I think, nice for Dad too maybe."

Natty ruffled Ruth's hair and left.

"Oh brilliant, now I have to do my hair again, thanks Nat, why is everyone trying to make me late?" Speaking very loudly Ruth stomped up the stairs, needing Glenn to be finished in the bathroom more than ever: she had a toothpaste stain to get rid of and a full head of blonde hair to do again.

"I'm definitely leaving now or I will be late like the rest of my mad family." Natty slammed the door shut behind her, inhaling a huge breath of fresh air, as she left her sisters together.

"Glenn, please come out." Ruth stood outside the door as she pulled her flowery bobbles from her messy plaits.

"OK, I'm out. I do have things to do as well, you know, but then who gives a shit?" Glenn slowly glided past her. She was completely ready.

"Oh yeah, so you are." Ruth took her chance, leaping into the bathroom as though her prince was inside. She twisted her hair to make it presentable and left the bathroom again; this time she was ready.

"Anyway, your language is getting really bad lately!" As Ruth stood at the top of the stairs, shouting, she could see Glenn putting her coat on. And her wonderful orange scarf. She thought how good it would look with her own black jacket.

"Oh, who gives a bollocks chop?" Glenn laughed as she buttoned up her grey raincoat.

Suddenly finding the whole morning funny they began to chuckle. It was a good beginning to another day.

Outside college, Natty sat alone on the wooden bench. Feelings from her birthday came flooding back. They had all sat there waiting that evening, anxious and strangely excited for when their father would return home with her, picking at the food their father had placed beautifully in the centre of the table, which had been laid to restaurant standard. He had arrived home without her. His body slumped into a chair next to them. She couldn't make it after all, said she didn't feel like it in the end. Sent her greetings though. The dinner was eaten slowly. Each wondering what they had done that was so bad, for her not to even want to share a small meal. They all sang "Happy birthday". It was a beautiful birthday cake, you could see how much work had gone into it once the candles had been lit.

Natty made one wish and one wish only. A wish where her birthday could begin all over again. Her father would walk in with her mother. They could laugh with her and joke together. Eat and drink wine, she could even stay until the morning. She knew her wish was already wasted when the candles went out.

"You coming in Nat?"

"Oh, hi Katie."

Walking to class with a fellow student Natty's mind was full of everything else rather than a hard day's claustrophobia in the classroom.

46

Matthew would dress the girls each morning while singing songs to them, forcing himself to act as though he was happy, but as he would never be in the mood to sing it was almost excruciating. He wanted to make amends to his girls for all the tears they witnessed each and every day. For all the times their arms had been grabbed hard or they had been hurt by Eve. It was a relief when they would help him pick up the books Eve had thrown at the walls. Matthew was always the preferred target. The girls would find the books everywhere, counting each one as they put one on top of the other. The next day there'd always be more books to count.

Natty was going to be a big seven years old and Glenn had started school. Like her elder sister she enjoyed the freedom of play and knowing they were going to be greeted with a smile. Slowly gaining confidence and gradually believing that the people who greeted them were not going to become angry or hurt them at any given moment. The consistency of the day enthralled them both. Little Ruth was nearly two and still tiny as ever. She really was a pretty little girl. As Matthew looked at her he could see she resembled her father greatly. Matthew would never be far from her. At a very young age Ruth chose not to be far from his side, clinging to his leg whenever it was in reach. Natty and Glenn always looked like a train. Glenn was always hanging onto Natty's blouse or pretty dress. They were always so close. Eve would be in her usual place, wrapped in a blanket looking out of the window admiring her wonderful garden. It needed attention: the grass needed cutting and the trees needing taking back a bit. She worried that the apples wouldn't be any good this year. A little more colour would have been nice; a few more bulbs could be planted before the coming spring. Eve often asked Matthew to take care of it; in the middle of his busy day she would complain about how upset her father was to see in such a way.

It wasn't going to be another thing Matthew was going to get around to. He would leave it deliberately sometimes simply to annoy her. If her father was so bothered why didn't he do himself? He seemed to visit so often. He knew he was playing a silly game and being unfair to cause her such worry, but really he didn't give a shit; he had lost his business, his brother, his wife and was trying to keep his remarkable girls secure. Matthew would stand at the front door after taking the girls to school and take a deep breath, gazing at all the other houses and wondering if there were really people inside, and if there were what did they do with themselves all day? He would often get a picture of how they might be only by looking at their gardens or even their nets. He knew without a doubt all his guessing would be wrong; you only had to look at his wonderful home from the outside and assume the happiest family in the street lived there.

It made him chuckle to himself; it could have been the only laugh of the day, any day.

He had planned to write to Harry for some time, allowing him to take complete control of the garage and handing over the whole premises and earnings to him. It seemed to be a gift to his brother somehow, knowing he didn't deserve it. But Matthew needed to get rid of it quickly to end any form of connection to the Hopkins family business whatsoever. He would be very clear in his writing, stating the facts and reminding him there was no reason, no reason at all to have contact, everything would be sorted.

The letter would be to the point, as it should be. Not let him know too much. Keep it simple. Matthew sighed, thinking of how much fun they used to have working together. Inhaling deeply he began to write again. It had taken him nearly an hour to put his address on the page, flicking the pen nib up and down, remembering them as small boys. Harry would always get him into trouble. Climbing over garden walls and knocking on old ladies' front doors, scampering over their garden gates laughing, until they got caught. Many a penny chew did Matthew have stuffed into his grey school shorts by Harry until they got caught. But trying to sell their mother's brooch caused the biggest trouble for sure. The ludicrous idea was all in good faith, they would never have hurt their own. Their mother had died when Harry was born, and they wanted to buy lots of pretty flowers to put by her gravestone. Their father didn't find it honourable as he had bought her the brooch. To him they were scoundrels. From that moment their father was so very strict with them, making them do chores all day every day, not letting them out of his sight.

"Daddy!" Ruth wanted to have a go at the new game, trying to grab the pen from his hand, disturbing his thoughts.

"Ruth it's dangerous and I'm busy, you can't have it."

Ruth let out a loud cry – she wanted the pen her father had and felt the need to let the neighbourhood know.

"What's going on?" Eve stood at the door, her face full of disgust, her grey blanket at her feet where she had let it fall from her shoulders.

"Nothing Eve, Ruth wanted the pen." He wondered why Eve had responded to Ruth's crying, she never normally did.

"Well what's the problem? Why can't she have it? What are you making her cry for? You always make her cry." Eve grabbed the pen from Matthew's hand and gave it to Ruth who instantly stopped crying.

"Eve, I said it was dangerous, why are you giving it to her?" Matthew looked on the side for some juice, hoping he could do an exchange.

"She's two years old for heaven's sake man, she can take care of herself."

"I'll get her some soft crayons. What's got you so mad again, Eve?" Matthew felt belittled. He began to feel stressed while trying to speak calmly.

"You Matthew! You, my father is trying to sleep and what do you do? Deliberately make her cry so she wakes him up."

"He's been asleep for years, you fucking fruit cake." Matthew thought he had spoken under his breath, but Eve had heard every single word. He decided to get Ruth a drink while she sat happily scribbling on the unfinished letter to Harry with his pen, watching her while taking her favourite apple juice from the fridge.

"What did you say Matthew? What did you say? How can you be so unkind? I can't believe it. All the things I do for you and the children and this is how you behave." Eve picked up her blanket and quickly turned away from him in disgust yet again. "Fool." Eve went into the dining room.

That was it. Matthew couldn't take it any more; words and emotions bubbled up inside him. Screwing up the letter, he squeezed it for a few seconds desperately trying to get rid of the rage. Looking down and seeing Ruth in dismay as he had snatched her scribbling from her, fuelled his rage even more. Matthew pushed everything from the table, apple juice splattering up into his face. He frantically wiped it with his shaking hands. He stormed into the dining room where Eve was making herself comfortable.

Matthew began to shout at her louder than ever before. He was instantly aware of how loud; he knew it didn't matter any more.

"You do what for me Eve? You do nothing for me; all you do is fuck me up, fuck the girls up. I do everything and more for you, you are a fucking delusional mad fucking woman, a pill-popping lazy bitch. All I have ever done is try to help you, and that's not enough is it? I want you to get better, for you to be my Eve again. But you're too fucking mad. All you do is hurt me and our girls. That's all you ever do. Get over your father will you? He's dead, fucking six foot under, just where I will be if I stay with you a minute fucking longer than I need to!" Matthew stood strong, looking down at Eve. Feeling out of breath, slowly being immersed in fear.

Eve sat and stared into his eyes. She wasn't unsettled by his actions or Ruth crying as she hung onto his leg. She began to laugh at them both.

"See Dad, see what I have to put up with?" Eve looked away, picking up her lukewarm tea that Matthew had made for her earlier.

"That's it Eve, no more, no more for me or our girls. I'm going, I'm taking them away from you, from you and your mad father." Picking Ruth up, trying to prise her small arms from his leg, he pulled her up to his strong heavy chest.

"Is the doctor at the door Matthew? Better get yourself composed, don't want to be seen as a failure now do we? Chop chop, off you go." Eve sipped her tea, appreciating how kind it was of him to make it.

"What happened to you Eve?" Matthew had lost her, he had

235

failed. She was right. He felt like he was in a dream, he could see himself from up high but wasn't in his own body.

Matthew went to answer the door; the doctor may well have been the sixth member of the family.

"Hello Matthew, how are you today?"

"Bloody swell Doctor, like every other day in this fucking mad house." His voice was stern and hostile. Matthew turned his back and made his way to the kitchen and the doctor was left outside. He wiped his feet and closed the door. Looking into the dining room he saw Eve but decided to follow Matthew.

"How's things Matthew? Getting hard I can imagine?" The doctor stood with his hands in his pockets. He was wearing the same blue pinstripe suit that he wore every time he came to their house.

"That's it Doctor, I can't do it any more. You're going to have to take her. I'm not going to be able manage another moment with her, with that crazy person in my wife's body." Matthew was trying to make coffee with one hand as Ruth was still perched on his waist sobbing, clutching a pen lid in her small hand. Hearing Ruth crying again reassured Matthew that he was finally going to do the right thing.

"She will have to go into hospital Matthew, is that what you want?"

"Does it look like that's what I want? I haven't put us through this for her to end up in goddam hospital, but there is no other way is there? The professionals are going to have to do it. They will do a better job. I can't give her what they can. I have never been able to. I can only love her. I don't really know what's best." His voice began to sound croaky as the tears fell from his eyes once again. His hands were shaking as he poured the water into the cups, conscious of how near Ruth was to the hot steam and only half filling Eve's as she never liked it too hot. He always made the rest up with milk. It was always easier for her to digest her tablets that way.

"You have done a marvellous job; you and your children have made lots of sacrifices for her."

"Oh yeah, and how unfair is it? It's sheer madness Doctor. I'm an adult, at least I have the chance to make a decision. The only thing they know is sadness. I have to take them from here, from all the bad."

"The bad being Eve? If she's going to be taken to hospital there's no need for you to take your children anywhere."

"If it's a case of money, I will be earning more soon. I have another job lined up, I found it in the paper, and it pays loads more than the garage. I will pay for her to have the best in hospital! Can you arrange it to happen soon, Doctor? Can you take her today? I don't think I can share the same room with her." Matthew spoke in a panic, almost automatically. He was asking someone to take the woman he lived for away, and feared he might regret it when he calmed down.

"I think we should be able to make arrangements in such circumstances."

"Thank you Doctor." Matthew knew he had to do it, if only for a while. It meant there was going to be a chance to relax for more than ten minutes, not having to wait for the next slap. He also didn't have to see his perfect Eve so sad and alone. He couldn't imagine being without her, but couldn't be with her, his beautiful Eve.

"Oh, hello Eve." Dr Peters turned and acknowledged her presence at the kitchen door; she had heard everything yet again. She looked lost and like a small child. Vulnerable and alone. Matthew couldn't look at her, he dare not. She had always got him back this way, the guilt and responsibility for her would begin to overtake him.

"Where are you taking me? Can my father come too? He needs me to take care of him."

"Yes Eve, your father can come, only for a while if that's OK with you? You can come home soon, what do you think of that, eh?"

"But what about Matthew and the girls, can they come?"

"No Eve, they're going to stay here."

"OK, I'll go and get my things." Eve was almost whispering. Wondering how her family were going to take care of themselves, thinking before she left she must tell Matthew to read them a bedtime story, and to make sure he gave them a big kiss goodnight.

"That's it Matthew, she's coming with me today. It was all you had to say and I would have taken her."

"That was all Doctor, I simply had to ask you to take her and, hey presto, all would have been over. I couldn't let her go. I don't think I can now really. I'm her husband goddam it. I'm meant to look after her. I love her so much Doctor. I hope you can imagine how very much, because if you can then whoever you love is the luckiest woman alive. She is my life, what will I do without the other piece of my life? Will she be OK? Will she be looked after properly? Please Doctor, take care of my Eve." He cried so many tears his whole body was numb. Ruth was gently wiping the tears from his cheeks and kissing his wet face.

"Daddy, Daddy, cry Daddy."

"I'm OK my little Ruthi. We're going to be OK, Daddy promises." He managed a gentle smile.

"Matthew, you have done very well. You should be very proud of yourself. I'll let you know how she is when we get her settled."

Matthew felt comfort from the doctor as he touched his shoulder, a silent reassurance that Eve was going to be fine at the hospital.

Eve was waiting in the hall for her chaperone to take her and her father away. She was calm and unsure of what she was really doing. But she was willing to take her father to somewhere new; they would not be disturbed by anyone.

"Ready Eve?"

"Yes, bye Matthew, goodbye Ruthi, be a good little girl." Eve waved slowly, smiling softly at Matthew and Ruth. I love you very much, she thought.

The door slammed, rattling every bone in Matthew's body.

"Go and play, Ruthi. Daddy will be in soon." Matthew let Ruth run off to play. She could make as much mess and noise as she wished and finally be the child she had longed to be. Matthew put his head on the table and cried, for the woman he was in love with and for the chance to feel completely free.

"What do I do now girls? Where do I start?" He cried as though he was a very small child who had fallen over and hurt his knee. He wanted his mum to come and help him, he wanted someone to take him in their arms and say it was going be all right, that was all he had wanted for so long. He was left crying alone like always.

"Daddy, have fun?"

"Yes Ruth, I'm coming." Wiping his eyes on the tablecloth and taking an extremely deep breath, he glanced at the clock, realising it wasn't long before his beautiful daughters came out of school. In the meantime he had a castle to build.

47

They all sat around the large pine table, the chairs deliberately placed close to each other. The multicoloured light lit the kitchen with a wonderful glow. With all the colours together it had a rainbow effect across the ceiling. A tin of biscuits and three glasses of lemonade were in the middle of the table, to be devoured at any moment. Their father's preferred radio station echoed softly in the background, each sister listening out for her favourite tune, wanting to turn up the volume till the radio crackled. They never could on a Sunday, as their father was usually asleep on the sofa. They tried to persuade him it wasn't going to wake him, it was only the radio after all. He always shook his head and smiled as he made his way into the living room where he was going to nap.

"When are you going to call your new-found sex partner, Nat?" Glenn asked excitedly as she began to lick the chocolate from the biscuit.

"Put it like that Glenn and I don't think I'll bother. Why do you have to make everything so Glenn's world?" Natty shook her head, grabbing at two biscuits, having a feeling Glenn was going to eat them all; she always managed to eat more than anyone else.

"Glenn's world? I don't understand." Glenn shook her head, her mouth covered in chocolate.

"I mean revolting." Natty smiled at her messy sister.

"Have a day off, I'm only joking. Give him a ring will you? He won't hang on for ever."

"I wasn't asking him to." Natty spoke abruptly, knowing she was being defensive.

"Nat, what have you got to lose? Only a gorgeous yummy man."

"OK I will, give it another day. I don't want to seem like I'm desperate."

239

"Yes Natty, we know you are. That's the thing. Where the hell is the number? I can't take the anticipation for you any more." Glenn jumped up, rushing over to Natty's huge tartan bag.

"Get out of my bag! Anyone would think he gave you the number. Actually, forget it, I haven't got the time to see anyone, I have college and with everything going on, it isn't the time." Natty pulled her bag from Glenn by the straps.

"Nat, your favourite song's on, do you think Dad would mind?" Ruth went to turn up the radio slightly.

"YES!" Glenn and Natty spoke together, turning quickly to Ruth.

"OK calm down will you, anyone would think I'm jumping off a cliff." Ruth sat back down, taking her lemonade.

"Will you stop talking shit? Just ring the man will you? For the love of God Natty, call him." Glenn's patience was wearing thin, as she blew her cheeks in and out.

"Oh, for heaven's sake, whatever makes you happy. I'd better get the number." Natty instantly felt nervous.

"What? You haven't got it printed on your best knickers?"

"Not very funny are you?" Natty ignored Glenn's jokes and went to retrieve the number. Deep down she had longed to call, but she had been too afraid of making a fool of herself. Natty wondered if it was possible he thought she was prettier than she actually was, and when they met he would want to walk past her. It was bound to end in disaster, surely, and she was always so good at putting her foot in it. Never having been on a date or even kissed a young man, it seemed that fear stirred in her, as she stood and opened the serviette.

"Nat, have you found it?" Glenn stood holding the phone wiggling her toes in her shoes, desperate for her far-too-relaxed sister to return and set the wheels in motion.

"Shh! Dad's asleep. Will you give me the phone please? Right, here goes." Natty's legs were shaking, she felt like she wanted to throw up. It was madness, she was only ringing a boy.

"Oh hello, is Ben there please?" Natty spoke really quickly, almost in a panic.

"Who shall I say is calling?" The voice on the phone sounded strong.

240

"Oh, it's Natty." Inside she wanted to say "the skinny ugly girl with the messy hair". Covering the phone with her hand Natty let out a huge sigh of relief – she was finally in reach of the lovely guy. Her legs began shaking erratically; she was finding it impossible to control her nerves.

"Hello, I'm really sorry, he can't come to the phone at the moment. If you leave your number he will ring you back, he's in the shower. I'm sure he won't be long."

"Oh OK, thanks." Relaying her number to the stranger, being ignored seemed most realistic. The thought of him in the shower made her blush.

"So come on, what happened then, did you speak to him?" Glenn was nearly sitting on Natty's shoulder, trying to speak quietly.

"He's in the shower; he's going to ring back when he's finished." Natty let out a huge sigh, feeling slightly deflated.

"Yummy, can you imagine such a thing?" Glenn fluttered her eyelashes, looking up at the ceiling.

"I know he's not going to call, why did I ring? I've gone and made a complete knobhead of myself. See? I look flaming desperate; it's flipping a waste of time. Oh shit! Why did I have to call? Mother would have never made such a mess of it."

"Calm down will you? You'll wake Dad. Anyway there's no reason why he shouldn't call, it's his loss if he doesn't." Glenn rubbed Natty's arm.

"Thanks Glenn! Do you know it's probably one of the nicest things you have said in a long time." Natty spoke in shock, feeling a sudden comfort from her sister's compassion.

"No, you dimwit; I meant he won't get a chance to meet fabulous me." Glenn fluttered her eyelashes at Natty.

"Oh, I thought it was too good to be true." Natty stood by the phone table close to Glenn, fearful of moving. If the phone rang it might wake their father. Natty couldn't believe her sense of timing.

"What are you two still doing out here?" Ruth walked quietly into the hall, tapping her hands on her hips as her favourite song had just been played. She was still moving to the rhythm.

"Natty's gorgeous fella is in the shower."

"Sorry?" Ruth came to a standing position.

"Don't worry Ruth; Glenn's being her usual self. Just put the kettle on could you?"

"You put the kettle on." Ruth folded her arms in dispute.

"Yeah Ruth, your big sisters are busy. Two sugars."

"No, do it yourself Glenn, I'm busy."

"Busy doing what, being nosey?" Glenn leaned forward, nearly touching Ruth's nose with hers.

"Will you both shut up? Glenn don't be out of order." Natty touched the numbers softly, pretending to make the call again.

The beginning of an argument brewing was disturbed by the ringing of the phone; it seemed to be the loudest ring they had ever heard. It filled every space. All they could picture was their father rushing out into the hall and being cross.

"Quick! Get the phone, it's him." Frantically Natty and Glenn reached for the phone.

"Can I listen?" Ruth walked forward.

"I thought you were busy." Glenn gave her a smirk.

"Oh, bugger off Glenn." Ruth smirked back.

"Hello."

"Hi, is that Natty?" The stranger's voice sounded gentle.

"Speaking." Natty wanted to burst into laughter. Of course it was her speaking, if only he could have seen her hovering over the phone like a wild animal ready to pounce.

"I'm glad to hear from you, sorry about earlier, going off to work soon."

"Oh, oh that's fine, I was busy anyway. Was going to go out in a minute, too, it's lucky you caught me." Natty smiled at Glenn and Ruth trying to tell them to go away, by only moving her lips, moving her head slightly, looking almost cocky. Not believing how cool she sounded. They both stood laughing hysterically at their sister. Knowing they had to be quiet made it harder; Ruth had her legs crossed in case she wet herself.

"I'm a fireman. I know, before you say it I don't look like one."

"Well, what are they meant to look like?" Natty couldn't believe what she had said – she didn't feel so great any more.

"Not like me, they've usually got a few muscles. Anyway enough about my physique; what are you up to Monday week? I have the evening free if you would like to grab something to eat."

242

"That sounds really nice. Shall I meet you in the coffee bar?" Natty was full of excitement. She couldn't wait to get off the phone and wind Glenn up about it.

"I'll come and pick you up if you like."

"Um, coffee bar sounds OK. What time?" She dreaded the thought of him knocking on the front door. What would their father say?

"Seven to seven thirty."

"Great, see you then."

"See ya then."

Natty placed the phone down in disbelief. She wanted to burst, her body filled with adrenaline.

"Have a date Monday." All three sisters began to jump up and down in the hall, grabbing at each other, trying not to laugh too loud.

"Guess what he does, he's a fireman."

"Doesn't look like one." Glenn continued to jump up and down.

"I'll make that cuppa." Ruth went back into the kitchen, rubbing her hands together.

As they sat round the kitchen table they seemed exhausted after all the jumping up and down and the energy which had been pumping through them. They drank their warm lemonade while the kettle was boiling. Glenn finished off the chocolate biscuits. They even forgot to listen for their favourite songs through all the giggling and chatting.

"I don't know what to wear, I haven't got anything." Natty put her hand over her mouth, thinking she actually might have to do some shopping for real.

"You can go and get something which covers your face quite easily, shouldn't be a problem. What do you think, Ruthi?" Glenn banged on the table, enthralled with her joke, laughing until her stomach ached.

"I think you're being a knobhead Glenn." Natty raised her eyebrows, feeling full of worry, her mind on the clothes she had hanging in her small wardrobe. She became anxious about having to begin the whole dating thing.

"Knob, oh yeah, Natty's going to see his knob or shall I say hose." Glenn banged on the table once more, laughing harder than before. Licking her finger and reaching for the crumbs on the plate.

"Ruth, what did we do to deserve such a sister,? Maybe it's something we did in a previous life, which we are going to be eternally punished for."

"Come to think of it Natty, I think we probably did." Ruth got up from the table to make the tea.

"Stick it up your bum, you two, just kidding. Actually stick it up your bum, Nat remember that." Glenn had laughed so hard she felt as though her ribs were going to break.

"See what I mean? Eternally punished." Natty looked over at Ruth, full of anticipation, how could she wait for such a long time with the worry she was feeling? It was guaranteed she was going to have diarrhoea come on or the biggest spot ever appear.

Glenn continued to laugh, completely oblivious that no one was laughing with her any more.

"Shall we go and see Mother? Ruth, what do you think?" Natty's voice lifted.

"Yes Natty, I think it would be a really great idea." Ruth wanted to see Glenn's face while they were on a wind-up.

Glenn's laughter came to a sudden halt. She was now looking at her sisters in the same disbelief they were earlier.

"Are you serious Natty? You really want to go and see her? We're having so much fun." Glenn became deflated.

"No Glenn, I wanted to see your reaction. I think we should make the effort – we haven't been since before my birthday and it was months ago."

"She couldn't even come to see you for your dinner. I really thought she would, she let us all down, even Dad." Glenn wasn't in the mood for laughing any more.

"Come on Glenn, Ruth, let's go. Why wait?" Jumping up from her chair Natty was hoping her sisters would show the same enthusiasm. Ruth left the tea bags brewing in the hot water as she went to get her shoes and coat. Glenn slowly made her way from her chair. Huffing and puffing but making her way to the coat hook all the same.

Natty took a piece of paper from the kitchen cabinet and left a note for their sleepy father. "Dad, gone for a walk, love girls. Xxx"

*

244

They all stood outside her front door, quickly glancing at each other, sending each other silent messages of reassurance. Natty took a huge breath and knocked on the door. The paint was beginning to chip and the brass knocker had tarnished.

"Hello Mother, it's us." Natty felt sick like she had earlier in the hall.

"Hello girls." Their mother smiled at them, she was clean and her hair was styled. There was no sign of Coco the clown anywhere. "I'm so glad you all have come. I would like to apologise, Natty, for your birthday, and I really hope I didn't ruin your dinner." Their mother smiled.

"No Mother, you didn't." Stupid woman, of course you ruined it, she thought, sighing.

"More like her life," Glenn muttered under her breath.

Their mother led the way into the dining room. They wouldn't feel as comfortable in there. The kitchen was closer to the front door. They felt unsure as they were taken too far into the house. Ruth kept looking at the front door, as if she was never going to find the escape route again. They slumped on the chairs and looked around for a moment. It seemed cleaner than their last visit. Their mother brought in some cool orange juice.

"Here's a drink, one for each of you." I hope they like it, the oranges were freshly squeezed this morning, she thought, happy that her girls were there.

"Helps." Glenn was lucky yet again that she was not heard.

"I'm glad you have come, I was thinking about having a chat with you all soon, and now you're here I may as well get it out of the way. That's if your father hasn't told you. Maybe he has, never mind, you see he was always the one who organised things. He always made sure things were done properly." She realised how much she missed him. Wondering what it would be like if she was to kiss him now. Looking at her girls she was amazed to see how much they had grown up. They were extremely pretty; that must be something their father had given them. Eve didn't think she was pretty at all. A sense of pride rushed through her. As she looked at Natty she frowned, wondering why she had agreed to a name she didn't like. She hoped Glenn would grow her hair long like her sisters, it irritated her the way her daughter was the prettiest by far

245

but didn't care about her appearance. It simply wasn't good enough. Their mother sat on the sofa, holding a cup of lukewarm tea.

Not having seen her for such a long time, they really didn't know where to start. How were they going to begin any conversation? They sat listening to the ticking of the clock and looking at the three untouched glasses of orange juice on the tray.

No one said a word. Their mother kept moving her hair from her face, and brushing the front of her trousers with her hands. She kept sighing and tutting over and over again.

"Mother, what's wrong?" Natty reached for her drink.

"Oh, nothing dear. I'm sure your father has already spoken to you about Ruth, so I will leave it in his capable hands." Their mother looked at Natty's pink nail varnish and smiled, and then quickly checked her own. She could have painted them properly that morning, she could have been a better example.

"What about Ruth?" Natty moved her body forward. Glenn and Ruth both sat up straight, Ruth especially – she was almost standing.

"You know – Ruth, how things are with her. You know how she is different to you and Glenn."

"Mother, you're not making it very clear. What do you mean, why is Ruth different?" Natty frowned, feeling nervous for her sister.

"Please don't worry yourselves, any of you. How have you all been, would you like some more orange juice? I could easily squeeze some more." She spoke gently, not understanding why her girls suddenly seemed on edge.

"No thank you, Mother, I think it's time we went. We were only going to stay for a drink and to see if you were OK. Dad's home and we really should be there." Natty's voice became harsh, knowing their mother was obviously OK and she was leaving them all confused as usual. Natty stood and was instantly followed in her actions by her sisters.

They all rushed outside and stood at the front door, breathing heavily, staring at each other with uncertainty.

"What the hell was that about? Ruth, are you OK?" Glenn tapped her sister on her arm.

"NO I'M NOT BLOODLY WELL OK!" Ruth looked like she

246

was going to burst into tears as she kicked the plant pots over, the dried earth covering the porch.

"Ruth, calm down, Mother's on one of her mad moments." Natty began to walk back down the steps.

"Nat, she didn't say you were different did she? She said I was, for Christ's sake we have to get home and see Dad. What do you think she meant? Glenn, what do you think she meant?" Ruth questioned her sisters in desperation.

"I think she meant you were knitted at birth." Glenn smiled.

"This really isn't the time, OK? Ruth's upset."

"I'm only trying to cheer her up, that's all. I wouldn't hurt her."

"Please you two, what do you think she meant?"

"We really don't know, you shouldn't take too much notice of her, remember she has said some strange things in the past. We haven't seen her for quite a while and yet again she is ready to turn us all upside down. Let's go home, but you can't say anything to Dad – we're not even meant to be here." Natty wasn't sure what to say, she rubbed her sister's back, hoping she would not tell their father of their visit. Her mind was making up all sorts of stories. What did their mother mean? Why did she pick on Ruth?

Glenn and Natty were fixed on each other, wondering if they were thinking the same.

Ruth began walking in front, her head down. She couldn't wait to get home. It had been a stupid idea in the first place, they should let things be. Ruth was mad at herself for agreeing to go again.

"Glenn, hurry up will you? What do you think's really going on? Why would Mother say Ruth is different from us?" Deciding to walk quickly to catch her up, Natty felt fearful Ruth was going to reach home before them.

"Glenn will you hurry up? She's going to see Dad before we do."

"Stop panicking, she won't say anything, and if she does it may not be a bad thing. I've had enough of the stupid secret anyway, makes you feel shit after a while."

"I was only thinking about how Dad would feel, that's all, and of how much crap we're going to be in. Catch her will you?" They ran together to meet their smaller sister, she needed them now

247

anyway. They all had to walk into their father's house together whatever happened.

"Dad!" Ruth dashed in and out of each room.

"Oh shit, she's going to tell him. Will you grab her Nat?"

"Changed your tune all of a sudden, young Glenn." Natty was full of sarcasm.

"Ruth, come here will you and calm down, Dad's obviously not here." Natty held her sister by her arms, gently she pulled her to her chest and held her tight.

"He is here, I know he is, I can hear him, I think he's in the bathroom. I'm going to have to ask him as soon as he comes out. What Mother said about being different – I know it's mad but for some crazy reason I have felt that way and now she has simply added to it. I have to ask him Nat, please don't stop me." Ruth's body was shaking on Natty's chest.

"Listen, I understand what you're saying, but how do you think he will feel if he knows we have been seeing her behind his back? It's really going to hurt him. Ruth, you don't want that do you?" Natty's heart was beating hard, she knew it was wrong of her to request such a thing. Ruth had a right to feel and ask exactly what she wanted, and of whom she wanted. But the thought of their father having any more heartache was far too much for her to bear.

"This isn't about hurting our dad; this is about me, little thirteen-year-old me. So if you wouldn't mind I have to see Dad, are you coming with me or not?"

"Ruth stop being so bitchy, it's not Nat's fault." Glenn stormed forward to stand next to Natty.

"What's all the commotion about; I will be down in a minute!" Their father's voice echoed from the top of the stairs.

"Sorry Nat, sorry to you too Glenn. Are you going to stay with me?"

Her elder sisters looked at each other; they both let out a huge sigh, they were all going to be in the biggest trouble and they knew it.

Their father came slowly down the stairs, his hair still damp from his bath. His aftershave surrounded them. It was always his favourite. It was lovely – the girls would close their eyes and take in the fragrance. It would always be the smell which would remind them of him if they smelt it in a supermarket or on the bus. They would look at each other and smile.

"Hello girls, how was your walk?" He greeted them all with a kiss.

"Dad!" Ruth stared at him longer than necessary.

"Ruth, have you been crying? What's the matter?"

There was a long pause. Looking at each of her sisters, Ruth's eyes filled with tears.

"I'm sorry you two. Dad, I have to talk to you." Her tears fell slowly down her cheeks.

"What is it?"

"Dad, I need to talk to you."

"Yes, Ruth, you have already said. What is it?" Their father waited in anticipation for her to begin. Natty and Glenn's stomachs were turning. The thought of her new fireman friend had gone completely out of Natty's mind.

"Dad ..."

"Yes Ruth?"

"Why am I different to Natty and Glenn?" Ruth waited for their father to answer, watching him standing as if almost frozen.

"I'm sorry, what do you mean?" Their father made his way to the sofa. How could this be? Why would she ask such a thing? It was all going fine, everything seemed to be going fine. Damn it. Thoughts rushed through him in seconds, his head becoming instantly full.

"Mother said you know why I'm different from Natty and Glenn, why is she saying that? What did she mean?" Ruth's tears had stopped falling. She became full of wonder. There was no going back now; their father would have to speak to her.

Their father looked up from the sofa and rubbed his eyes. They seemed to be full of sadness. He knew Ruth was going to hate him if he spoke honestly, he knew he was going to be hated by them all.

"Your mother said this did she? And how is it you seem to know what she has to say?" Their father felt a little angry.

"Mother was going to tell us. But then she said she was going to leave it to you, as you kind of have everything sorted. You know how organised you are?"

"I've got everything sorted, eh? Don't be silly Ruth, there isn't anything different about you, any of you. I don't really understand. And you still haven't told me how you know what your mother has to say, did you seen her out at the shops yesterday?"

There was a silence.

"We go to see her Dad, now and then, keep in touch a little." Natty stepped forward and spoke on her sisters' behalf. She could see Ruth's shoulders beginning to drop as their father's had already.

"YOU DO WHAT?" Their father leapt from the sofa, full of fury.

"Dad, it's OK you haven't got to get cross. She hasn't harmed us, we're bigger now, we can leave when we want and go to see her when we want." Natty stepped forward, reaching for Ruth's fingers. She finally got a hold of them. She held her hand tight.

"Oh well Natty, I am so very pleased for you that you feel so at ease with lying and going behind my back. I surely didn't think I brought up a bunch of liars!" He didn't want to make them upset, he couldn't bring himself to shout at them for too long. He began to lower his tone so they wouldn't be scared in his presence. What if they ran away, he thought? They were all he had.

"Dad, please hear us out, it's OK, we wouldn't lie to you, well not to hurt you anyway."

"So lying was to protect me? So you must have known it was wrong. I'm sorry girls but I can't listen to any more of this, filling your heads with mumbo jumbo."

"Dad, please listen, Ruth's really upset about today." Glenn stepped forward to be in line with her sisters. They all stood side by side ready to defend themselves, ready to help each other.

"Yes Glenn, I can see that." Their father suddenly burst into tears. He held his hair with both hands and rocked to and fro like a baby, his body slumping back on the sofa.

"Dad, please don't be sad, we didn't mean to hurt you, we are so sorry, we all are!" Natty ran forward and wrapped her arms around him. She held him so tight. Ruth and Glenn looked at each other, their tears beginning to fall. As usual they followed their elder sister.

They all cried together. Their father had always been the strength in their lives, now he was a broken man. He seemed overwhelmed with sorrow. They had never seen him like it before. He rarely showed them his weakness and never let them see how he was truly feeling inside. Ruth cried harder than ever before. She needed her prince to come and rescue her right at that very moment.

"Sorry Dad, I'm sorry I asked such a thing. I'm being silly, I know Mother is doing this to mess us all up, like she always has." Ruth's voice was soft between crying. She was frantically swallowing. She could barely breath.

Their father raised his head, allowing his girls to feel they could let him go. Allowing them to be the children once again. He composed himself as much as he could manage and looked at his smallest child, heartbroken. It was time.

"You weren't being silly, you were doing what one day I knew you would. I'm so sorry Ruth, but you are different, you don't belong to me. You are the most beautiful little girl but my brother has you really, you are his daughter, my brother Harry." Their father wanted to be sick. He held himself strong for them once more, pushing his shoulders back; he was the adult and he had to let them see it. They were always being so strong for him. By looking at them he had always managed to get through another day, from the moment they were all born.

"Dad, what are you saying? How can that be." Glenn wiped the tears from Ruth's eyes.

They all knelt in amazement, completely in shock. They didn't know whether to get up, or to find a seat to sit in, everything was a blur.

"Dad please, please tell me it isn't true. Oh God, please tell me I'm yours!" Ruth's pain erupted inside of her, her cries and pleas bellowed through the house.

Their father wanted to scream and cry with his child, but he couldn't allow her to see him. He owed it to her; in her eyes she had lost a father she had always adored and loved more than anything. He wasn't going to take away her right to be mad. He held her chin in his strong shaking hand and brought her closer to him, his voice reassuring.

"Ruth, you are mine, you have always been from the moment you were born. I have always loved you as I do your sisters. It wasn't meant to turn out like this. I promise you it wasn't your fault. You

251

are the most amazing, beautiful child anyone could ever be gifted with." His throat was hurting, trying to hold back his tears. He wanted to cry for her also.

"Turn out like this Dad? Are you saying Mother was with your brother? I can't believe it. Ruth, I am so sorry." Natty was still kneeling on the floor – her feet had gone numb and were beginning to hurt. She wanted to feel the pain. She couldn't keep her eyes from Ruth; her little sister who she loved so much. She feared Ruth might leave them, go away for ever. She used to wish Ruth was never born, purely for the fact that she was their father's favourite and she was always going to be much prettier and cleverer than both of them put together. Natty wondered if Glenn felt the same way.

"You don't have to be sorry Nat. I'm OK, truly I am." Ruth had slowly calmed herself down and as usual portrayed complete maturity.

"I know Ruth, you always are." Natty smiled at her vulnerable sister and thought how typical her behaviour was.

Their father felt as though his heart was being ripped out once again. Everything he had ever tried to be, everything he had tried to hide, was wasted in one moment. Ruth's eyes reminded him of all of the pain he had endured just to try and make it all OK, just simply OK.

He felt that his brother was almost looking back at him, laughing, finding the whole mess funny.

"Dad, what's going to happen? Please say it's all going to be OK. You're not going to let me go anywhere are you? Please let me stay with you, please." Ruth began to sob once again.

"Ruth, I am so sorry this has happened to you, all I have ever wanted to do is protect you from harm. I have never loved you any less. I am sorry my little Ruthi, truly I am. I will never let you go, ever." Their father realised she was part of them all. She wasn't his secret any more. He wished he had never tried to fight what he had always instinctively felt for her.

"If Mother hadn't said anything, you wouldn't have would you?" Ruth wiped her face with her hands, wiping the tears into her hair and making her fringe wet.

"I didn't think there was anything to say, why would I need to hurt my beautiful child so badly, for what reason? For whose reason?" Why did their mother want to cause them all to hurt so much? he wondered.

"Yeah, you're cool Ruth." Glenn smiled quickly at her distressed sister, and hastily looked back to the floor, feeling bad for all the times she had been mean. She wasn't sure what to say to her or how to be suddenly, so she simply kept smiling.

"Dad, please help us understand what happened, especially with Ruth's situation." Natty knew it was time they were all told the truth.

"Natty, Ruth doesn't have a situation; she is the same as she has always been."

"But I'm not really, am I Dad? I am not the same as the others. We can all pretend but it will never be the same again, not ever. Why did this have to happen? Why did I have to be the mess up of the whole family?" Her anguish had built up again and Ruth could barely speak through her tears.

"Ruth, my dear Ruth, you are the same, you must never think any differently ever."

The emotions and cries that echoed through the living room were intense.

"I don't know what to do. Please, I can't stand it; you all must have it wrong. Where is he then, this so-called father of mine? Why didn't he want me? If I'm so special as you say how come I have never seen him?" Ruth stood as her family remained seated. They all watched her in pain, crying with her.

"He's just not around, it has nothing to do with you and how special you are. It has been his misfortune he has never been a part of your life. Please don't hurt yourself any more. It was so very hard for you to live as you did with your mother. Please, could this be another thing you may one day be able to forgive me for?" Their father spoke to her softly; he felt nervous. What if he couldn't reassure her that everything was going to be OK? Maybe one day she would want to find her father and stay away from them all, then she would finally be taken from his grasp. His thoughts went back to Dr Peters who was going to take her away. Their mother must have wanted Ruth to be taken away from them all; she wouldn't have made her so sick if she hadn't. He had promised her he was going to keep her safe, but she didn't look as if she felt safe now,

253

as she stood above them all, crying with all the strength she had left in her young body.

"You left us there Dad, you left us to get hurt by her." Ruth looked at her elders, all of them just looking. Not one of them could tell her the answer to anything.

The reality had hit their father, the thing he had hidden away for so long. It always sat dormant in the pit of his stomach. He had learnt very quickly how to hold on to pain, but it was slowly releasing itself from his aching stomach. He knew full well he had left them in a helpless position. Each night as he closed his curtains he had known he was closing them out, they were alone at their mother's house, needing him to come and take them away from it all; they would be asking for him as they lay on their small beds alone and hurting. It had suffocated his mind every day.

"Natty, I question myself every second. If only I knew what I was thinking. There seemed to be so many things going on, some days I couldn't even think straight. We kind of make decisions in life which may or may not affect others. The decisions I made affected you all in ways I shall never be able to mend. It looks like I am leaving your own mending to you."

"We are sorry your life was such a mess, you did what you had to at the time. We all mess up sometimes." Glenn's voice was assertive. She knew she was talking crap as it was surely the goddam adult's responsibility to get it right.

"My life wasn't a mess, how could it have been when I had you beautiful, wonderful girls to keep me going? You all are the most precious angels anyone could ever hope or dream for. You were the ones who suffered; you all were the ones that kept my heart beating each day. I thank you all for being part of me, and I thank you for allowing me to explain myself. I ask for your forgiveness. Ruth I ask for your forgiveness, I have kept this from you for such a long time." Their father cried like Ruth had earlier. He couldn't look at them; the shame he had carried for so long consumed him.

"But how come Dad, it was always about you and our mother?" Glenn sounded stern, even though she was crying.

"Ease up Glenn!" Natty hit Glenn's knee.

"Its OK Natty, Glenn is right, it was about us for so long, I was so wrapped up in your mother at the beginning, I only wanted her to get better. There wasn't anything in this world that was going to stop me. You know I wish I could say something or show you somehow how to make it all go away from you, erase it from your lives, but I cannot. We do our best with what we have, and we didn't have a lot to work with. Most of the time we are just bigger versions of you, children in big shoes. We get it wrong sometimes. We don't have anyone there to correct us." He moved back into the position he was in earlier, rocking to and fro, pulling at his hair, wishing it had all never happened. How it could have been so very different for his children. Wondering why all their bad memories couldn't be washed away with the heavy rain outside, praying they could all diminish into the gutter, and once the rain stopped the warm sun would shine brighter than ever before on their beautiful innocent selves.

"Dad, I have always waited for a Prince Charming to come and take me away from this life. Each day it has kind of kept me going too. As young as I am I felt like I wanted to disappear some days simply because I felt so sad. I know now my Prince Charming is never going to come and rescue me, because he already has. You held me tight and took care of me. You didn't have to Dad; you could have left me alone. You're my prince Dad, you." Ruth knelt in front of her father. He looked up, his wet face leaning into hers. "I love you Dad, I'm glad I belong to you."

48

Matthew would smile to himself now and then, and it would end up with him chuckling – it had all been over a little pen. It seemed unreal, as he had been given the chance to start all over again. It would take him some time to absorb the situation as he wandered from room to room. His body ached, he knew he could finally relax but he simply didn't know how to. When Eve was home he was always fearful of leaving his girls with her for too long, even if he had to disappear for a moment to make coffee or a peanut butter sandwich. The feeling would often overwhelm him, the simplest of tasks would fill him with tears and a relief he hadn't felt for such a long time. He missed her more than he ever thought he would; he missed her smell. Trying to understand his thoughts, he knew it was her and not her behaviour which would make him want to call the hospital and get her home again, only so he could look at her, just so he could have her one more time. With all the things which consumed his day, he would manage at least two visits a week. His taking her girls to see her would always make her smile; she was getting better, she was taking control little by little. The doctors said that she had finally said goodbye to her father and would sit waiting for the days when she could pack her things and leave. Soon, he would tell her, she could leave with them soon. Sometimes it was the only way of getting her to let the girls leave again.

Matthew was beginning to struggle financially. He had made arrangements so that he could work from home, but being so busy he could only put in a couple of hours each day. He needed to get back to full time, he wanted to provide for his girls but it was just the way it was, as everything had been for years. Swallow and walk with your head high, his father had once told him. Matthew took some advice from him, as much as he hated the thought of it.

It had been the longest year. Putting some chocolate in a bag he went to find his girls. They sat close together on the sofa holding hands, watching the magical scenes on the television which enthralled them. There wasn't a movement to be seen.

"Girls, come on, we're going to see Mummy for a while."

Being quickly taken out of their trance, they all jumped off the sofa and went to find their shoes.

"Is Mummy coming home?"

"I am sure she will soon, my little Natty."

"Oh." Natty pulled on her little shoes and continued to help Ruth.

With a sigh Matthew left the safety of his home, all the girls holding onto him, looking up into the sky wondering where the next test was going to come from.

The drive to see Eve took a little over forty minutes and the girls sat comfortably listening to the music or reading from the choice of books permanently scattered on the floor of the car. It would bother him every time he got in, but he knew he was going to clean it soon so he tried to ignore the mess.

The girls happily ran in to see her, jumping from the car, their little hearts racing, full of excitement. Being small their bad memories of their mother before then were few.

Dodging the clusters of chairs and hurrying to find her, they saw their mother's new acquaintances mostly sitting quietly, although some weren't so, holding on to curtains, speaking out loud, praying someone, anyone, would hear them and reply. Each time Matthew went inside the haven of sadness he still felt calm and safe; he knew by looking around he hadn't been the only one dealing with such misfortune. He felt comfort when he would be acknowledged by other helpless husbands and wives, mothers and fathers; they all understood him without even having to pass a single word. They were all dealt the same cards, and they were now putting them in the correct order.

Eve sat alone, her bag upon her lap, her legs tight together as prim as could be. She looked so gentle and small. She had sat in the same position for the last four hours, knowing she had been

257

given permission to go home. Matthew was still to be informed of the news when he arrived.

The same rules applied: she was to stay on her medication, though the dosage had been cut somewhat. She wasn't to be left alone too long with the girls, which of course would continue to put pressure on Matthew. She had improved immensely, she was like a different woman. The thing was, Matthew didn't want her different; he just wanted his beautiful Eve to get better.

"Do you know why cold water disperses bubbles and hot water makes them get bigger?" Matthew's jacket was grabbed by a young man, no more than twenty.

He looked pale, and was alone. Matthew hadn't seen him there before. He was one of the new ones, and by the looks of it he was in for the long haul.

"Sorry mate, I have never thought about it." Matthew gently pulled his jacket from his grasp.

"Oh, OK, thanks anyway." The young man sat back again and thought hard.

"What is your name?" Matthew turned and leant down slightly.

"Lucas."

"Bye, Lucas, take care of yourself."

"Yeah."

Matthew walked towards Eve, the sense of protection overwhelming him as he felt the desperate need to spend more time with the young man. He wanted to help him, to let him know everything was going to be OK.

"Hello Matthew, I'm coming home today, I'm not staying here any more. Isn't it the most fabulous news? It's great!" The girls were all perched on her lap, balancing on any space possible.

"Girls, jump off Mummy's lap a minute, she needs to speak to me." Matthew bent over and kissed Eve on her small soft lips. He grabbed at a chair and moved it closer to his beautiful lady while holding on to her hand.

"Are you really coming home, Eve? How do you know?"

"I am Matthew, they said so this morning. Someone else was going to be in my room, they took my flowers out and everything. I don't know where they are now, I will have to get them, they are

258

so pretty. My mum always knows what flowers to buy. Make sure you find them Matthew, we can't leave them here it's not right, such pretty things in such a place."

"Eve, calm down, we will find them and you can take them home with you." He took a quick glance around; there were so many pretty things there, the most young and attractive people you could see in one place. Why had it all happened to them? Why such beautiful people?

"Lucas, your room is ready now." Two gentlemen in white coats approached the young man and he held their hands, fearful of letting go as if, should he get lost he would never be found again. Ironically he was the new person who would take up residence in Eve's room.

As he passed Matthew he gave a small smile.

"Do you know why cold water disperses bubbles while hot water makes them bigger?"

"No, we have no idea," the two gentlemen replied to the young man as they took him out of sight.

Eve sat quietly in the car; the music was on low, books still scattered on the floor.

Matthew had had to sit and discuss her progress for the last hour and all of the dos and don'ts. They felt she was well enough to leave, after Matthew had been given the third degree of course. He felt as though he was the one who had done something wrong and it was his fault she had had this happen to her. He was full of apprehension, full of excitement too. The girls held the flowers in the back; they looked as if they needed to go in the bin, but Eve insisted they were still in bloom and they were to go in front of the window once they reached home.

"Don't they look lovely there Matthew?"

"Yes Eve, I'll go and get some water for them, shall I?"

49

The atmosphere in their father's home had not been the same at all since the great secret wall had been knocked down. Their father would continuously ask Ruth if she was all right, her usual reply being "Of course I am." Deep down she wasn't, they all knew she was only acting and carrying on as before to make them all feel better, not wanting any of them to feel awkward because of her situation. It had the reverse effect on Natty and Glenn. They couldn't keep up treading on eggshells with her, and they wanted her to be honest with them, not treat them like strangers. They were sisters after all.

"For goodness' sake, why can't Ruth say she feels shit?" Natty sat on her bed, pulling the threads from the embroidered flowers which covered it. They all had brown duvets with cream flowers sprawled across every inch of the shiny material. Their father had bought them when they had moved in; they had never liked them. Three brown and cream beds with dark blue walls; it wasn't the most calming room or the prettiest, but with their little bits on the dressing table it was bearable. And it was their room. Their father never came in. If they had decided to hide all the good-looking boys from the school's football team under the bed, he would never have been any the wiser. Natty finally decided to get organised and began sorting her washing, trying to cram more in her drawer. Her drawer which couldn't possibly hold any more – already it looked like it was about to explode.

Glenn sat next to her clean clothes. She was always the last one to do anything.

"Nat, it's not happening, you're going to have to throw some bits out. Or give them to me; I could always help you sort out if you like?" Glenn touched her washing, wondering what items of Natty's

260

would look good with hers, knowing she had completely changed the subject from Ruth. She felt tired of talking about it.

"Glenn, I was thinking how worried I am. Ruth hasn't spoken to us about how she feels." Natty began to feel stressed. Pushing her clean washing in, she finally realised that what Glenn said was right; she threw a handful of clothes in the corner. And let out a scream.

"Natty, they're only clothes, give them over here."

"Stupid drawers!" Natty became flustered, knocking over the lamp.

"Natty, will you be careful. You'd better not have broken it!" Glenn was dreading the thought of not having the light on when she slept. It quickly brought back a memory of when she was very small. She was so hungry because their mother hadn't fed them. She had crept into the kitchen and tried to make something to eat, pulling one of the heavy wooden chairs across so she could climb upon it to reach the work surface. She was in the dark the whole time, having to find her way back to her room, her bread and jam squelching through her tiny fingers. Everyone was asleep, she was all on her own. She sat in her bed under the covers eating her sticky bread and licking her strawberry-flavoured hands. Her room was full of the dark shadows, but she was too hungry. She had been scared of the dark from the moment she had finished eating her rations. The fear overwhelmed her as she couldn't move from under her covers all night.

Ruth had put her washing away and finished all her chores earlier. She had taken it upon herself to take a stroll down to the supermarket get some more cake ingredients. Now there were eggs and flour everywhere, as Ruth loved making cakes. She'd made chocolate, jam and coconut. The next task was to bake some butterfly cakes. It kept her busy and she seemed to like being on her own. Natty and Glenn would always look out of the window as she left, simply to make sure she wasn't going in the direction of their mother's. They had not visited since the day Ruth became somebody else's daughter. She was back in no time at all.

The smells coming from Ruth's baking were giving Glenn and Natty an appetite. After tidying their room and managing to find a place for all the clothing they made their way down to the kitchen, rubbing their bellies and licking their lips.

"Will you let them cool down at least? I have to cut the tops off, put buttercream in and make little wings." Ruth sighed and gave Glenn a dirty look.

"Ruth, as if you have the patience for biddy little wings." Glenn tried to grab one while Ruth was still staring at her. She gained a slap to her hand.

"I have more than you Glenn, I know for sure."

"Let's lick the bowl then?" Glenn was chasing Ruth like her shadow, trying to stick her fingers in the bowl.

"Will you get out of here Glenn?" Ruth tried not to laugh.

"Sorry Ruth, I don't mean to hassle you. If only I could have a little taster. Anyway, you have made enough to feed the neighbourhood."

"I'm going to take some to Mother. I thought she would like some." Mixing frantically, Ruth waited for her sister's disapproval.

"Cool, she likes coconut." Natty spoke with a mouthful of cake, she also liked coconut and was happy they had another excuse to visit.

"Coconut! Are you mad? You're the nut. Natty she's the nut, you're all nuts." As much as Glenn wished she had her sister's enthusiasm she couldn't hold on to any feeling for longer than the length of a visit. She wanted to bond, she wanted to try and forgive the whole mess-up of her childhood, and stop blaming their mother for the way she felt. She would often lie in bed at night and say over and over again to herself "Tomorrow will be different, tomorrow I will stop blaming her." But tomorrow would always come and she would still feel the same. The fact was, Ruth was not even their father's and she still managed to deal with her childhood much better. Wanting to take her some home-made cakes, especially coconut ones, was surely incredible.

"In the reality of things Glenn, I don't think a few cakes are going to matter or change anything." Natty sneaked another cake from the plastic tub, and shoved it quickly into her mouth.

"Natty I know, it is never going to change and we could shit gold and it wouldn't change, I just think what happened to Ruth is kind of the icing on the cake. Pardon the pun and everything." Glenn looked at Natty standing with her mouth full. They were all mad like Mother. Let them all sit around eating cake pretending everything was all

262

right, hope they all fucking choke on them she thought, as she tapped her foot on the lino.

"What's happened to me Glenn? Grown six heads have I? Bloody hell I'm still the same, I wish you could forget about it." Ruth put more cakes into the oven. She wanted to burst into tears, she wanted to open the front door at that very moment and run until her legs were unable to move any more, away from the truth, from the feeling of not belonging.

"Look you two, I didn't mean it like it sounded, I was trying to say how everyone is acting like nothing's happened or been said. You're all OK with it." Glenn's head felt like it was going to burst, she felt like she was going mad too.

"Christ Glenn! You're the one who said keep stum about everything, not to upset Ruth and you're putting it up on billboards." Natty raised her voice and also her eyebrows.

"Excuse me you two, I'm still here you know, I haven't disappeared. At least have the decency to go into another room and discuss the fact I don't have Dad the way you both do." Ruth was becoming upset, wrapping the oven gloves around her arm again and again and feeling unsettled.

"Ruth, we're sorry we can't understand how you must feel because you haven't said anything." Natty hoped she would finally open up. She wanted to help her, but unless Ruth accepted it Natty felt useless.

"Maybe there is nothing to say, but then even if there was, why should I have to talk about it just so you can both feel better? Natty I really thought you would understand." Ruth put the washing-up in the bubbles and began to swirl the cloth in the bowl, the sleeve of her checked blouse getting wet.

"You are really grown-up Ruth, really mature for your age." Natty smiled with sheer pride.

"I obviously get it from my father." Ruth turned around and smiled at her sisters.

They all began to laugh. Ruth dried her hands and picked up a plate of coconut cakes and handed them out.

"Cakes, Ruth, you will want to live with her next." Glenn spoke with a mouthful of warm sponge.

The laughter came to a sudden halt.

263

"I was kidding, don't look so serious." Glenn grabbed at another cake.

She was beginning to feel sick. But one more should be all right.

"Actually, thinking about it, we are old enough to go and live with her if we want to, aren't we? It might be what's needed." Natty's mouth was open as she was deep in thought; a sudden determination rushed through her.

"What's needed Nat? Have you gone completely round the twist? Amazing, just fucking, piss bollocks amazing, completely unbelievable." Glenn thought she was in a nightmare. Surely they were pulling her leg? They were playing a joke on her.

"Eat another cake Glenn, as mad as it does sound Natty does have a point." Ruth smiled at Natty, as she imagined the scenario. Imagining as if their mother behaved as her friends' mums did.

"I haven't heard you two crazy people correctly have I? You both want to leave Dad and go and have some more psycho fun? How could you even think of it? Dad's done everything for us. She's mad, you two. What the hell, give me strength! Why don't you really become heartless bitches and inform Dad of your superb idea while he's eating his Sunday roast, he might even choke on his frigging Yorkshire pudding. Stop bloody laughing at me. You both make me sick!" Glenn paced up and down the messy kitchen, hitting herself on her head, holding on to her short hair. She wanted to do something crazy. Throw the cakes up into the air or something. Her body was shaking in anger inside, feeling as though it was screaming at them.

"Glenn, you are funny when you're mad." Ruth watched her frantic sister, hoping she could calm her down with her sarcastic comment.

"Funny, you are so funny, the both of you. Ruth's making cakes for the starving world and you're sitting there Natty, waiting to pack your suitcase, with too many clothes may I add, and leave Dad. I can't believe it! Look! If there was a chance a little magical, really magical fairy with all the powers of all the other fairies with pretty little wings was to fly past and sprinkle a miraculous magic dust over Mother and she were to be totally obliterated, I would have no problem going back to live in our superb house, but while she is there it's a *no, no, no, no!*"

264

"Have you finished, Glenn?" Natty went to make some tea.

"No, no, no!" Glenn was still pacing up and down.

"You're going to put a hole in the lino in a minute if you don't stand still. Cuppa, dear?" Natty tried not to laugh at her lunatic of a sister.

"I'm going upstairs. Bunch of fucking crackpots." Quickly pinching another cake Glenn stamped her feet as she made her way up to their tidy bedroom.

The kitchen instantly became quieter. Natty continued making tea and Ruth stood back and finally realised she had probably made far too many cakes. Shrugging her shoulders she went to wash up again, the draining board was full of cutlery and bowls. She would never be able to add another thing without the whole lot crashing down onto the worn-out lino.

"Nat, were you serious about, you know us going to live with Mother?" Ruth moved the bubbles over her hands as she dipped them in and out of the water. She quickly caught a cup which fell back into the water from the wobbly stack of tins and glass, wondering what her sister's answer was really going to be.

"No, don't be daft. What, did you think I was being serious?" Natty stopped putting sugar in the tea and looked at Ruth. She began to ponder.

"I thought you were, got a little worried for a moment." Ruth balanced bubbles on the back of her hands. She blew them into the air, and watched as they fell onto the side.

"You don't really think it could work do you?" Natty was inquisitive.

"I'm ..."

"Ruth, do you think it could work?" Natty went and stood next to Ruth who was still blowing bubbles into the air.

"Why are you asking me? After all I'm the youngest and I'm not even Dad's." Ruth blew a bubble into Natty's face.

"Stop being a tit. What shall we do? Do you know, you have really got me thinking now, do you think I should go and ask Glenn, you know, to see what she thinks about it?"

"You're missing a huge factor here Nat, she thinks you meant it, so the ice has kind of already been broken."

"Look, I am nineteen, surely I can make my own mind up where I live, don't you think?"

265

"Just bail out on us all? Is that what you mean?"

"No Ruth, you're still being a tit. I mean living with Mother was the hardest thing sometimes, but now we know the problem we maybe could deal with it better. You know, understand why Mother behaves as she does." Natty knew she was sounding irrational, because it still happened. Did it really matter if you understood why someone smacked you in the mouth or not?

"So if she hurts us again, you know starts hitting us and making us clean all the time? I don't think I could ever take it again. Not ever. We're safe here, and she said the thing about Dad to me to mess it all up." Ruth stopped playing in the sink and began to feel nervous.

"She wasn't trying to hurt you when she gave you a little glimpse of the truth. I think she wanted to finally release herself from it. As much as it hurt you, it released you also, if you know what I mean."

"Oh thanks." Ruth thought Natty's comment was ridiculous.

"Ruth, you're fourteen, you're not silly, you are the cutest and brainiest out of all of us. It's your mad arse of a sister who doesn't seem to know what's going on."

"Old cow," Glenn said softly as she sat at the top of the stairs, listening.

"Look Nat, I kind of get what you're saying, if we live there again, it will be OK because we are really close to Dad now too. And we could be one big happy family. Maybe even have a Christmas dinner and all the normal stuff. I just don't know how you begin to make it happen. Don't forget we can't do it without Mother and Dad."

"Stop washing up for a minute Ruth and listen. We've been doing it without them for years in a funny kind of way. I'm not saying Dad hasn't looked after us, and given us a safe haven, before you throw one of your cakes at me. I'm saying we have gone along with how they have done things for such a long time. Why can't they go along with how we want things for a while?"

"I think you have got a point Nat," Glenn said as she came down the stairs, stomping her feet on each step again.

"Listening were you Glenn?" Natty pushed her tea towards her on the table.

266

"Too bloody right Nat. I actually think you have a point, why not see if we can sort it out, put all our hurt away in the cupboards, and like Ruth says all have Christmas dinner together. Maybe if we are good Mother might even read us a bedtime story, and when its finished hit us over the head with the book." Glenn began pacing the floor again. There was only a certain amount of punishment any lino could take.

"Look, we don't need you to be silly about it Glenn; I was speaking seriously to Ruth."

"Oh sorry, I didn't think it mattered what I said, considering I'm a mad arse." Glenn wanted to go and squeeze Natty's head. She was feeling angry again and close to tears.

"Look Glenn, I know it's hard for you, and I'm sorry, but why not? Why can't we all just give it a go, and see what happens? You never know."

There was finally silence, each sister not saying a word. They all stood taking quick glimpses at each other, wondering if it was going to be a yes or a no.

"OK I'm in. After all she has put us through I will be a glutton for punishment and have a go, as long as Dad doesn't think it's because of him, and we aren't thankful and we love him still." Glenn waited for her sister's decision.

"Well if Glenn is prepared to give it a go, then so am. I" Ruth looked directly at Natty, feeling sick.

"OK dear sisters, for whatever reason I'm in also." What on earth were they thinking, she thought?

"OK, OK, OK." Glenn began her chanting and pacing up and down. Her body began to shake with nerves.

"GLENN WILL YOU STOP MOVING!"

"Sorry Ruth, only trying to figure out how to tell Dad, oh shit how do we tell Dad? Shit, shit, shit."

"I could always give him one of my cakes first." Ruth gave a nervous smile.

"Don't worry, I will tell him." Natty placed her cup in the sink, feeling like the big sister again.

"Tell who what?" Their father's voice echoed through the hall as he came in the front door.

50

"It's been so lovely being home again with you all, Matthew, thank you. Dinner smells nice, what are we having?" Eve sat at the kitchen table with Natty, Glenn and Ruth, while Matthew stood at the oven adding vegetables to the saucepan to mix with the chicken. He was making chicken soup for them all. It was full of goodness. He was hoping they would all enjoy it as much as he always did as a boy.

"What are we having Matthew? You didn't say." Eve wrapped her soft grey dressing gown around her, as she smiled at him; it was so kind of him to take care of her like this. He really didn't have to. She wished he would go out for longer than half an hour, then she could surprise him with his favourite meal. She remembered how much he loved chicken soup with big slices of crusty bread.

"We're having chicken soup, Eve." Matthew placed the lid on top so the delicious mixture could simmer. He turned and looked at his Eve sitting with their beautiful girls. He couldn't believe how happy she looked.

"Chicken soup." Eve spoke aloud. That's what I will cook him, she thought. As long as he doesn't spread too much butter on his bread like before. Eve's mind was full of all the wonderful things she was going to do for them all. She simply couldn't wait.

"Are you OK Eve?" Matthew stood behind her, wanting to kiss her on her glossy black hair. If only he could touch her; what if she was waiting for him to? The unbearable thought that she might not want him any more overwhelmed him every day. He found it sexy, how she never got dressed but always tied her hair back and put on her perfume. It made his thoughts go off track as excitement rushed through him.

"I am, Matthew. Time has gone so quickly. I miss my little room sometimes – it was so easy to keep tidy, not like this large place. We have always had far too much space here. We simply don't need it." Eve spoke softly. She could barely be heard over the chatting and laughing of the girls, as they sat near her, painting pictures.

"That's a lovely sunshine Natty, a big bright yellow sunshine, how lovely. Can I keep it after you have finished?" Eve touched Natty on the head, hoping she would grow up to be pretty like her sisters.

Natty looked up from her masterpiece and smiled.

"What are you drawing, Glenn?"

"A seaside." Glenn looked up to absorb the attention.

"Very nice, what about you Ruth?" Eve completely discarded what Glenn had to say – she didn't even look at her picture. It annoyed her constantly the way Matthew had her hair cut so short. There was no need for it, especially as she was a pretty thing; she was prettier than Natty by far. It irritated her, why her daughter wanted to ruin her looks.

Ruth had drawn the biggest castle, surrounded by red roses, it was wonderful for someone so small. Her imagination was far beyond her age, she was only three. She would draw the same picture each time, and try to fold them all up neatly and keep them in her drawer in her bedroom.

Matthew stood in the doorway, watching his family together. He couldn't believe she was so calm and was slowly building a bond with them all, like she surely hadn't for such a long time, if ever.

"I'm going to have a shower before dinner, Eve. Are you going to have some?"

"No thank you Matthew, I'm not feeling very hungry."

Matthew sighed – she never was hungry. He couldn't work out why he even bothered to ask her, some days she wouldn't even drink. He was concerned that she could become sick, she was already so small and slim, she would waste away if he didn't manage to get something into her soon. Every day Matthew would make small snacks and place them on the table next to her, but when he went back the food had only been rearranged on the plate. He wasn't going to give up, not with something as simple as that.

*

269

Matthew would worry constantly about the bills; if he could work full time then they would be sorted, his wages were really great if he put the hours in, even though working in accounts didn't really match the freedom of the old family business. He would sometimes call Dr Peters to let him know how things were going, but mainly to make sure he was doing a good job. He needed someone to tell him how well he was doing. He wouldn't leave her for too long, but sometimes he managed to get to the supermarket and back while the girls stayed with her. When he arrived home everything seemed to be how he left it. He enjoyed walking slowly around their garden picking ripened apples and giving them to the girls to hold. They placed them in the front of their floral dresses, holding the front up so they didn't drop any. When they got back into the kitchen they would let the tight grip on their dresses go and the apples would roll around the floor.

Sometimes as he stood among the apple trees he wondered to himself how the young man was getting on, hoping he wasn't lonely. After their brief encounter, the bubble question would often come to his mind.

A few days had passed since Eve hadn't wanted the chicken soup. She decided to sit in the dining room while they all ate, looking at the picture Natty had painted. Now as Matthew stood in the garden his thoughts were disturbed by Eve touching him gently on his shoulder.

"Hello Matthew, are you happy?" Eve's face had a healthy glow; her eyes had a twinkle in them, her voice was full of excitement.

Matthew looked at her. She was the young woman he had seen in the coffee bar, full of energy and happiness, and she was flawless. It took him a little time to respond, he was fixated on her.

"Yes Eve, I am, it's really good to see you with the girls." He felt nervous. His voice was croaky, and he had to cough quickly to clear it, feeling embarrassed.

"That's good. I've invited Harry over for dinner, I thought it would be a nice idea, you know, now everything is back to normal." Eve tapped him on the arm and walked happily back into the house.

Matthew stood looking up into the tree, the branches swaying in

270

the wind, the sun shining through the branches. How wonderful it looked. How freely the trees moved. His life had been frozen in time once more; he couldn't move freely like the leaves rustling above him. Another moment in his life was far too much for him to bear: fooling himself like he always had that everything was finally OK. He stood in the wind, his hair blowing around; his eyes began to water as the wind blew into his face. Taking a deep breath he walked back indoors. Not to discuss anything, not to try to help or work anything out, just to pack his things, and simply walk out of the front door.

Organising the girls' things, placing them with his, the only thing on his mind was to start again with them. How he was going to, or where he was going to live didn't seem to be a huge concern, going was enough. It didn't take long to put his girls' things into a large bag. Matthew threw the heavy bag at the front door. He looked at it and shook his head, he had felt the same emotion before. He wondered if he was ever going to learn.

"Where are you going, Matthew? Your brother's coming over soon, you will miss him." Eve stood in the kitchen, her apron tied around her skinny waist. Beginning to cook a wonderful meal, she had peeled the potatoes and the vegetables, all she had to do was brown the chicken and leave the soup to simmer.

"That's the whole point Eve, I will miss him." Matthew understood quickly why Eve suddenly looked so vibrant.

"But he's Ruth's dad, how can you be like that?"

Matthew's breathing became hard, his chest felt tight.

"Have you finished Eve? Have you finished taking the piss out of me? I can deal with you being unwell, I can deal with having to do everything, but I can't deal with you taking the piss out of me. I can imagine your cosy little chat on the phone to him. How grateful he must have been to be invited over after what he has done. How much do you think I can take? Why do you want to sentence me to a life of punishment? Don't ever say he's Ruth's dad again, I don't want them to know or to hear such a thing."

"But where are you going?" Eve's voice seemed full of confusion.

"I'm simply going Eve, I will come and see you with the girls. I have been a failure to you. I have tried, Eve. But you taking the piss, oh no!" Matthew raised his voice slightly; he didn't want to upset his daughters.

"Oh don't overreact, stop being such a silly billy and sit down. It will be nice for you both to catch up."

"*Eve*, I'm going with the girls, I don't want to see him. I don't want to be anywhere near him."

"But you can't go, can you? You know what will happen if you take the girls. How would you explain it to them? One day you would have to look them in the eyes and explain the reason why they haven't got a mother. Simply because you took them away from me. It's a hard thing to have on your conscience. Surely that's worse than having Harry over for tea, isn't it?" Eve stirred the vegetables, wondering why Matthew was being so selfish. It was his brother after all and she was taking the time to make them a meal. What was she meant to do to try to get Matthew to love her again?

"Girls, come on." Matthew put a coat on each of his unsure children. He had been ridiculed enough. The feeling as though he was going to cry began to hurt his stomach.

"Where are we going, Dad? I want to read." Natty looked into his eyes.

Matthew felt Eve standing behind him.

"Where are we going? Are we going to get some sweets?"

Matthew stood up and looked at Eve. He stared at her; he really didn't know what to do. What if she took her life because he took the girls away? How would they be if they didn't have a mother; how would he be? He knew he'd take them to see her, he would never stop them. How could he chance it?

Eve raised her eyebrows at him; it was an unspoken threat that Matthew already took seriously.

"Actually Daddy's changed his mind, you all carry on reading and doing things and I will see you soon." Quickly taking each one of his girls to his chest he squeezed them so tightly, their little bodies could have burst. Kissing their heads he whispered to them, saying how much he loved them, and how he was going to see them soon.

"Eve?" He looked at her for a few seconds. A sudden urge to pull her into his arms rushed through him, it was crazy. He was

272

consumed with trepidation as he frantically picked up the bag and left. He closed the door quietly.

He got into his car and drove away, full of desperation, seeing the house in the mirror.

"*Oh God no*! You have to keep driving, oh God what have I done? Drive you selfish arsehole! I love them I do, I'm so sorry. Drive, just drive Goddam it." Finally he could release his tears. They rolled into his mouth, and his nose was running. He quickly wiped his face dry and placed his hands back on the wheel. He would be in trouble for leaving them like he had. He knew it, as much as he knew he had to keep driving. His own life depended on it. He was going to see them soon – he realised he had their clothes and they would have to be taken back. Pulling over at the side of the road to wipe his face properly, he unzipped the bag and took out a small jumper. He felt how soft it was, he had never noticed before. He leant over and smelt all of their clothes placed neatly on the top, crying onto them, holding them tight in his hands. He leant over and used the bag as his pillow, the cars racing past; he sobbed alone, seeing the clouds moving above him. He could smell his children around him.

"Please forgive me; please God let them all be OK." His whole body felt numb. He felt like he was the only one in the world.

He wasn't sure where to go. Remembering the place where he felt safe, he began to drive.

"Hello Mr Hopkins, how are you?"

"Yes I'm fine thank you." Matthew didn't want to speak to her.

"Is your wife keeping well?" The nurse spoke with eagerness as she enquired after Eve.

"Is it possible for me to see Lucas? I'm not sure if he's still here." Matthew had a heavy feeling in his stomach, wanting to inform the oversized lady that his wife was still crazy.

"I can't see any reason why not." The nurse led Matthew to a room that Matthew was already too familiar with.

The young man was sitting looking out of the window. Matthew could only see the top of his hair; his brown curls would be noticed anywhere. Not wanting to startle the young man he walked slowly in to get a full view.

"Hello Lucas."

"Have you been crying?" The young man could see the aftermath on Matthew's face from the day's earlier events. He sat with a red blanket on his lap.

"I'm OK. How are you keeping?" Matthew's face was tingling from where it had been so wet. He was finding it hard to breathe as the room was so warm. Looking at the window, he wanted to open it for a minute but remembered the bars which prevented anyone from reaching the handle. The young man must have been boiling in his dressing gown and slippers.

"I'm keeping OK, the custard isn't up to scratch, but you can't have it all in life can you?"

"You certainly can't." The young man's comment brought a warmth to Matthew. He wanted to smile.

"How is your lady friend, is she happy?"

There was a pause in the conversation.

"She seems to be happy in her world, but not really in mine. If that makes any sense to you." Matthew's throat began to hurt again as he wanted to burst into tears.

"I understand, I'm the one sitting in this chair remember. Anyway I don't even know your name and you have been kind enough to visit. You are the only visitor I have had, my parents walked away from me a long time ago."

Matthew's knees felt weak, he urgently reached for a chair. He could envisage his daughters saying the same thing of him.

"Have you made any friends in here Lucas?"

"I haven't really mixed with anyone yet. They all seem a bit crazy." He chuckled to himself.

Matthew felt a funny sense of reassurance, understanding sometimes life was bearable whatever was thrown at you. Knowing the young man who sat alone each day simply wanted to get better, as he wanted his perfect Eve to.

Two hours had already passed while they were deep in conversation. As Matthew looked at the white clock, it reminded him of the one that had been in his old school classroom. He knew his girls had been without him for quite some time.

"I'll come and see you again Lucas, if it's OK with you?" Matthew stood and put the chair back. As he looked on the small shelf he could see a photo of an older man and woman standing at either side of Lucas. They all appeared to be so happy, all wearing hats they had got from their Christmas crackers. Matthew's heart sank for the young boy with huge brown curls who stood safe between the smiling adults. If only Matthew could have reached into the picture and let him know what his future held.

"That would be very nice of you; maybe we could work out the bubble theory next time you come. I hope it all works out for you, try not to be so sad. It will all be all right – I have a feeling about it, I get them sometimes." The young man gave Matthew a warm smile, his eyes glistening in the sun's reflection which just managed to come through the barred windows.

"Thanks Lucas, I'm very happy we have become friends, I'll come again soon." Matthew placed his hand on the young man's shoulder and squeezed it slightly.

Before he left his room Matthew turned around to see the back of Lucas's chair once more, his curly hair still sticking up over the edge.

The feeling of safety was soon to disappear as he sat in his car once more, the opened bag full of girls' colourful clothes next to him.

51

"Natty will you get the phone, it's bound to be for you again." Their father washed the dishes after supper while the girls relaxed in front of the television.

"Ruth, get it will you? I'm going to miss the good bit." Natty sat with her feet up, slowly working her way through the tin of biscuits on the table.

"And so will I." Ruth threw a piece of biscuit at her reluctant sister.

"Oh, for goodness' sake you two, I'll go, it's going to be for you Nat anyway!" Glenn pulled herself from the sofa, pushing Natty's legs from the table, and went to answer the phone. The ghastly brown shades in the hall diminished any glow the bulb tried to give out but Glenn turned the light on anyway.

"Lazy lot they are," Glenn said softly to herself. "Hello." Her voice was abrupt.

"Hi, it's Ben, is Natty there please?"

"Oh hi Ben, it's Glenn. I'll go and get her for you before she eats us out of house and home." Glenn giggled, sounding almost bashful.

"Who is it?" their father's voice bellowed from the kitchen.

"It's Ben." Glenn's tone of voice had risen with enthusiasm. She was thinking how sexy Natty's boyfriend was, but under no circumstances could she ever let her elder sister know.

Without any hesitation at all, Natty threw her handful of biscuits into the tin, wiped her mouth and ran to the phone, quickly taking a glimpse at herself in the mirror. She had to make sure she looked good enough to talk to him.

"Hi Ben!" Natty had butterflies in her stomach; she still shook with nerves every time she spoke to the most gorgeous man she had ever seen. It had been a year since their first date in the coffee bar and her affection for him was growing more intense. She had worn her favourite black trousers and borrowed Glenn's red blouse; she did look very cute, even Glenn complimented her before she left. Most of their date was spent giggling with nerves, and she hadn't looked back since. She was worried about bringing him home to meet their father; she didn't want him to embarrass her so she opted out of the idea. As they were always both so busy with work and studying whatever time they did have was together precious. The meeting place was always for coffee. So when he called it was a huge bonus.

Glenn left her over-loved-up sister drawling down the phone to her fella and sat back on the sofa, finally getting a chance to grab at the biscuits herself. "How desperate is she, she never plays hard to get," she said sharply. but as her sister spoke on the phone a sense of envy rushed through her.

"It's got to be love, that's all I can say. It would be cheaper for him to come to dinner and then he could see her properly." Their father walked back to his chores, trying to find his daughter a reason to bring him over. He felt annoyed that she disrespected his judgement on the whole thing. He did understand clearly what his beautiful daughter was feeling. When you find the person of your dreams you don't want to share them with anyone. She was twenty years old with her whole life ahead of her. Their father prayed for them all every day, he prayed that their lives would be different, that they would make the choices which would allow them to be happy and to grow. He wanted them to be individuals in a busy world, knowing how to make their own decisions, not caring what anyone thought of them. All the things he felt he was, he couldn't bear his daughters to be.

The thought entered his head often after his girls had spoken to him about living with their mother. He had known that one day the conversation would happen; he just wasn't prepared for it so soon especially with Ruth having such heartache. He knew it was something completely out of his control. He had felt let down for a while, but who was he to judge when he had let them down so very much in their lives? His father had once said to him, what you give out in life you will get back; so he accepted what they had to say with grace.

277

They had all been shaking in their boots as they spoke to him that day, Natty obviously beginning the discussion, Glenn throwing in all sorts of comments throughout and Ruth mostly sitting watching her family make decisions for her future again and keeping quiet. He'd had to inform them it wasn't going to be straightaway but if it was something they really wanted to do, he would contemplate it through the coming year. He knew he was going to agree, after he had sat and devoured a whole tub of coconut cakes once they had all gone to bed, on that very same evening a year ago. Each time they passed him on the stairs or they were having dinner together, they would stare at him with raised eyebrows, waiting for his decision.

Finally the kitchen was spotless. He was so absorbed by his thoughts he didn't realise his job had been finished so quickly. He made four cups of tea and took another packet of biscuits from the cupboard to add to the slowly emptying tin. He wanted to spend some time with his girls. He went to join them. Natty was still in full conversation.

"See you tomorrow then, bye." Natty blushed. She was already thinking of what she was going to wear. But she had to study a whole day in college before she could meet him at the gate.

"Bye Natty."

"Bye."

"Bye angel."

"Bye." Natty wished he didn't have to go.

Not being able to take it any more Glenn ran to her own rescue. "Will you just say goodbye to him, for goodness' sake!"

"Bye my darling."

"B—"

Glenn grabbed the phone from her sister and spoke sternly into the mouthpiece. "Ben, she said Bye, nice to chat to you and everything."

"How dare you, how rude are you? I can't believe you have done that, I will have to call him back to apologise." Natty stood in complete disbelief.

"Please do us the great honour of not doing that. Maybe if you saw him more you wouldn't be so mushy."

"Glenn we are both busy, if only we could see each other, but it still doesn't give you the damn right to act like a complete selfish bitch! You wait until you find someone you care about, you'll see then." Natty wanted to punch her in her pretty face, feeling as though she wanted to scream.

"Natty, lighten up."

"I can't believe it, you are the most irrational person I have ever met, I can't even argue with you. You only want everything to be the way you flaming want it! I can't stand being around you any more. I will go to Mother's without you; at least she doesn't mean to hurt us!" Natty was raising her voice more each second.

"Hey girls, come on, your tea's getting cold." Their father walked out to see his girls at boiling point.

"Fight! Fight!" Ruth leapt from the sofa to witness the excitement of the day.

"But Dad, what she did was inexcusable."

"Natty a lot of things in our lives are that way. Come and sit down." He felt like banging their heads together. He wished they could stop hurting each other. They were always so close when they were small, if only they realised how close.

"Sorry Dad, I'm going to Mother's. I can't live with her if she is going to keep doing stupid things like this, thinking the whole thing's flaming funny."

"Glenn, stop laughing. If anyone is going to stay with your mother it will be all of you." Their father felt like he was going to faint. There was a pain building up in his chest, his palms becoming sweaty.

"Are you serious Dad?"

"Yes Glenn. No matter what has happened you have never been separated. You certainly aren't going to start now."

Ruth stood behind their father quietly.

"What made you decide we could, Dad?" Natty's disagreement with Glenn was instantly forgotten.

"Natty you are all wonderful young ladies who will make choices I am afraid even a parent can't do anything about. Who am I to stop any of you doing as you want? I have made too many choices for you, which unfortunately have been wrong, let's hope this one's right. Let's hope you all make a better job of the challenges which will come your way." Their father held his arms out. They all

279

rushed forward and he held them; his life in his arms, being protected. Could he really bring himself to let them go again, to go into a world they despised so much? It was their request to go, he had to remind himself of that.

"Dad, Glenn still gets on my nerves though, I think she should stay here. What do you think?" Natty's comment made everyone laugh.

"Let's go and finish that tin of biscuits, eh?" Their father released them from his grasp.

"That won't be hard for Natty, she's already eaten the last lot." Glenn stuck her fingers up to Natty as she walked away.

"Glenn, I think you have said enough to your sister this evening, don't you?"

"No Dad, I have only just started, race you to the best seat." Glenn pushed through them, all wanting to reach the soft chair nearest the television, it was the best seat in the room. Natty would normally take up residence in it, but tonight it was going to be her turn.

They all sat comfortably, though not so much as Glenn. They all felt happy and calm together. The atmosphere in the living room was serene. They happily chatted and ate together, laughing at the television programme.

"Dad, when do think we could go and live with her?" Natty drank the last dregs from her cup.

"Has it really been that bad living with me?" Their father sat with the biscuit tin on his lap and realised it had been four years since his beautiful girls came to stay. It had been the best four years of his life. He looked at them as the lights from the television screen lit up their angelic faces. He was the luckiest man alive. He inhaled a huge breath and thought of their mother being alone for such a long time.

"No Dad, only thought we could let her know, that was all." For all the things that had happened to them in their young lives, the choice they made to go back to her had to be the most absurd. No one in their right mind would chance going back into a life of pain and neglect, however old they were. Natty sighed in disbelief.

"Don't let her know. It's easy to turn up, isn't it? You have done it before. You are her daughters after all. I'm sure she will be happy to see you again. All she has ever wanted is to be a good mother to you all, this might be her time." Their father hurt inside, he felt dazed. His lips began to wobble and his throat began to burn.

"Dad, what about you?" Ruth touched his hand softly. She wanted to sit next to him, there wasn't much room on the armchair, but she squeezed in all the same.

"What about me Ruth? I will fine, I'm big enough and ugly enough to be on my own. I have done it before you know, but don't forget I'm here, don't stay away for too long, that's all." Their father felt a lump in his throat; he couldn't cry now, not when they were happy, and finally felt they could be without him for a while. He had to make sure they weren't going to feel responsible for him any more.

"When were you thinking Natty? I have just absorbed the idea." Glenn sat in the comfy chair, with all the soft pillows on her lap. Her sister could only see her face.

"Do you think the weekend would be too soon Dad? Do you think it would be all right?" Natty couldn't believe she felt so at ease speaking in such a way with her father – she had hidden feelings and secrets for so long, it was the most amazing relief to be able to speak so freely. But the strangest thing of all was not feeling guilty about it. She knew how much she loved and respected her father and would continue to until the end of time. There wouldn't be anyone in this world who could ever replace him.

"If it's your wish then I will understand," he said, his stomach feeling like it was being squeezed, as he took deep breaths.

They all took a long look at each other, not another word needed to be shared. They were simply together, safe and warm. Their father quickly wiped a tear from his face, he was desperate to hold them back until he went to bed, but one managed to escape.

The week took its toll on their father, each day he seemed to be counting the hours. Each meal they all sat down to he would spend most of the time watching their every mouthful, as they chatted and argued amongst themselves. They had all grown up, he had never really taken any notice of it before, but this felt somewhat different. He knew he only had another day with them, and then they were going away. Without doubt he'd be seeing them again, but they wouldn't be in their bedrooms with the music playing and the smells of perfume wouldn't engulf the bathroom in the mornings. It would be the little things he had always moaned about that he would miss the most. His three beautiful daughters were not going too far away. It didn't matter – they were going because of a decision they made themselves. The first choice they ever had and it was to be with their mother, after everything.

"I love you all."

"We love you too Dad," they all replied together and went back to making lots of noise around the dinner table.

Ruth laid her knife and fork at the side of her plate. Rubbing her hands on her trousers she looked at their father and spoke softly. "Dad, do you think I should say to Mother that I know about your brother?"

"Ruth, you will know if you should say anything or not. I trust you will make the right judgement one day. Have the same belief in yourself." It was really happening. As close as it was to them going, he still prayed one of them would change her mind. He was already dreading the thought of turning the key in his front door and knowing there wouldn't be anyone waiting for him inside. He already missed the little notes they would leave him to read. Sometimes they'd put a chocolate bar next to the note. The thought made him smile, looking at them once again.

"I don't see the point. You're my dad; no one else." Ruth picked up her cutlery again and continued to eat her pasta. Sucking it up to her mouth, red sauce splattering onto Glenn's green sweatshirt that she had pinched from her sister's drawer. The drawers they would all be emptying after dinner.

"Well, there's your answer." Their father felt a huge sense of unspoken loyalty.

The pain he felt at them going was eased somewhat by Ruth's statement. He was their father, wherever they were. And whoever they were with. He felt as though a weight had suddenly been lifted from his shoulders. He was always going to be in their wonderful futures, to witness them become the intelligent beautiful women he always knew they would be.

*

282

"Natty, do you think we ought to call Mother before we all turn up on her doorstep? I was only thinking last night. We have only ever gone for tea and now we are expecting her to make beds for us. I feel really nervous, that's all. I wish Dad was coming too, but I know he won't and really I'm not sure why the hell we are. Nat, are you listening? Why are we really leaving Dad? He hasn't done anything wrong." Ruth spoke quickly, she was full of nerves, packing a large bag on her unmade bed.

"Ruth, I think this will be what we need, to put it all to a close – the whole thing. We understand how Mother's been so unwell for such a long time so it's going to help us. Dad will be fine, I really feel it. I know it's the best thing for us to do. Don't worry, we can always come back if it gets too much." Natty zipped up her bag. She had started packing long before the others. She was petrified but couldn't share her feelings with her sisters. They'd only follow her and get back into bed and forget about the whole idea.

"Glenn, have you packed?"

"Yes I have Natty. I suppose you have my knickers in your case because I can't find most of them," Glenn said sarcastically while she put her lamp in a plastic bag.

"Oh, and I really think your fat arse knickers are going to fit me." Natty threw her pillow at Glenn.

"Um, yes I do actually. Will you watch my flaming lamp?" Glenn began huffing and puffing, hearing their father coming up the stairs.

"Girls, I have called your mother to let her know you are coming to see her for a while, I thought it best." Their father had spent all morning building up the courage to pick up the phone to his Eve. When he heard her soft voice he knew how much he missed her.

"What did she say Dad?" Glenn held the brown pillow Natty had thrown at her. She was going to wait for their father to leave the room before she went and smacked her in the head with it. Looking at Natty's hair she was desperate to mess it up.

"She said she is going to bake an apple pie. I remember it used to be my favourite." He remembered the apple pies well. Sometimes he got to eat them and other times he'd spend the evening cleaning the carpet where it had been thrown.

"So why don't you stay for a slice Dad?"

283

"Let's deal with one thing at a time Glenn, shall we?"

Their father disappeared downstairs once more; it was obvious to them he had been crying, but not one of the girls dare admit it.

"Are we ready then, you two?" Natty held her belongings and looked at her sisters. "It's all going to be all right, I promise." As she walked towards the stairs she felt the force of the pillow hitting her on the back of the head.

"Glenn!" Natty put her hand to her hair. Now she wouldn't be going downstairs for at least another five minutes. She realised she had packed her brush.

"Hold on, this is heavy." Ruth dragged her bag to the furthest point of their bare bedroom.

"What the hell do you have in there, bricks?"

"Yes, to build my castle." Ruth laughed with Glenn

"Dad, we are ready now, we will come over in the morning if you like?" Natty stood in the hall, tears beginning to well up in her eyes.

"Eh? You haven't gone yet, you're still here, I can see you right now, all of you, I will see you when you're gone and I will see you when I sleep." Their father drifted off into an emotional daydream, the fear of such a reality becoming almost unbearable. He had spent so much of their childhood holding them tight but then letting them go.

"Dad, it's all going to be all right." Glenn hadn't said too much to him that morning.

"I know, I know, you're all doing what you have to do, I won't stand in your way. Just remember, if you sense the first moment of fear you come straight back. I will even decorate your room, maybe we could do brown walls this time." He let out a false chuckle.

"Dad, was it next week we were going?" Natty felt sick, she wanted to try and bring humour to the moment.

"Sorry Nat, I will get my car keys. Now where can they be? Oh yes here they are, worse luck, only kidding." Their father was flapping about; he tried to hide his panic but to no avail.

They parked in the street not far from their mother's front door and all sat quietly, each one full of nerves and anticipation for the next move; who was going to make it? Who would be the first to get out? They could turn back and go home, it wasn't too late.

Their father turned off the engine and inhaled a huge breath.

"Right girls, you'd better be off, you have apple pie to eat." Don't cry, not now, wait until they've gone, he thought.

"Are you not coming in to say anything Dad?" Glenn leant forward, her face peeping through the middle of the front seats.

"Glenn, I have spoken all of my life to her, I shouldn't think she will listen now, do you?"

"Dad, it's only a chat." Natty's tears rolled down her face, her mascara had run onto her cheeks.

"You'd better clean your face Natty. You know your mother, she won't like to see you that way." Ruth gave her an overused tissue.

"Go on girls, I will see you tomorrow then, eh?" Their father's emotions overwhelmed him. He needed them to get out of the car quickly or he would drive away with them. He wanted to go to where he felt safe, but the opportunity to gain a friend and feel safe had been taken away from him as well. Lucas had been transferred to a more secure home. He had only smashed a few things in a moment's fury, but he was apparently a danger to himself and others.

"See you tomorrow Dad." Natty kissed him on the back of the head.

"Just go, go on. Your mother is waiting."

They all kissed him and left, the farewell was too casual for their liking. Their father watched them walking to the door, his little girls walking to her again with heavy bags and tears in their eyes.

"Hello Mother, how have you been?"

"Hello Ruth, hello to all of you." Their mother stood at the door, admiring her beautiful daughters who were now young ladies. Why would they want to be with me after everything I have done to them? After I have taken away all the good things from them? How do I deserve this? How do I thank them for coming home? their mother was thinking.

"Hello." Natty greeted their mother again, smiling.

"Come in, come in. I haven't touched your rooms, they are still the same. Where's your father? Is he not coming in for a while?" She spoke softly, thinking of how much she would like to have seen him again. "I didn't think he would want to see me."

285

"No, he had to go home." Glenn spoke firmly.

"No Glenn, I didn't have to go anywhere." Their father stood on the doorstep gazing around, admiring his perfect wife and his three wonderful daughters. He couldn't believe how alike they all were. Their mother was still the most amazing woman he had ever seen, he had wanted her from the first moment he saw her when he stood at the door of the coffee bar. Standing at the door of her home, he loved her still. The love had always consumed and exhausted him, now he gazed at her in the same disbelief. Looking around he remembered when he had hung the stripy yellow wallpaper in the hall. She hadn't liked it, but he put it up anyway. She never liked the decor in any of the rooms. He had never realised it before. A sense of guilt rushed through him, wondering how hard it must have been for her to live with him. He had always wanted his way.

"Dad, you've come back for us." Natty knew he would, how could he simply let them go without making a fuss?

"Natty, I should have a long time ago. If it's OK with your mother I could stay for some pie?" Their father closed the door and walked slowly through to the kitchen.

"Are you coming home, Matthew? Are you coming home to stay?" Their mother stood next to her daughters, her voice full of anticipation. Her hands were clasped together: she could have been praying.

Their father stopped and looked in her eyes. He was strong and tall over her petite flawless body.

"Eve, I have to be with you all, we don't work apart, we never have." He longed to take her into his arms and hold her close to his chest. To stroke her hair and kiss her on her soft flushed face. It was crazy, he knew it, after everything. He wished he could stop wanting her, but he couldn't. He was to die loving her, it was as simple as that.

Their mother put her hands over her mouth; she couldn't believe her family were with her again, standing uncertainly together in the crowded hall.

"It will be OK. We will all be OK." Their father took all the bags from his girls, and placed them at the bottom of the stairs. The thought rushed through him of how many times he had had bags

286

ready to leave, but this time he was leaving them at the bottom of the stairs to stay.

They all dashed into the kitchen. Apple pies covered the table.

"I didn't know how many to cook, so I kind of kept going."

"Yes, we see what you mean." Glenn laughed as her thoughts went back to Ruth's mountain of cakes.

"Mother, they are really nice, they look lovely." Ruth placed her little finger onto the sugar and sucked it clean.

"I'm better now, I really am. We can be happy all of us. I can't believe you are all here. Eat up, don't let them get cold." Their mother stood and admired her family once more.

"Thank you Eve, they look very nice." Their father smiled at her. He could smell her perfume as he sat next to her at the table.

"They're not as good as your cakes though. Are they Matthew?" Their mother spoke in a comical tone, her eyebrows raised. She wanted to burst into laughter. Their father blushed.

"No, I don't think they are." Their father laughed, hoping their mother wouldn't go any further.

"What are you two laughing at?" Natty asked her parents in amazement, feeling nerves and excitement building up in her stomach. She had never seen them laughing together before. There weren't any ashtrays she could see, which pleased her even more. It was the best day ever.

"Your father and I used to make cakes. They were very good I must say, especially for beginners."

"Don't listen to her," their father told his girls.

"It was Mother's Day and your father and I thought it would be nice to make some for my dear mum. We had lots of different coloured icing and wanted to decorate them really carefully. I had to go out for a while so I left your more than capable father to ice them. Well, we had quite a few so we decided to keep some for ourselves. It was only when we sat down on the evening of Mother's Day, that your dear father realised he had given her the wrong box. We had flowers on our cakes you see but your poor Nan had pictures of little willies and boobs. We couldn't eat through laughing, I think it's what killed her off in the end." Their mother spoke while staring at their father the whole time, becoming hysterical with laughter.

"Your mother thinks it was the shock which stayed with her for years but I kept telling her it was old age." Their father remembered how hard it was for Eve when her mother passed away. She still took it better than her father's death. She didn't speak for nearly a month. It was another crazy time in the life of the Hopkins family.

"Dad, no way, you didn't, how embarrassingly wicked." Glenn had to cross her legs in case she wet herself. The thought of hunting for a pair of knickers in one of the bags was far too massive.

"OK, if we want to be like that, I think your mother could share the time when she got into someone's truck at the market where she used to work"

"Dad what's so funny about that?" Ruth spoke in the middle of eating.

"It was my truck she was meant to be getting into. Because I was always on time your dear mother saw a blue truck and jumped in. To her amazement the man in the driving seat nearly had a heart attack. He was old enough to be your great-great-grandad, he must have thought his luck was in. I pulled up to see your mother apologising profusely to him, and for the record I wasn't late, your mother was early." Their father roared with laughter, banging his knee with his hand. He felt relaxed everyone seemed to be happy in each other's company. They all sat joking and laughing around the table, eating slices of pie. The bags still remained in the hall.

Deep down they were all praying it would be OK, they could all begin again.

"I'm so glad you are home, I'm so happy to see you all again." Their mother sat at the table with her chin on her hands. She was so excited for their future together. How she loved her girls so much. She couldn't wait to tell her father how they were all going to go shopping, and have wonderful lunches together. Enjoy each other as she wished she always had. She wasn't going to waste any more time.

"We are happy to be together again, all of us." Natty touched her father's hand. He was shaking slightly.

They had been speaking for hours; the darkness drew into the room.

288

"I hope you don't mind, but I'm going to get into the bath, with all that's been happening I simply haven't had time to look my best."

"You look fine Eve, you always have." Their father held his stare as she went to leave.

"Flattery will get you nowhere." Their mother left them in the kitchen, and turned on the light before making her way upstairs. He's trying to be charming again, she thought, smiling as she walked up the stairs.

"Dad, I think it's going to be OK, I can't believe you are here, thank you Dad."

"Glenn, I think it will be OK with time. Let's clear this up for your mother." They all began to clear away. As they rose from the table they stopped to cuddle, standing in their mother's kitchen holding each other tight. Their father began to cry and his beautiful girls who were full of uncertainty began to cry with him. As they all let go of each other they inhaled deeply and began to wash the plates.

Their mother could hear them chatting, the house felt lived in again. She began to run the bath adding a few bubbles; she wanted to relax. Wanting desperately to feel everything was going to be fine, she took a look at herself in the steamed-up mirror, wiping it away with her hand. She looked at herself for a while.

"You have them all home; it's going to be OK. You can do this, young lady. Dad, you have to go now. My daughters are home," she said sternly.

Turning off the taps she went into her bedroom. As she sat on her bed she could hear muffled voices through the floor. Her family were all together; she was alone sitting in her bedroom. She looked at her red covers and pillows. Her wonderful dressing table with the most beautiful carved mirror. It was something Matthew had picked up from an old antique shop. It was all very classy. She had always disliked the white wallpaper with red roses printed all over it, but for some reason that evening it didn't look so bad. She could have finally got used to it. She shrugged her shoulders, confused as to why she was worrying about such silly things as colours anyway.

"It's going to be fine, young lady. Yes fine, all of it. You will be great with them." She began to feel anxious and rocked gently back and forward, tapping her feet and finding the smallest thread on her bedcover to undo. Hearing the voices getting louder, the situation became difficult for her to deal with. She took a deep breath and wiped the tears slowly falling onto her face.

"You won't hurt them any more. You know you can make them happy. You don't have to cause them any pain. You can do it." Her voice was soft, in her heart she could never promise such a thing. She longed to be good to them, they were the most precious things in her existence. She was desperate to be the mother she had always dreamed she could be. Her own mother had shown her how to be the best; she was another person she had let down.

Sliding off her bed she walked over to her dressing table, her trembling hands opening a drawer. Inside, a wooden box had been hidden. It had once belonged to her father, his well-organised paper-work would be kept inside. She touched each corner gently. She sat back on the middle of the bed, her legs crossed, with the box perched on her knees. She opened it slowly, taking each item from its place and laying it on the duvet with precision. She looked at them all and smiled. Her stomach felt heavy as she placed her small hand on each one. A picture of the sunshine bigger than her hand. It brought a small smile to her face, remembering the day when Natty had painted it for her. Picking up the sunflower and holding it to her nose, she closed her eyes, longing to gain a scent from it as the dried petals fell onto her lap. The petals broke as she tried to pick them up and put them back into the box, blending in with the old confetti which lay at the bottom. Everything became a blur. She desperately wished she could bring herself to read the love letters Matthew had written to her, but as she blew Ruth's first curl from them, Harry came to the very front of her mind. She knew from the second their lips touched it was the moment she had fallen out of love with Matthew. Tears fell from her eyes, as she shuffled her keepsakes together, holding them to her chest. She closed her eyes and cried, for everything that could have been. Wiping her face with the back of her hand, as she opened her eyes she could see her tablets lying at the bottom of the box.

Letting her scrunched-up cards and drawings fall around her, grabbing at each packet and bottle, twisting the lids off, five bottles had been emptied into her wet shaking hands. She cupped them to her face. Multicoloured shapes being protected by her. Her heart was breaking, her body felt numb. She couldn't allow anyone to see her cry any more, it just wasn't fair.

"Girls, be free, fly over the oceans of the world." Each swallow brought more tears, the ones she wanted to keep inside; they were her feelings and she wanted to keep hold of them. Each sob gave her fragile body the strength to swallow more tablets.

She stared into her hands – they were finally empty, only white residue remaining. Lying down, she reached for all the things she had kept so very safe, holding them to her lips. She was feeling safer than ever before, as though her father was holding her in his strong arms. She could rest now, and so could her girls. She couldn't cause them any more harm.

Wishing she could hold them one last time, bathe them and kiss them goodnight, she closed her eyes.

"Please don't forgive me." Her voice was weak.

She lay alone as she always had. Her bedroom cold and silent, muffled voices and a dripping tap were all that could be heard. The array of memories lay around her, moving only slightly with the rhythm of her breathing.

Finally, it all became still.

52

The house felt warm as Glenn and Ruth walked in from the garden. As they walked into the hall, they could see Natty and their father huddled together on the stairs, where they had been speaking for some time. Natty's head was in her hands, she was crying so very hard, their father's arm around her shoulders. The tears they both had cried had been frozen in the bottom of their aching stomachs for so many years.

"Dad, Natty, are you all right?" Ruth stood with her arms folded, trying to warm herself up. She was wearing Glenn's black blouse. They had had an argument that morning. Glenn didn't want her to continue helping herself to her clothes. But she didn't listen, she took it anyway.

"Hello you two, sorry we took so long, got chatting. Has the doctor gone?" Their father took his hand from Natty and wiped the tears from his face. His voice was shaky.

"No he's still outside with Mother." Glenn decided to sit down in front of Natty, tapping her on the knee, being cautious not to ladder her sister's tights.

Their father got up and went into the dining room, looking out of the window. The doctor was the only one who came that day, the only one who cared enough to say his goodbye. Their father watched as the doctor laid flowers next to the grave. Natty, Glenn and Ruth stood at the door and watched him.

"That's kind of him, don't you think girls, that he took the time to come?" Their father couldn't believe how someone so beautiful and perfect had no one else who cared for her. She was buried in her life, hidden away from the rest of the world, how unfair to them all he thought. He couldn't cry any more, his face was too sore, and he didn't have the strength. His body was so tired.

292

"It is, Dad; I can't understand why Mother didn't have any friends. I can't imagine what that must have been like for her, to have no one but us." Ruth flicked the fluff from her sister's blouse, she couldn't get into any more trouble with her. She knew she was already in far too deep. For some insane reason she had invited Harry. She had spent the morning of the previous day plucking up the courage to call him. She had hidden their mother's address book under her pillow while she slept, hoping it would give her the strength. She found his name clearly written inside, and next to his name was a red heart in thick red pen. Ruth knew it was him. She didn't know if she was doing the right thing when she dialled his number, full of apprehension. It was good of him to come; he stood in front of the house in a smart black suit, pacing up and down. Ruth's heart skipped a beat when she saw him. She wanted to go and say hello. But she couldn't, their father would be too let down by her. Their father was only out with him for a few minutes, he wouldn't let him come in to see her to say goodbye. He wouldn't even take the beautiful white roses. They were placed at the front door.

"I'm sure your mother had someone keeping her company and looking over her most of the time, when we didn't even know it. They are lying together now. Come on girls, let's go down and see her." Their father took a huge sigh, and walked up to his girls, wiping the tears from each of their faces. They had cried from the moment they had woken. They were to cry until they slept again. Kissing them all on the head, he pulled them close to him one at a time, each one crying into his chest as he did so.

"Dad, I wish it could have been different, I wish it didn't have to end like this, she was so young Dad, she was only fifty-two, how can that be fair?" Natty held on to him as he walked out of the dining room. He stopped in the hall to speak.

"We all wish it could have been different, and sometimes life isn't fair. But it is life Natty and we have to deal with each day and whatever is put in our path. It kind of makes us who we are in the end; life has a funny way of transforming people. I know your mother didn't want her life to end like this; she just couldn't do it any more, that was all. It's no one's fault, it was what life put in her path." He held the tears back for their sake, though he wanted to scream out in sorrow.

"I don't understand Dad, why did she give in to it? Why couldn't she have changed her path, not give in to it? Why couldn't she just get better and not give in, why Dad?" Natty cried in desperation. She felt alone and afraid, just as she did when she'd waited in the school playground for her father to arrive; she waited until the school was empty. As her tears began to fall her mother had tapped her on the shoulder.

"Natty, I'm sure in hindsight she would have, but sometimes it's too late to discover what to do. We are only human, remember." Their father thought of his brother having to walk away from his only family again.

They all made their way to the back door and walked out on to the soft grass. The sun shone down on them all but there was a chill in the air. Their father closed his eyes and put his face up to the sky. He could hear the birds singing like never before, they could have been singing to his Eve. She had always loved the sound of the birds singing on a summer's evening. They knew she wasn't coming back this time, they had pleaded with her to wake as they stood around her in her bedroom, looking at her small still body on her bed. All alone, no one was with her to hold her hand. They had stayed in the kitchen for nearly an hour, waiting, until their father decided to go up and check her. It was in vain. He let out a screeching cry and on hearing their father's distress they ran up the stairs. That was when they knew that they truly loved and wanted their mother.

Their father knew his Eve was finally going to be safe. She could be held by her parents while she slept, they would be together for ever, and she would never feel any more pain, not with them beside her. He had to find comfort in something.

"Thank you for coming, Doctor. We can't thank you enough for everything you have done. And I mean everything." Their father shook the doctor's hand, gently smiling. He was the third person in their marriage.

"Matthew, I obviously didn't do enough did I?" The doctor wiped a tear away with his handkerchief as he looked at the grave and walked away.

Their father knew they were never going to see him again.

Natty, Glenn, Ruth and their father didn't have to say anything, each lost in their own thoughts.

294

Their father took his wedding ring off and held it tightly in his hand. Putting it to his lips he kissed it and laid it softly upon the ground, his fingers touching the fresh cool earth which was covering her ashes. Their marriage could never be harmed. There could be no more hurtful words or actions, they could both be at peace.

A few months had passed slowly from the day they all had to say goodbye to the woman who had always been the other part of them. She was the part of them they could never be allowed to get close to, the part of them who could hurt them beyond belief and still they wanted her to hold them close, yearning for her to sing them a lullaby. They were all in her home; they were free to touch all the ornaments and belongings they had not dared to before.

"What are you doing, Natty?" Glenn held their mother's make-up bag as she spoke to Natty from the hall.

"Nothing." Natty stood at the cupboard, opening and closing all the drawers, each time she closed one she opened another. She began to wipe her hands over the furniture, she was able to walk freely in the family home for the very first time.

"It isn't fair Glenn, it could have really worked, do you know that? Mother said she was better, you heard her didn't you?" Natty saw her sister near the door and raised her voice slightly for her to hear.

"I think so Natty. I'm going to have Mother's make-up bag if it's OK with you and Ruth." Glenn raised her voice back and went into the garden.

Natty shook her head and went to sit near the window. Grabbing the old grey blanket and laying it across her lap, she cried as she watched Glenn in the garden. Glenn would always go to the garden, even in the rain, wandering around and climbing trees. She would always organise their mother's flowers. She seemed to know how their mother would have liked them to be. Glenn would chat to her for a short while, trying to understand, trying not to cry.

Natty cried, sitting on her own in her mother's chair. The arms were tatty, the flowery pattern worn away, just like the butterflies on her apron which still hung in the kitchen, apple stains still on the front.

Natty felt lost. She could finally relax, knowing she wasn't going to be hurt any more, just as her sisters weren't. It had been part of her existence for so long, and now she felt scared because she didn't have to be frightened any more.

Their father was upstairs. As he walked around the large rooms he tried to see what he could begin sorting out. He could throw a few things away, make it nice again. He had to do something, get it to the standard his Eve always deserved. It was messy. As he went into the bathroom he sat on the toilet seat holding an empty black bag. His shoulders slumped forward. It was meant to be the best time of their lives; he remembered how they had painted the bathroom together. Eve found it funny putting the paintbrush in his face, cream paint covering his black hair, she'd laughed so much. It brought a smile to his face as he thought of her happy. He looked around at the cream walls; they did finally manage to get it finished after the paint fight. They had spent the rest of the day making love. Their father looked up at the cabinet, knowing it must have been full of tablets. His throat began to burn, as he was suddenly aware that he was in the room where his beautiful Eve had hurt herself so very badly. She must have been in pain from that very day. He huffed and rustled the bag in his fingers; he got up and opened the cabinet, water stains obscuring his reflection. Grabbing at old pots and packets he threw them all in the bag. "Please now leave my Eve alone." Swallowing hard he tried to hold back his tears again.

Ruth was never too far away from their father. She wanted to look after him – he had looked after her for so long, treated her like his own. He didn't have to any more, their mother had gone. She was scared he was going to leave her, just like their mother did, and like her real father did, even on the day of their mother's funeral. He had known she was inside the house, if he had taken the time before walking away he could have seen her at the window, even if it was for a few seconds.

"Dad, what shall I do with this?" Ruth called from the bedroom.

"What's that, Ruth?" Their father took a deep breath.

"This old thing, I found it under the bed." Ruth spoke inquisitively.

"I threw that away ages ago." Their father could remember as if it were yesterday how he had put her china doll in the bin, just thrown her doll away, as if it were nothing to her.

The guilt rushed through him; he couldn't believe how he could have done such a thing to her. How was he ever going to make it

296

up to her now? He burst into tears as Ruth handed it over to him. Eve's doll had sat under her bed for years, untouched and unnoticed. Ruth watched as their father cried, wiping the dust from the doll's pretty face. He had only ever seen something as perfect and beautiful once before. Slowly walking past Ruth he gently placed the doll on the pillow.

"Goodnight my perfect Eve."

They both left the room and closed the door.

1979

As he stood on the warm, echoing stage he wished he'd managed even the small slice of toast he'd left on his plate at home that morning. If his belly rumbled he knew everyone in the softly lit theatre would hear. He stood calmly and breathed heavily, hoping the eager onlookers wouldn't notice. He took a deep breath as he heard the vibrations of the music under his feet. He tapped his foot on the stage, closed his eyes and inhaled the deepest of breaths, absorbing the moment of pure freedom. The smell from the previous performer's sweat and perfume whirled around him. He moved his body slowly from one side to the other, which brought a smile to his face. The lights left a pleasant, tingling sensation on his warm glowing skin. He danced across the stage, tapped his feet hard, and moved with all his force. The audience would stand and cheer at such a spectacle of elegance and skill. His blood pumped hard and vibrantly around his quickly moving body. It flowed and swayed with elegant movements. Every space of the stage used, he smiled and absorbed the wonderful attention. Flowers were thrown in gratitude on to the stage, which landed at his feet, as the over-contented audience applauded him with wide eyes. He could hear the sound of the applause from the happy onlookers, who stood with their hands above their heads. Each time the heavy red velvet curtain was pulled back they would still be cheering, another standing ovation, every night the same.

"Encore, Encore!" the audience cheered. Their roared demands to see him again filled the theatre and the noise echoed through his tired and exhilarated body, which overflowed with adrenaline and excitement.

"Lucas! Hey Lucas!"

Lightning Source UK Ltd.
Milton Keynes UK
UKHW010004230819
348409UK00001B/352/P